Rendezvous
Eighteenth

Also by Jake Lamar

If 6 Were 9

Close to the Bone

The Last Integrationist

Bourgeois Blues

Rendezvous Eighteenth

Jake Lamar

St. Martin's Minotaur ✄ New York

www.minotaurbooks.com

Book design by Nick Wunder

Library of Congress Cataloging-in-Publication Data

Lamar, Jake.
    Rendezvous eighteenth / Jake Lamar.—1st ed.
        p. cm.
    ISBN 0-312-28920-0
    1. Montmartre (Paris, France)—Fiction.   2. African American men—Fiction.   3. Americans—France—Fiction.   4. Paris (France)—Fiction.   5. Runaway wives—Fiction.   6. Pianists—Fiction.
    I. Title.

PS3562.A4216R46   2003
813'.54—dc21

                                                              2003046820

First Edition: November 2003

10   9   8   7   6   5   4   3   2   1

For Dorli

Acknowledgments

I could probably fill a book with the names of all the people who have taught me invaluable lessons about life in Paris over the years. For brevity's sake, I will thank just a few great friends who helped make this novel possible: Ted Joans and Laura Corsiglia, C. K. Williams and Catherine Mauger, Christophe Ortega, Maggie Doherty, David Harmon, Velma Bury, Tannie Stovall, Odile Hellier, James Emanuel, Hart Leroy Bibbs, Bob Swaim, Craig Preston and Nicole Johnson.

Merci mille fois à tous.

PART 1

Cousin Cash
Comes to Paris

One

WHAT CAN I TELL you? Ricky Jenks was the family embarrassment. The fat kid. The bed wetter. The C student who broke your heart because you just *knew* he could do better. If only he would "apply" himself. Laughable athlete. Luckless with girls. Not that he lacked talent. He was a naturally gifted pianist. That, in any event, was what Ricky's parents always said, as if to excuse all his obvious shortcomings. Whatever modicum of artistry Ricky Jenks possessed, he was by no means a musical prodigy. In most families, Ricky's ordinary imperfections might not have been a badge of shame. But he was the progeny of one of the fabulous Pendleton sisters of Norris, New Jersey: three famously smart and ambitious black beauties who all married "well" and prided themselves on breeding "well" the next generation, the blessed black children of the 1960s, who would be trained to stake their claim in mainstream American society. Ricky's kid sister grew up to be a judge in Miami. All of his cousins were prominent in their fields as well. Ricky, on the brink of 39, knew he was considered a bit of a fuckup. Back in America, anyway. But Ricky, despite all his ostensible privileges, felt he'd been dealt a pretty weak hand in life. He figured he had made the best of the raw human material he had to work with. Ricky Jenks was not a proud man, nor did he suffer from self-pity. Yet he always found it somehow fitting that the place where he felt most at home in this world was called the Street of the Martyrs.

April in Paris, 1999, had been typically dreary: leaden gray skies, a chill wind blowing spitty drizzle in your face. May tends to be the truly beautiful month in this town, the time when the sun reappears and the cafés fling open their doors, round-top tables and rattan chairs taking over the sidewalks. "This song should have been called 'May in Paris,' " Ricky Jenks often said before launching into his rendition of the famous standard at the crêperie where he played piano. "But 'April' scans better." The sun was shining boldly, though, on this last Thursday morning in April, filling Ricky's studio apartment with brassy yellow light. The tall narrow windows were open wide. Ricky sat in a chair, wearing a T-shirt and gym shorts, tiny cup of fierce espresso in hand, his bare, chubby knees pressed against the intricately wrought little iron railing over the window ledge, looking out on the rue des Martyrs, a steep, mile-long street that climbed through Paris's northern precincts. Ricky's building, number 176, was smack in the middle of a precipitously inclined stretch of Martyrs. At the bottom of his block was an intersection where the neighborhood of Pigalle, the neon-bathed commercial sleaze district, boasting round-the-clock peep shows, leather underwear shops and the International Erotic Museum, bordered the neighborhood of Barbès, a buzzing network of African and Arab communities. At the top of Ricky's block was Montmartre, the hilly, cobblestoned neighborhood that combined a bohemian grit with a village-like quaintness tourists found irresistible. The main boulevard of Pigalle and the whole of Barbès and Montmartre were the three key regions of Paris's sprawling Eighteenth Arrondissement, a city within a city: eccentric, hard-bitten, robustly alive.

The telephone rang but Ricky had no intention of answering it. Fatima groaned. Ricky turned and saw only a tumult of jet-black hair poking out amid the white sheets and pillows on the sofa bed. The phone rang a second time and now the sheets undulated in the bold late-morning sunshine. There would be one more ring before the answering machine clicked on. Ricky hated disturbing Fatima's sleep but he couldn't bring himself to pick up the phone. The caller had either dialed the wrong number or was someone Ricky wouldn't feel like talking to. No true friend of Ricky Jenks would phone him before eleven in the morning. The third ring. Fatima grumbled loudly. Ricky saw two burnished-bronze arms emerge from the tangle of white sheets, slender hands groping. Fatima's black hair disappeared beneath a plump white pillow. Her arms were splayed atop the pillow, behind Fatima's covered head, crossed awkwardly at the wrists. Oh, well, Ricky thought, it was time for Fatima to get up anyway. She had another day of relentless studying ahead of her.

"Bonjour," Ricky heard his voice say jauntily on the answering machine. As his greeting played on the tape, Ricky returned his attention to the rue des Martyrs. He sipped his potent coffee, the caffeine tingling in his brain. He felt the sunlight on his face, prickling the skin on his cheeks. His eye wandered across the motley array of establishments across the street: the seedy cafés and popular nightclubs, the bread and pastry shop, the Chinese, Senegalese and Lebanese restaurants, the fruit and vegetable store, the transsexual/transvestite whorehouse, the nursing home. Ricky Jenks loved his block and in that brief interval of time between hearing the electronic beep on his answering machine and the voice of the caller—a one-second pause during which he gave no thought at all as to who might be phoning—it dawned on him, like a pleasant whisper in his ear: "Hey, maybe I'm a pretty lucky guy after all."

Then he heard the voice of the caller, rising above the static, the aural clutter of a public place. "Yo, R. J.!"

A sudden twinge of panic, a tightening in Ricky's throat. Nobody called him that—"R. J."—anymore. Before he recognized the voice, he knew this was someone from his distant American past. But he could not bring himself to believe that the voice belonged to . . . no, couldn't be . . . not him . . . not *here!*

"It's your favorite cousin! Heh heh heh."

Ricky felt as if he had been pushed backward into a swimming pool. Though he remained seated in his chair in his cramped and tiny Paris apartment, he imagined he was flailing, tumbling blindly, falling through the air, then splashing down, helpless, shocked, unable to breathe, submerged in the cruel, cold past.

"Are you there?" the voice on the machine asked. "It's Cash."

Ricky, submerged, could hear the old confidence in his cousin's honeyed baritone—and the expectation, the undoubting assumption that Ricky, when he learned who was calling, would hurry to pick up the phone.

"Maybe you're not there. I hope this is the right number. I only heard someone speaking French on the machine. I'm calling for R. J., Ricky Jenks. This is his cousin, Cassius Washington. I just arrived in Paris. I'm at Charles de Gaulle Airport and I need to talk to him. It's an urgent matter. I will only be in Paris for a few hours and I need to speak with Ricky, so if you're there, man, please pick up . . . Ricky? . . . Are you there?"

A violent kicking and tussling in the sunny sheets. Fatima bolted upright on the sofa bed and, at that moment, Ricky broke to the surface, emerged from his icy blue trance. He could breathe again. Fatima was rubbing her eyes, scratching her lush and unruly black mane. "Rahr rahr rahr," she said in a needling whine. That was Fatima's imitation of American speech, a grating nasal drone. No real words. Just noise. That was how all Americans sounded to Fatima. But Cassius Washington sounded nothing like that. Cash had a mellifluous, Michael Jordanesque voice to go along with his smooth and sculpted good looks. That beautiful voice now had a desperate edge to it on Ricky's answering machine.

"Okay, well, maybe you're really not there. I got your phone number from your mom. She said this would be a good time of the day to reach you but . . . whatever. Maybe you don't want to talk to me. After all the shit that's gone down between us, I guess I could understand that. But, you know, I thought we'd gotten past all that shit."

Now Ricky was aquiver with rage. He saw the little cup of espresso trembling in his hand. *How dare you! How fucking dare you come to my town, to my side of the ocean, and talk about all the shit we've supposedly gotten past!* Fatima was out of bed now, standing, stretching and yawning with a feline languor, one of the white sheets wrapped around her lithe, cinammon-skinned body like a sari.

"All right," Cash said on the answering machine. "I'll be staying at the home of a business associate. On the Left Bank. Like I said, I'm just here for the day. But I'll try you again later. I could give you the number on my cell phone but I . . . No, I better not. I'll just call again in a little while." Ricky heard a horn honk obnoxiously in the background. "I need your help, R. J. You're the only person in the world who can help me right now. I need you, man. Okay. Anyway, I—"

The answering machine beeped three times in rapid succession, cutting off Cash's voice.

"Rahr rahr rahr," Fatima said irascibly, turning and walking into the bathroom, slamming the door behind her. Even sleepy-eyed and grouchy, Fatima was the most beautiful woman Ricky had ever known. He hated to admit it, but he was deeply, achingly in love with her. He hated to admit it because she was not in love with him.

Slowly, Ricky's rage subsided. He felt strangely soothed by the sound of streaming water from behind the closed bathroom door. He drank the last of his bitter coffee, rose from the chair, slipped into a pair of baggy black pants and sneakers, put a New Jersey Nets cap on his prematurely graying head. While Fatima showered, he would go out to buy their daily bread. But first he pushed a button on the answering machine, erasing Cassius Washington's message.

"I'm antisuccess, antitechnology, antiexercise, antiself-improvement, antistock market and antisobriety. But I am not anti-American. I actually like most Americans. I just can't stand living in America."

That was how Ricky Jenks liked to answer the questions of why he had come to Paris, France and why, after nine years, he was determined to stay here. Like a lot of what Ricky said it sounded only half-serious. Ricky laughed when folks wondered if he had been inspired by the great black American jazzmen who had lived in Paris before him: the Bud Powells, Sidney Bechets and Kenny Clarkes. Ricky would cheerfully explain that he was a pretty mediocre piano player and that he harbored no aspirations of greatness. He could see the shock in the faces of his fellow Americans when he spoke of his mediocrity and lack of ambition.

In America, Ricky Jenks would be considered a loser. In France, he was simply himself.

"You are too lazy for America," Fatima would chide him. "You are like a Frenchman. Or an African. You live for pleasure. Americans live for work." Fatima would nod vigorously, endorsing the American way. She wanted nothing more than to emigrate to the United States. She was in her last year of studies at Paris's elite Institute of Political Science. Once she got her degree, she was determined to find a job in New York, the city Ricky had once called home. The daughter of a Moroccan man and an Cameroonian woman who had grown up in the southwestern French city of Toulouse, Fatima thought Ricky was foolish to have left the United States. "You black Americans," she scolded, "you don't know how good you have it."

"Maybe you're right," Ricky would say with a shrug. "Maybe you're right."

He never told her how France had saved him. How he had come to Paris a broken, humiliated young man. How he had needed to be a stranger in a foreign land, his old identity obliterated, his American past extinguished. He didn't speak of the catastrophe that had, at once, shattered and redefined him. Ricky never told Fatima about his cousin Cash and how he had, more or less, destroyed Ricky's life.

"What the fuck does he want from me?" Ricky muttered under his breath as he climbed the steep slope of the rue des Martyrs. "Why the fuck doesn't he leave me the fuck alone?" For Ricky Jenks, one of the bonuses of living outside the United States was not having to see, talk to or hear about his cousin Cassius Washington, who, in Ricky's eyes, was an immoral scumbag but who was, in the eyes of America, a glorious black role model: not simply a success, but a doctor. And not just a doctor, but a surgeon! Absence of Cash had been a wonderful aspect of Ricky's life in Paris. Now here was Dr. Washington, barging in with no advance warning, leaving a mysterious, melodramatic message about *needing* Ricky. About Ricky being "the only person" who could help him. What kind of shit was Cash trying to pull now? Cash had never seemed to need anybody in his life, least of all Ricky. And even if he did need

Ricky, why in the hell would Ricky lift a finger to help him? Fuck Cash!

Ricky's mood improved as soon as he turned the corner and began walking across the Place des Abbesses, a courtyard-like open space full of trees and pigeons; benches occupied by gossiping little old ladies leaning on their canes, a leather-clad couple, bodies entwined, kissing hungrily and a few ragged street people swigging from green-glassed wine bottles; young toughs standing in clusters—white French, black French, brown French—ostentatiously loitering, smoking cigarettes, tryin' to look bad, talkin' shit; a girl with dirty-blond dreadlocks rollerblading in circles, Walkman headphones plugged into her ears; a noble-looking, ebony-skinned man handing out leaflets and rotely, wearily demanding an end to the war in Sierra Leone; befuddled white American, German and Japanese tourists, maps in hand, cameras strapped around their necks, struggling to get their bearings in Montmartre, this curious puzzle of a neighborhood, full of hills and outdoor staircases with iron bannisters, hidden alcoves, ivy-lined nooks and crannies, narrow, labyrinthine, cobblestone streets. An ornately crafted iron-and-glass canopy presided over the center of the little plaza, the Art Nouveau entrance to the Abbesses metro station. The bells of St-Jean, the imposing, orange-bricked, Byzantine-looking Catholic church that towered over the shady public space, sounded eleven o'clock.

Ricky smiled. There was just this thing he had with Paris, with the Eighteenth Arrondissement in particular: No matter what else was going on in Ricky Jenks's life, whether he had money or not, whether he had a woman or not, whether—back in his first days in the town—he was abysmally depressed or not, once he stepped into the swirling nebula of this *quartier*, he felt better. Ricky saw, in the near distance, the sun shining brassily on the white apartment buildings that stretched down the rue des Abbesses, the long street that originated at the busy square. His heart felt full. He knew that he was in exactly the place where he needed to be. His beloved Eighteenth.

"Bonjour, monsieur," trilled the pert young woman behind the counter at Ricky's favorite bakery. *"Comme d'habitude?"* she asked. "The usual?" Ricky greeted her and nodded yes. They talked about the improvement in the weather as she pulled a baguette, one of those long batons of hard crusty bread, from the row of them along the back wall.

Ricky had never known the name of the girl behind the counter and she did not know his, though they had developed a jokey, ever-so-slightly flirtatious rapport since she had begun working in the place a year earlier. She was twentyish, with quick, birdlike gestures; olive-complexioned but of indeterminate ethnic origin. To Ricky's eye, she could have been Algerian, Turkish, half-European and half-African or some sociogenetic mix beyond his powers of perception. A lot of people in the Eighteenth looked like that. Ricky watched her scoop up a buttery croissant and a golden brown *pain au chocolat* (Ricky's mother had been horrified when he told her he ate "chocolate bread" for breakfast most mornings) from under the glass display case. As Ricky paid, he noticed the girl was staring quizzically up in the air. "What does it say?" she asked in English. She stood on the tips of her toes, leaning across the counter, reaching up and tugging gently at the bill of his cap.

"New Jersey Nets," Ricky said in his native tongue. "It's a basketball team."

"Ah," the bakery girl said, with a familiar, coquettish little gleam in her eye. "Shouldn't you wear it backwards?"

Ricky laughed and responded in Franglais: "*Je suis* old school."

As he walked out of the bakery, Ricky felt a buzz from his little encounter with the girl behind the counter. You have to realize that Ricky Jenks was a guy who didn't know he was good-looking until he was thirty. Though he had lost his roly-poly figure by late adolescence, Ricky carried a fat-kid complex with him right up until the year he moved to Paris. He would always be a husky man, a wide body at six feet tall and two hundred twenty pounds. But, despite his high-calorie diet and lack of exercise, there was little flab on Ricky. He had the sturdy, solid, strong-shouldered build of a shorter Charles Barkley, the pro basketball player once dubbed the Round Mound of Rebound. Though plenty of women back in the States had found him attractive, Ricky could never quite believe it. But in the nine years he had lived in Paris, Ricky had lost most of his insecurity around women. Popularity will do that. And, for some reason, Ricky found that his popularity with the ladies had soared in Paris. The only woman who could make him feel the timidity and awkwardness of his younger days was the one back in his apartment, awaiting breakfast. Fatima Boukhari.

Stopping at a newsstand just off the Place des Abbesses, buying the English language *International Herald Tribune* for himself and the French left-wing daily, *Libération,* for Fatima, Ricky wondered if his cousin Cash had phoned again. Cash said he would be in Paris for only a few hours. So all Ricky had to do was screen his calls for the rest of the day, just not pick up the phone if he heard Cash's voice on the answering machine. But what if Cash had called since Ricky went out? And what if Fatima, having emerged from her shower, had picked up the phone? The idea of Cash talking to Fatima made Ricky suddenly very afraid.

Ricky walked a little more quickly as he turned onto the rue des Martyrs and headed downhill. Grace Kelly, he instantly noticed, was trudging uphill, on the same side of the street. What a surprise to see her at this hour. Grace Kelly was part of the night shift of transvestite and transsexual hookers who stood in doorways, here and there, up and down Ricky's long block. The day shift was just beginning to gather at eleven A.M. Familiar neighborhood faces, particularly the two hookers who seemed to be the veterans of the afternoon corps looking always a bit matronly, a certain Dustin Hoffman-in-*Tootsie* aspect in their chunky bodies and curly wigs. These were men or former men, dressed as suburban moms who had put on their best outfits and got all made-up for a big trip to the city. The night shift on the other hand, consisted of hookers done up in more of the tawdry showgirl mode with miniskirts and fishnet stockings, short leather or fake fur jackets.

Grace Kelly was the regal blond princess of the night shift. One look at any of the crew and you could see they were not organic women. According to Valitsa the Serb, most of the hookers on Martyrs had gone under the knife, switching gender by surgical means. Valitsa herself was a woman by birth and had never been a hooker, but she had, years ago, lived in the same building on the rue des Martyrs where the whores took their johns and she had gotten to know a few of them. It was Valitsa, Ricky's sometime French tutor and one-time-only lover, who had named the tall, leggy prostitute with the golden, shoulder-length hair and movie star haughtiness "Grace Kelly."

"She's really a very nice woman," Valitsa the Serb had told Ricky. "You should get to know her."

But where Ricky came from you didn't talk to a hooker on the street unless you were interested in a business transaction. Sometimes, when Ricky had still been new to the area, the hookers would whisper to him from their shadowy doorways as he walked past. Ricky assumed they were offering their services and did not reply. After a while the hookers stopped saying anything to Ricky. He figured they'd seen him around a lot, seen him in the company of different women and realized he wasn't a potential customer. But the longer he lived on the rue des Martyrs, the more Ricky saw that the shopkeepers, housewives, young professionals and policemen who lived or worked on or regularly traversed the block often said *bonjour* or *bonsoir* to the prostitutes.

One winter evening, walking up Martyrs on his way to work, Ricky spotted Grace Kelly standing and smoking majestically in a doorway. He realized then that what made her distinctive among the hookers on his block was the way she so fully inhabited her femininity. Grace Kelly seemed to *own* her adopted gender in a way that the other transsexuals did not. Ricky impulsively decided to be friendly. As they made eye contact, he smiled and said, *"Bonsoir."* Grace Kelly's reaction was immediate and theatrical. She rolled her eyes and let out a loud, exasperated groan. She then shot Ricky of look of utter scorn, as if he were an ugly bug she had just squished beneath one of her stiletto heels. She shook her big, yellow head and sneered extravagantly. Ricky had never received such a contemptuous, wordless put-down before. Rather than being offended, though, he thought it was hilarious. And probably well-deserved. Where did Ricky get off suddenly trying to be neighborly after living on the block for years? Ricky never said anything to Grace Kelly after that. But sometimes when he would pass her on the street, she would suck her teeth in annoyance or mutter something inaudible but clearly insulting. Ricky, though, remained more tickled than affronted.

Now, on this Thursday morning in April 1999, Ricky couldn't help but wonder what Grace Kelly was doing out and about so early. Was she currently working the day shift? No, from the heaviness of her steps as she climbed the street, her disheveled hair and the hungover slackness in her face, Grace Kelly looked like she was returning home after a particularly rough night. She was trudging past the long, pale façade of the nursing home that sat amid the nightclubs and restaurants of Martyrs when a prim, little nun in gray veil and habit stepped out of the building. Nuns and ambulances were always coming and going through the wide green doors that swung open onto the courtyard of the nursing home. As the prostitute and the nun passed each other they both nodded and said, *"Bonjour."*

Ricky decided that he, too, would greet Grace Kelly this morning. As they approached each other, Ricky was startled by how deeply lined, rugged and masculine Grace Kelly's face was in daylight and without makeup. He suddenly sensed something bottomlessly sad about Grace Kelly. A sympathy welled up inside him. He was opening his mouth to say "good day" when the hooker, not even glancing at Ricky as she trudged uphill and he plodded down, blandly uttered one of the more severe slurs in the French language: *"Pauvre con."* There is no precise translation for this in English, at least not one that captures the withering disdain of the expression. It's sort of like saying, "You pathetic asshole."

But Ricky didn't mind.

"So—why do you not wish to speak to this cousin of your?" Fatima Boukhari said in her lilting, scolding voice. She sat across from Ricky at the small round-topped table wedged into the corner of his studio that constituted the kitchenette. Fatima was dressed in her blue workshirt and black jeans, her turbulent black hair still wet from the shower. She spoke while staring at the newspaper spread out on the former café table in front of her. She took a sip from a small ceramic bowl of tea, waiting for a response. Ricky held his tiny cup of espresso in one hand, his carefully folded *Herald Tribune* in the other, pretending not to have heard the question, absorbed in his morning newspaper. "Ree-KEE!" Fatima squealed impatiently.

"Yes, dear?"

"Why do you disrespect a relation so?"

Cash had indeed called while Ricky was out buying the bread and newspapers. But Fatima, fortunately, was still in the shower at the time. Ricky had listened to the second message on the answering machine as soon as he walked in the door. "Hello, this is Dr. Cassius Washington calling for Richard Jenks." Traffic noise in the background. "Yo, Ricky, pick up the damn phone, man." Cash's voice had changed instantly from authoritative to combative and now, in a split second, switched again to high-pitched whiny: "C'mon, man, don't do me like that! Please, Ricky, pick up the phone." A pause; the motorized cacophony of the highway. "Okay," Cash said dejectedly. "Be like that." Honking horns. "But I *will* call you back." Click. Dial tone. Ricky erased the message.

"It sounded like your cousin is in need," Fatima said.

"Then I guess he'll call back," Ricky replied in a disinterested tone, trying to concentrate on his newspaper, sipping his espresso.

"Will you answer when he does?"

"I dunno."

"Why not?"

"He's a jerk."

"That is no excuse!" Fatima cried. "He is your relation—in blood!"

Ricky finally looked up from the paper. Fatima was staring fixedly at him, her dark brown eyes sparkling the way they did whenever she felt argumentative, which seemed to be more and more often. "He probably won't call again."

"But you just said he would!" Fatima fired back.

"What's it to you, anyway?" Ricky said, trying not to sound too annoyed, but just annoyed enough to end the discussion.

Fatima paused, seeming to stop and wonder why she should, in fact, care. Then she smiled. "I don't know," she said, "I think maybe I just like to—how do you say?—bust the balls."

Ricky let out a huge laugh. "Well, you certainly do a good job of busting mine!"

Fatima's smile was a radiant sunburst, all the more precious because she displayed it so infrequently these days. She thrust a fist into the air. "I am queen of the Busters of the Balls!" Fatima, who had been so stern and hypercritical the past few weeks, was giggling uncontrollably.

Ricky, at first, was thrilled to see Fatima enjoying herself so freely, so fully. But he began to wonder if her mirth was due to the fact that she had just discovered some essential truth about herself. "So that's why you keep me around," Ricky said in his half-serious tone, "just to bust my balls."

Fatima was beside herself with laughter now, slapping a palm down on the copy of *Libération* spread out on the table, her eyes closed, crinkling at the corners, tossing her magnificent head of black hair that managed to be, in different places, straight, curly and kinky. "I like to bust the balls," she wheezed. Slowly, Fatima calmed down. She sipped her tea, took a bite out of her buttered slice of baguette, returned her attention to her newspaper. Back to business. "I have to go soon. I have a class."

Ricky always had to remind himself that, no matter how much he was in love with her, Fatima was not in love with him. She was in love with the Frenchman who had dumped her a year ago. Ricky was Fatima's diversion while she got over Bernard-Henri. This was something that Ricky had to force himself to keep in mind: *She is not in love with you. Memorize that fact. She is in love with the rich French yuppie, the former management consultant she met during a summer internship, the Gauloise-smoking motherfucker who traded in his business suits and ties for an all-black wardrobe, shaved his head, grew a goatee and, with an immense subsidy from Papa and Maman, started up an Internet company. He dumped Fatima for some skinny blond chick from the posh Seventh Arrondissement and Fatima still can't believe it. But she uses you to cover up the hurt. You're not her boyfriend. You're a Band-Aid. And she will never love you.*

Yet, even if Bernard-Henri dropped his posh girlfriend and came crawling back to Fatima, even if he demonstrated his undying love for her and no matter how deliriously in love with him Fatima might be, she would never marry Bernard-Henri. Just as she would never marry Ricky Jenks. Fatima Boukhari had sworn she would only, ever, marry a fellow Muslim. Fatima's inflexibility on the issue surprised Ricky. Because he had always seen her as a fairly secular Muslim. She was certainly no fundamentalist. Yes, she had been to Mecca and she fasted during Ramadan. But she also drank wine and engaged in premarital sex. Ricky would never have thought that someone as intelligent and broad-minded as Fatima would be adamantly opposed to religious intermarriage. He was wrong. Fatima had her convictions. They had been ingrained in her, she said proudly, by her family.

Ricky and Fatima ate their breakfast and read their newspapers in silence. Ricky hoped the telephone would not ring. He did not want to

feel pressured by Fatima to answer it. Ricky wanted to ignore Cash, to
pretend his cousin had not even called, or that he had just happened to
be away from the studio during those few hours when cousin Cassius
had just happened to be in Paris, missing those urgent messages. He
knew Cash would call back. He just wanted Fatima to be gone before
the phone rang again. It was the first time in the ten months of their
now-we-see-each-other-now-we-don't quasi relationship that Ricky was
eager for her to leave his apartment.

Killings were splattered all over the pages of Ricky's newspaper. For
more than a month already, an international war had been raging on
European soil—the worst in fifty-four years—just a few hours away
from where Ricky and Fatima sat. Bombers, refugees, the slaughter of
civilians. And just a week or so earlier, a couple of rich white boys in
Colorado walked into their high school, armed to the teeth, gunning
down their fellow students. They had specifically targeted jocks and
black kids. Kosovo and Columbine. So this was the *fin du siècle*.

The telephone rang. Ricky almost jumped up to answer it, but forced
himself to remain in his chair. Fatima locked eyes with him. The phone
rang a second time. Ricky pretended to read his newspaper. Fatima rose
from the table. The third ring. Fatima slid her newspaper into her knapsack, strapped the knapsack over her shoulders. *"Bonjour,"* Ricky's voice
said on the answering machine.

"I have to go," Fatima said as Ricky's recorded greeting played on
the tape. She stood above him. "Just remember: Your family is all that
you got."

She leaned forward and kissed Ricky roughly on the forehead. The
electronic beep on the answering machine sounded. There was a long
silence on the tape. Fatima opened the door to Ricky's apartment. He
wanted to believe that what she had just told him was true. But he
couldn't. Fatima softly closed the door behind her.

"Yo, cuz." Cash's choked voice on the answering machine. "I've
arrived. I'm here. On your turf. And I gotta see ya, man."

Ricky Jenks sat rigidly in his chair, thinking of what Fatima had
said to him—and trying not to reach for the phone.

"You gotta help me, Ricky." Cash seemed on the verge of crying.
And Ricky felt tears sting his own eyes. "I'm dyin', man. For real."

Two

THE STREET OF THE Fishmongers, that is to say, the rue des Poissonniers, was not the sort of place a tourist like Dr. Cassius Washington was likely to visit. Ordinarily, when American sightseers ventured to the north of Paris, it was to visit scenic Montmartre, not the neighborhood it bordered: Barbès, the rambling Third World unto itself that dominated the eastern area of the Eighteenth Arrondissement. Barbès was one of the few places within the Paris city limits where one could walk for blocks and blocks and still more blocks, through bustling crowds of humanity, and not see a single white person (unless it was a cop). The streets of Barbès were full of amber-toned women in billowy black, white or beige veils and dark brown women in vibrantly multicolored headdresses and gowns, with tiny, doll-eyed babies, swaddled tight in *kente* cloth, strapped to their backs; men wearing kufis, turbans and small, delicately embroidered, skull-fitting caps, men striding in ankle-length robes and sandals. The outdoor marketplaces resonated with the beautifully jagged rhythms of Arabic, and the bubbling musicality of the French language in the mouths of pure-blooded Africans whose family lines—unlike those of Ricky Jenks and Cash Washington and just about every other American of African descent—had never been mixed with the blood of whites: a polyphony of vendors hawking their wares, women laughing and haggling, groups of bantering, gesticulating men, and shiny warm-up–suited Barbès homeboys in jewelry, shades and backward baseball caps babbling importantly into their mobile phones. If Ricky was going to let himself be coaxed into meeting Cash in Paris, he was at least going to make sure they met someplace his sophisticated cousin would never go unless he absolutely had to: the thumping black heart of the Eighteenth.

"Thanks for answering the phone," Cash had said that morning, sniffling, pausing, seeming to suck back a dry, suppressed sob. "You there, man?"

"I'm here."

"Can you see me? Today?" Cash seemed to have gotten a grip. He still sounded desperate, but less pathetic. He wanted to make a plan. "I'm leaving town at six."

"I can meet you at five," Ricky had said. He was surprised by the frost in his own voice.

"Where?"

"Do you know the Eighteenth?" Ricky asked, assuming Cash did not.

Now Ricky sat in the cool and dark of a small, obscure café, around the corner from a crowded street market, at the nexus of rue des Poissonniers and rue Poulet—that is to say, Chicken Street—waiting for Cash. The nearest metro stop was named Château Rouge—or Red Castle, though there was no such distinctive monument in sight. Ricky sipped his glass of bittersweet Belgian beer and discreetly checked out the clientèle: a couple of Arab men in long robes and skullcaps drinking mint tea and engaged in solemn discourse; a man and a woman, both thirtyish, both black, he urgent in his neatly pressed open-collar shirt and blue polyester pants, nursing a glass of pink wine, whispering, imploring her, and she hardly touching her little cup of espresso, impassive and un-impressed in her floral-printed sundress, nonchalantly tossing her long, lustrous braids, crossing and uncrossing her bare legs. Ricky wasn't sit-ting close enough to hear their conversation, but he wondered where the couple was from. Did they hail from one of the former French colonial countries in Africa? Or were they from Martinique or Guadeloupe in what was once known as the French West Indies? Or maybe the nation that used to be called "French" Guyana in South America? Or had they been born and bred right here in Barbès? One thing was clear to Ricky: this beautiful black couple was definitely not from the U.S. of A.

Everyone in the café—the Arab men, the black couple, the Algerian bartender and Ricky—looked up when Cash Washington suddenly ap-peared in the doorway. Cash paused for a moment, standing on the sunny sidewalk, peering uncertainly into the shadowy café. He wore an expensive-looking double-breasted charcoal-gray suit, a crisp yellow shirt and blue silk tie; he carried a brown leather briefcase in his left hand and raised his right hand above his brow to blot out the glare of the sun. As soon as he spotted Ricky, Cash broke into his broad, confident grin. The bartender and the other customers continued to stare at Cash as he strode into the café, beaming at Ricky. It was freakishly rare that someone like Cash—obviously American, obviously wealthy, and obvi-ously a tourist—should walk into a Barbès café. But as the bartender and the other customers fairly gawked at Cash, Ricky detected something other than surprise in their eyes. They all seemed to wonder where they had seen this tall, handsome black American before. It was that celebrity aura that Cash radiated. He just *looked* like somebody famous.

"R. J.!" Cash yelled. He stopped in front of Ricky's table, set down his briefcase and held out his arms, as if he expected Ricky to leap into his embrace. "Gimme some love!"

Ricky remained in his chair. "Hello, Cash."

A sudden look of dismay rippled across Cash's face but he quickly recovered and, smiling broadly again, bent over and put his arms around his cousin. Ricky stiffened in Cash's awkward embrace, his nostrils quiv-ering from the smell of Cash's cologne. He remembered the last time he'd seen his cousin, five years earlier, during a brief visit to America when—with their mothers and fathers, brothers, sisters and other family watching—Ricky and Cash had also hugged, tentatively, clumsily, in false reconciliation.

Cash stood upright again, gave Ricky a querulous look, then sat down at the table, taking care to slide his briefcase underneath his chair. The other customers finally stopped staring at Cash. Who knows? Maybe they *did* recognize him. Maybe, unbeknownst to Ricky, Cash had appeared on French television. In America, Dr. Cassius Washington was a not-infrequent TV interviewee. Still only in his late thirties, he had become the favorite orthopedic surgeon of a small galaxy of sports stars. He was the accomplished black doctor famous black athletes sought out to repair their shredded tendons and ligaments, their corroded cartilage and battered bones. When franchise players were sprawled on the turf or the hardwood, writhing in agony, it was Dr. Cash who was summoned to assess the damage, heal the wound and then give a press conference explaining it all to reporters who invariably used the same word to describe the young surgeon, that adjective white Americans habitually employed when they were astonished by the intelligence of a black American: "articulate."

"I'm glad we could have this time together, R. J.," Cash said, flashing his winning grin.

"Call me Ricky," his cousin replied, taking a sip of his beer.

The bartender walked up to the table, greeted Cash and asked what he would like. Cash suddenly stopped smiling. He turned to Ricky, a helpless, puzzled look on his face. "What do you wanna drink?" Ricky translated.

"Oh, I don't know, just a mineral water. Do they have Evian in this country?"

As the bartender left to fill Cash's order, the cousins sat uncomfortably at the table, casting quick glances at each other, then looking away. The bartender placed a cold bottle of Evian and an empty glass on the table. "Thank you," Cash said.

"*Merci,*" Ricky corrected him.

Cash stared out at the rue des Poissonniers as he took a thirsty gulp of his drink. "I thought all the slums were on the *outskirts* of Paris," he said with a brittle chuckle.

"Just 'cause black folks live here doesn't mean it's a slum," Ricky snapped.

"I'm just joking, R. J., I mean Ricky."

The cousins fell back into their tense silence. Ricky had been somewhat surprised to see that Cash was the picture of perfect health. "I'm dyin', man. For real," Cash had whimpered on the answering machine this morning, just before Ricky picked up the phone. Right up until the moment Cash appeared in the doorway of the café, Ricky had entertained a perverse fantasy: he envisioned his once strong and handsome cousin showing up wan and shriveled, suffering from some fatal, organ-devouring disease. He had imagined that Cash wanted to finally set things aright before his imminent demise, that maybe Cash would say to Ricky the words he had never said before, had refrained from saying during their false reconciliation five years earlier: "I'm sorry." Ricky had even taken his daydream further into the realm of TV movie banali-mentality, seeing himself standing beside Cash's hospital bed, tearfully bestowing his forgiveness as his repentant and pitiful cousin lost consciousness and the electronic heart monitor that had been bleating rhythmically suddenly emitted a single, ominous, high-pitched death note.

"You're lookin' good, Ricky," Cash finally said, grinning winningly again. "Real good. I can see that Paris was the right move for you. Am I mistaken or have you lost a lot of weight? You know, your parents still worry about you sometimes, living in a foreign country but I say, hey, diff'rent strokes for diff'rent folks, you dig? Sometimes it takes a man a while to find himself. Maybe you've found yourself here—in Paris. Am I right?"

Ricky downed the last of his beer. He knew Cash was accustomed to disarming people with his charm, but he wasn't playing along. Not here. Not in this town. "You said on my machine that you don't have much time. Neither do I. Now, what is it you wanted to see me about?"

Cash stared down at the floor. He seemed genuinely hurt. "Damn, Ricky."

"You told me you were dying."

Cash paused for a long moment. "I am," he whispered. "I am dying . . . of heartbreak." He looked up again, his eyes glassy. "Serena . . . my wife . . . she left me."

Ricky had to restrain himself. *WELL, WELL, WELL,* he wanted
to shout. *How you like it, Cash? How YOU like it, you slimy muthafucka?!*
He wanted to leap from his chair, to dance on the table, pointing and
jeering at his cousin, exulting in his misery. But Ricky stayed in his
seat, struggling to control his facial muscles, to stop the huge, shit-eating
grin that threatened to split his face in half. The image of Serena Moriarty Washington flashed across Ricky's mind. He had never met the
woman and, naturally, he had boycotted Cash's wedding two years earlier. But on Ricky's last visit to the U.S., his mother had forced him to
watch videotaped highlights of his cousin Cash's big day. He had seen
the trophy bride, had seen that his sister Isabel had been accurate when
she described Serena as "a dead ringer for Mariah Carey." Oh, how he
wanted to gloat, to say, *Yo, cuz, what goes around comes around, don't it?*

And yet . . . and yet . . . despite all the venom he felt for Cash, looking
at his glass-eyed cousin, seeing the hurt in his face, his trembling lower
lip, Ricky could not help but feel sorry for the man. Even after all the
pain Cash had caused him, Ricky felt a rush of sympathy for his cousin.
As his kid sister, Isabel Jenks Douglas, the hard-assed Miami judge, had
said many times, Ricky Jenks was "too tenderhearted." Instead of all
the justifiably cruel things he could have said to Cash upon hearing that
his wife had abandoned him, Ricky stared at his cousin and simply asked,
"When?"

"Last week," Cash said, his voice cracking. He took another gulp of
water, then closed his eyes for several seconds, as if to force back tears.
He bowed his head and took a deep breath, trying to compose himself.

"What happened?"

Cash raised his head again but stared into space as he spoke, as if
he were afraid that looking Ricky in the eye would cause him to break
down. "It was my fault, Ricky. Well . . . mostly my fault, anyway. I didn't
realize how things were going wrong. I thought we were happy. I've
been workin' like a dog, you know? Trying to make a good life for us.
Hoping that we might be able to start a family soon. But there's just so
many things I didn't see, didn't know. Couldn't have known. I guess I
was just too focused on my career. I've been building a hospital. Not by
myself. But with some partners. We've been raising money for years.
Finally broke the ground a few weeks ago. A beautiful spot in upstate

New York, right on the Hudson River. It's gonna be called the Center for Athletic Wellness. A full-service place of healing, not just for the athletic elite but for any sportsman who needs help. And not just rich folks, either. I've got all sorts of plans for community outreach, you know. For dealing with young people from the inner city, serving their athletic health needs. This has been a dream of mine for so long, Ricky. And, finally, in just the past two or three years, I've begun to see my dream come to fruition."

Cash paused to take a sip of water, then continued to stare into space, avoiding eye contact with Ricky, as he spoke. "I'm an ambitious man, Ricky. Maybe a little too ambitious. Anyway, I thought Serena understood. I thought she appreciated the fact that I was trying to build something. Not just for me. But for both of us. For our future. For the . . ." Cash stopped suddenly, swallowed hard before continuing. "For the family we might have someday. But I guess I just got too caught up in it all. All the traveling, the consulting, the fund-raising for the Center for Athletic Wellness. Maybe I was too distant, too wrapped up in my work. You know how sisters are always bitchin' about how they can't find a good man who brings home the bacon. Well, shit, I am such a man. I thought I was being a good black husband to my beautiful black wife. And with all the time I spent away from home, despite all the temptations that were out there, I never once cheated on Serena."

At that moment, Cash finally looked directly into Ricky's eyes. "Never," he said. "Not once." Then he averted his gaze again. "But even that didn't make Serena happy. I guess she felt neglected. She started acting out. Screaming and carrying on. Throwing tantrums. I tried to reason with her. I really did, man. I told her I was doing my best. But she just kept nagging me. Nag, nag, nag. She wanted to go into couples counselling. Can you imagine? Like I got time for that shit. But she just kept after me about this fucking couples counselling. Nagging me about it. Constantly—like I was some kinda fuckin' head case. Nag, nag, nag, nag, nag. Till finally I just couldn't take it anymore. And, one night, I just . . . well, I . . . I guess I musta just snapped and . . . I hit her."

Cash Washington bowed his head, closed his eyes again. There had been times, over the past ten years, when Ricky had truly despised Cash, when he had hated him as much as he had hated anyone in his life.

But even when his feelings toward his cousin were most bitter, Ricky had never imagined Cash to be something that their mothers had taught them to regard as the lowest form of male: a wife-beater.

"That's disgusting," Ricky said.

"I know," Cash whispered, his head still lowered, eyes shut tight. Ricky saw a single tear slide down his cousin's cheek. "But it was just one time. And you gotta understand—she provoked me."

"How?" Ricky said hotly. "By suggesting couples counselling? For Christ's sake, Cash, half of America's in some sort of therapy! It's the goddamned national religion!"

Cash lifted his head again and continued to stare past Ricky as he spoke, though now his eyes were burning red. "There's more. More to it than that. Serena had misled me. For a long time. She had a secret. A secret she never told me till last week. It's too painful for me even to talk about, Ricky. But a secret like that . . . a secret like that is like . . . a poison. I know I was wrong to do what I did. But I was always honest with Serena. It was her secret that had poisoned our marriage."

Cash pulled a blue silk handkerchief from his breast pocket, blew his nose loudly, soggily. Ricky noticed the black couple, the Arab men in robes and skullcaps and the bartender all staring brazenly at his cousin. When they noticed Ricky noticing them, they all looked away.

"Okay, Cash," Ricky said, his voice turning frosty again. "I understand you're upset. There was a time when I thought I was gonna die of heartbreak, too. About ten years ago."

"I know, man, I know," Cash said, nodding, his voice sounding even more anguished. "And I want you to know how much I regret what happened. I want you to know that I'm really, really sorry. I'm so sorry about what I did to you, man."

At last, Cash had said it, uttered the apology Ricky had longed to hear. But Ricky was surprised to find that when his cousin's guilty plea was finally spoken, it meant absolutely nothing to him.

"Look, Cash, I know you're going through hell right now but . . . um, well . . . what do you want *me* to do about it?"

Now Cash's eyes zeroed in on his cousin's and when he spoke there was a startling steel in his voice. "She's here. Serena is in Paris. I don't know where exactly. But she's somewhere in this city. I need you to find her."

"Why don't you find her yourself?"

"I'm the person she's hiding from, Ricky! Serena doesn't want to see me. If she knew I was here, she'd go even deeper underground. And, besides, I don't know this town. I wouldn't even know where to begin looking."

"How should I?"

"Serena used to live here. For three years, back in the eighties. I know that was before you came to Paris but I thought you two might have some mutual friends. Especially in the African-American expatriate community."

Ricky shrugged. "It's possible."

"Look, man, all I'm asking is for you to make a few inquiries. Ask around. Find out what you can. And if you do locate Serena, maybe you could talk to her. Serena knows all about you, Ricky. From the family. She really admires you."

"We've never even laid eyes on each other."

"I know. But she thinks you're this hip, adventurous dude who bucked all our family pressures and followed his bliss to Paris. That *is* what you are, isn't it?"

"If you say so."

"Please, Ricky. I'm begging you," Cash said, his voice sounding more determined than pleading. "Find Serena. Tell her how sorry I am. Tell her I'll do anything to make up for my sins. I'll make any sacrifice to save our marriage."

Now it was Ricky who avoided eye contact. Staring down at the stained wooden table, he said, "Why should I want to help you, Cash? I mean, our past aside, if you beat up your wife and she doesn't want to see you, why in the world would I help you find her? Maybe she's better off without you."

Ricky looked up to see Cash pull a white, letter-sized envelope from his inner jacket pocket. He slid the envelope across the table. "There's one thousand dollars in there. In cold, hard *me*," Cash said with a self-conscious laugh.

"Are you trying to bribe me?"

"No, Ricky, I'm trying to pay you. I'm asking for your help and I believe in paying the people who help me. You will also find inside that envelope a recent photo of Serena. Show it around to the folks you know. Maybe somebody will recognize her."

Ricky stared at the sealed envelope on the table. He didn't know whether or not to feel offended. "I don't get it."

"Sure you do, Ricky. I'm asking a favor of you. Besides, your mom told me you live from hand to mouth. An extra thousand bucks couldn't hurt now, could it?"

"I guess not," Ricky murmured, regarding the envelope on the table almost fearfully, as if it were a live grenade.

"I'm leaving Paris in half an hour," Cash said in a businesslike tone. "I'll be back in three days. Find out what you can on Serena's whereabouts. When I get back I'll give you a call and you can tell me what you've learned. Okay?"

"Where are you going?"

Cash paused, seeming, for a moment, reluctant to answer the question. "Switzerland," he said. "Zurich."

Ricky chuckled. "Zurich? What, have you got a Swiss bank account?"

Cash stared hard at Ricky, unsmiling. "Why do you say that?"

"I'm just kidding, Cash."

"Oh." Cash smiled thinly. Then he was all business again. "Like I say, I'll be back in Paris Sunday night. You get a thousand dollars, up front, for three days of light detective work. That's not a bad weekend's pay, is it?"

"Not for me," Ricky said, still afraid of touching the envelope on the table. "But I'm just a piano player."

The sudden toot of a horn startled everyone in the café—except Cash Washington. Ricky saw a black sedan out on the rue des Poissonniers. "That's my ride," Cash said.

"You hired a limo?" Ricky asked incredulously.

"It belongs to my business associate. You didn't think I'd try to negotiate the Paris metro on my own, did you?" Cash gave Ricky a mischievous wink. His old self-assurance had returned.

"Guess not."

"Hey, man, I don't have any French money on me." He gestured toward his empty bottle of Evian.

"My treat," Ricky said.

Dr. Cassius Washington rose from the table, picked up his brown leather briefcase. Smiling his winner's smile again, he looked down at his cousin and asked, "Need a lift?"

"No thanks. I can walk home from here."

Cash held out his hand. Ricky shook it. As the bartender and the four other customers watched in apparent awe, Cash strode out of the café, into his waiting car. The sleek black limousine—which was about as common a sight in Barbès as a flying carpet—disappeared down the Street of the Fishmongers.

Now all eyes were on Ricky Jenks. His face felt hot with embarrassment. He left forty francs on the table for the Belgian beer and mineral water. Rising quickly, he waved to the bartender. *"Merci, monsieur. Au revoir."* Ricky was almost out the door when he suddenly realized what he had forgotten. He turned around, retrieved the envelope full of money from the table, stuffed it in his pocket, then walked briskly out of the cool, dark café.

Three

THE SKY HAD CLOUDED over by the time Ricky returned to the rue des Martyrs. Despite the change in the weather, he felt oddly jolly after his meeting with Cassius Washington. Why? Was Ricky, his tender heart aside, cheered by Cash's anguish? Was he excited by the prospect of tracking down his cousin's runaway wife? Or did he just like the feel of that envelope stuffed with American currency in his pants pocket? Maybe seeing Cash pathetic and heartbroken here in Paris was the final salve Ricky needed for his own ancient heartbreak, the trauma that had sent him in flight to this town in the first place. Whatever the reason for his glee, Ricky had a merry little bounce in his step as he climbed the steep slope of his block. He thought he might even show up early for work tonight. But first he had to stop by his apartment to stash his payment from Cash.

Entering the darkened lobby of his building, Ricky slid a hand along the wall and pressed the light button. Ordinarily, at the push of the button, the lobby and stairwell would be illuminated for two minutes before the lights switched off again. It always struck Ricky as a smart, electricity-saving custom. But, for the past week, the light buttons in his building had been malfunctioning. With the first push, the lights would come on for only about five seconds before switching off again. Ricky had just started walking up the stairs to his third-floor apartment when he was plunged back into shadows. He pushed the next light button on the second-floor landing but before he climbed the stairs to the third floor, everything had gone dark once again. By the time he turned the key in the lock of his apartment door, he'd had to push the light buttons four times just to see what he was doing.

Once inside his studio, he carefully opened the envelope Cash had given him. He counted the twenty crisp $50 bills. And there, amid the greenbacks, was the small photo of Serena Moriarty Washington. It was a color head shot, two inches by three inches, a miniature version of one of those professionally composed pictures that actresses and singers send out with their résumés. Once again, Ricky was struck by Serena's resemblance to the pop star Mariah Carey. Like Mariah, Serena had a multicultural look about her, neither unambiguously black nor white, maybe biracial with a dash of Latin blood, long light-brown hair, soft cheeks and a slightly upturned, little round nose. As with Mariah Carey, Ricky thought Serena was objectively gorgeous yet he was not subjectively attracted to her. There was an artificiality, a show-biz phoniness in her expression that he found off-putting. What Ricky saw in Serena's face was cunning without deep intelligence; sexiness without real passion; openness but not a trace of kindness. She was definitely not his type. Yet, by the time Ricky remembered to look at the little digital clock on the side table next to his sofa bed, he realized he had spent ten minutes staring at Serena's picture. He slipped the photo back into the envelope full of money and locked the envelope inside the trunk that he had brought with him when he first came to Paris in 1990.

Instead of having time to spare, Ricky was now running a bit late for work. Hurrying down the stairs of his apartment building, he almost took a tumble when the lights suddenly switched off five seconds after he had pushed the button on the wall. Back out on the street, as he strode up the rue des Martyrs, Ricky spotted Grace Kelly leaning casually in a doorway, talking to a potential customer. At ten minutes to six in the evening, it was still early for a member of the night shift of transvestite and transsexual prostitutes to make an appearance on Martyrs. But this was obviously no ordinary day for Grace Kelly. She seemed to be in much better shape, though, than she had been this morning. She wore a leopard-print miniskirt, black nylon stockings and high heels, a black leather jacket with the collar turned up. Her hair and makeup were meticulously done and in the cloudy early evening light she had regained her feminine panache. The would-be client chatting with her was comically nerdy-looking: a balding, wiry man in his fifties with thick, round-lensed spectacles and a droopy gray mustache. Wearing a wrinkled beige trenchcoat over his bland brown business suit, he seemed the ultimate anonymous *fonctionnaire*, maybe a lifelong clerk in some obscure department of irrelevant records.

Grace Kelly and the nerdy man seemed to be in deep discussion. Ricky wondered if they were negotiating a price. But as he drew closer to the couple, he was careful to look away. He wanted to stare straight ahead and stride quickly past them without drawing attention to himself. After all, it had been only a few hours since Grace Kelly had called Ricky a *pauvre con*. He didn't want to do anything that might incite more hostility from her. Yet, just as he was about to pass the couple, he felt the hooker's eyes on him. He cast a reflexive glance her way. At that moment, Grace Kelly smiled generously at Ricky. *"Bonsoir, monsieur,"* she said, with a gracious nod of her blond head. Ricky was too startled to say anything back. He just smiled at the prostitute and kept walking. But Ricky felt warmed by the hooker's greeting. He was glad that, for whatever reason, Grace Kelly didn't seem to hate him anymore.

Where Ricky lived all hills climbed toward, fed into, the one Huge Hill, or the Butte Montmartre. Here, at the highest altitude in Paris, the immense, white, domed basilica of Sacré Coeur loomed over the city. To walk through the streets surrounding this massive church of the Sacred Heart, in the middle of a winter's night, when all the hilltop was asleep, felt like walking through an abandoned movie set. Indeed, Gene Kelly had pranced across these cobblestones in *An American in Paris*. In the

last years of the twentieth century it was impossible for Ricky Jenks, an
American child reared, in part, by television, to walk past the cafés and
small cottages encircling the Place du Tertre, with their red or gray tiled
rooftops, their shutters and chimneys, and not instantly associate the
scene with Golden-Age-of-Hollywood, stylized quaintness—but only on
those deserted, moonlit nights, at two or three or four o'clock, when all
the shops were closed, and especially on the rare occasions when the
rooftops and cobblestones were dusted with snow. Ricky would eventually forget American kitsch and remember that the likes of Renoir and
Toulouse-Lautrec, Van Gogh and Picasso and Henry Ossawa Tanner had
once prowled the narrow, bumpy streets of the Butte Montmartre—back
in the late nineteenth and early twentieth centuries, back when much
of the sprawling hillside was pasture. Ricky would stare up at the dome
of Sacré Coeur, at the golden light that capped it, glowing against a blue
velvet sky, and forget the structure's disconcerting resemblance to the
U.S. Capitol building. Forget the art historians who laughed at the
church's grandiosity. On those cold, late, empty nights, Sacré Coeur was
the proud summit of one of the earth's more indomitable towns, visible
from myriad spots all around the City of Light.

If the alabaster vastness of the basilica was an Olympian vision, particularly when seen from the low-slung neighborhoods of the rest of the
city—Paris's nineteen other arrondissements—then up-close, eight
months of the year, anyway, the area just behind Sacré Coeur was Tourist
Hades. From the end of March until the end of November, to walk across
the Place du Tertre was to engage in a roiling body slam of sightseers, chattering people outfitted with caps and sunglasses, whining children, snarling parents, men—always men—holding camcorders to their faces, one
eye squinting shut, the other obscured by the glass bubble eye stretching
forward for the zoom-in shot. By the peak of the season in mid-August, the
Place du Tertre and most of the streets around Sacré Coeur were, in early
evening, a steamy phantasmagoria of multinational consumption. The
consumers babbled in German and English, Spanish and English, Italian
and English, Japanese, Chinese, Russian and English, provincial French,
Parisian French, painstaking, stammering phrasebook French, Arabic,
Farsi, Hebrew and English: British English, American English, most often a heavily if obscurely accented, broken English.

The doors of all the souvenir shops shooting off the Place du Tertre gaped open during the season: posters, scarves and T-shirts, soccer jerseys, glass and porcelain figurines, cuckoo clocks and marionettes, little replicas of the Eiffel Tower and the Arc de Triomphe, plastic snow bubbles containing a miniature Cathedral of Notre-Dame, plates and ashtrays and shot glasses painted with the image of one of the butte's decrepit brown windmills: it was all part of the hilltop bazaar. *Artistes* were everywhere, their easels carefully arranged, displaying corny, oily representations of the surrounding monuments; pencil-and-crayon portraitists toting their drawing pads under their arms, offering to create your likeness, in ten minutes, for just fifty—or was it a hundred?—French francs. There were African vendors, wearing umbrella hats, selling postcards and wind-up plastic toys. And lots of heavily painted street mimes.

This was where Ricky Jenks earned his living.

The past, some wise person wrote, is a foreign country. But on this Thursday night in April 1999, Ricky's past seemed more like a distant planet. Playing in a zone, his chubby fingers gliding across the keyboard, his body swaying to the music he spun out into the air, Ricky kept laughing to himself, seemingly apropos of nothing, like some benign madman on the metro. He was laughing at the past that had once caused him such grief, chuckling as he played the scratched and battered old black piano at Le Bon Montmartrois, bemused by the memory of people who had wounded him, people who suddenly seemed as irrelevant to his current existence as bacterial life on Neptune. Giddily tickling the ivories, Ricky imagined his cousin Cash not as a visitor from another country but as a being so alien as to hail from another galaxy, a tragicomical, E.T.-like figure.

Despite Ricky's inscrutable, private laughter, the audience in the crêperie was zoning along with him. Tourist season was just hitting its stride. Turnover was fluid tonight, the clientèle a shifting mix of wintertime regulars and first-and-probably-only-time visitors who had either stumbled upon this low-ceilinged, wood-beamed, candlelit, red-and-white checkerboard-tableclothed one-trick pony of a restaurant or had seen it listed in a guide book. François was squeezed between the double counter, a nimble maestro, orchestrating tonight's cuisine on the two circular, hot metal griddles before him. He took orders from the tourists standing out on the rue Norvins, who leaned into the wide window of his cooking space; then François would turn around and take orders from the waitress for the customers sitting inside Le Bon Montmartrois, who were listening, unusually raptly tonight, to the piano player and munching their crêpes.

Crêpes were the only food served at "The Good Montmartre Dweller." Sad-eyed François, with his long, chalky, unsmiling face and brisk yet unfailingly polite manner, would make hundreds—and in deepest summer, thousands—of crêpes in the course of a day, ladling the yellow liquid mix onto the wide, steaming griddles, watching the dough turn into golden brown, crusty-edged, wafer-thin circles. Before folding the circle into a tri-cornered sandwich with his trusty spatula, François would fill it to your liking: ham and cheese, butter and sugar, chocolate syrup and banana slices, Grand Marnier and apple chunks, chestnut marmalade or a fried egg: You could have your crêpe your way at Le Bon Montmartrois.

"Nice Work if You Can Get it": By around midnight, Ricky was playing his version of Thelonious Monk's version of the classic Gershwin tune for the second time. He had already charmed and puzzled his audiences with his idiosyncratic renditions of such standards as "I Love Paris" and "April in Paris" and "Misty" and "La Vie En Rose" and "As Time Goes By." He had then, taking the pulse of the ever-changing crowd, switched to the mellow menace of Miles Davis: "So What" and "All Blues." He had already dipped into his Prince Suite: lulling the audience with "Sometimes it Snows in April," arousing them with "Let's Go Crazy," then zapping 'em with the funk of "Dirty Mind" and "Sexy Motherfucker."

Yes, Ricky had the crowd tonight: its attention, its appreciation, its generous tips. In the hierarchy of jazz musicians living in or passing through France, Ricky Jenks ranked himself somewhere between the second and third tiers. He was not one of those esteemed second-tier artists: a good interpreter if less than great composer, who had put out a few albums, gave the occasional solo concert and regularly played with first-tier artists (those household names with major recording contracts who headlined at the premier spots in Paris and did the rounds of the European jazz festivals every summer). Ricky had met precious few first-tier musicians in his life. He knew a number of second-tier players in Paris, though, and he was honest enough to admit that those musicians just had it, or had *more* of it—whatever *it* was (Talent? Discipline? Ambition? Inspiration?)—than Ricky would ever possess. But at least Ricky wasn't one of those poor bastards on the third tier, blowing their saxophones in the metro stations, or fingering a portable electric keyboard on the banks of the Seine. Ricky was content to occupy his little niche of mediocrity, between tiers.

"You have a funny kind of a life, don't you?" Fatima had said to him on one of their first dates. It was true. But it was the life he had chosen. And, wriggling his ample butt on the piano stool at Le Bon Montmartrois, banging away on his funky, if clunky, version of Prince's "1999," Ricky believed he would never wish to trade places with anyone. Certainly not with his cousin Cash: the success, the role model, the batterer whose wife had fled across the ocean to escape him!

As closing time approached, Ricky considered fucking Cash over. Maybe he would just take the money and . . . sit. Do nothing at all to find Serena. Ask no questions, make no inquiries. And keep Cash's thousand bucks all the same. But Ricky's curiosity had been piqued. Maybe he really would locate Serena Moriarty Washington. And what would he say to her when he did? She might not even be that hard to find. After nine years, there were rarely more than two degrees of separation between Ricky Jenks and any other member of the black American community here. That is to say, if you were a brother or a sister from the States living in Paris and Ricky did not know you personally, chances were he knew at least one other black person who did. It was large, the African-American expatriate contingent. It was diverse. But it was highly interconnected.

A pummeling rain was coming down when Ricky walked out of the crêperie at 2:15 A.M., huge drops exploding on the cobblestones like water balloons. Capless and without an umbrella, Ricky ducked his head low, turned up the collar of his denim jacket, stuffed his hands deep in his pockets and feet splashing, plodded his way downhill, squinting from the rain streaming down his forehead and into his eyes.

He felt that familiar pang, that longing. Oh, how he would love to cuddle up with Fatima tonight. If only they had that sort of relationship—if only he had a key to her apartment! If only he could walk in

at any time, to slip in the door in the middle of the night, to slip into
bed with her, to feel her naked body entwined with his as the rain
battered the zinc rooftop, to fall asleep in her arms. Fatima lived in the
Eighteenth as well, but on the opposite side of the Butte Montmartre,
in a quiet, residential part of the arrondissement, devoid of tourists and
nightclubs and as ethnically and economically well-integrated as any
section of Paris Ricky knew. But they didn't have that kind of relationship. Ricky had no key to Fatima's apartment, and though he had given
her one to his, she never used it. Fatima let Ricky know she did not
enjoy surprise visits. She would most definitely not find it romantic if
Ricky rang her doorbell at two thirty in the morning wanting to cuddle.
Fatima was the one who decided when they would see each other and
what the terms of intimacy would be. Ricky hated feeling so dominated.
But he knew if he complained, Fatima might stop seeing him, sleeping
with him, completely and forever. And that would be the worst thing
of all. So he acted like he didn't care. He would never tell her how
lonely he felt, how much he longed for her, walking home in the rain.

By the time Ricky arrived at a deserted rue des Martyrs, his feet felt like
they were floating in his soggy, high-top, old-fashioned canvas basketball
shoes. So he was a bit unsteady as he entered the darkened lobby of his
building, slid a hand along the wall and pushed the light button. His feet
had already left the ground as the lights snapped on. At first, Ricky, in mid-
air, saw only red. He turned his body slightly before landing and hit the
floor, with a tremendous splash, on his left side. Blood was spreading across
the white tiles of the lobby floor. Ricky was sloshing about in it, trying to
right himself. Then he saw her, on the other side of the lobby, sitting in the
expanding puddle of blood, the upper part of her body half-propped, half-
slumped against the wall. Grace Kelly, her eyes closed, had an almost peaceful expression on her face. But there was a ghastly, unnatural tilt to her head
and her blond hair was matted with blood. Her throat, her leather jacket,
leopard-skin skirt, her splayed-out legs: blood soaked everything. Ricky was
sitting up, on the other side of the lobby, staring in horrified incoherence at
Grace Kelly, under the stark fluorescent lights. Suddenly, after five seconds,
the lights switched off. Ricky Jenks could see nothing. And all he could hear
was his own scream, ringing in his ears.

Four

"YOU LIKE ZE BEESH Boys?" Inspector Lamouche asked. *"Everybody go surfeeeeeeng, surfeeng U.S.Aaaaaaaaaay...."*

Lamouche's raspy voice echoed in the dimly lit Hall of Marriage. A high-ceilinged, wood-paneled cavern of a room with rows of antique-looking chairs arranged before an imposing mahogany dais and towering stained-glass windows, the Hall of Marriage looked to Ricky Jenks like a combination of a church and a courtroom. Why had the police detective chosen this place to question him? Was it to make the witness feel more comfortable? That had seemed to be Inspector Lamouche's intention. But like Lamouche's cheery warbling of Beach Boys lyrics, the grand setting only added to the bad-dream surrealism of Ricky's situation.

"No," Ricky said as pleasantly as he could. "I was never much of a fan." He shifted his weight in the fancy chair, tried to look as alert as

possible. It was nearly five in the morning, two and a half hours since
Ricky had slipped in Grace Kelly's blood, seen her body sprawled in the
lobby of his building for only a couple of seconds before the lights
switched off, screamed, then fainted. He had only passed out for half a
minute or so, but ever since one of the neighbors who poured into the
lobby revived him, Ricky had felt foggy-headed, abstracted from himself,
as if he were floating in a semiconscious state. He blinked hard a couple
of times, tightening his focus on Lamouche's faintly smiling, pale moon
of a face.

"Iz true, zey were not a very good band," the plainclothes cop said.
"I like zem only because I live in San Diego. Back in ze years of ze
seventies, I was high school exchange student. Zis is how I come to
speak English."

"Ah, yes," Ricky said, nodding politely.

"You are not from California. You are from where?"

"New Jersey."

Lamouche continued to smile at Ricky, a mysterious, knowing little
glint in his eye. The detective's face was so powdery pale and so perfectly
round, framed with short, oily black hair, that he looked like an actor in a
silent movie. Lamouche pursed his lips and mooed, "Bruuuuuuuuuuuuce!"

Ricky nodded politely again. Was this a police interrogation or fucking *American Bandstand*?

"I find it always interesting zat both Sinatra and Springsteen come
from New Jerzee. I also find interesting zair very corporate nicknames.
One is ze Boss. Ze ozer is ze Chairman of ze Board! Ze next star from
Jerzee, he will be ze Chief Executive Officer!" Lamouche smiled broadly
at his own little joke, his moony face glowing. "And you are musician
also. I remember now from your dossier."

The word made Ricky feel even woozier. *Dossier!* What the hell was
Lamouche talking about? What did they *have* on Ricky? He imagined
some ominously thick black binder filled with transcripts of wiretapped
phone conversations, grainy, black-and-white, furtively snapped photos,
printed denunciations signed by neighbors he'd never even met. Ricky
wondered if he should demand to speak with the American embassy.
He regretted not having insisted on seeing a lawyer. In America he

would have. But this, as Inspector Lamouche had reminded him earlier, was not America.

Ricky was losing his French. It often happened in stressful situations. He stood in the crowded lobby, feeling his body swaying slightly, feeling as if he had been kicked in the head. His mind was taking in all the images around him, but haphazardly, like a handheld camera manipulated by a deranged documentarian, twirling here, focusing, then spinning around, zooming in blurrily on another detail, another face, over there, focusing briefly, then diving to glance at the floor, now swooping up to stare at the ceiling. The camera took in the tubular fluorescent bulb above, noted the fat wad of black electrical tape over the light button on the wall. Pointing downward, it lingered on the sight of Ricky's wine-red, blood-and-rain-soaked sneakers. Bodies jostled in and out of the frame: neighbors in bathrobes and pajamas, black-clad Montmartre trendies, and lots of pointy-faced, blue-uniformed police officers. Faces pushed toward the camera, babbling in tight close-up, pink mouths contorting energetically, spitting out questions in French.

Ricky struggled to respond in kind. He groped for words, formations of verbs sliding in and out of his grasp. He spluttered phrases, then stammered haltingly, trying to correct his grammar. How to say "I slipped in blood"? He heard himself say it in English, to one of the cops scowling at his denim jacket. "*Sang,*" Ricky suddenly remembered. The cop nodded in agreement. Yes, the left side of Ricky's jacket was drenched in it, heavy on his shoulder with thickly dripping blood. "*Je suis trompé,*" Ricky blurted out. That was how you said it, wasn't it? I am fallen. Or was it "*Je me suis trompé*"? I myself am fallen. No—that actually meant, "I myself am mistaken." What he had really wanted to say was, "*Je me suis* tombé." I myself am tumbled. No! There was no reflexive *me* in that construction. "*Je...suis...tombé...dans...le... sang,*" Ricky said, stressing each word like a rhythmic hammer blow.

"*Levez les bras!*" the cop ordered gruffly.

Ricky raised his arms above his head and the cop briskly frisked him, reaching under Ricky's jacket, running his hands up and down his torso, then his legs. This was when the deep, specific dread welled up inside Ricky Jenks: *Do they think I killed her?*

"*Je suis innocent,*" Ricky said.

The cop sneered, then literally turned his back on Ricky, as if he were snubbing some pesky tourist asking for directions.

Now it was Monsieur Hashemi filling the shaky frame of Ricky's vision. At least Ricky thought the portly Algerian man with the trim little mustache who lived on the second floor was named Hashemi. For years they had greeted each other, passing on the spiral stairwell or in the lobby, entering or leaving the building: "*Bonjour, monsieur,*" "*Bonsoir, monsieur*": perfectly polite, discreet and anonymous. In one of those connections an urban neighbor can make without being consciously aware of it, Ricky had assumed that the name on the lobby letterbox below his belonged to the man who occupied the apartment directly below his: the fiftyish, vaguely wary, dusky-toned man who seemed to live alone and kept hours as irregular as Ricky's. He'd always seemed like a nice enough guy, this Hashemi. It was Hashemi who had revived Ricky when he was laid out on the lobby floor, his knuckles tapping on Ricky's cheeks, his voice wheedling insistently: "*Ça va, monsieur? Ça va, monsieur?*" What Ricky mainly felt was embarrassment as Monsieur Hashemi helped him to his feet. The lobby was already filling with people. Ricky thanked Monsieur Hashemi, thanked him again and again. He was grateful; and he felt shamefully vulnerable, having lost consciousness like a damsel in distress.

"*Merci, monsieur. Merci beaucoup, monsieur.*" Ricky, struggling to get his bearings, had said the words over and over again. For several moments, they were the only words in the French language he could remember. Next thing Ricky knew he was bumblingly trying to explain himself to the cops. Then, after the cops ignored him, Ricky was focusing once again on Monsieur Hashemi in his shiny, purple bathrobe, the look in his neighbor's eyes at once compassionate and guarded. "I am tumbled in the blood?" Ricky said, in French, to his neighbor, his voice rising interrogatively at the end of the sentence, like a suburban American teenager's. Ricky realized how uncertain he must have sounded: as if he were asking what had happened; as if he did not quite know whether he had really tumbled in the blood. Monsieur Hashemi squinted at Ricky and shook his head. "I don't understand you," he said.

Ricky's herky-jerky vision locked on the face of Grace Kelly. People seemed to be clearing out of the tight lobby space, making room around the dead body slumped against the wall. The expression on the victim's face was still sleepfully serene, eyes closed, lips slightly parted. But the complexion had turned ashy gray and the bloody husks of blond hair seemed stiff and sharp, like painted straw.

Now, except for Monsieur Hashemi, Ricky and the body of Grace Kelly, all other civilians seemed to have been cleared out of the lobby. Police officers ringed around the corpse, creating a cross-armed barricade. Now Ricky was sure of it: *They think I killed her.*

"You should want to change out of zose bloody cloze."

English! Those few heavily accented words of consideration in his first language formed an aural life preserver, a linguistic flotation device that kept Ricky from drowning in miscomprehension—just when he felt he was about to go under. Ricky's camera eye zoomed in on the English-speaker, the pasty-faced, greasy black-haired man who looked like the unholy offspring of Harold Lloyd and Napoleon Bonaparte.

As in a dream, there are abrupt shifts in time. Ricky is standing on the third-floor landing, unlocking his apartment door. But he does not remember climbing the stairs to get here. The moon-faced English-speaker seems to have escorted him upstairs. The man is wearing civilian clothes, a dark green suit, with a gray wool sweater underneath the jacket, a frizzed and itchy-looking brown scarf tossed casually around his neck. He looks like a young professor at the Sorbonne. Ricky has given almost no rational thought as to who this man might be. All he knows is that this pallid, pleasant-mannered Frenchman about his age spoke to him considerately in English. In Ricky's trancelike state, this is enough to instill a sense of trust.

"Here, please," the Frenchman says, handing Ricky a large, folded-up gray plastic garbage bag. "Put your bloody cloze, and ze shoes, in zis. I come back for zem later."

Another disorienting jump cut in time: Ricky finds himself standing in the center of his apartment, barefoot, in gym shorts and T-shirt. He stares at the gray plastic garbage bag on the floor. He assumes his clothes are in there but he does not remember undressing.

A red number 3 glows in the tiny window on Ricky's answering machine. He pushes a button and three times hears the same thing: the faint sound of someone breathing; the gaping, expectant pause; finally, a click and a dial tone. Only then does Cash Washington pop back into Ricky's mind. He is sure it was his cousin who called and left three straight hang ups on his machine.

Now Ricky is standing in one of the long narrow windows of his darkened studio, looking down at the rue des Martyrs. A white ambulance, blue light spinning silently atop it, is parked in front of his building. He sees one blue, white and red police car and a boxy, tri-color police van behind it. The crowd milling in front of the building is subdued. The curious clubgoers, the drunken street people, a cluster of cops and medical workers crane their necks and mutter among themselves. The violent downpour is over but it is still raining lightly. Ricky sees two transsexual hookers from the night shift, in short leather jackets and miniskirts, standing on the edge of the crowd. He recognizes one of them as Carmen—at least "Carmen" was what Valitsa the Serb had always called this particular hooker. Tall and broad-shouldered, with jet-black hair running down her back, Carmen had a long, gaunt, tragic mask of a face, dominated by enormous dark brown eyes that—even when the prostitute was smiling at a potential client—looked haunted, filled with an implacable sorrow. Ricky and Carmen have never said a word to each other. Many times over the years, though, he has spotted her standing in doorways up and down the rue des Martyrs, chatting with Grace Kelly. Suddenly, Carmen looks up, focusing her traumatized gaze on Ricky's window. Ricky quickly closes the shutters.

Doorbell rings. How much time has passed? Ten minutes? An hour? Ricky has no idea. He is standing now in the open doorway, barefoot, in his gym shorts and T-shirt, clutching the garbage bag filled with his blood-soaked laundry. He hands the bag to the moon-faced Frenchman.

"Maybe you should want to change into some new cloze," the man says in his pleasant rasp, the scarred voice of a veteran smoker. "I need you to come wiz me."

"Who are you?" Ricky's voice sounds, to his own ears, echoey, disembodied.

The Frenchman flashes his badge. "Inspector Lamouche. Buzz buzz buzz. I am ze housefly. Very annoying."

Ricky gets the joke but doesn't smile. "Am I under arrest?"

"Not at all," Lamouche says, with a reassuring little shake of his perfectly round head. "I just need you to come to *ze mairie*. For a few questions."

"I'd like to talk to a lawyer."

Lamouche furrows his brow and throws back his head, looking startled and confused. "Do you need a lawyer?"

"I would in America."

Lamouche gives a lavish shrug, smiling benignly. "Zis is not America."

Cops were never the good guys—not to Ricky Jenks. His earliest memories of police officers came from black-and-white images on television, images of white cops in helmets beating people who looked like Ricky and his family. He watched in horror from his New Jersey living room as black Americans, marching peacefully, demonstrating for their civil rights in faraway cities like Birmingham and Selma, were attacked by cops wielding billy clubs, cops charging at them on horseback, cops unleashing vicious German shepherds, blasting tear gas and water cannons. By the age of ten, in 1970, Ricky commonly referred to cops as "pigs." During his adolescence he grew accustomed to being stopped by police as he walked through the streets of suburban Benson, New Jersey. "What are you doing here?" they always wanted to know. "I *live* here," Ricky would reply. He would wait beside the patrol car as the cops radioed in to the station to make sure that the Jenks family did indeed own a house in the neighborhood. When he was in his twenties and lived in Manhattan, Ricky marched in protest against the racist brutality of the NYPD blue.

He had spent his thirties in Paris, France, and, so far as Ricky could tell, cops were the same everywhere. In African-Arab Barbès, police harassment of the citizenry was a daily occurrence. Ricky had been stopped by officers a few times in his years in the Eighteenth Arrondissement.

"Your papers, please," they would demand gruffly. Once Ricky showed the cops his American passport, he was sent on his way. Black folks from the United States were generally treated with respect here. But God help, say, the Senegalese, the Algerian, Guadeloupean or Moroccan who was stopped by the cops in the wrong place at the the wrong time and did not have his or her papers in order.

Inspector Lamouche was one of *them*—wasn't he? Sitting with the casually dressed Frenchman in the passenger seat of a perfectly nondescript gray Renault, Ricky, in his dreamy state of mind, found it hard to believe that Lamouche really was a cop. Ricky was still having trouble remembering the very recent past. He wondered if, when he had slipped and passed out in the lobby, his head had hit the tile floor too hard. Had he suffered a concussion? He did not recall putting on a fresh set of clothes. He only vaguely remembered walking with Lamouche through the lobby of his building. Grace Kelly's corpse had been removed but the half-circle of cross-armed cops was still guarding the pool of blood, the spot where the butchered body had lain. Out on the rue des Martyrs, Ricky saw the ambulance, felt a light drizzle on his face, sensed the eyes of Carmen, the haunted hooker, on him (though he dared not glance up to meet her creepy stare) as he followed Lamouche into the compact gray car. During the short drive to the *mairie*, Lamouche whistled a bouncy little tune. Ricky thought he recognized it, then rejected the recognition: Why in the hell would a French cop be whistling "California Girls"?

Lamouche parked in front of the *mairie* of the Eighteenth. Paris was divided into twenty distinct arrondissements—twenty big neighborhoods. And each arrondissement had its own *mairie*: a sort of town hall, a center of civic bureaucracy. The *mairie* of the Eighteenth was a massive, courthouse-like building that took up an entire block. On the imposing façade of the building were inscribed the three words of the French national motto: LIBERTÉ, ÉGALITÉ, FRATERNITÉ. Each *mairie* was a bureau of records and a communal nucleus: the place where marriages and divorces, births and deaths, applications for everything from citizenship to incorporation were certified, made official and legal. There was, of course, a police station located inside the *mairie* of the Eighteenth.

But Inspector Lamouche did not take Ricky there. Instead, they walked through the darkened, palatial lobby of the building and climbed the grandiose staircase. The detective opened an enormous set of double doors and stepped across the threshold. Lamouche clicked on a few lights, but the huge room remained spookily chiaroscuro.

"La Salle des Mariages," Lamouche said with a ceremonial flourish. "Wait here. I come back soon."

Ricky lumbered aimlessly about the room. He admired the stained-glass windows, remembered that Fatima Boukhari lived quite close to the *mairie*. Just as he was wondering what time it was, Ricky, who had never in his life worn a wristwatch, noticed a clock on the wall behind the dais: a quarter to four. Ricky decided there was no reason for him to stay here. He marched toward the double doors, swung them open. Two uniformed cops stood before him, cross-armed and glowering. Ricky closed the double doors. He shuffled over to one of the antique-looking chairs, plopped down and, before he knew it, fell asleep.

"You are a guest in zis country," Inspector Lamouche rasped. "And a good guest—he don't shit on ze carpet."

Ricky was startled by Lamouche's instant transformation. Only a moment earlier, the detective had been speaking cheerily of American pop music. He had left Ricky alone in the Hall of Marriage for an hour. As soon as Lamouche returned through the big double doors, Ricky awoke from his fitful snooze. Just as he was remembering where he was, realizing that this was not some weird nightmare, Lamouche had started prattling about the Beach Boys, Sinatra and Springsteen. But the chumminess had suddenly disappeared. Lamouche was now all cop.

"You have no official status here. No card of residence," Lamouche said sternly. He sat across from Ricky, flipping through notes in a thin cardboard folder. "At your job, you are paid in cash. You pay your landlady in cash each month. If you were African you would have been kicked out of ze country long ago. But you are American, so we let you stay. You like it here?"

"Yes," Ricky croaked.

"Good. We do not mind having a guest like you. You pay no taxes but you take no zing from ze state. You seem to obey ze laws. Is it not true?"

"It is true."

"Like I said, you are not under arrest. All ze same, we can, by French law, keep you in custody for seventy-two hours. Just if we want to. You have no right to remain silent. You have no right to a lawyer. No right to make phone call. Your ass, it is ours. So I say to you, Richard, it is in your best interest to cooperate wiz us."

"All right," Ricky said warily. He could feel his senses slowly sharpening again.

"So where were you tonight?"

"At my job. Playing piano at Le Bon Montmartrois. I left after closing time, just after two o'clock. My boss François Penin can vouch for me."

"I know François," Lamouche said. "And after you left ze crêperie?"

"I walked down the hill to my house. I entered the lobby and turned on the light. I slipped and fell in the blood. I saw . . ."

Ricky paused, stopped himself from calling the prostitute "Grace Kelly."

". . . the dead person," he continued. "The lights went out. I must have lost consciousness. When I woke up, the lobby was full of people."

"Zat's all?" Lamouche asked.

"That's all."

"And did you know ze dead person?"

"No. I mean, I had seen her around, on the rue des Martyrs. I sometimes said hello to her. But we had never had a conversation."

"Okay," Lamouche said. He had taken a pen from his jacket pocket and was scribbling in a small notepad. "We are just about finished here. You say you saw zis person sometime in ze street. Do you remember when you last saw ze victim alive?"

"Yeah, I do. It was last night. On my way to work."

"*Ah, bon?*" Lamouche said—the French version of "Oh, really?"

"I saw her on the rue des Martyrs, about six o'clock, talking to a guy."

The cryptic little smile had returned to the cop's face. "And what did zis guy look like?"

Ricky described the nerdy man with the droopy gray mustache, his thick eyeglasses, his rumpled beige raincoat and brown suit. Lamouche scribbled furiously as Ricky spoke. The detective asked if Ricky had anything to add. Ricky said no, then, after a moment, he could not contain his curiosity. "What was her name?" he asked. "The dead person."

"*Her?*" Lamouche sneered. "Perhaps one should say 'him.' Or even '*it.*'" Lamouche stared at Ricky, as if he expected him to share his contempt. Ricky did not react. Finally, the cop shrugged. "Sorry, but, by ze law, I am not allowed to give ze victim's name."

"Oh. All right."

Lamouche looked at his wristwatch as Ricky stole a glance at the clock on the wall: ten after five. "Ze metro is not yet in service. Would you like a ride home?"

"No thanks," Ricky said with a magnanimous wave of the hand, trying to conceal his desperation to get away from Lamouche as quickly as possible. "I can walk home."

They rose from their chairs and Ricky followed the cop to the double doors. "Well," Lamouche said, holding out his hand, "have a good life."

Ricky took that to mean there would be no occasions for further questioning. "*Merci, monsieur,*" he said, shaking Lamouche's cold and clammy hand.

"By ze way," the inspector said just as Ricky was reaching for one of the shiny door handles, "I receive an e-mail zis night from Interpol. You know, ze international police. Zey are looking for a man, a black man from America, like yourself. He is a fugitive and zey believe he has come to Paris. Interesting case. He is a medical doctor who stole money from a hospital. He had a funny name. Ze same name as one of your American presidents. Lincoln? Jefferson? Some zing like zat."

Ricky felt as if he were about to swoon again but he struggled not to show it. "*Ah, bon?*" he said casually. Meanwhile his mind was racing: Lamouche could only be talking about Dr. Cash Washington. Was this the truth? Cousin Cash an embezzler on the lam? Was such a thing possible? Did Lamouche know that Ricky and Cash were related? Was he only pretending not to remember Cash's last name? Did he know Ricky and Cash had met this afternoon? Was this some kind of a trap?

"Yes, really," the detective said, that enigmatic smile creeping across his powder-white face again. "He stole nine million dollars."

"Huh," Ricky grunted. "Nine million isn't that much money in America these days."

"Yes, but it is not *his* money." Lamouche was staring intently at Ricky now, as if searching his face for clues. "You would not know of such a man, would you?"

Ricky had a millisecond to decide whether or not to tell the cop the truth. Straining to keep his face a mask of neutrality, Ricky shook his head and said, "No."

Lamouche seemed to believe him. "Okay. Bye bye."

Outside the *mairie*, the sky was still nighttime dark. Across the street, the huge Café Jules Joffrin was just opening. Ricky felt that if he did not get some caffeine into his body immediately he would pass out right there on the sidewalk. Standing at the café's zinc counter, Ricky sipped a double espresso. The only other customer in the place was a burly butcher, in immaculate white coat and apron, also standing at the counter and nursing a strong coffee, staring absentmindedly into space, seeming to brace himself for the long, bloody day ahead.

Ricky's thoughts were swirling. He remembered the horror of tumbling in Grace Kelly's blood, tried to blot out the image of her corpse in the lobby. He was relieved to have escaped the Lamouche interrogation—it seemed he was not a suspect in the prostitute's murder after all. But what was this shit about the fugitive doctor? Twelve hours earlier, Cash Washington had been boasting about his Center for Athletic Wellness. Had Cash really stolen from his own dream facility? Was Cash not only a wife-beater but a thief as well? Ricky recalled Cash's wary reaction when he joked about a Swiss bank account. Maybe Cash really was in Zurich laundering stolen money. And what about those three hang ups on Ricky's answering machine tonight? Why hadn't Cash left a message? And what of his runaway wife Serena? Where did she fit into this embezzlement scam? Did Inspector Lamouche suspect that Ricky was somehow involved in the scheme?

Stepping out of the café, Ricky was powerfully tempted to drop by Fatima's apartment. She lived just two blocks away, on the rue de Trétaigne. Finally, he thought the better of it. He climbed the vertiginous rue du Mont Cenis, traversed the Butte Montmartre and, once again, plodded down the rue des Martyrs on the other side of the sprawling hilltop. The sky was lightening, turning a pearly predawn blue-gray, as Ricky approached his building. Three bouquets of flowers lay on the sidewalk, just in front of the doorstep. The friends of Grace Kelly had, evidently, wasted no time in creating a little memorial. Entering the lobby, Ricky saw the building's regular cleaning lady on her knees, vigorously sponging blood off the wall. The white floor tiles were still wet but clean. A bucket beside the woman was full of soapy, pinkish water. The light button on the wall was still covered by a fat wad of black electrical tape, keeping the lobby and stairwell illuminated.

"Bonjour, madame," Ricky said. The cleaning lady glanced up at him, gave an almost imperceptible nod, then returned to her scrubbing. Climbing the spiral staircase to the third floor, Ricky could feel the rousing effect of his double espresso already wearing off. He was in mid-yawn, pulling his keys out of his pants pocket, when he noticed that the door to his apartment was, ever so slightly, cracked open. Ricky knew he had been in a daze when he left his studio with Inspector Lamouche but he could not believe he would have neglected to lock his door, no matter how foggy-headed he had been. Then he heard a noise inside his apartment, a faint murmur. His curiosity barely outweighing his fear, Ricky pushed lightly on the door, watched it slowly swing wide open. He saw the back of his couch, saw the back of the head of the person sitting on the couch, the magnificent tumult of black hair. Ricky whispered, "Fatima?"

The unexpected guest did not turn around. "Reekee," she said softly.

As Ricky entered his tiny apartment, closing the door behind him, the dreamy sense of unreality returned. Only as he sat down beside Fatima did Ricky see her face, her bloodshot eyes and tearstained cheeks. Ricky had never seen Fatima cry before and the sight shook him to the core. "Sweetheart," he said. "What's wrong?"

Fatima pulled a Kleenex from the box that rested on her lap. She blew her nose, then crumpled the paper handkerchief and let it fall to the floor where it joined a small cluster of balled-up, discarded tissues. "I called you three time this night," Fatima said, choking back a sob. "But you did not answer."

"That was you on the answering machine?"

"Yes."

"Why didn't you leave a message?"

Fatima wiped her eyes with the back of her hand. She paused, then said, almost reluctantly, "I thought maybe you were with some other woman."

Ricky had to stifle a laugh. It was a laugh not of joy but of nervous confusion. He was pained to see Fatima in such anguish. Yet he couldn't help but be pleased by the revelation of her . . . there was no other word for it . . . jealousy! If she had been that worried about the possibility of another woman in his life, then she *must* love him. And Ricky was thrilled that Fatima had finally used the key to his apartment. But, at the same time, he felt scared. Something must have been terribly upsetting to Fatima for her to call him three times late at night, then show up at his studio before dawn. It couldn't be jealousy that caused her tears to flow like this. Had there been a death in her family? Was that why she had been so eager to speak with him? Or maybe she just felt like his company tonight, came over the hill on a whim, then learned about the murder in the lobby. Had someone told her that Ricky had been dragged off by the police? That he was a suspect in a homicide? Was that why Fatima was so overwrought? No—that didn't make sense. Ricky decided that someone Fatima loved dearly, a parent or sibling, must have died suddenly. It was up to him to console her, to reassure Fatima of his devotion to her, to let her know that he would be—as Americans were always saying—"there" for her. Even if he hadn't been home when she called.

"No," Ricky said sweetly. "I wasn't with another woman." He placed a hand on Fatima's shoulder. Was it his imagination or did Fatima's muscles seem to tense at his touch? "I worked late tonight. Until two o'clock. Then things got crazy here in the building. I had to go out. Did you hear about the murder?"

"Yes," Fatima said. She pulled another Kleenex from the box, blew her nose again.

"But that's not what you're upset about—is it?"

"No," Fatima said, dropping the tissue on the floor. "It is not that."

Ricky stroked Fatima's shoulder. Her body seemed to stiffen even more. "What then?" he said gently.

"Ah, Reekee. There are things I have not told you." Fatima paused, bowed her head. "I have not told you, for example, that, recently, I have seen Bernard-Henri."

"Oh." Ricky withdrew his hand from Fatima's shoulder. At least a couple of months had passed since Fatima had last mentioned the French yuppie who had dumped her so coldly for another woman. For most of Ricky's ten-month quasi relationship with Fatima, she had talked incessantly about Bernard-Henri. So Ricky should have known that once Fatima finally stopped complaining about her ex-boyfriend there must have been trouble afoot.

Fatima raised her hands to her head, grabbed two tight fistfuls of her hair. "What a chaos I have made. What a terrible chaos."

"Listen, Fatima, if you want me out of your life, just tell me. I'm a big boy. I've been burned before. I can handle it. Let's just not drag it out. You want to stop seeing me? Is that what you came here to tell me?"

"No, no," Fatima said, still clutching hunks of her black mane, now slowly shaking her head from side to side. Ricky feared she was on the verge of a nervous breakdown. But he was rapidly losing sympathy for Fatima.

"What then?" he said again, only this time not so gently.

Fatima's hands dropped into her lap, collapsing on top of the cardboard tissue box. Now she looked directly at Ricky, her beautiful face grimacing, her features contorted as she burst once more into tears and wailed: "I am pregnant!"

PART 2
The Runaway Wife

Five

SUMMER, 1968. THE BIG family Fourth of July gathering took place in Eagleton, Pennsylvania that year. All the aunts and uncles and cousins were there. This might have been the first time that Ricky Jenks was keenly aware of being the oldest member of the new generation. He had just turned eight. Uncle Bill and Aunt Jackie Grant were the hosts of the party and they were obviously—maybe even a bit obnoxiously—proud of the swimming pool they had just had constructed in their backyard. Ricky, shy and overweight, hovered near the edge of the pool, in his tight and itchy swimming trunks. He did not want to venture into the shimmery blue water. He preferred listening to the grown-ups, who, while they joked and drank and smoked, prepared the potato salad and grilled the burgers and the hot dogs and kept their eyes on the scrambling children all around them, seemed, at the same time, sad and worried, talking about the recent murders of Martin and Bobby; civil rights and deadly riots; the pointless war in Vietnam and some clearly evil man named Nixon.

Ricky's little sister Isabel was dog-paddling with their cousin Samantha in the shallow end of the pool. Meanwhile, cousin Cash, not yet seven years old, was, to the amazement of everyone, swimming laps like a little Olympian. Cash's mother, Aunt Lenora, tall and gorgeous in her white, one-piece bathing suit, was the designated lifeguard, chatting with the other adults but always acutely conscious of what was going on in the pool. Twice already, she had urged Ricky to wade into the water. He had tremulously refused, not wanting to admit that he did not know how to swim. Aunt Lenora hugged him and cooed, "Ooooh, my little butterball!"

It happened so fast. Aunt Lenora had disappeared into the house. Ricky was standing with his back to the pool. His gaze was focused on the adults. None of them were paying any attention to him. They were talking about the Black Panthers and Ricky had just figured out that they were referring to a political organization and not a bunch of ferocious big cats. Suddenly, his little cousin Cash, soaking wet, his footsteps splatting noisily on the poolside tiles, came running up to him.

"Humpty Dumpty had a great fall!" Cash squealed.

Ricky felt the tiny palms press against his fleshy chest. Next thing he knew he was flailing, tumbling blindly, falling through the air, then splashing down, helpless, shocked, unable to breathe, submerged in icy blueness. Water filled his mouth, his nostrils: the sharp smell, the taste, of chlorine. Instead of the deep voices of grown-ups, the high-pitched chatter of children, he heard only bubbles, the glub-glub-glub of water bursting in his ears. He turned upside down, knees above his head. His eyes burned so he shut them tight. He was suspended in liquid. Upside down. The sensation was distantly, prenatally familiar, but mainly horrific. Ricky was barely eight years old and he knew, as chemical blue-tasting water filled his nose, his mouth, his lungs, that he was about to die. Then there was flesh touching his flesh. Arms in the pit of his arms. Air. Noise. Brightness. People's cries all around him. The voices of his family. Out of bubbly blue solitude he found himself in screaming sunlight. Water pouring out of his nose, his mouth. He was gasping at the air, his eyes stinging as he saw his parents above him, yelling, reaching out to him, pulling him out of the water.

Many years later, he would remember sitting on the grass, his ass wet, shivering in the blanket that was wrapped around him. Everybody was thanking Aunt Lenora for rushing out of the house, diving into the pool and saving Ricky's life. Ricky's parents and all the grown-ups were very nice to him, stroking him, hugging him, asking if he was okay. But beyond the circle of adults, Ricky could see the other children. They were all gathered around his cousin Cash, whispering, snickering. Except for Isabel, who stood apart from the others, hands on her hips, glaring at Cash.

"It wasn't Cash's fault," Aunt Lenora kept saying. "He was just playing around. He didn't know Ricky couldn't swim."

Everyone understood. Cash was never blamed. And Ricky would never learn how to swim.

Do you know what it is to feel like a bad joke? To be a human punch line? A living, breathing comic standard? To know that the most excruciating tragedy of your life will be a corny, squirmy source of mirth for others? *Didja hear the one about the groom who was left standing at the altar?*

This was Ricky Jenks's wedding day, in the summer of 1989. He stood up there, on the platform at the front of the church, sweating in his tuxedo, waiting. The organist played the tune over and over again, that Telemann piece that most Americans thought of as the theme from the movie *Ordinary People*. He looked out at that sea of faces, the three hundred family members, friends, colleagues and acquaintances gathered in that sweltering Presbyterian church in Benson, New Jersey. He saw the proud, expectant smiles turn anxious as people twisted around in the pews, craned their necks, peering down the long empty aisle, then looked back at the altar. Soon the whispering started. People kept on smiling, but the grins now were false, forced. People were questioning each other, shrugging their shoulders, shaking their heads, glancing at their watches, twisting and turning. The organ continued to grind out the stately tune: *Deeeeee-daaaaah, deeeeee-daaaaah . . .*

Ricky kept on smiling, too, his hands folded in front of him, microscopic beads of sweat prickling across his forehead. He looked at Reverend Emerson, a formidable oak tree of a man, who stood before the altar, clutching his battered, old bible, staring straight ahead. Ricky was hoping Reverend Emerson would cast a reassuring glance his way, but the snowy-haired old preacher, whom Ricky had known since his early boyhood, seemed reluctant to turn his large, dark-skinned, lionine head. Did Reverend Emerson know something Ricky did not?

Ricky kept on smiling, though his facial muscles now ached from the strain. He tried not to look at the chattering masses in the pews, kept his his gaze focused on the archway at the back of the church. At any moment, his lovely bride Clementine would come waltzing through that archway—in her lacy white gown, the gown which, adhering to tradition, Ricky had not been allowed to see, gauzy veil covering her sweet, round pixie face—arm in arm with her father, the noble patriarch who would "give her away." Ricky, feeling his shirt clinging to his sweaty chest, was absolutely certain that Clementine and her father would soon appear in the archway. How could anything possibly go wrong? They had just rehearsed the entire ceremony the night before last. He very slowly realized what the nervous people in the pews must be saying: "What if she doesn't show up?"

Deeeeee-daaaaah, deeeeee-daaaaa . . .

Instead of Clementine and her father in the archway, Ricky saw his sister Isabel in her pale pink bridesmaid's gown speaking with one of his ushers, Zack Zimmerman. Isabel had her hand on Zack's shoulder. She was whispering urgently in his ear. For some reason, Ricky felt relieved. He was certain that some unforseeable delay had popped up. A problem with Clementine's wedding outfit, perhaps: a torn stocking, a faulty zipper. Nothing to worry about. Standing at the altar, Ricky turned to his best man—his diminutive, cross-eyed cousin Byron (better known as "Tiny") Jenks—and gave him a confident wink. But Tiny stared up at Ricky with a profound sadness in his crooked gaze. Ricky looked to the back of the church again. The four other pink-clad brides-maids had joined Isabel, all of them whispering and gesticulating ani-matedly. The other ushers joined the group. Ricky tried to figure out what the hell was going on by the faces and gestures of his tuxedoed buddies: Zack, Yussef, Vance, Lloyd. . . . Wasn't there someone missing? Ricky had had five ushers, hadn't he? Ricky suddenly remembered who was absent from the group and, with an escalating sense of dread, he wondered what the fuck had happened to that fifth usher: his cousin Cash Washington.

Oh, how Ricky loved her, his darlin' Clementine. Everything about her was so right. So perfectly correct. He knew it as soon as he laid eyes on her in the corridors of the law firm Ayton Schenker Harmon & Thicke. Even though he was only a lowly paralegal and Clementine Yerby was a driven young attorney on the fast track to making partner, Ricky Jenks was determined to woo and to win her. She was no great beauty, this Clementine, but, somehow, that made her all the more appealing, all the more right. She was a serious young lady, a studious black woman from a respectable family, full of ambition and old-fashioned common sense, mother wit—a "good head on her shoulders," as Ricky's parents would tell him the first time he brought her out to Jersey for Sunday dinner. The fact that his parents were so charmed by Clementine was the clincher. For Ricky, this was not just a romance, it was a form of redemption. After years of aimlessness, a lifetime of doing wrong, Ricky was ready to do right, to become one with his family of achievers, to get with the program at last—a black sheep no more! Nothing would represent Ricky's personal transformation more distinctly than his marriage to the bright, sensible Ms. Yerby, his darlin' Clementine.

Ricky could pinpoint the exact moment when he had decided—in the words of the old Nat King Cole song his mother always played—to "straighten up and fly right." After six years and three different colleges, Ricky had managed to eke out enough credits for an undergraduate degree. He then spent another three years bouncing around America, mainly out West, playing piano in a variety of sleazy venues. In the spring of 1987, he was the house pianist in a strip club in the Tenderloin district of San Francisco. He'd found the gig through the house sax player, an old pal from Vymar College named Zack Zimmerman. One afternoon, sitting in a barbershop, waiting his turn for a haircut, Ricky thumbed through a copy of *Esteem* magazine, a monthly general-interest journal targeted at African-American readers. Just about the only time Ricky perused *Esteem* was when he was sitting in a barbershop. He was carelessly flipping through the pages when he stumbled upon an article titled "The Ten Most Eligible Black Bachelors in America." And there, ranked number five—with a full-color photo of the subject in his white intern's jacket, stethoscope around his neck—was Ricky's cousin Cassius Washington.

Ricky's first reaction was to laugh. He had never expected to come across Cash in an article like this, yet, at the same time, coming across Cash in an article like this really wasn't such a surprise. With his good looks, brains and charm, Cash had always seemed destined for some kind of celebrity. Still chuckling, Ricky read Cash's brief biography, his list of favorite movies *(The Godfather, Rocky, Star Wars),* hobbies (exercise, chess, fine wines), the attributes he was looking for in a potential mate (beauty, class, sense of humor). But once he stopped laughing, Ricky felt the piercing twinge of an unfamiliar yet undeniable emotion: envy.

He knew how ridiculous his envy was. Ricky would never have wanted his own picture in *Esteem* magazine; and he had never aspired to a career in medicine; he didn't exercise, didn't play chess and didn't drink fine wines and had never dated classy beauties no matter how good a sense of humor they had. It wasn't that Ricky wanted to be like Cash or to be in his position. While Ricky knew he was considered a bit of a disappointment—at least on his mother's illustrious side of the family—he had always been content with who he was. He could never remember envying anyone. But, sitting there in the Frisco barbershop, Ricky felt himself longing for, coveting, something cousin Cash had always seemed to possess, something as insubstantial as it was recogniz-able: an air of success. How strange that, staring at a photo in a slick magazine, Ricky suddenly began caring about something he had never cared about before. He had never thought of life as a race—but now he felt as if he were lagging far behind. Ricky was a few weeks shy of his twenty-seventh birthday. Cash was a full year younger—yet cousin Cash was almost finished with his medical training! And here Ricky was, banging on the keys in some seedy strip joint. Suddenly, his envy was mingled with a sense of guilt: Had his parents raised him for *this?* They had sweated and strained to give him a good education, showered him with unconditional love—and this was how he repaid them? Ricky decided right then and there, with *Esteem* magazine still open in his lap, his cousin Cash grinning smugly up at him, that he would go to New York and do anything he could to make his family proud of him.

That night at the club, Ricky told Zack he was going Back East to pursue a more respectable career. "I don't want to spend my life playing piano in a San Francisco strip joint," Ricky said.

Zack flashed his skeletal grin. Tall and pale, with thinning hair and hollow cheeks, Zack Zimmerman always looked somewhat unhealthy, undernourished, though he was actually in pretty good shape. "How about playing piano in a strip joint in Paris, France?" he said. "I just heard about a gig over there. I think I'm gonna go. Wanna join me?"

Ricky shook his head no. "I'm going to New York to get a job as a paralegal."

"Oh well," Zack said. "Better a paralegal than a quadrilegal."

"So what happened to *you*?" Clementine Yerby asked.

Sitting across from Ricky at a table in the steak house a couple of blocks from the midtown Manhattan office of Ayton Schenker Harmon & Thicke, Clementine scrunched up her plump, girlish face and stared quizzically at her dinner companion. Ricky was sure she had not meant for her question to sound as obnoxious as it had. Ricky had just been telling her about his family: his father, the successful architect; his mother, the successful real estate agent; his sister, who, after graduating near the top of her class at Columbia Law School, was now clerking for a judge in Chicago. Ricky hadn't even bothered to mention his first cousins on his mother's side: the nuclear engineer, the biochemist, the television producer, the award-winning literary scholar, the software entrepreneur, the orthopedic surgeon. But Clementine was in awe just hearing about Dad, Mom and Sis. Since Ricky had already told her a bit about his aimless past, since she knew he was only a lowly paralegal, she couldn't disguise the arrogant dismay in her voice when she asked how he had come to be the man he was. Ricky was certain that her grating tone of voice was unintentional. At least, he was willing to give her the benefit of the doubt.

"I don't know," Ricky said. "My mother must have dropped me on my head when I was a baby."

Clementine burst into giggles. Ricky maintained his deadpan delivery. "Or maybe I just missed out on the ambition gene."

Clementine was laughing hard now, hiding her face in her napkin. "Oh, God, I'm so sorry," she said between giggles. "I didn't mean to say . . . oh, my Lord, you must think I'm such a . . . such a . . . *witch!*"

Actually, Ricky was enchanted. Clementine was like no other woman he had dated before—if you could even call this dinner a date. Ricky had had to ask her three times if she would deign to have a meal with him. Clementine, the workaholic associate, had, on the first two occasions, looked at this overaged paralegal with a naked contempt in her eyes. "I'm too busy," she had replied coldly. Finally, late on a Friday night in September, long after most of the lawyers in the office had gone home and Ricky had dutifully delivered to Clementine a brief which one of the senior partners had demanded she redraft, the pitiful peon asked his superior, for a third time, if she would dine with him. For a long moment, Clementine simply stared down at the thick legal brief, her hands folded across her forehead, fingers entwined, forming a sort of visor over her bent brow. At last, she looked up. "Okay," she sighed.

"No, no, no," Ricky said reassuringly an hour or so later, at the steak house. "I don't think you're a witch at all. Maybe just a little overworked."

"That's for darn sure," Clementine said, dabbing at her tears of laughter with the white cloth napkin. Ricky silently marveled at Clementine's outfit, her whole upstanding demeanor. Over the past three years, Ricky had grown accustomed to wild, wanton women with chaotic hair, skimpy clothes, nose rings and tattoos. But Clementine wore a dark blue jacket and skirt, a silky white blouse with a bow at the collar; her black hair was neatly straightened, tied in a bun at the back of her head.

"I don't know what's happened to me since law school. I feel like I've become so . . . so . . . *hard.*"

"Don't feel bad about it," Ricky said. "I think it's a good thing. You ask what happened to me and I think maybe I've always been too soft.

Too easy on myself. That's why I haven't done more with my life. I admire people like you."

"Do you?" Clementine was obviously flattered.

"Absolutely. In fact, I'm thinking of applying to law school. First, of course, I have to take the LSATs. I've never had very good study habits, though. But I want to change all that."

"I could help you."

"Really? Would you want to?"

Clementine locked eyes with Ricky and nodded eagerly, like the exemplary pupil she had always been. "Yes. I would. Let me help you. Please."

She's the best thing that ever happened to you. That's what everyone told Ricky about Clementine. She had taught him how to study, spending endless weekend afternoons drilling him on the finer points of the law school entrance exam. She taught him how to dress, dragging him to Brooks Brothers, getting him to give up his scruffy T-shirts, raggedy jeans and tattered sneakers for crisp white button-down Oxfords, pinstripe suits and shiny black wing tips. It was Clementine who taught Ricky how to straighten up and fly right; to quit drinking liquor and smoking pot; to stop listening to those nasty Prince records. By the end of their first year together, Ricky had ceased playing the piano altogether. Just about the only music in his life, the only music he needed, were the hymns he and Clementine sang together at church every Sunday morning.

Yes, everyone knew that Clementine was the best thing that had ever happened to Ricky. What they did not understand was what a good thing *he* was for *her*. But Ricky knew. He knew he had brought love and passion to Clemmy's lonely life. She had told him about her wretched adolescence, the isolation she had always felt as the smartest girl in the class, the bespectacled Plain-Jane who was never resented, never mocked—but who was also never asked out on a date, never even invited to a party. Clemmy had had a couple of boyfriends at Yale, a couple more at Harvard Law School—but nothing, as she said wryly, to write home about. "I'm kind of a late bloomer," Clemmy had whispered, almost apologetically, the first time they made love. Ricky never told her that he had felt like a sexual outcast, too. At least, Clementine had excelled academically. Ricky had been a loser when it came to both hittin' the books *and* hittin' the skins. Most of his lovers had been drugged-out sluts, most of his relationships one-night, or one-week, stands. But he let Clemmy think that he had been a suave ladies' man. He didn't tell her that she was for him—as he was for her—a first: an enduring, "serious" partner. He brought her candy and flowers. He listened to her problems, gave her sage advice, massaged her weary muscles at the end of a long workday. He told her she was beautiful. He watched her blossom in the light of his affection.

On Christmas Eve, 1988, while they were visiting her parents in a suburb of Atlanta, he proposed marriage. Following tradition—knowing how much Clementine adored tradition—he had asked her father, a retired Marine lieutenant colonel, for permission beforehand. Later that night, Ricky dropped down on one knee before his darlin' Clementine and popped the question. Thankfully, she said yes. The wedding date was scheduled for late June. Ricky was certain it would be the happiest day of his life.

A decade later, when Ricky would, just about literally, stumble upon the body of a murdered prostitute in the lobby of his Paris apartment building and enter a strange state of dreamy unreality, he would remember that there was only one other time in his life when he felt so bizarrely disconnected from the here and now, only one other moment when the cruelly factual seemed so distantly, so abstractly, fictional: the day he was supposed to have married Clementine Yerby.

Ricky sees his sister Isabel hurrying down the aisle, alone in her pale pink bridesmaid's gown, her quick pace conflicting with the stately Telemann: *Deeeeee-daaaaah, deeeeeee-daaaaah . . .*

Before Ricky can understand what is happening, Isabel is up there at the altar, whispering in his ear: "Go into Reverend Emerson's office. I'll explain everything to you there, in a few minutes. Go!"

As he moves slowly, reluctantly, toward the mahogany door at the side of the altar, now turning around to face the crowd, then reaching for the polished gold doorknob of the minister's private chambers, now suddenly casting a glance back at the altar, Ricky sees his sister waving her hand up at the balcony. The organist continues to grind out the tune—*Deeeeee-daaaaah*—until Isabel draws an index finger, with an abrupt brutality, across her throat. The music instantly stops. Isabel stands in front of Reverend Emerson, addresses the crowd in her ringing, authoritative voice: "We're sorry, everybody, but there's been an unexpected change in the program. You all should go straight to the reception. We'll have more information for you there."

"Clementine is crazy," Isabel tells Ricky. They sit across from each other, their knees almost touching, in leather armchairs in the minister's dark and woody office. Reverend Emerson is hovering somewhere in the room and Ricky feels the presence of one other person—maybe his best man, Tiny—somewhere nearby, but his attention is entirely focused on his sister, who speaks in a stern and even tone. "I know she has never seemed crazy, but Clementine is a very unstable young woman and, in the past twenty-four hours, she has had a nervous breakdown."

Ricky feels as if he is floating in his chair. As in the most disturbing dreams, what Isabel tells him seems, at once, completely impossible and inescapably actual: *This cannot really be happening, yet it is really happening, happening to me.* He feels a desire to speak, but, somehow, he cannot open his mouth. He can only listen.

"It's not the first time Clementine has cracked up," Isabel continues. "She had another breakdown during her second year at Harvard Law School. She had a brief relationship with a student at MIT and when he dumped her, she totally lost it. She almost had to drop out. Eventually, she pulled herself together, but she never got over this boyfriend. For seven years, she has continued to be obsessed with this guy. Has she ever mentioned this to you?"

Ricky slowly shakes his head, says nothing.

"I didn't think so. I've only been able to piece together the whole story since last night. Nobody told you but Clem didn't show up for her bridal shower last night."

Isabel pauses, which is good because it takes Ricky a moment to digest this fact. They were sitting here, in Reverend Emerson's office, early on Saturday afternoon. Ricky reminds himself that he has not seen Clementine since Thursday night, at the rehearsal dinner. He remembers that he spoke with her briefly on the phone the next morning, but they spent Friday night apart. Ricky was among other men, at his bachelor party in Manhattan. Clemmy was supposed to have been among women, at her bridal shower.

"When she didn't show up," Isabel continues, "her girlfriends from law school told me about this trauma from the past, about this guy from MIT she's been carrying the torch for for seven years, even though their relationship lasted only a few weeks." Isabel pauses again, biting her lip. Ricky has the feeling that she does not want to go on, but knows she must. Isabel takes a deep breath, then says, "The guy was cousin Cash."

CASH CASH CASH CASH CASH CASH: the word echoes in Ricky's head. He is not really thinking anything. He just keeps hearing the name, reverberating: CASH CASH CASH. . . .

"They're together right now. Cash and Clementine took off last night. They're up in Massachusetts, at an inn in the Berkshires."

CASH CASH CASH CASH CASH . . . Ricky suddenly remembers that Cash did not show up for the bachelor party. He told Tiny to tell Ricky that he'd come down with a migraine headache . . . a result of all the pressure he was under in his surgical residency . . . he needed to rest up Friday night so he could be at his best for the wedding on Satur- day . . . Ricky had thought nothing of it . . . Now the name continues to reverberate, bouncing off the walls of his mind: CASH CASH CASH CASH CASH . . .

"I talked to him a little while ago. Clem was asleep in the next room. Cash is very upset about this, Ricky, but he says there was nothing he could do. Clem was all over him after the rehearsal dinner. Then yesterday, she was harassing him. She said she would kill herself if he didn't get her away from here. Apparently, she was hysterical, out of control. She demanded that he take her to this inn in the Berkshires where they had had a romantic weekend seven years ago. Clem said if Cash didn't take her there she would kill herself, commit suicide on the morn- ing of your wedding. It wasn't an idle threat. She had tried to kill herself back in 'eighty-two, when Cash broke off their relationship. He says he was scared, didn't know what to do. So they drove off early last night."

Now Ricky feels seasick. He fears he will either pass out or throw up. He thinks back to the rehearsal dinner. Yes, he saw them, during the cocktail hour, sitting together in a corner of the banquet hall. Cash seemed to be pouring on the charm, Clementine listening raptly. Cash, Ricky had assumed, was talking about himself. Ricky had been surprised that Cash had come solo for the wedding festivities. At other family events in recent years, Cash had always shown up with some stunning brown beauty on his arm, some aspiring model-actress-singer type. Ricky had embraced his cousin warmly that night, even teased him about not having a babe in tow. Had it been Ricky who introduced Cash to Clementine earlier that evening, at the church, where everyone gathered for the run-through of the upcoming ceremony? Hadn't the usher and the bride-to-be shaken hands as if meeting for the first time? Now, dizzy and nauseated, sitting in Reverend Emerson's office, Ricky opens his mouth to speak but the only thing he can think to say is: "But Clemmy isn't even Cash's type!"

Isabel smiles sadly at her brother. "I know, Ricky, I know."

"This, too, shall pass," Reverend Emerson intones, his voice coming from somewhere behind Ricky's leather armchair. "Your cousin found himself in a difficult situation, Richard. He had to do what seemed best. As painful as it is to acknowledge now, you must forgive him. As the good book says, 'To err is human, to forgive divine.' "

Ricky does not turn to face the preacher, but he sees Isabel shoot Reverend Emerson a nasty look as she says curtly, "That's not the bible, it's Shakespeare."

"Remember," Reverend Emerson says, ignoring Isabel's correction, "we black folk, we are a very forgiving people."

Isabel looks at Ricky again. Her eyes narrow and when she speaks, Ricky hears in her voice the steel of the public prosecutor his kid sister has become: "You know what I say: Forgive . . . but never forget."

"Can I go home now?" Ricky hears himself say.

"Not yet," Isabel replies. "You have to make an appearance at the reception."

It is there, in the ballroom of the Benson Hills country club, that Ricky Jenks feels like a bad joke. He knows his world has been shattered. Clementine's abandonment of him is not just the end of a relationship—

it is the end of the life he has meticulously constructed over the past two years, a whole way of being that he had considered his Real Life, the life he had finally discovered after his first twenty-seven years of aimlessness and underachievement. After his Roman honeymoon with Clementine, they were supposed to move into an apartment in Brooklyn Heights; Ricky was to begin, in September, the first of three years at New York University Law School. Everything had come together, the future was all planned. Now, in one afternoon, Ricky's whole life has been blasted into dust.

But the guests in the country club ballroom do not realize this. Oh, they know how sad Ricky must feel, left standing at the altar on his wedding day. As Ricky mills through the crowd, shaking hands, accepting kind words of commiseration, consoling hugs and pats on the back, he knows he has the sympathy of these people. But he sees something else in their faces, in their sorrowful smiles, their downcast eyes and furrowed brows: it is a painful sense of embarrassment. A feeling, never expressed, at least not to Ricky, of personal relief: "Thank God this didn't happen to *me!*" Or: "This would *never* happen to me!"

And Ricky knows that these members of his family, his friends and colleagues, will inevitably tell his tale of woe to others—and will not be able to stop themselves from laughing when they relate this Wedding Day from Hell story. Ricky's tragedy will be their "Can-you-top-this?" anecdote. Putting on his bravest face, greeting everyone in the ballroom of the country club that his parents boldly integrated twenty years earlier, Ricky notices that Colonel and Mrs. Yerby, and all other members of Clementine's family as well as her friends, are nowhere to be seen. It is just Ricky's "people" here. And mixed in with the embarrassment, the suppressed humor of their commiseration, is another unsettling sentiment, a subtext to all the kind words directed at Ricky: that this is not Clementine's fault; nor is it Cash's. Clementine, after all, is a disturbed young woman. And Cash, well, everybody here knows Cash, knows how irresistible he is. Cash is certainly not to blame for Ricky's catastrophe. He did his best under very trying circumstances.

A bride ran off with her groom's first cousin. This was the tragicomic fact. And the hidden message of the guests at this grim farce of a reception was that if anyone was to be blamed for what had happened, then it was, somehow, the groom himself: the eternally hapless, congenitally unlucky Ricky Jenks.

Ricky got drunk—for a year. He holed up in his studio apartment in the East Village, occasionally venturing out to buy food, toilet paper and booze. He rarely attended classes and managed to flunk out of NYU Law School after a single semester. He spent a great deal of time in bed, sleeping, weeping, jerking off, watching TV. He almost never picked up the telephone unless he heard his sister's voice on the answering machine. Isabel, who was working in the district attorney's office in Miami, kept Ricky informed—with what little information she had—of the ongoing saga of Cash and Clementine. In the weeks after the aborted wedding day, Clementine had taken a job in Ayton Schenker's Washington, D.C. office so she could be closer to Cash, who was a resident at the Georgetown University Medical Center. Cash and Clem did not live together but, in the fall of 1989, their rekindled affair was, apparently, still burning bright.

In September, three months after Ricky had been left standing at the altar, he received a brief letter from Clementine. It was a short litany of banalities about how much he would always mean to her, how sorry she was about what had happened but how she had needed to follow her heart. She assured Ricky that he was "a good person" and that she would always wish him well. There was no mention of Cash. And Ricky never received a letter or a phone call from the cousin who had run off with his bride. Cash, evidently, had nothing to say for himself. Not a word.

For several months, Ricky kept Clementine's banal little letter by his bedside. He would read it over and over again as if it could somehow explain what she—what she and Cash—had done to him. He often wondered: When did Clemmy know he was related to her old flame? Was that why she had stayed with Ricky, why she had agreed to marry him: in order to get back in contact with Cash? One night, as Ricky tossed about in his sleep, he knocked over an open bottle of beer, spilling its contents all over Clementine's letter. He awoke with a start and, as he tried to salvage the beer-soaked note, it disintegrated soggily in his hands.

By late April 1990, Ricky felt paralyzed. He had not yet told his parents he had flunked out of law school. His savings from the two years he had spent at Ayton Schenker were drying up. Constantly agonizing over his past, he could not even imagine a future for himself. Lying in bed one night, drunk and bleary-eyed, he watched an old black-and-white desert epic, full of dashing men in white uniforms and trooper caps with white handkerchiefs hanging at the backs of their heads. Yes! That was what he needed to do: join the French Foreign Legion! Weren't desperate men always doing that, in order to forget some woman who had done them wrong?

It was around this time that Isabel called with the news that Cash and Clem had broken up. Ricky's ex-fiancée was on her way back to New York. For a month, Ricky fantasized about a reunion. Maybe that would be the only way to rebuild a Real Life, to find a path into the future. He could only hope that Clementine might take him back. She had abandoned him for a better man, a far more successful and desirable man. Ricky, like everybody else, recognized that. But maybe, just maybe, Clementine could lower her expectations again. Maybe she could find it in herself to accept Ricky once more, to continue to try to mold him into the sort of man she wanted him to be. But would Clemmy even call him?

Ultimately, it was Isabel who made the call, acting as a liaison. Clementine would like to meet with him in a West Village coffee shop on the afternoon of June 1, Ricky's thirtieth birthday. Naturally, Ricky agreed. The last thing Isabel said to him before hanging up was: "Be careful."

"Cassius is the devil," Clementine hissed. She leaned across the table in the Bleecker Street café. Aside from a brief greeting when he arrived— Clementine was already there, waiting for him—Ricky had barely uttered a word. They had not kissed when he came up to the table, did not shake hands or touch at all. They ordered their cappuccinos, then

Clementine started monologuing away, in a low, queerly unfamiliar voice. It occurred to Ricky that, after a year of obsessing on his ex-fiancée every day, he might not have even recognized her had they passed each other on the street. The once plump and girlish face had become drawn, almost haggard. The big brown eyes that, only a year earlier, seemed full of shy innocence, now looked stricken, haunted. Yes, Ricky thought, Clementine was indeed crazy. And, at this point in time, probably anorexic, too.

"I know you must hate me," Clementine said, in her new gravelly whisper. "Most of the time, I hate myself. What you have to understand is that I was seduced. Cassius seduced me back in Cambridge and he seduced me again before our wedding. You've *got* to believe me!"

Clementine wore the same conservative business clothes as before, only now they hung loosely on her body. Her hair, though still knotted in a bun, looked frayed and dishevelled. Ricky did not want to think it, but he had to admit, silently, only to himself, that he was actually afraid of Clementine.

"Cassius knew how much he would hurt you. He knew that by seducing me, he would destroy us both—both you and me, I mean. Cassius *knew*. He knew that! But he did it. Do you know why? Because he *could!* For him, this was just . . . *sport!* Our destruction was your cousin's diversion. This is what I'm trying to tell you, Ricky. There is evil in this world. I know it now. Evil inhabits certain people. And it inhabits Cassius. This man is the *devil!*"

Finally, Ricky spoke. "Are you on medication?"

Clementine cast a joyless smile. "Is that all you have to say to me?"

"Because, if you're not," Ricky said, "I think you should seek professional counselling."

"You're not even hearing me, are you?" Clementine said bitterly. "You're not even hearing the truth about your blood relation."

This was when Ricky knew what he had to do. He did not make the decision. It presented itself to him, of its own accord. The idea came to him like a line from a song he had once loved but had forgotten and now popped back into his head, out of the blue. This was how Ricky made a life-altering choice. He felt healthier, more sane and coherent, than he had in nearly a year. He suddenly knew what he had to do to get away from these totally fucked up people, this totally fucked up place. Ricky rose from the table, started walking toward the door of the coffee shop.

Clementine shrieked, "Where are you going?"

Ricky turned to face her. He saw his ex-fiancée twisted around in her chair, haunted eyes staring crazily at him. He answered her; or rather, the word sprang from his lips, at once plainly matter-of-fact and irrevocably decisive: "Paris."

Awake. Ricky Jenks had never felt so completely awake, so wide-eyed and alert, so attuned to the peculiarity of everyday life as he did during his first months in Paris, in the summer and fall of 1990. After a year of bedridden depression in lower Manhattan, he found himself in a strange and beautiful place, dazzled by blazing sunshine, revived by the newness of it all, his senses tingling like a baby's.

The first thing he noticed was the sky. How much of it there was. Paris was not a vertical city like New York, crowded with steel-and-glass towers aspiring to blot out the sun. Throughout most of Paris, the tallest buildings were only seven or eight stories high and the majority of them were off-white, or the color of sand, brilliantly reflecting the sunlight in their door-sized windows. On his first day in town, Ricky stood on the Pont des Arts, the wooden footbridge stretching across the Seine, and gazed at all the pale buildings on the Left and Right Banks, the spires that rose above the slanted gray metal rooftops, the sunlight shimmering on the water and the vast, cloudless sky. Ricky turned to his old college buddy, former San Francisco strip-joint band mate, wedding-day usher and current Paris host, Zack Zimmerman. All Ricky could do was shake his head and laugh.

Zack, balding and bony-faced, grinned and said, "I know what you're thinking: It makes every other city look like shit."

"Exactly," Ricky said.

He saw all the famous sights, each one—the Eiffel Tower, the Arc de Triomphe, the Notre-Dame cathedral—more spectacular than any film or postcard image could possibly convey. But from the very start of his life in Paris, Ricky lived up north, in the Eighteenth Arrondissement. He and Zack shared a two-bedroom apartment in the crook of what the French called an "elbowed" street, the rue des Trois Frères. Zack had been making good money playing saxophone in a strip club a few blocks from the flat, near the Place Pigalle. Ricky, when he had phoned Zack the day after his thirtieth birthday—the day after his last meeting with his wrung-out and traumatized ex-fiancée—thought there might be a job for him playing piano in the club. But just before Ricky arrived in Paris, Zack and the rest of the musicians had been fired, replaced by a DJ and state-of-the-art sound system. Zack broke the news to Ricky minutes after he'd landed at Charles de Gaulle Airport, wheeling his trunkload of possessions past the customs desk.

"This is the trend," Zack griped. "Same thing that's happening in Frisco, in the Tenderloin, in Times Square. Now it's crossed over to Paris. Strip-joint musicians—we're being downsized, man, made obsolete! But don't worry, I've got a few leads. I'll come up with something for us."

Something turned out to be a full-time gig with Pierre Defenestre. "A Montmartre legend": That was what Zack Zimmerman told Ricky Jenks when they got their jobs as members of the French *chanteur*'s band. Pierre performed three sets a night, Tuesdays through Saturdays at Le Coucher du Soleil, the Sunset café, on the rue Houdon. Pierre Defenestre wore a bright red suit, starched white shirt and cowboy-style string tie. Ricky figured he was at least sixty years old but it was hard to tell for sure—Pierre's pompadour hairdo was always dyed midnight black and a dense layer of powdery makeup concealed the cracks in his craggy face. Pierre had his cult, from leather-clad trendies to aging ex-hipsters to neighborhood barflies, who frequented Le Coucher du Soleil to see him warble his versions of American classics—"Hound Dog," "Tutti Frutti" and "Twist and Shout" were among his favorites—as well as his renditions of golden oldies by the great French showmen Johnny Hallyday and Eddy Mitchell, those widely revered geezers who had adopted Anglo-American sounding names to lend a measure of rock 'n' roll authenticity to their acts. As the night wore on, Pierre would segue into mellow mode, singing melancholy tunes by Jacques Brel and Serge Gainsbourg. And on those nights when Pierre had downed one or two too many bottles of Bordeaux, he would dip, slurringly, into the Sinatra *oeuvre:* "When zumbody luv you, eet no good unless she luv you, aaaaaaaaall ze waaaay..."

Ricky Jenks was having a blast. The apartment he shared with Zack on the Street of the Three Brothers was a sort of twenty-four-hour hangout for musicians from all over Africa, Europe and Asia. They relaxed, drank wine, smoked hash, jammed together and blathered away in that bizarre amalgam of French and English known as Franglais. Ricky always understood the other players and their friends and hangers-on, however badly they mangled English; and they always seemed to understand him, however brutally he massacred French.

It didn't take long for Ricky to realize that this was the life he *should* be leading. Not the life of American professional propriety or alienated outsiderness. His life in Paris defied the categorizations he was accustomed to. Questions of acceptance or rejection were beside the point. And, perhaps best of all, Ricky was getting laid. A lot. With women from all over the world.

Then, in the fall of '93, the management of Le Coucher du Soleil changed hands and Pierre Defenestre abruptly decided to retire to the South of France. Ricky and the rest of the band were fired and, within a year's time, the famous café was transformed into a McDonald's. Zack Zimmerman, meanwhile, had fallen ecstatically in love with a Danish punk rocker and emigrated to Copenhagen to be with her. Once Zack moved out of the apartment on the rue des Trois Frères, the owner decided to turn the place over to his college-aged nephew. Ricky, in the space of a few weeks, found himself confronting the specter of being both jobless and homeless. Fortunately, after three years in Paris, Ricky had made some very good friends. One, Valitsa Karodovic, had heard about a studio for rent on the rue des Martyrs. And another, Marva Dobbs, arranged an audition for him at Le Bon Montmartrois. Ricky was saved. But even when his situation had been most dire, the one option he never considered was going back to live in the United States.

When was it that Ricky Jenks began to feel like a foreigner in his native country? During his first couple of years in Paris, when Ricky would return to visit the States, he felt as if he was getting back to reality. After a few days in America, his life in Paris began to take on the texture of some weird fantasy he had had. But, at some point, Ricky's sense of place was turned inside out. America became the weird fantasy land. It was in the States that things seemed other-worldly—the bigness of it all: huge buildings; enormous cars; grotesquely fat people, people so humongous that they made Ricky, who seemed so large in Paris, feel puny. And everyone everywhere speaking English—or maybe Spanish, but never French, the language that had become so everyday familiar to him.

It was not that Ricky had become some sort of pseudo-European. He was proud to be an African-American. And New Jersey was in his bones, in his blood and tissue. But, after a certain amount of time living in Paris, France, he found that something inside him, some fundamental notion of belonging, had changed, changed irreversibly. He wondered if he had entered some psychic state of nonaffiliation. Had he become the ultimate ambiguous and ambivalent creature of betwixt and between-ness? A nowhere man?

When he was most honest with himself, Ricky knew precisely when he began to feel this way. It was at his parents' thirty-fifth wedding anniversary party, in the summer of 1994.

The smell of charcoal and barbecue sauce. All those happy people on his parents' lawn. All those familiar faces, subtly transformed. Some folks were plumper, some grayer. A few more chins of his cousins were hairier, a few more heads shaved. There were fewer perms and more dreadlocks. New wives and husbands; squealing babies; and sulky adolescents who used to be cute little kids. Isabel, the prominent Miami prosecutor, was there with her new boyfriend Harold Douglas, a nice if somewhat nerdy Negro accountant who was a perfect fit for this family.

Everybody asked Ricky about Paris: How was the food? Had he seen all the sights? Did he speak the language? How were black folks treated over there? They were sincerely interested and he enjoyed answering all their questions. But this was the first time Ricky had seen many of his relatives since his catastrophic, tragicomical wedding day five years earlier. Their curiosity about his life in Paris was genuine but it was laced with a sort of grim concern. The subtext of every question seemed to be

"Are you doing all right? Have you recovered from that horrible incident we all witnessed?" Ricky played along, trying to answer the unasked questions by expressing to his uncles, aunts and cousins how truly happy he was. Nobody seemed to believe him. Through all the toasts and speeches and reminiscences about the thirty-five-year marriage of Henry and Matilda Jenks, there was a palpable sense of anticipation at the gathering. Nobody said it but Ricky knew they were all waiting for Cash to arrive. And everybody wanted to see what would happen when he showed up.

Cash made his entrance at the party three hours late. Ricky watched his cousin working his way through the crowd, dispensing hugs and handshakes, talking about his busy schedule at the hospital, how lucky he had been to catch the shuttle from D.C. when he did. Watching Cash, seeing him move as if in slow motion, Ricky felt nothing. No love, no hate, no envy, no resentment. At that moment, Cash seemed to him a perfect stranger. Suddenly, the cousins were facing each other across an empty expanse of lawn. The eyes of all the family were on them. Cash, flashing a lopsided grin, strode across the grass and threw his arms around his cousin. Ricky hugged him back. No words were spoken. The family burst into applause. Ricky, embracing Cash, smelling his cologne, still felt nothing.

This is so corny, he thought. *Like a TV commercial. But this is what they all want. So let the family have this contrived little moment, their false reconciliation.*

Afterward, Ricky and Cash retreated to their separate corners of the lawn. People congratulated them, patted them on the back, told them, with tears in their eyes, how moved they were by their embrace. But Ricky and Cash said nothing to each other. Another five years would pass before they would sit down and talk, face-to-face, in a Barbès café.

But on that day in 1994, on his parents' lawn in Benson, New Jersey, Ricky Jenks realized that when you are an expatriate you don't just leave your country. You leave your family.

Six

"Reekee. Reekee... are you awake?" He had been dreaming of the past. Blinking, yawning, groggily getting his bearings, Ricky felt as if he had been away on a long and arduous voyage. Seeing Fatima's lovely face above him, seeing the sun—just behind her head, through the open windows—barely, bravely, managing to break through the light-gray cluster of clouds, Ricky felt that very specific sense of enveloping relief: the inimitable joy of a homecoming.

"I have made you a coffee," Fatima said. "Here."

"*Merci,*" Ricky croaked. He sat up, gently took the little cup of espresso Fatima handed him. Only with that first sip of fierce coffee did he remember the new reality into which he was awakening.

He remembered how, some hours earlier, Fatima had collapsed into his arms after telling him she was pregnant; how he held her tight as her body convulsed with sobs; how he could think of nothing to say but,

"It's okay, it's okay. Everything is going to be all right." Finally, he had suggested they go to sleep. He pulled the folded-up bed from out of the couch, undressed, and got under the covers. But Fatima wanted to remain in her clothes. She stretched out, still dressed in her blue workshirt and black jeans, on top of the sheets and blanket. Ricky was disappointed that Fatima did not want the intimacy of curling up naked together beneath the sheets. But he was too exhausted to worry about it.

"I must go soon," Fatima said. "I have a class." Sitting cross-legged atop the blanket, sipping tea from a ceramic bowl, Fatima had recovered from her predawn anguish, but she was still a long way from seeming like her sparky old self. Glancing at the clock beside the sofa bed, Ricky saw that it was almost 10:30. "I am sorry about last night," Fatima said.

"There is absolutely nothing to be sorry about," Ricky assured her.

Fatima stared down into her bowl of tea, a curtain of lush black hair falling across her face. Ricky, still naked beneath the sheets, sipped his coffee and remembered the strange sense of anticipation he had felt over the last few months. For most of the past decade, just about his entire time in Paris, Ricky's life had felt like an exciting but pleasant ride, full of surprising discoveries yet essentially calm, free of drama and trauma. He could not discern when, exactly, this ticking sense of expectancy had begun. But, since at least the beginning of the year, Ricky had had this feeling that something—some big "It"—some watershed event, either cathartic or cataclysmic, was waiting for him, just around the corner of his life's carefree Parisian amble. Now, in just the past twenty-four hours, a rush of bizarre events had blindsided him all at once: Cash Washington shows up in Paris, asking Ricky to find his runaway wife, Serena; Ricky stumbles upon Grace Kelly's body in his lobby; Inspector Lamouche tells him of a fugitive embezzler who can only be cousin Cash; Fatima Boukhari shows up in his apartment, telling him she's with child. Did all of these sudden developments constitute the big "It" Ricky had been, more or less, waiting for? Sitting up on his sofa bed, Ricky felt somewhat overwhelmed, trying to make sense of everything that was happening to him. But he also felt a peculiar exhilaration. Whatever else this life was about to hit him with, Ricky Jenks was ready for it.

At this moment, what he needed was more information from Fatima—but he knew he had to approach the situation very, very carefully.

He couldn't pepper her with questions. Couldn't ask: "So when did you start seeing Bernard-Henri again?" And he certainly knew better than to pose the most painful question—though it hung, unasked, in the air like a swaying pendulum—concerning the baby Fatima was carrying: "Is it mine?" Ricky could remember only one occasion when he had made love with Fatima without wearing a condom. But he could not recall precisely when that night of careless passion had occurred. He knew it was fairly recent—but when?

"How are you feeling?" Ricky asked.

"I think I am fine," Fatima said. "Though, I must say, I don't really feel pregnant. However it is one is supposed to feel I don't think I really feel it."

Ricky nodded, though he did not understand what Fatima meant. "When did you find out?"

Fatima continued to stare into her tea. "Yesterday afternoon. I had a regular appointment with my doctor and she told me."

"Your gynecologist?"

She winced. Ricky realized that Fatima was so modest—so archaically pre-feminist, so non-American, at least when it came to the subject of what was going on inside her body—that the very word caused her discomfort. "Yes," she said.

"And how far along are you?"

Fatima sighed, then said, "She think two month."

Ricky gulped, hoped Fatima did not hear it. "So what happens now?"

"I have another appointment. At a maternity hospital. Tomorrow morning."

"I'll go with you."

Fatima finally looked up, her eyes filled with an almost bewildered level of surprise. "You will?"

"If you want me to."

Fatima nearly smiled—but not quite. "Okay. I come by here at nine tomorrow morning. Then we can go there together."

"All right."

While Fatima packed her knapsack, Ricky rose from the bed, slipped into his gym shorts and T-shirt. Standing in front of the door of his apartment, they embraced. Ricky thought that he should not say it, the

words he had not uttered to any woman since Clementine. But, holding
Fatima in his arms, his face buried in her hair, Ricky whispered, "I love
you."

Fatima gently pulled away from him, that expression of puzzled
surprise in her eyes again. She quickly stared down at the floor, seemingly embarrassed, uncertain of how to respond. Finally, Fatima said,
"Thank you."

Ricky tried to go back to sleep after Fatima left his apartment but it
was impossible. After an hour and a half of lying on the sofa bed, staring
at the peeling ceiling, Ricky felt the need for some sort of solace. Feeling
a sharp pang of hunger, he knew what he had to do. He would go to
Marva's Soul Food Kitchen.

Comfort and nourishment were Ricky's main objectives but it occurred to him that a visit to Marva's place could also help in his
"detective work." Marva Dobbs, the most famous black American *restauratrice* in Paris for the past thirty-odd years, might very well have
been an old acquaintance of Serena Moriarty Washington. After a quick
shower and a shave, Ricky decided to take the photo of Serena with him
to the restaurant. If Marva could not recall Serena's name she might
remember her face.

Ricky gasped as he removed the decorative *kente* cloth from the top
of the trunk that served as his de facto coffee table. The padlock on the
trunk had clearly been tampered with. It looked as if someone had
battered the metal face of the lock with a hammer. Quickly dialing the
combination, Ricky assumed that French police officers must have
searched his apartment while he was at the *mairie* with Lamouche but
before Fatima arrived. Yet there were no other signs of a ransacking of
his studio. And, as he opened the lid, Ricky saw that everything inside
the trunk was in its proper place. Serena's photo was still inside the
white business envelope, and so were the twenty fifty-dollar-bills his
cousin Cash had given him. Ricky left the money where it was but
slipped the photo into his wallet and relocked the trunk.

The lobby of Ricky's building looked completely normal—not a single spot of Grace Kelly's blood on the wall or the floor. But out on the

sidewalk, there were now a dozen bouquets stacked in front of number 176. Ricky paused to stare down at the pile of roses, carnations, daisies, lillies and irises wrapped in clear plastic and tied with brightly colored ribbons. He thought of the so-called Princess Diana memorial downtown at the Pont de l'Alma, the Bridge of the Soul. Since September 1997, just after Di's fatal car crash in a nearby tunnel, an enormous gold torch at the foot of the bridge had been appropriated as a shrine to the princess. Never mind that the accident had occurred underground, clear on the other side of the busy intersection. Nor did the mourners who were always gathered by the torch seem to mind that the monument, in reality, had nothing to do with Diana at all. It was a replica of the torch held by the Statue of Liberty, donated to the city of Paris back in 1987 by the *International Herald Tribune* in commemoration of the newspaper's hundredth anniversary. A plaque on the side of the torch clearly explained this. But nobody cared. For nearly two years, the torch had been plastered with images of the photogenic dead royal. People had scrawled tributes to her, in red and black ink, in at least half a dozen languages, all over the gold flame. Worshippers from around the world came to lay bouquets at the base of the monument, the monument that most of them believed had been placed there specifically for Diana. Ricky wondered if the murdered transsexual prositute, whose real name he did not even know, would now acquire a sort of divine celebrity status: the Diana of the rue des Martyrs.

As Ricky looked at the assortment of flowers on his doorstep, he remembered the grisly sight of Grace Kelly's corpse. A lump swelled in his throat as he thought of how painful her death must have been. Suddenly, Ricky felt that he was being watched. Looking up, he saw, across the street, the two matronly queens of the day shift, eyeing him suspiciously. He had always thought of them as Little Tootsie and Big Tootsie, these middle-aged transsexual prostitutes with their heavily rouged faces and wigs that recalled the stiff, conservative-lady hairdos of a Nancy Reagan or a Margaret Thatcher. They had none of the sleazy glamour of the night-shift hookers. Ricky imagined that the clients who were drawn to the charms of the two Tootsies must have had serious mother fixations. There was a demure quality about Little Tootsie, with her velvet gloves and patent-leather handbag. Big Tootsie, however, was

even taller and wider than Ricky, an imposing "brickhouse" of a gal
who strode up and down the rue des Martyrs in her high heels, her
cloth overcoat usually unbuttoned, revealing a tight-fitting, low-cut dress
and bountiful, silicone cleavage. The Tootsies and their colleagues on
the day shift had never paid Ricky any mind. That was why he felt all
the more disturbed as the two hookers stood directly across the rue des
Martyrs, brazenly glaring at him. Little Tootsie muttered something to
Big Tootsie who nodded slowly in response, keeping her gaze riveted to
Ricky. He considered walking up to the prostitutes and explaining that
he had had nothing to do with Grace Kelly's murder. But he quickly
decided that anything he said might be horribly misconstrued; any claim
of innocence he professed might make him seem all the more guilty. So
Ricky simply turned and started climbing the rue des Martyrs, feeling
the hookers' laser eyes burning little holes in his back.

Marva's Soul Food Kitchen was jam-packed this Friday noontime, filled
almost to capacity with Japanese tourists. They chattered merrily, slick,
jet-black heads nodding, beautifully tapered eyes shining as they chowed
down on fried chicken and black-eyed peas, cornbread and chitlins, cat-
fish and gumbo, juicy pigs' feet and Marva's finger-smackin' sublime
barbecued spareribs. Ricky carefully worked his way through the
crowded tables, edging toward Marva Dobbs who was standing by the
bar, glass of mineral water in hand, holding court. Several of the Japanese diners were clustered around her, occasionally snapping photo-
graphs.

"Oh, Alain Ducasse comes in here all the time," Marva said grandly.
"I knew him when he was just starting out, an apprentice chef. Now he
says to me, 'Marva, *ma chérie*, I may have all ze Michelin stars but it
is you who are ze *vrai génie!*' "

Marva was, as always, the picture of nonchalant elegance, dressed in
a Chanel suit and a string of pearls, tall and lean, her black hair, flecked
with gray, worn short and natural, her deep brown, high-cheekboned
face noble and ageless, reminding Ricky of that old American expression:
"Black don't crack." Nobody knew Marva's actual age. But she was happy
to tell you that she had arrived in Paris in the summer of 1962 as the

lead singer of an up-and-coming girl group known as Marva Dobbs and the Marvalines. They wore silk dresses and bouffant wigs and had just scored their first and ultimately only Top Forty hit in the States, "When Oh When Will You Be Mine?" Marva and the three Marvalines were in the midst of a six-city European tour when their manager, Sid Abramowitz, suddenly dropped dead of a heart attack while strolling along the Boulevard Saint Germain. Sid's body was taken away in an ambulance and the girls were overwrought. Sid had been handling everything. They had no money on them. Sid had even been holding onto their passports. Neither Marva nor any of the Marvalines spoke a word of French.

"We were a mess," Marva liked to recall. "I was trying to keep everybody together but the Marvalines were hysterical. Weepin' and shriekin', mascara runnin' down their faces. Thank God for that young assistant manager at the hotel. His name was Loïc. He spoke English fluently. He was smart and kind and efficient and he sorted everything out with the authorities. And he was also *fine!* I mean, *so fine!* One of those Bretons, you dig? The best mixture of French-Latin and Anglo-Saxon features. Blond-haired and blue-eyed but delicate, smooth. The Marvalines went back to the States but I stayed in Paris with Loïc. I would sing with the American bands that came through town but my heart was never in it. What I really loved was cooking for the musicians after their gigs. We'd all get together at the hotel where Loïc worked and everybody would stay up all night, drinkin' and smokin' and eatin' my food. After a few months Loïc asked me to marry him. I said, 'Baby, I didn't stay in Paris to marry no assistant hotel manager.' So he went back to school and became a tax lawyer. We got married and in 1965 I opened this little restaurant of mine. *Et voilà!*"

Three decades later, that little restaurant, on the rue Véron in the Eighteenth Arrondissement, was a Paris institution. As Ricky maneuvered his way toward Marva, through the throng of happily munching Japanese, he nodded to the two busy waitresses as they rushed past him holding aloft heaping platters of dessert (cheesecake; pecan pie; fat, glistening slices of watermelon) and glanced at the walls of the restaurant, at the framed black-and-white photos taken during the 1970s, the heyday of Marva's place. There was Marva with her arms wrapped around Muhammad Ali; Marva posing between Liz and Dick; Marva clinking Champagne glasses with James Baldwin; sharing a sly smile with François Truffaut; seemingly engaged in serious discussion with an aging but absolutely gorgeous Josephine Baker; hugging Chester Himes; kissing Catherine Deneuve.... Ricky, like everybody else, was impressed by Marva's Walls of Fame. But a far less renowned FOM—or Friend of Marva's—had meant the most to Ricky Jenks. It was Marva Dobbs, you see, who had introduced Ricky to Fatima Boukhari.

"Well, look what the cat done drug in!" Marva boomed joyously when she spotted Ricky. She kissed him once on each cheek, then, with a long arm draped around his shoulders, introduced Ricky to the group of tourists surrounding them, several of whom quickly snapped his picture. "This is one of the finest jazz pianists in all of Paris," Marva proclaimed, somewhat ironically since, though she often featured live music in her restaurant, she had never once asked Ricky to play there. Ricky was never sure if this was because she did not want to complicate their friendship by hiring him or if she didn't think he was good enough. He was content not to know. "Now, y'all sit back down and get some dessert," Marva said warmly to her customers. "I'll come back around later."

Marva led Ricky to one of the few free tables in the restaurant, in a shadowy corner near the kitchen doorway, and sat down across from him. "So how's my big ol' bear?" she asked.

"Can't complain," Ricky said with a shrug.

"Well, that sure makes you different from most folks around here, Richard." Marva pronounced his name, lovingly, in the French way: Ree-*shar*. "Your typical Parisian can *always* find something to complain about. So how's that beautiful girlfriend of yours?"

Ricky felt a hot rush of blood, a blushing, in his face. "She's not my girlfriend."

"Well, she oughta be. If you had any sense you'd ask Fatima to marry you."

"You know Fatima will only marry a Muslim."

"So convert!"

Ricky laughed. "Really, Marva, one religion has been more than I could handle. I'm not lookin' for another one."

"But how is she?" Marva asked, a note of serious concern in her voice.

For a moment, Ricky wondered if Marva knew about Fatima's pregnancy. Was it possible that Fatima had told Marva, their canny matchmaker, of the new development/dilemma? Was Marva subtly inviting Ricky to share his thoughts on the matter with her? No. Ricky decided that Fatima had not told Marva of the pregnancy. And Fatima might be angry with him if he spilled the beans. So Ricky decided to say nothing significant about his "girlfriend." He just waggled his head and told Marva, "She's all right."

"So what's the matter then? And don't tell me nothin', 'cause I know you, Bear, and I know somethin's up."

Ricky knew he could hide some of what was going on in his life from Marva but not everything. So he told her about coming home from work and stumbling upon the body of the transsexual prostitute. He told her of his questioning by Inspector Lamouche at the *mairie* of the Eighteenth. He told her how shaken up he was by the whole experience but he did not tell her about finding Fatima sitting in his apartment at six in the morning.

Marva took it all in, nodding slowly as Ricky told his strange tale. Finally, when he was through, she asked, "Do you have a lawyer?"

"I was gonna call Archie Dukes."

Marva frowned. "Now, you know I love Archie. He's an upstanding brother you can always count on. I've known him for thirty-five years. But Archie's a black American corporate lawyer. And semiretired. You need a *French* lawyer, Bear. A French *criminal* lawyer."

The way Marva said "criminal" made Ricky want to cringe, but he tried not to. "Okay," he said as evenly as he could.

"Loïc, of course, is a tax lawyer," Marva continued. "But we have a neighbor who practices criminal law. And he's damned good. Lemme call Loïc." She paused, seemingly lost in thought, then said, "What do you wanna eat, Bear?"

"Oh, I don't know. I'm usually only having breakfast at this hour."

"Fine. I'll order you up a Sunday brunch."

"But it's only Friday."

"Yo, Bear, I own the joint."

Marva Dobbs rose and disappeared into the kitchen. Five minutes later, she reemerged, gave Ricky a conspiratorial wink, then plunged into the crowd of stuffed and thoroughly satisfied Japanese customers. Having enjoyed one of the best meals of their tour, everybody wanted to have their photo taken with Marva. The master chef was only too happy to oblige. Just as the flashbulbs starting popping, Ricky's Sunday brunch on Friday arrived. He dug into his generous pile of scrambled eggs, his crisp and consummately greasy slabs of bacon, his home fries and grits—the only genuine home fries and grits you could find in Paris—his towering stack of exquisitely browned pancakes, slathering them in genuine, imported Aunt Jemima maple syrup. And Ricky Jenks was happy. As happy as he had been in a long time. Because he was in the place where he belonged, eating the comfort food he loved. Everything feeling, tasting of home. His chosen home.

"There are three types of Afro-Americans in Paris," Marva informed Ricky back in his early days in town, September 1990, the second time he'd been to the famous restaurant but the first time the owner had been there to meet him. It was near closing time and Ricky and Charlie Jackson—dreadlocked bass guitarist, Cleveland homeboy and longtime black expat—sat with Marva at a table cluttered with smeared, bone-filled plates, empty beer and wine bottles and glasses. They were onto the after-dinner drinks now—the *digestifs*: Cognac, Armagnac, Calvados. Around their table, customers were paying their bills, retrieving their jackets from the coatracks, waving good-bye and saying *"Merci, au revoir, Mar-VAH."* The great lady waved back, shook a few hands, kissed a few cheeks, exchanged pleasantries with an array of regulars as they headed out into the night; but after every interruption, she would pick right back up where she had left off in her discourse, Ricky and Charlie listening closely like honorable schoolboys though Ricky thought Charlie may have heard Marva's social theories before.

"First there are the brothers and sisters who want Paris to be just like back home, or think it can be, or assume it is when it ain't. They wanna hang out just with other black Americans. If they bother to speak French at all it's the bare minimum for survival. They enjoy seeing the sights and eatin' the food but the whole time they're here they're always bitchin' about the way the French do things. They can't get out of the American mind-set. They assume a white Frenchman is exactly the same as a white American, not realizing how often nationality trumps race, or how race can be something different, more strange and subtle and nuanced and ambiguous than a mere question of black versus white. These are the black folks who often complain the most about America but who are, at the same time, hopelessly in love with the place. They can't stop thinking about, talking about America. It's as if they're living in Paris but have left their brains in Oakland, or St. Louis, or Manhattan! You always wonder why these folks stay in Paris at all and the fact is they always go back. Back to the devil they know, back to America. *Home.*"

Marva orders the waitress to take away the dirty plates, bring a fresh ashtray and a bottle of Cointreau. More liqueur is poured. Marva fires up another Marlboro Light. The cash register clangs. The *grande dame* bids another farewell to another couple of regulars, continues discoursing, Ricky and Charlie completely focused on the words of this charismatic woman the age of their mothers, now listening with the attentiveness of fawning suitors.

"Then there's the second type. These are the black Americans who disappear into France. As best they can, they shut America out. Often they have French spouses, socialize almost exclusively in French circles, express themselves entirely in the French language. Don't get me wrong, these brothers and sisters ain't tryin' to be white! They might have friends from all over Africa, or from Martinique or Guadeloupe or Guyana. They just don't want to have anything to do with Americans, black or white. They have simply disappeared into France. They are the Virtual Frenchmen. I run into them, by chance, here and there. Sometimes one of them will show up, in a group of French people, at this restaurant. I can usually spot a member of our tribe—that is, as an old friend of mine used to like to say, 'the North American cohort of the African diaspora'—on sight. And as I talk with the Virtual Frenchman—or Virtual Frenchwoman—I find that sometimes they've forgotten how to say certain basic words in English. Or, stranger yet, they speak English with a French accent. You don't know what bizarre is till you've heard a sistuh from, say, Fayetteville, Arkansas, speaking English and sounding like Jeanne Moreau!

"Finally there's the third group—the rest of us. The betwixt and between. We may love America but we also love not living there. We celebrate our roots but savor the freedom of rootlessness. We may not speak French as fluently as the Virtual Frenchmen but we blunder along valiantly. We live in that spiritual country that is home and not-home: the chosen home. We want to have our cake and our *tarte*, too! We revel in the pleasures of displacement. And yet ours is a transient community. You always hear about some brother or sister who, for whatever reason, had to *go back*. They may have been perfectly happy here in Paris, in France, but maybe they ran out of money, or they had a family crisis stateside, or experienced some personal epiphany that told them it was time to *go back*. And that's what we old-timers, the expatriates-for-life, always say about them. 'Yeah, Greg and Tanya went *back*. . . . Leroy went *back*. . . . Alexandra went *back*. . . . Don't know when we'll see them again. They were in Paris six, or twelve, or nineteen years. . . . But now they've *gone back* . . .' Maybe to return to Paris. Probably not.

"Meanwhile, the rest of us stay. And we create the community, each in his or her individual way. We need to be around our people, our brethren and sistren, but we also need that intoxicating air of international independence. I speak only of Paris. But you'll find Afro-American folk like us all over Europe—certainly in all the great cities. I love America like I love my family. You don't choose your place of birth any more than you choose your family. But I love Paris in the way that you fall in love. It's romantic, it's sensual. It's chosen. It's like Josephine Baker sang: 'I have two loves: my country . . . and Paris.' "

The last of the Japanese tourists had filed out of the restaurant and a different wave of lunchtime clients was slowly taking their places. Having devoured his Sunday brunch on Friday, Ricky was nursing another mugful of American coffee—weak stuff by European standards, but tasty enough for Ricky and one of the pleasures of dining at Marva's place. Ricky had watched Marva bowing her head respectfully and bidding *"Sayonara"* to the tourists. Then she was rushing in and out of the kitchen, up and down the stairs. When she finally sat back down at Ricky's table, she had a Louis Vuitton handbag hanging on her arm. "How was everything, sweetheart?" she asked, sounding slightly out of breath.

"Perfect as always, Madame Dobbs."

"You want a dessert?"

"No room for it."

"Well, if you change your mind, tell one of the girls. You're my guest today, everything's on the house."

"Marva, I can't," Ricky began to protest but the *restauratrice* held up a regal hand, cutting him off. He knew there was no point arguing with her.

"Sorry I can't stay, Bear, but I've got a rendezvous down in the Fifth. But, listen, I talked to Loïc. The criminal lawyer is out of town right now. He won't be back till Monday night. From what Inspector Lamouche said to you I doubt the cops will be calling on you over the weekend. But they will eventually. We just have to hope this lawyer, Olivier, is back in Paris before they do."

"Marva, I can't thank you enough. It's great of you to do all this."

"No trouble a-tall. Let me know if there's anything else I can do."

"Well, actually, I did want to ask you about something, unrelated to the murder. Just another weird thing that happened yesterday. But if you have to go . . ."

"I can wait a couple more minutes," Marva said. She was being kind but Ricky could see from the little glimmer in her eye that her curiosity had been aroused.

"Well, a cousin of mine came through town yesterday and asked me to do him a favor. It seems that Cash's wife——"

"Cash?"

"That's my cousin's name. Cash Washington."

Marva beamed. "Dr. Cash Washington is your *cousin?*" she exclaimed, clearly impressed.

Ricky suddenly felt queasy. "You know him?"

"Sure! He was here in this restaurant back in, oh, it must have been early 'ninety-seven. Don't you remember? When he was on his way back to the States. He'd just been to Africa with a group of doctors. They were making a few stops in Europe trying to raise consciousness, and money, of course, for land-mine victims. I'll never forget Dr. Washington talking about how moved he was, outfitting little children in Mozambique with prosthetic limbs. Weren't you here that night?"

Ricky tried to play it cool but he was actually stunned. "No," he said blandly. "I must have been working." The fact that Cash had been in Paris two years earlier, had even been in Ricky's neighborhood, eaten in his favorite restaurant, was startling news. But the real shock was his cousin's altruism. Dr. Armani tending to the poor and mutilated?

"But you must have seen him sometime during that visit."

"Actually, he was really busy and our schedules couldn't quite match up. . . ."

"Oh, what a shame."

"But I did see him just yesterday."

"And he's your *cousin*," Marva said, still glowing at the memory of her encounter with Cash. Marva Dobbs had rubbed elbows with her fair share of Nobel Peace Prize winners and the look of awe on her face was the same one she wore when recounting her meetings with the likes of Martin Luther King Jr. and Nelson Mandela. Ricky knew that Marva cared deeply for him. She was as good a friend as he had had in his nine years in Paris. But there was no mistaking the fact that Ricky had now risen in Marva's estimation. As if the accident of birth that made him Cash's cousin was some kind of noteworthy accomplishment. "You must be so proud."

"Of course, we all are," Ricky muttered.

"And Dr. Washington is in town! Shame on you, Ricky! Why didn't you bring him by?"

"He was only here yesterday afternoon. Anyway, he asked a favor of me and I thought maybe you could help me out."

"Anything for that cousin of yours. And for you, too, of course, Bear!"

"*Merci*, Marva." Now Ricky had to stop himself from smirking as he said, "Cash's wife left him."

"No! What's *her* problem?"

"Cash admits it was all his fault," Ricky rushed to say.

"Hmmmmmmm." Marva hummed skeptically.

"Anyway, she ran away from their home in New York and Cash has reason to believe that his wife might be here. She used to live in Paris, back in the eighties."

"Really?" Marva straightened up in her chair, her eyes twinkling expectantly. She reminded Ricky of a contestant on a quiz show who was certain that she knew the correct answer before a question was even asked. "What's her name?"

"Serena. Her maiden name was Serena Moriarty."

Marva paused. She pursed her lips and stared down at the table for a long moment before looking up and asking querulously, "A black girl?"

"Yeah. Maybe *métisse*," Ricky said, using the French word for biracial.

Now Marva looked up at the ceiling. From the concentration in her eyes, Ricky could see that she was rapidly scrolling through a vast database of names in her mind. He was already reaching for his wallet when Marva lowered her eyes and shook her head in stumped disappointment. "Sorry, Bear, I don't think I know her."

Ricky handed Marva the photo. The shock of recognition was immediate, obvious, and a little frightening. As Marva held the small photo between thumb and forefinger, staring hard at the image, a strange, disoriented look fell across her face like a shadow. Her eyes seemed to go out of focus then concentrate again, her gaze frozen. It was the petrified gaze of someone standing at some great height who had just looked down and realized what a steep drop lay beneath her feet: a vertigo stare. Yet, Ricky was excited by Marva's reaction. With his first line of inquiry, he'd hit pay dirt. Clearly, Marva knew Serena and seemed to know, through experience, that the girl in the photo was trouble. Maybe, Ricky thought, he was a natural-born detective.

But then, just as suddenly as Marva Dobbs had silently freaked out, she pulled herself together. Quickly but carefully composing a look of neutral indifference on her face, Marva handed the photo back to Ricky. "Never seen her before," she said.

"What?" Ricky almost shouted.

"Now I really do have to run." Marva leaned forward, kissed Ricky once on each cheek. She rose from the table and bolted out the front door, leaving Ricky paralyzed in his chair, clutching the little photo of Cash's runaway wife.

And Ricky began to turn the question over in his mind: Why did Marva lie?

Seven

VALITSA THE SERB WAS ranting again. "You Americans and your childlike sense of time! How can you say thirteen eighty-nine was a long time ago? To a Serb thirteen eighty-nine is a living memory! Of course this is not the case for you Americans." Valitsa pronounced the words *you Americans* with a twist of indignant revulsion, in the same way one might say *you child molesters*, or *you mass murderers*. "Because you have no history. Or you have no conception of what it means. To the American mind, history is something contemptible. What does an American say when he wants to make an event sound meaningless? *'That's history!'* When someone's career is over, you Americans say *'He's history!'* History is your way of saying something does not matter, has no relevance! You live in the eternal present. Like ignorant little children!"

Ordinarily, Ricky just listened to Valitsa's tirades and did not bother debating her. But on this Friday afternoon, he could not resist barking back. "So are you really going to sit here and tell me that thirteen eighty-nine was *not* a long time ago?"

"To you Americans," Valitsa snarled, "even nineteen sixty-eight is a long time ago! World War Two is the dark and distant past and anything before the twentieth century is caveman days! You can not understand that to a European nineteen sixty-eight is the equivalent of last week to *you*. World War Two was like a month ago! It is an entirely different conception of time, of history. This is why you can never understand that to a Serb the events of thirteen eighty-nine could not be more relevant to the events of nineteen ninety-nine! Six hundred and ten years ago Serbian culture ruled supreme! And Kosovo was our seat of power. But the Turks overran us. The brave Prince Lazar led seventy-seven thousand men to their deaths against the Turks. They knew they were doomed. But they went into battle singing, proud to die for Kosovo! It was the finest hour of the Serb people!"

"But you lost," Ricky said.

"Of course."

"So how could that be your people's finest hour?"

"Acch! You Americans will never understand the nobility of defeat. That is why you and your NATO bombs think you can crush the Serb spirit today! The Albanians have been trying to do to us what the Turks did to us six hundred and ten years ago, to take Kosovo away from us. Now the Americans and NATO and all your bombs are helping the Albanian oppressors. And once again we will lose the battle of Kosovo!"

"And you will be proud?"

"Prouder than you can ever imagine!" Valitsa cried, actually shaking her fist at Ricky. "You with your puny American sense of time, of history!"

"Okay, okay. Can we have our lesson now?"

Ricky wanted to remind Valitsa that he was paying one hundred francs an hour to learn the complexities of the French language, not to listen to her rant about Balkan politics. But Valitsa's rants were part of her identity, the reason why people who knew her automatically added her ethnicity to her name: *la Serbe.*

Valitsa lowered her fist. She seemed chastened. "Sorry," she whispered. Ricky's tutor started digging into the pile of books and papers stacked haphazardly on her desk, searching for the text they had been studying for the past few sessions. Ricky knew Valitsa was crazy but he couldn't help feeling a certain affection for her. Valitsa the Serb was one of those peculiar women who was not in any way conventionally pretty but who, for a certain type of man—the type of man who was not obsessed with notions of conventional prettiness—possessed an over-powering sexual magnetism. Gaunt and pale, with lank black hair, parted down the middle, and immense, dark, Picasso eyes, small breasts and a flat bottom, Valitsa never flirted with men. Just the opposite. She was gruff, brusque, even hostile in manner. Yet men were inexorably drawn to her. Maybe it was that she exuded passion. The same passion that fueled her political diatribes gave her a carnal glow that a certain type of man found enticing. Ricky Jenks had allowed himself to be enticed only once. He could barely remember that one drunken, hashish-smoky night with Valitsa back in the early 1990s. But he remembered the afternoon after, when he was alone in his apartment and noticed the blue-black spot on his left biceps, the blood swelling beneath it, the little dental indentations above and below the achy bump. Valitsa had left her mark. He and the Serb remained friends but he was never tempted again.

For better or worse, Valitsa Karodovic was an excellent tutor of French. She had patiently helped Ricky put together the language's tricky building blocks of basic grammar. By April 1999, their meetings were irregular, but always constructive. Mainly, these days, they read together. They were currently working on a collection of short stories by Marcel Aymé, a writer who had spent his entire life in Montmartre and set most of his tales in the bumpy hills and crooked alleys and dark corners of the Eighteenth Arrondissement. In addition to teaching, Val-itsa earned money as a mime near the Place du Tertre, painting her face and dressing up as Cleopatra or Sainte Catherine or the Statue of Liberty. But teaching and miming were only a means of survival for Valitsa, a way of feeding herself, of paying the rent. It was something else that defined her, gave meaning to her life: the politics of her tor-tured homeland.

Valitsa found her volume of Marcel Aymé, then paused, staring down at the book. Ricky worried that he had hurt her feelings. "I'm sorry," he said. "I didn't mean to cut you off. I know it's terrible, this war."

"No more talk of Kosovo," Valitsa said. "But I must ask you. Did you murder Grace Kelly last night?"

"What?" Ricky, walking from Marva's Soul Food Kitchen to Valitsa's small and shabby apartment on the rue Berthe, had decided not to mention the killing to his French tutor. He figured that even if Valitsa had heard of the prostitute's murder, she probably would not know about his stumbling upon the body. And since, as soon as he had entered Valitsa's place that afternoon, the proud Serb had started railing against the bombing of Belgrade, Ricky had managed to put Grace Kelly out of his mind. Now, flabbergasted by Valitsa's question, Ricky stammered: "B-b-b-but . . . No! . . . Of course not! J-j-j-esus, Valitsa! Me? How could you think that?"

"It is not I who think it," Valitsa said calmly. "It is the prostitutes on the rue des Martyrs."

"But why?"

"You were taken away by the police, were you not?"

"That's because I found the body. The cops know that!"

"But she was killed in your building. The prostitutes do not normally take their customers into your building. Someone must have led her in there. What else would she have been doing there? How would she have known the door code?"

The door code! Like most apartment buildings in Paris, Ricky's had a panel of numbered and lettered buttons just to the right of the front door. Ordinarily, only the residents of a building and their guests knew the door code—Ricky's was currently 46A79—and he had to punch it in to unlock the entrance. The manager of a Paris building usually changed the door code every year and a half. Ricky had given no thought at all as to what Grace Kelly was doing in his building or how she had managed to enter it. "How the hell would I know?" Ricky answered Valitsa, his voice rising defensively. "Maybe she had a friend in the building."

"Maybe you were that friend." Valitsa shrugged, her pallid face impassive. "I tell you only what the prostitutes are saying."

"And how do you know what they're saying?"

"I have my sources," the Serb said cryptically.

Now Ricky was angry. "Well, I hope you're telling your sources that you know me and that you know I'm no fucking murderer! What possible motive could I have had for killing Grace Kelly?"

"The motiveless crime is a *spécialité* of the late twentieth century."

Ricky buried his face in his hands. "Damn, damn, damn," he murmured. When he looked up again, Valitsa had a curious little half-smile on her face.

"So," she said, "when are you going back to live in the U.S.A.?"

This was a running joke of theirs. Valitsa the Serb liked to taunt Ricky with his conventional, middle-class background. She would tell him that his life in Paris as a bohemian piano player was just a pose; that deep down what he really wanted was to return to Suburbia, U.S.A. buy a house with a white picket fence and a lush green lawn, get a safe, boring job, get a safe, boring wife, have a couple of kids, a couple of cars, a couple of weeks vacation per year. Valitsa had no idea that this was, in fact, the sort of life Ricky might have led had Clementine Yerby not left him standing at the altar. "You are not cut out for this improvisational Parisian life," Valitsa would jeer at Ricky. "You will not admit it but you are as American as Wonder Bread. When are you going back to live in the U.S.A.?"

Valitsa and Ricky had had this exchange for years. And now, when she asked him her snide little question, after having told him he was suspected of murder, Ricky gave her the same answer he always had, year after year, only today with a fierce edge of determination in his voice: "Never."

Valitsa lit a long, thin brown cigarette. Soon she was shrouded in a cloud of smoke, giving Ricky her intense, black-eyed stare. Like the first time they met, back when Ricky was the house pianist at Le Coucher du Soleil. Like most of the bars and restaurants and clubs Ricky frequented in Paris, The Sunset Café was usually filled with voluminous clouds of tobacco. The attitude toward smoke was another example of how France was like a funhouse-mirror version of the States. In America, even in the "smoking section" of a café, no one would be smoking. In France, even in the "nonsmoking section" of a café, everyone would be smoking.

One night, banging away on the piano on the little stage, Ricky noticed a solemn-looking woman drinking and smoking up a storm, alone, in a corner of the joint. Something about her reminded him of Dora Maar, Picasso's dark and brooding lover and model. During a break between sets, Ricky couldn't resist sitting at the mysterioso woman's table and chatting her up in French. Valitsa kept staring at him, squinting and tilting her head as if she did not quite grasp what he was saying. Ricky had lived in Paris for two years at the time and thought he spoke the language reasonably well. Finally, Ricky said, "I'm sorry, my accent is not very good."

"Your accent is fine," Valitsa replied. "Your grammar is atrocious." She said she could help him, for a price. He took her up on the offer.

Now, seven years later, on this Friday afternoon, the last day of April, Ricky could not concentrate on French during his class with Valitsa. Instead, he told her, in English, about all the bizarre events of the past twenty-four hours: his meeting with Cash Washington in Barbès; the discovery of Grace Kelly's body and his subsequent grilling by Inspector Lamouche; Fatima's pregnancy. He even divulged that his cousin Cash had confessed to battering his wife and might be an embezzler on the lam. Valitsa the Serb listened attentively. When Ricky was through with his recapitulation, he felt almost like crying. The gravity of it all, particularly of Fatima's pregnancy, was finally hitting him with full force.

"You know what I think?" Valitsa said, after seeming to have given serious thought to everything Ricky had told her. "I think you need to protect yourself."

"How so?"

"Come."

Valitsa led Ricky down the short, dark, narrow corridor that stretched between her apartment's living room and bedroom. She opened the door of the closet in the middle of the hallway, knelt down on the floor. She reached into the back of the closet, then slid a small wooden crate across the floorboards. Ricky saw U.S. ARMY stamped on the side of the crate. Valitsa lifted the lid and Ricky found himself staring at a little pile of dark green objects, vaguely pineapple-shaped. He immediately thought of toys from his childhood, back in the days when little boys were unabashedly allowed to play with such macho models. It took him a moment to realize that he was staring at the genuine article, here in Valitsa's hallway: a box full of hand grenades.

"What the fuck," Ricky whispered.

"I am a conduit for these weapons," Valitsa said matter-of-factly. "Someone passed them to me. I cannot tell you who. And I am supposed to find a way to pass them on to someone else. I can not tell you who. In truth, I do not even know myself. But I am to wait to learn the name of my contact. These grenades will end up in the hands of the Serb freedom fighters in Kosovo."

"Now wait a minute. It's the Serbs who have the army in Kosovo."

"Yes, but they are short of supplies. And after we lose this war our forces will have to go underground. We must supply the needed weapons to the secret militias that will continue the struggle."

"And how did you acquire a box full of hand grenades?"

"Like I said, I cannot tell you. I am waiting for the word so I can find out who to pass them on to. They are the original property of your American army."

"So I see."

"I hear they are somewhat defective."

"How so?"

"I do not know. All I know is that the Serb freedom fighters need all the weapons they can get. But, of course, I am somewhat under suspicion. I would like to know: Could you keep these weapons in your apartment, until I receive instructions from my contact?"

"Fuck no."

"Ah, yes, you are one of those apolitical Americans, aren't you, Ricky?"

"Not apolitical. Just nonviolent."

"And did your people in America achieve freedom without violence? America had to go to war to free the slaves. We Serbs must wage war for our freedom, too."

"I'm not going to get into an argument with you about the American Civil War," Ricky said. "It was too complicated. And, as for what's going on in Yugoslavia, I just don't know enough about it."

"So you will not keep these weapons for me?"

"No, I won't."

Valitsa lifted a grenade from the box, thrust it at Ricky. "Then here. Take one for yourself. I have twelve in the box. You can take one for your own protection."

Ricky stepped away from Valitsa who held the grenade in her out-stretched hand, casually, as if she were offering him a hard-boiled egg. "I told you no. I'm not gonna throw a fucking grenade at someone to protect myself."

Valitsa shrugged, put the explosive little missile back into the crate, slid the crate back into the dark recesses of her closet. "Suit yourself," she said.

Though they had spoken almost no French that afternoon, Ricky paid Valitsa two hundred francs for the time they had spent together. Leaving the apartment, he decided he would no longer be taking lessons from this nutty Serb.

At first glance, it was just another pasty face in the crowd. But as Ricky jostled his way through the churning groups of tourists, painters and sketch artists filling the Place du Tertre, the sense of being watched caused him to turn around and take a second look at the man sitting at a sidewalk café table. Yes, the man was waving at him. Ricky was thrown by seeing the pale, moony face out of the fever dream context of the Grace Kelly crime scene and the Salle des Mariages in the middle of the night. But there was Inspector Lamouche, sitting alone at a table, at a café just around the corner from Le Bon Montmartrois, a small cup of espresso in front of him, gesturing for Ricky to come over. Ricky could feel his paranoia kicking in as he approached Lamouche's table. Was he now under police surveillance?

"Good afternoon, my friend," Lamouche said in his cheery rasp. "Will you join me for a drink? Coffee, an apéritif?"

"I was just on my way to work."

Lamouche looked at his wristwatch. "Yes but you are not due at your job for another fifteen minutes. Join me, please. I will take only a moment of your time."

Ricky took a seat, tried to sound casual. "What's up?"

"Well, a funny zing happened on ze way to ze autopsie. Our murder victim, ze prostitute, she was wearing a very short, tight skirt. But zere was one pocket in ze skirt and inside zat pocket, we find zis."

Lamouche dropped a small clear plastic baggie on the table. Inside the baggie were two silver keys, partially encrusted in blood. A little slip of paper was tied around the key ring. Written, in a familiar hand, on the thin strip was "M. Jenks."

"I believe zese are ze keys to your home. My question is, did you give zese keys to ze prostitute?"

"Hell no," Ricky said, struggling not to sound too excitable or defensive. "I told you, I barely knew her."

"Zen she must have got zem from Madame Lavache. Perhap zat is madame's writing on ze paper."

Ricky gave a knowing nod, as if this all made perfect sense to him; but he was still struggling to understand. Madame Lavache: ah, yes, he often forgot the name of his concierge. She was part of the contemporary breed of Paris apartment-building caretakers. Traditionally, French concierges were combination superintendents, security guards and servants who lived on the ground floor. They cleaned the lobby and stairwells, changed the lightbulbs, received the mail for each and every tenant and kept watch over who entered and exited the building. The concierge in Ricky's building, however, did not have such sweeping responsibilities. Madame Lavache only occupied the studio apartment on the ground floor for eight hours a day, Monday through Friday, from nine in the morning to seven in the evening (with a two-hour lunch break). There was a regular cleaning lady to keep the building neat and tidy and letter boxes for the mail. Ricky could never understand what exactly it was his concierge did except gossip with the elderly residents who habitually dropped by her studio. But the concierge possessed, as a matter of course, keys to every tenant's apartment. Ricky remembered that Madame Lavache had posted a note in the lobby saying that she would be taking Friday off, for the May Day weekend. Since Madame Lavache played no significant role in his life, Ricky did not care. He never imagined that, before she left on holiday, the concierge would lend some prostitute her copy of the keys to his apartment.

"Why would Lavache do that?" Ricky wondered.

"You mean to say you do not know?" Inspector Lamouche asked, his voice laced, ever so finely, with suspicion.

"That is exactly what I mean to say. Why don't you ask Madame Lavache?"

"We cannot find her. She and her husband, zey go to Bretagne for ze holiday. We have a phone number for her zere. We call many times but zere is no answer."

"You know, I could tell this morning that someone had tried to break into the trunk in my apartment." Ricky did not tell Lamouche he had figured it was the police who had battered the padlock.

"*Ah, bon?*" Lamouche rasped, curling his lips in that cryptic little smile of his. "And what is in zis trunk?"

"Nothing much. Papers, old clothes and photos. Souvenirs."

"Hmmm. Well, of course, zis complicates your relation to ze case."

"Why?"

"Because now zere is a direct connection between you and ze victim."

"Are you trying to tell me I'm a murder suspect?"

"No no no no. *Pas du tout*. Let us say zat you are a *potential* murder suspect."

"Oh, that makes me feel much better."

"Do not fear. I tell you what. Come to ze police station at ze *mairie* Monday morning. I would like you to talk to some of my colleagues. And you can bring a lawyer if you like."

"Can we make it Tuesday morning? My lawyer won't be back in Paris until Monday night."

Inspector Lamouche threw back his head and scowled. "Already you have retained a lawyer?"

Ricky felt as if he had just flipped the GUILTY switch in the cop's brain. "Well, um, yeah, just as a precaution. You know?"

Lamouche glanced at his watch. "Now you must go," he said, his tone turning frosty. "Or you really will be late for work."

As soon as Ricky saw the cowboy hat, he knew he would not be American tonight. It was almost six o'clock and he had just arrived for his eight-hour gig at Le Bon Montmartrois. Dominique was at the crêperie's soarred old piano when Ricky walked in. As usual, he was reading a newspaper—at this hour of this day, it was *Le Monde*—while he played, the journal propped in front of him where sheet music might have been placed for another musician, his omnipresent glass of wine, almost empty, resting just to the right of the keyboard. Dominique, gray-haired and grizzled, flashed a tobacco-stained grin when he saw Ricky walk in the door. He tilted his head, seeming to finish reading the article in front of him, picked up his glass and knocked back the dregs of his wine, then ended the song he was playing, Cole Porter's "I Get a Kick Out of You," with a tingling flourish.

"Merci, mesdames et messieurs," Dominique exclaimed. Rising from the stool as the customers applauded, Dominique flung out his bony, hairy right arm. He bowed and awkwardly genuflected to the audience. Then, picking up his single steel crutch and a cloth-lined straw basket, Dominique hobbled away from the piano. Ricky walked up to his colleague and patted him on the back. Before Dominique plunged into the crowd, he leered at Ricky and said, *"Tes compatriotes."*

That was when Ricky spotted the tall, white Stetson, something he had never seen in the crêperie before. Beneath the John Wayne headgear, a fat, ruddy, beady-eyed face was perspiring. "And Ronald Reagan said, 'Mr. Gorbachev, tear down this here Berlin Wall,' " the cowboy tourist pronounced. "And guess what? Gorby did it!"

The restaurant was about half-filled with people eating and talking but once Dominique had stopped playing piano, the voice of the man in the Stetson drowned out all other sounds in Le Bon Montmartrois. Sitting beside the cowboy tourist was a woman Ricky presumed to be his wife, a prim, schoolmarmish figure with thick, plastic-framed glasses, a sticky-looking hairdo and an eerie, frozen smile. Her husband was addressing a couple at the table next to theirs. Dark-blond-haired with aquiline features, the thirtyish couple listened politely to the cowboy and said, "Oh yes?" in an accent Ricky could not quite define. He guessed that they, too, were tourists but they might have been from anywhere in the middle of Europe: Belgium, Germany, Switzerland—it was hard to tell.

"We're from Texas," the man in the Stetson boomed. "Well, my wife, she wasn't born there. But I'm a real Texan. And us Texans, we loooooove Ronald Reagan. Don't get me wrong. We were proud of George Bush, too. It just wasn't the same thing. But now George Sr.'s son, George Dubya, is our governor. And folks like me are gonna see to it that Dubya's our next president!"

"Oh yes?" the European couple said politely.

"We think Dubya could out-Reagan Reagan!" the Texan gushed, his big grin causing his little eyes to squinch tightly.

"S'il vous plaît," Dominique said, standing above the two tables, leaning on his single steel crutch, thrusting the basket at the couples. *"Pour la musique."*

The Texan looked up, stared at Dominique with beady-eyed suspicion. "Come again?"

His wife nudged him and said, in a loud stage whisper, "He's the piano player. Give him a tip."

Seeing the European couple drop two five-franc coins into the basket, the Texan pulled out his wallet. He held up a twenty-franc note. "You speak English?"

"Non, monsieur," Dominique replied.

"Hmmph," the Texan grunted. "You play good," he shouted, as if raising his voice would cause Dominique to understand the language. "Piano!" He dropped the bill into the basket, then mimicked playing the instrument, his thick, sausage-like fingers tapping at the air. "You play very good pi-AN-*oh!*"

Dominique scowled, then turned away, pivoting gracefully on his crutch, and hobbled toward the tables near the back of the restaurant. Ricky, sitting down in front of the keyboard, had to bite the insides of his cheeks to keep from laughing. He glanced at François, squeezed between his double counter, pouring crêpe mix onto the steaming griddles. François smiled and winked at him. Ricky started playing a rollicking Charles Mingus number, "Better Git It In Your Soul." The hard bop seemed to startle the Texan and his wife. Meanwhile, Dominique limped among the tables, holding out the basket and murmuring, *"Merci."*

Ricky always enjoyed watching Dominique work the crowd. There was nothing actually wrong with Dominique's leg. He never arrived at work with the crutch and always left the crêperie, through the side entrance, without it. Ricky had occasionally run into Dominique on the streets of Montmartre. The sly old piano player usually had a young woman on his arm and a lively bounce in his step. The steel crutch was simply a prop that Dominique kept in the pantry of the restaurant's kitchen. Ricky could only guess whether it induced the sort of sympathy that led to bigger tips. Dominique swore by the crutch. But, as a frail-looking sixty-year-old, he could get away with it. Ricky, meanwhile, never even ventured into the crowd to collect his tips. He thought it better to have one of the pretty waitresses pass around the basket, *pour la musique*, while he went to the *toilettes* or disappeared into the kitchen during his breaks. And, unlike Dominique, Ricky would have found it impossible to drink excessively and read several newspapers while playing the piano. But Ricky and Dominique maintained a friendly collegiality. While they never fraternized outside the crêperie, they had an excellent professional relationship. Six days a week, Tuesday through Sunday, one of them worked the noon to six shift and the other worked the six in the evening to two in the morning shift. They were always amenable to trading shifts and taking on each other's hours on short notice. Dominique, for instance, owed Ricky a day shift, so he would put in the full fourteen hours the coming Sunday. François, though he had employed Dominique for two decades, actually preferred Ricky as the house pianist since the American at least seemed to be making an effort to entertain the clientèle rather than getting drunk and reading four daily newspapers—the right-wing *Le Figaro*, the left-wing *Libération*, the moderate *Le Monde* and the staunchly nationalistic sports journal *L'Equipe*—while playing tunes, à la Dominique.

The cagey veteran limped over to the piano while Ricky continued to do his Mingus thing. Dominique pocketed the tips, set the empty basket atop the piano, saluted Ricky, then hobbled into the kitchen. As Ricky finished the tune, he saw the cowboy tourist and his wife standing beside the piano. The man in the Stetson stared suspiciously at him. "American?" he asked.

"Non," Ricky said. *"Martiniquais."*

The Texan squinted at Ricky, his porcine face sweating. "Come again?"

"He's from Martinique," the wife explained. "It's a French island. He doesn't speak English."

"Oh," the Texan said. "Well, you play real good," he pronounced loudly. "We got a lotta people of your color in the U.S.A. And they play music real good, too. Only they cause a whole lotta problems."

Ricky glared at the Texan, unsmiling. It was rare that Ricky pretended not to be American. Ordinarily, he was happy to talk with his compatriots who walked into the crêperie, whatever their race, ethnicity or state of residence. But every once in a while, an American like this Texan wandered into the place and Ricky was reminded of so much of what he disliked about his homeland.

"We oughta get going," the prim wife said, her frozen smile gleaming.

"Awright, awright," the man in the Stetson grumbled. "Anyway, come to America sometime. You seem like a real nice fella. We could use more blacks like you in the States."

Ricky continued to glare at the Texan.

"He doesn't understand you," the wife said nervously.

"*Allez,*" Ricky said with a smile, "*et nic ta mère, pauvre con.*"

The cowboy tilted his head and stared uncertainly at Ricky while his wife's face turned almost as crimson as his. "Come again?" he drawled.

The wife, discombobulated, struggled to say, "He said that you're a very nice man and you must have had a very good upbringing."

The Texan grinned. "Mercy boo koo," he said. As the couple left the crêperie, Ricky could only wonder if the wife had understood that he had just told her husband "Go—and fuck your mother, you pathetic asshole."

Deciding to stay in Mingus mode, Ricky played "Fables of Faubus." Slowly, he began to lose himself in the music. It was just what he needed: to concentrate on his craft; to forget, for a few hours, anyway, all the strangeness that had suddenly taken over his life.

Midnight at Le Bon Montmartrois. The crêperie was packed and Ricky was having fun playing songs of ocular romance: "Angel Eyes," "I Only

Have Eyes for You," "Smoke Gets in Your Eyes" . . . He wasn't sure
when he noticed the woman sitting alone in the most distant corner of
the cozy restaurant but, after a while, he was certain that she was checking him out. She wore a khaki, logo-less baseball cap and black-lensed
sunglasses. Given the low lighting of the crêperie, Ricky wondered how
the young woman could see him at all—but she was definitely looking
his way. What with the cap and glasses, she could have been a movie
star incognito. Ricky tried not to stare back at her, through the crowd
of customers and the thick clouds of cigarette smoke. When he did steal
a glance, he thought he saw a wavy ponytail sticking out from the back
of the cap. Though the woman had a tan complexion, Ricky could not
discern her ethnicity or nationality. She could have been French or
American, Asian or North African, black or white or Latina or biracial.
It was impossible to tell. Still, Ricky couldn't help but feel flattered by
the way she seemed to be scrutinizing him from behind those pitch-
black shades. A year earlier, before he had met Fatima Boukhari, Ricky
would have been planning to approach the mysterious stranger during
his next break, to chat her up in either French or English and hope
she'd hang around until closing time when they might go to her place
or his for a few hours of exuberant fucking.

But not on this night, not when he had an appointment with Fatima
to go to the maternity hospital the next morning. During his last break
of the night, Ricky ducked into the kitchen for a glass of wine while
one of the waitresses went from table to table with the straw basket,
soliciting his tips. He took a quick piss, then returned to the piano. The
crowd was thinning out, as it always did between 12:30 and 12:45, when
folks wanted to catch the last metro before underground rail service shut
down at one in the morning. But the chick in the cap and the shades
stayed. Only now she wasn't paying any attention to Ricky. She seemed
to be staring into space, smoking a cigarette, sipping a glass of white
wine. Suddenly, something about her reminded him of someone he
knew; or had known; but he couldn't think of who it was.

Ricky played until just before two o'clock, knocking back a few more
glasses of wine, Dominique-style, as the night wound down. During most
of that last set, he had kept his head slightly bowed, his eyes half-closed.
He was in a melancholy zone, fingering lush, soaring renditions of "Cry

Me a River," "Summertime," "My One and Only Love," and "Stormy
Weather." He only really looked up when one of the waitresses brought
him his last basketful of tips. The other waitress was stacking chairs on
top of empty tables. François had disappeared from between his double
counter. Just about all of the customers had departed. But the strange
woman in the cap and shades was still there. That was when Ricky
knew, when he was absolutely certain who she was.

He rose from the piano stool, walked slowly over to the table. The
woman tilted her head in his direction but didn't appear to look directly
at him. Her eyes concealed behind those impenetrable lenses, she seemed
for a moment like a blind person, reacting tentatively to the sudden
presence of another. Ricky stood beside her table, his heart pounding
hard. "Excuse me," he said, "but do we know each other?"

Serena Moriarty Washington pulled off her sunglasses and stared up
at Ricky. Her left eye and upper cheekbone were encircled by a bluish-
brown bruise. "Save me," she said.

Eight

"MRS. WASHINGTON, Y'ALL!" the groom shouted exultantly. "Check out
Mrs. Washington, y'all! *Miss*-US *Wash*-ing-TONE!" Cash danced a
crazed jig around his bride, who smiled and curtsied in her frilly white
wedding gown. They acted out their pantomime on the uppermost deck
of the large white yacht, like figurines come to life atop a wedding cake.
As the vessel steamed majestically toward the shore, Cash's voice grew
louder, drowning out the hubbub of the two hundred guests gathered
on the dock. "Mrs. Washington, y'all!" he crowed as he kicked at the
air, twirling around his new wife. As the yacht drew closer to the harbor,
the faces of the bride and groom became sharper, more clearly defined
on the videocassette. Cash looked sweaty and delirious, beside himself
with emotion—not so much joyous as victorious, like a miler who had
just crossed the finish line in a hard-won race. The bride, meanwhile,
was cool, the smile on her face somewhat sardonic, as she raised the

hem of her gown and curtsied, again and again, to the waiting crowd. "Mrs. Washington, y'aaaaaaaaaall!" Cash hollered maniacally.

"Why does he keep saying that?" Ricky asked his mother.

"Serena didn't want to take his name," Matilda Jenks explained. "She had wanted to keep her maiden name: Moriarty. Apparently she was pretty adamant about it. But so was Cash. He insisted that any wife of his should carry his name. And you know your cousin. In the end, he got his way."

Ricky's mother said this in a perfectly neutral voice, sipping her sherry. It was the day after Christmas, 1997, and Ricky had come home to Benson, New Jersey for the holidays. Cash's wedding had taken place six months earlier and though Ricky had received an elegant engraved invitation, he had come up with some excuse not to return to the States for the big event. His absence amounted to a boycott. Ricky knew it and so did everybody else. Given what had happened on Ricky's aborted wedding day, people understood. But at Christmastime, Matilda insisted that Ricky watch the videotape of his cousin's wedding. After all, Ricky and Cash had made peace. At least, they had given the appearance of making peace, three years earlier, at Ricky's parents' thirty-fifth anniversary party. Ricky had absolutely no desire to watch the highlights of Cash's nuptials. But he knew it would make his mother happy. And he wanted to pretend that he had no hard feelings toward his cousin. So while Ricky's father and sister went out for a walk in the Jersey woods, Matilda brought out the sherry and the little heirloom glasses and loaded the VCR.

"Serena wanted a wedding at sea," Matilda said as the tape started to roll. "Don't ask me why. It had some personal meaning for her. So Reverend Emerson performed the ceremony on this yacht they had rented. Only the immediate wedding party was on board. The rest of us waited on the dock for the reception."

"Interesting," Ricky said, in a completely uninterested tone of voice.

He wanted to be a good sport. He knew how close his mother was to her older sister. He didn't want Matilda to think that he hated her favorite nephew—even if he did. And, though he might *always* hate Cash, Ricky felt he had pretty much recovered from his wedding day debacle. He had, at this point, been living in Paris for more than seven years. On those occasions when Ricky visited the States he thought it should be obvious to everyone how happy he was with his new life. But Ricky could see that, despite his obvious happiness, his family still pitied him. He wondered if, to them, he would be forever frozen in time as the jilted groom, the hapless chump who fled the country in despair.

On the television screen, Cash and Serena's wedding reception was in full swing, guests milling about on the lawn of the quaint Sag Harbor inn, under the billowy white tent, drinks in hand. Ricky could feel his mother casting anxious glances his way as he watched the videotape, as if she were afraid that viewing the reception might be too painful for him. But Ricky was actually enjoying himself. He pointed to relatives he spotted, asked Matilda how certain uncles, aunts and cousins were doing, chuckled at all the little speeches and toasts. Eventually, he realized that all the speakers and toastmasters were friends and family members of the groom.

"It is a bit strange, isn't it?" Matilda said. "Serena didn't seem to have any *people* there." Ricky knew when his mother said *people* she meant *family*. "She had some friends from New York, actors, singers and such. Did I tell you she's a singer? Or a wannabe singer, anyway. I think mainly she's a temp. Or *was* a temp—until Cash started supporting her. Last I heard she was working on her demo tape, or demo CD, or whatever. But anyway I asked your Aunt Lenora, 'Doesn't Serena have any *people*?' "

On the videotape, Cash clutched his bride's hand as, together, they lowered the large carving knife into the bottom layer of the mountainous white cake. They each licked the frosting from the shiny blade. Then they puckered their lips and kissed. Cash, with his eyes closed, had an ardent, rapturous look on his face. But Serena, during the stagey kiss, kept her lids wide open, tilting her head slightly. Ricky saw her big, fawnlike left eyeball roll searchingly in the direction of the camcorder.

"And Lenora told me," Ricky's mother continued, "that Serena never had any people, except for her mother and father. And they're both dead. Died in a plane crash, years ago. Serena was an army brat. Or maybe an air force brat. Lived all over the world, never knew her people in America. Isn't that sad?"

Now the bride and groom were dancing across the parquet floor of the platform that had been set up under the tent. They were a beautiful couple, no doubt about it: a Hollywood vision of black American perfection, Cash with his chiseled features and café au lait complexion, Serena with those gorgeous Bambi eyes and skin so light that, in another era, she might very well have "passed" for white. They danced to Whitney Houston's rendition of "The Greatest Love of All." For the most part, Cash and Serena gazed into each other's eyes. But every once in a while, the bride would turn her head and beam into the lens of the camera. "To looooove yourself," Whitney Houston wailed triumphantly, "is the greatest love of all. . . ."

"Imagine not having any family?" Matilda asked. It sounded, to Ricky, like a leading question. "Wouldn't that be terrible?"

Ricky turned to his mother. "Well, now Serena has *our* family." Matilda beamed. Ricky could see that his response was exactly what his mother had wanted to hear. He returned his attention to the videotape.

The reception seemed to be winding down. Darkness had fallen over Sag Harbor. Orange candles flickered beneath the vast white tent.

"I'm just soooooooo happy!" Serena enthused, her starlet's face framed by the wedding veil. "This is the happiest day of my entire life!" Though the bride seemed sincere, Ricky couldn't help feeling that there was something a bit practiced, a bit self-conscious, about the way she spoke. Her voice was throaty and theatrical. Serena, speaking intimately into the camera, reminded Ricky of a child playacting in front of a mirror. Watching Serena, the bride sitting alone at a round table, crumbs strewn across the white cloth, guests departing in the background, orange candlelight flickering in the nighttime sea breeze, Ricky felt disturbingly conflicted toward this woman he had never met. Serena, who seemed both utterly fake and totally genuine at the same time, inspired in Ricky a strange attraction-repulsion. As Serena blinked back tears of joy, looking not unlike one of those blandly beautiful women who had just been crowned Miss America, Ricky—who had never considered himself a man of overpowering passions—sensed a lustful violence stirring within him. Sitting beside his mother, Ricky felt a sudden surge of shame. He felt as if he was raping Serena with his eyes.

"I had wanted to use one of Mariah's songs for our dance," Serena confided to the camera. " 'Love Takes Time' from Mariah's self-titled debut album. But my husband—" Serena suddenly raised her hands, covering her mouth, her eyes popping wide in surprise. She lowered her hands, slowly, dramatically; flashed a mischievous, mock-lascivious grin. "That's the first time I ever said that: My *husband!*" Serena let out a delighted little squeal: "Ooooooooo!... Anyway, my husband didn't like the song and we both loved Whitney's 'Greatest Love of All.' We loved the message. What the song said. You know?"

What a bimbo, Ricky thought. He glanced at his mother. Matilda sipped her sherry, watching the video impassively.

"I love Mariah Carey," Serena said. "I mean, I don't just love her. I want to *be* her." Serena's voice was trembling with emotion now. "That's my dream. That maybe someday I could..." Serena paused, tried to compose herself. "Well, maybe not *be* her," she continued, Bambi eyes shining glassily. "But be *like* her. You know what I mean?" She dabbed her eyes with the gauzy veil. "Anyway, I just feel so blessed to have met Cassius. So blessed with this day. So very blessed."

"She's a special girl," Ricky's mother said. "Don't you think?"

"Oh, yes," Ricky said, trying not to sound sarcastic. "Very special."

Sixteen months after first seeing her on videotape, Ricky sat across from Serena at a small table in a Paris crêperie.

"Let's pretend we don't know anything about each other," Serena said. "That you don't know anything about me and I don't know anything about you."

"All right," Ricky said. "Tell me about yourself."

It was past closing time. Ricky and Serena were the only people in Le Bon Montmartrois, sitting at the only table that did not have chairs stacked on top of it. Ricky's boss, François, left him a set of keys to the crêperie, said he could lock up when he and his friend were ready to leave. A carafe of white wine and two glasses, a fresh ashtray, pack of cigarettes and lighter were arranged on the table. A single, orange-tinted lightbulb illuminated the space. Serena had put her baseball cap and sunglasses in the leather shoulder bag that hung on the back of her chair. She had also managed to squeeze a compact suitcase, one of those ubiquitous Samsonites with little wheels and an adjustable handle, under the table. Serena's wavy, light brown hair was pulled back in a ponytail. Even at two fifteen in the morning, wearing no discernible makeup and with a hideous bruise on her face, Serena Moriarty Washington was stunningly beautiful. Staring at his cousin's wife, Ricky had that odd, slightly incredulous sensation that the average person feels when meeting some very famous celebrity—someone you have known only from television or magazine photos—in the flesh, for the first time: *Is that really her?* Yes, here the star is, in three dimensions, like some figment of your imagination suddenly sprung to life, at once familiar and bizarre.

"Well, I'm a Gemini," Serena said in her theatrically throaty voice, "with a Cancer rising and a Aries moon, so I'm a bit of a split personality, you know, fire and water. I was born on June eleventh but ..." Serena smiled coyly. "I won't tell you what year. Do you believe in astrology?"

"Sometimes I do," Ricky said, "sometimes I don't."

"See? There's that duality! You're a typical Gemini, too." Serena suddenly raised a hand to her lips. "Ooooh! Sorry, I'm supposed to act like I don't know that!"

Ricky chuckled. "You made the rule, you can break it if you like."

Serena beamed. "You're so sweet. I knew you would be."

Ah, yes, this Serena was a charmer, all right, a razzle-dazzler, like her husband. Ricky could feel himself being seduced and, at the same time, resisting the seduction. Seeing Serena up close, he sensed that same contradiction he'd noticed on her wedding-day videotape, that show-bizzy combination of sincerity and artificiality. Serena, even in what had to be a desperate moment of her life—battered, in flight from her abusive spouse—was definitely "on," conscious of Ricky as her audience. She was giving him an act—yet the act seemed to be who she genuinely was. She had that smoky purr of a voice but there was also something bland and characterless about it. She spoke in what Ricky thought of as an American television accent, the sort of voice one heard in TV "personalities" all over the U.S., a finely modulated tone that gave no hint of race or region. Even sitting inches away from Serena, Ricky found her exact ethnicity unguessable. She was a multicultural mystery. He noticed that her eyes were not so much brown as ginger-colored. And though Ricky tried to look Serena directly in the eye, his gaze kept drifting to the bluish-brown bruise. How could his cousin Cash have committed such violence? How could any man?

"Do you mind?" Serena asked, reaching for the pack of Gitanes.

"How could I?" Ricky replied. "This is France."

Serena smiled, fired up her cigarette, took a ravenous puff. "It's a terrible vice, I know. In America, I do it in secret. Cassius hates it. I don't indulge very often but somehow my husband always knows. He has a sense of smell like a bloodhound's. When I'm in Europe, smoking just seems like the natural thing to do. And here you have that fierce unfiltered stuff that I just love." She drew on the cigarette elegantly, like a forties film star; exhaled with brio.

"So where are you from?" Ricky asked. "Originally?"

Serena's ginger eyes twinkled. "Would you believe I'm German?"

"Why not?"

"Well, I'm not, not really. I mean, I don't have German citizenship. I was born on an air force base near Hamburg. My papa was a flyboy—a major. One of the top African-Americans in the force."

"My ex was an army brat."

"Clementine?" Serena said eagerly. When Ricky frowned, she quickly caught her mistake, smacked a palm against her forehead. "Sorry—I'm not supposed to know that."

"Never mind."

"Let's have some more wine," Serena said, raising the carafe and refilling their glasses. "Anyway, where was I?"

"Hamburg."

"Right. So we moved around a lot. South America, the Philippines, Italy, more places, more bases, than I can remember. It made me a bit of a chameleon, you know? Always a foreigner, always the new kid, always trying to fit in." Now Serena sounded even more stilted to Ricky, almost packaged, as if she were giving a quickie interview on a press junket. "I guess that was why I was drawn first to acting, then to singing. That desire to make an impression, to get people to like me. Maybe even to be someone else for a while. You know what I mean?"

"So where are your folks now?" Ricky asked, playing along with Serena's game, pretending not to know.

"Somewhere at the bottom of the Pacific Ocean," Serena said, her voice tightening. She took a long drag on the cigarette, then paused, closing her eyes for a moment, as if trying to collect her emotions. "They had retired to Hawaii. But Papa still liked to take Mama flying. And one day, back in 'eighty-four, they went out for a spin in the Cessna, in dodgy weather. And crashed in the water. They ... I ..."

Serena's voice trailed off. She gasped, then bowed her head. At first, the gesture seemed a bit melodramatic; but Ricky soon realized that Serena was truly hurt by the memory. And he was ashamed of himself for having made her talk about her parents' death. "I'm sorry," he said, the words both an expression of sympathy and a guilty apology.

Serena raised her head again, seemed to force a weak smile. "It's okay," she said. "I think it must have been their time. At least they were together. My mama and papa, they were so much in love, you know. It's reassuring to me to know that they went down together, into that watery grave." Serena took a big gulp of wine, refilled her glass. "I was here at the time, in Paris. I went back to Honolulu for the memorial service. But there was no funeral, no burial. They never recovered the bodies. And so, I guess, in a way, I've never had any real ..." Serena paused again, then pronounced the word with pregnant importance: "... closure."

After a respectful silence, Ricky asked, "What were you doing in Paris?"

"I was a student," Serena said, perking up. "At the Corbeau School. Do you know it? It's one of the best theater schools in all of Europe."

"Oh, yes," Ricky said, though the name sounded only vaguely familiar.

"Anyway, I was never much of an actress. Corbeau had a two-year program and I didn't make the cut for the second year. That was when I finally realized that my true love was singing. There's no purer form of self-expression than music. You must be able to relate, as a musician yourself."

"I thought you weren't supposed to know that."

Serena laughed, stubbed out her cigarette in the ashtray. "Oh, you," she trilled, as if they had been old friends since back in the day. "Ricky, Ricky, Ricky ..."

"Yes?"

"Do you know what it is to really burn for something? To want so badly, so painfully, to do something, to make a mark, to be somebody? A real somebody?"

"No."

Serena ignored his response. "Ever since I was a little girl, I had the feeling that I was put on this earth to do something . . . something special. Every one of us, every one of God's creations has a destiny. I believe that. But there are certain people among us who have . . . I don't really know how to say it. . . . A special destiny. We're made for something different, something extraordinary."

Ricky could imagine how his cousin Cash would have been captivated by this woman. At first, anyway. Beguiled not just by her beauty but by her outlandish self-esteem, a grandiosity commensurate with his own. Cash would have been spellbound by Serena, consumed by the thrill of finally meeting his match, his twin tower of narcissism. But the appeal could not possibly last. Sooner or later, Cash would have felt threatened by a woman who was his equal. But did he have to hit her in the face?

"And what is your destiny?" Ricky asked.

Serena sighed, reached for another cigarette. "I feel I was meant to give something to people. A gift. Maybe the gift of entertainment. To lift people's hearts with my music. Don't you feel that way, Ricky?"

"No. Playing piano is the only thing I know how to do, so I do it."

Serena took another Lauren Bacall–like drag on her cigarette, stared piercingly at Ricky. "I think you know better than that. I heard you play tonight. I heard the depth of feeling in your playing. You pour your heart out on that piano. You know you do. Why don't you admit it?"

"So what do you sing?" Ricky asked, wanting to shift Serena's attention back to herself.

"Everything!" she enthused. "Jazz, rhythm and blues, pop, rock, gospel, even classical! I've dabbled in all forms. I just love music, you know? And growing up all over the world, I had this idea that embracing all forms was a good thing. Then I went to live in America . . ."

Serena shook her head and paused meaningfully, but Ricky didn't catch her drift. "And . . . ?" he asked.

"And you know how it is over there! The obsession with categories, genres, classifications! Everybody always wanting to know what you are, always telling you who you're supposed to be. I know you know what I mean. If you're black in America you're only supposed to sing certain things in a certain way and if you don't conform to some narrow image of blackness then you aren't really black. It's just all so stupid, so shallow and limiting!" Serena was lip up now, practically sputtering in her fury. This was when Ricky felt he was seeing the true woman, the purest distillation of Serena. "There's no breadth of vision there! Look, my father was half black and half white. My mother was half black and half white. That makes me half black and half white. And I am totally comfortable with that. All over the world, people I've met are comfortable with that. Only in America did I ever get shit for what I am!"

"Or what you're not."

Serena shot Ricky a dubious look. She took a sip of wine, then said, "Exactly."

They were silent for a while. "What about Cash?" Ricky finally said. "How does he deal with who you are?"

Serena stared into her glass of wine. "Cassius," she said softly. "I do believe Cassius loved me for who I am. Or who he thought I was." Now, when Serena took a puff of her cigarette, her hand trembled slightly. "I've thought about this a lot. And sometimes I think Cassius didn't really fall in love with me but with some idea of me. Some idea of how I was supposed to fit into his life. And when the idea didn't match the reality . . . he freaked."

"What was it that Cash . . ." Ricky paused, then corrected himself: ". . . that Cassius couldn't handle?"

Serena, still gazing into her half-full glass, said, "I fell so hard for your cousin. You know? For a time, back in the early days, he was so good to me. He treasured me. Then something began to change. After we got married. I became . . . objectified. I know that's a big, high-falutin' word, but I don't know how else to say it, how to describe the way Cassius's attitude toward me changed. I wanted to be treasured . . . I *loved* being treasured . . . but I'm nobody's trophy bride! And that's how he began to treat me. Like I was just some shiny prize on his mantel."

"Was he supportive of your music?"

"Up to a point. As long as it seemed like a hobby, a harmless little pastime, he was supportive. But after we got married and I quit my office job and started writing more of my own songs and recording tracks for a demo disk—then Cassius stopped being so supportive. He just wanted me to sit at home and start breeding! Like my only purpose in life was to produce the offspring of the great Cassius Washington!" Serena was fuming again, revealing that rage that seemed to come from someplace deep inside her. "I mean, really, do I look like a fucking housewife to you?"

"Not particularly."

"Okay, so I know Cassius gave me money to work with engineers, to buy studio time and whatnot but that didn't give him the right to shit on my feelings, to dis my songs and tell me I would never make it, to stomp all over my dreams!"

"Why was he so negative?"

"Insecurity!"

Ricky was startled. "Cash? Insecure?"

"Yes! Don't tell me you never saw through his I'm-so-great-and-confident act! Your cousin's ego is as fragile as an eggshell. Don't you realize how jealous Cassius is of you?"

Ricky let out a hoot of disbelief. "Why the hell would Cash be jealous of *me?*"

Serena took another long drag on her cigarette, fixing Ricky with her piercing, ginger-eyed stare. She exhaled slowly, then said, "Because you're free."

Serena continued to stare evenly at Ricky, as if she wanted the notion to sink in. Ricky, meanwhile, could not take his eyes off the bruise. "Does it hurt?" he asked quietly, knowing that Serena would know exactly what he meant.

As Serena took a slow sip of wine, Ricky could see that her hand was trembling again. "It still throbs a little."

"Why did he do it?"

"It was my fault."

"Do not say that." Ricky was surprised by the anger he heard in his own voice. "There is never any excuse for violence."

Serena bowed her head again. "But Cassius had reason to be upset with me. I kept a secret from him. For a long time. I had never told him before because I was afraid that if he knew, he might not want to marry me. So I kept it from him. Until last week."

Ricky waited a moment, then, as gently as he could, asked, "What was it?"

When Serena looked up again, tears glistened in her eyes. She seemed to struggle to get the words out: "I can't have children."

Now Ricky felt as if he was the one who had just been punched in the face. Almost dazed with shock, all he could manage to say was, "Huh?"

"I knew it was wrong. I knew I should have told him. But I kept hoping against hope that some miracle might occur. That all the doctors would be wrong and I would be able to bear children. I knew how much it meant to Cassius. How much he wanted to have kids. And I loved him so much. I was so afraid of losing him. But, finally, after two years of trying to conceive, I thought I had to tell him the truth."

Ricky was still trying to make sense of what Serena had told him. When Cash, back in the Barbès café, had spoken of his wife's poisonous secret, Ricky had assumed it had something to do with infidelity. Cash's violence in reaction to his wife's unfaithfulness would have been awful enough. But now that Ricky knew what the secret really was, knew that Cash had beaten his wife because, through a cruel fluke of nature, she happened to be infertile . . . this was domestic horror of a different order. Ricky reached across the table—unable to stop himself even as he wondered if it was an inappropriate thing to do—and laid his hand against Serena's soft cheek, the tips of his fingers touching the tender, swollen flesh at the outer edge of the bruise. "Oh, Serena," he said, his voice choking.

Serena smiled faintly, seemingly soothed by Ricky's touch. Some sensation, a low-wave erotic charge, passed between them, and Ricky carefully withdrew his hand. After a while, Serena said, "Anyway . . . I guess I have only myself to blame."

"Please don't say that," Ricky protested. "Cash should have reacted to your news with sympathy, not brutality."

"Maybe you're right. I suppose, when you get right down to it, Cassius is a very destructive person. He's a double Scorpio, you know."

Ricky nodded and said, "Okay," as if he understood what that meant.

"He's also got a serious . . ." Serena let her voice trail off, didn't seem to want to go on. Ricky leaned forward, letting her know, through the tilt of his body, the trusting look in his eyes, that he wanted her to continue. "Cash," Serena said, "has a serious coke problem."

"Really?" Ricky tried to sound surprised, though, somehow, he wasn't.

"He was doin' a half a gram a day," Serena said. "That's part of the reason why he had these—what do you call them?—delusions of grandeur. That's what fueled his mania, his violence."

"So what happened after he assaulted you?"

"He stormed out of the house, drove off somewhere. And I thought, for my own safety, I better leave. I packed my bags, got a taxi to the airport and caught the first flight I could get for Paris."

"Why Paris?"

Serena shrugged. "It's the place in the world where I've always felt safest."

"So what now? Are you going to file for divorce or try to reconcile with Cash?"

"Oh, God, Ricky, I don't know. My head is spinning right now. All I want is to have some peace until Monday. After Monday, I'll be able to think more clearly."

"I'm sorry," Ricky said, furrowing his brow in confusion, "but maybe I missed something here. What happens Monday?"

Serena grinned and Ricky felt relieved to see the obvious joy in her face. "This dark old cloud does have a silver line around it. A long, long time ago, after getting a ton of rejections in the States, I sent my demo disk to a producer in Paris, DJ Fabrice. Do you know him?"

"No," Ricky said, adding, apologetically, "but I don't know any-body."

"Well," Serena continued, "about a month ago, I got an e-mail from Fabrice. He said he'd love to produce dance versions of a couple of my songs. He said we could do it next time he came to New York or we could hook up in Paris. Anyway, I called him when I got to town and he's really excited to work with me. We're supposed to meet at his studio on Monday, at three o'clock. I'll record a few new vocal riffs and he'll remix the tracks on his computer. He says we could release a dance single here in France and he's sure it would go over big time! Do you realize what this means, Ricky?"

"No."

"If the song catches on here, it'll soon get played in clubs in London as well. Then it's just a matter of time before it crosses back over to the States. This is the big break I've been waiting for! DJ Fabrice is totally hot. And French producers are the cutting edge right now. You know Madonna's last album was produced by a Frenchman."

"No, I didn't know that."

Serena made a sour, disappointed face. "Never mind," she said, excusing Ricky's ignorance. "The point is I need to focus all my energy on this recording session Monday. I'll worry about the situation with Cassius after that."

Ricky was amazed by how Serena's mood had instantly changed, how the possibility of fulfilling her ambition seemed to blot out her marital meltdown. "Well," he said, groping for the right words, "good luck."

Now Serena seemed to smirk at Ricky as she gave him a long, appraising look. "Aren't you wondering why I'm here tonight? Why I sought you out?"

"I was a bit curious, yes."

"Someone came looking for me today. I was staying at a hotel near the Place de l'Alma. Some guy in a chauffeur's cap asked for me at the front desk. Fortunately, I'd registered under a fake name. But this chauffeur guy kept pressing the hotel manager, describing what I looked like, saying he urgently needed to find me. The manager began to get suspicious, told the chauffeur to get lost. Apparently, the chauffeur had a Russian accent. I was out shopping at the time but the manager told me all this when I got back to the hotel. Anyway, I'm sure this must have been someone Cassius sent after me. So I checked out and came up here to look for you. I didn't have your address but your mother once told me you played piano in a crêperie near the Place du Tertre. I'm sorry to just show up like this, Ricky. I really hadn't planned on getting you involved in this whole crisis. But all my old friends in Paris are either no longer my friends or have disappeared. You were the only person I could turn to. I don't want to be an imposition but do you think I could stay in your apartment? Just until after my session with DJ Fabrice on Monday night. After that, well, I don't know what I'll do. Maybe return to the States to face the music. Get a good divorce lawyer. I don't know what. I just need a place where I can crash for three or four nights, someplace where none of Cassius's goons would come looking for me." Serena smiled sweetly. "I know you don't know me, Ricky, but do you think you could find it in your heart to do me this favor?"

"I would love to—" Ricky had not finished his sentence before Serena started to rise from her chair, as if she were going to lunge across the table and throw her arms around him. Ricky quickly raised a hand and said, "But!"

Serena dropped back into her seat, looking crestfallen. "But what?"

"I don't think it's a good idea."

"Why not?"

"Because I just saw Cash. Yesterday. Here. In Paris."

Serena's mouth popped open but no sound emerged. At this moment, she looked strangely childlike to Ricky: small and helpless, and completely terrified.

"Don't worry," Ricky hurried to say. "Here, drink some more." He raised the carafe, poured what was left of the white wine into Serena's glass. She continued to stare at him in openmouthed terror. "Calm down," Ricky said. "Please. Drink."

Serena seemed to break out of her trance, took a thirsty swig of wine.

"Let me explain," Ricky continued, speaking gently, patiently. "Cash just called me out of the blue."

"I didn't even know you two were on speaking terms," Serena rasped.

"We weren't. Until yesterday. I suppose you could say you were the one who brought us together. He was desperate to find you. He thought maybe I could somehow locate you."

Serena slowly shook her head. "Did he pay you?" she asked, a trace of acid in her tone.

Ricky had to think fast. He didn't want to lie to Serena; but he also wanted her to trust him. He took a deep breath, then said, "He offered to."

Serena downed the wine in her glass. "And?"

"And he wanted me to tell you, when I found you, how sorry he is for what he did. How much he loves you and, er, wants you back."

Serena puckered her lips, sucking the insides of her cheeks and nodding skeptically. For a long time, she said nothing. Finally, she asked, "Is he still here?"

"No. He said he was going to Zurich. That he'd be back in Paris Sunday night."

"Zurich, huh?"

"Yeah." After another lengthy silence, Ricky said, "Did Cash steal from a hospital?"

"A hospital?" Serena scoffed. "Are you talking about that so-called Center for Athletic Wellness?"

"Yeah."

"That's no fucking hospital! It's supposed to be a health spa for rich assholes. Cassius was trying to set up a whole network of them. Mainly in Eastern Europe."

"Really?"

"Really! And as for stealing, all I can tell you is your cousin is the biggest scam artist I've ever met and I've met an army of them, from all over the world!"

"Okay."

"Look," Serena said furiously, "Cassius might be a famous doctor but what he really wants to be is an entrepreneur. And the only way he can be an entrepreneur is by using his status as a doctor. What your cousin is into is money . . . and action. He loves the action. He's addicted to it. Just like he's addicted to cocaine. I've seen a million motherfuckers like him in my day, lemme tell you."

Ricky listened in fascination to Serena. He had already seen her anger but now he gleaned something else, yet another aspect to the ardent lover, the abused wife, the ambitious songstress, the international misfit: something street-smart and gutterwise, a knowledge so profoundly brutal that it had to be concealed. But it was always there, beneath the polished façade, burning at the core of this beautiful, battered woman: wary, incorrigible, unforgiving.

"Tell me more," he said.

"Why?" Serena asked suspiciously.

Ricky sighed. "Don't worry. I'm not gonna sell you out to Cash. I want to help you, Serena. I'll do whatever I can to help you." Pause. "Do you believe me?"

"I want to." Serena scrutinized Ricky's face for several seconds, as if trying to gauge his trustworthiness. Then she continued. "There's a lot I don't know. And whenever I would ask Cassius he would either be evasive or start launching into some sermon about global capitalism, about how globalization was going to make life better for everybody and black people had to be smart and jump on the bandwagon or we were going to be left behind. 'Black folks have to think globally. Just like the white folks!' He was always going on about this. Like I say, it's not good enough for Cassius to be a medical practitioner. He wants to be a medical tycoon."

"And these Centers for Athletic Wellness . . . that's his ticket?"

"So he says. But there's always been a nasty smell about this, if you ask me. He's part of this group, the International Consortium of Orthopedic Professionals—ICOP. I met a few of these jokers when they were passing through New York. They said they were orthopedic surgeons, from Russia, Poland, Romania. But they seemed like fucking mobsters to me. I've been around the block a few times, Ricky. We don't have time for me to tell you about some of the characters I met in my younger days but I gained a little more experience of the dark side of humanity living in places like Manila and Naples than your cousin got at MIT and Georgetown, okay? And as far as I could see, these self-styled doctors from Eastern Europe were nothing but stone-cold gangsters."

"But why would Cash get involved with people like that?"

"Yo, Rick, man," Serena said, her voice turning gruff and sandpapery, "are you listening to me or have you got fucking attention deficit disorder?" She paused and fired up another Gitane. When she spoke again it was in her usual bland purr. "Cassius thought these people were going to make him rich. I mean, really rich. You and I, we're artists. We don't understand this concept of megawealth. But to your cousin being a multimillionaire is small potatoes. He wants to make his first billion before he's forty. This is how Cassius—the healer—thinks."

"Okay," Ricky said, feeling somehow chastened.

"Look, this isn't stuff I should even be talking to you about. I'll have to tell it all to a lawyer when I get back to the States. But I think Cassius is involved in some pretty serious shit. I think he got greedy, I think he got in over his head. Ricky . . . it scares me to even mention this . . . but I found envelopes, parcels actually, of cash in our home. I mean, serious cash. Hidden away in closets and drawers. Fat batches of hundred- and five-hundred-dollar bills. When I would ask him about it he would speak to me in a way that he never had before, tell me to mind my own fucking business. I finally decided that if I wanted him to be honest with me I would have to be totally honest with him, too. That was what led to our crisis last week. I came clean, told him I couldn't have children. But when I wanted him to come clean, to tell me what was going on with these health spas and these shady characters, Cassius lost it. He didn't just beat me, Ricky. He threatened to kill me. Now you tell me he was in Paris." Serena shook her head and her eyes welled with tears again. "I think he must be at some kind of breaking point. I don't know, Ricky. I'm really scared."

Ricky was shaken by what Serena had told him. But his mind was clear. "Don't worry," he said. "I'll protect you."

"You know, I think Cassius feels a lot of guilt toward you," Serena said.

"Oh, yeah?" Ricky replied. "I thought my cousin was one of those fortunate conscience-free people."

They were walking across the Place du Tertre, which, at three thirty in the morning, had regained its abandoned movie-set aura. Ricky rolled Serena's suitcase behind him. The sound of its little wheels, grating along the cobbletsones, echoed throughout the deserted square.

"Most of the time, that's true," Serena said. She was wearing her khaki baseball cap again but had kept the sunglasses in the leather bag strapped over her shoulder. "But he does have these occasional pangs of remorse. I think he really does feel bad about what happened on your wedding day."

"Hmph."

"And after all these years, I think he still feels bad about pushing you into the swimming pool back when you were little kids."

"Uh-huh."

"You don't like talking about the past, do you?"

"You got that right."

"I guess that's one more thing we have in common."

They were silent as they descended the staircase on the rue du Calvaire, Ricky clutching the suitcase in one hand and holding onto the iron bannister with the other. Serena's outpouring of revelations at the crêperie had left him feeling exhausted. All he wanted now was to deliver Serena to her hideout, then go home and get in bed. At the bottom of the stairs, they followed a short zigzag path downhill, turning onto rue Gabrielle, walking a few feet before turning onto rue Drevet, then, just a few steps later, turning onto rue Berthe. Only then did Ricky remember the question he had wanted to ask Serena an hour earlier.

"Back when you lived in Paris, did you know Marva Dobbs?"

Several seconds passed before Serena said, "The name sounds familiar."

"Marva's Soul Food Kitchen?"

"Oh, yeah. I heard of her but we never met."

"You're kidding. I thought every black American who lived in Paris for more than a few weeks met Marva."

"Sorry, Ricky. To tell you the truth I never had any black American friends here. I hung out with French people and Africans."

Ricky said nothing, but, for the first time since he'd met Serena, he wondered if she was lying to him. From Marva's reaction to the photo, he had been certain she knew who Serena was. Yet, Marva said she'd never seen her before. So maybe Marva and Serena were both telling the truth. Maybe they really were total strangers.

Arriving at Valitsa the Serb's white five-story building, Ricky

punched in the door code on the numbered panel. A little electronic
beep sounded. Ricky opened the creaky wooden door and he and Serena
entered the vestibule. He pushed the light button on the wall and a
harsh fluorescent bulb illuminated the narrow corridor, the rickety-
looking spiral staircase. Serena took hold of Ricky's arm. "Before we go
upstairs," she purred, "I want to tell you how grateful I am for this,
Ricky. You may have saved my life tonight. *Merci beaucoup.*"

Serena stood on the tips of her toes and, with her mouth slightly
open, kissed Ricky, quickly, wetly, on the lips. "You're welcome," he
said.

Valitsa Karodovic had not sounded the least bit surprised when Ricky
phoned her from Le Bon Montmartrois at 3:20 in the morning. When
he told her the favor he needed to ask of her, she readily, if somewhat
grumpily, agreed. Now, as he rang Valitsa's doorbell, Ricky wondered if
he'd made a mistake. But he had had few alternatives. Serena needed a
place to stay, someplace where Cash would never think of looking for
her. Ricky's apartment wasn't safe. And he did not want to get Fatima
mixed up in all of this. He and Fatima had enough stress in their lives
already: in six hours they would be going to visit the maternity hospital
together. The crazy Serb was the only viable option in this emergency.

Valitsa looked liked shit when she opened the door, ravaged and
mucus-eyed, in a ratty plaid bathrobe. *"Bonsoir,"* she croaked.

Serena took over. She walked into the apartment with an uncanny
mixture of humility and privilege. She thanked Valitsa effusively in
French. Her accent, her rapid-fire delivery and command of grammar
were flawless. Valitsa, though groggy and naturally cantankerous, was
obviously charmed. She showed Serena the couch on which she would
sleep, told her—sternly but politely—that she kept irregular hours, so
her guest would have to always be quiet, and handed her a set of keys
to the flat. Their French dialogue was so effortlessly speedy that Ricky
had trouble keeping up. Serena excused herself and disappeared into the
bathroom.

"Thank you so much," Ricky said to Valitsa in English. "I really
didn't know where else to go."

"It is not a problem," Valitsa replied.

"I gave Serena my phone number and the number at Fatima's, too. I told her to call me if she needs anything and not to bother you. And, you know, she'll only be here for the weekend. Or until Tuesday morning at the very latest."

"That is fine."

"I don't know how I can ever repay you." Only as the words were leaving his lips did Ricky remember the box full of hand grenades in Valitsa's closet—and the fact that, just twelve hours earlier, the Serb had asked him to keep the weapons for her and he had refused.

Valitsa smiled wryly. "I am sure I will think of something."

Plodding downhill, on his way home, Ricky kept thinking about Serena's kiss. The way her lips had so furtively, so moistly, caressed his. After all she had told him, after all the memories and conflicted feelings their meeting had sparked, all Ricky could think of as he walked down the steep slope of the rue des Martyrs was the fleeting feel of Serena's soft, dewy lips on his. Only when he was about thirty yards from his doorstep did he notice the couple across the street, standing in front of the nursing home. He saw the woman first: the one Valitsa had dubbed Carmen, the Latin transsexual hooker with the haunted stare and the fine black hair that cascaded down her back. She was talking to the man but facing Ricky, her huge eyes locked on him as he approached his building. The man Carmen was talking to—Ricky could see only his back—wore a black beret, a black leather jacket and black pants. Carmen, her spooky gaze still focused on Ricky, said to the man, *"C'est lui."* Or: "It's him."

The man turned around and, at first, Ricky did not recognize him. The beret and Montmartre-hip, all-black wardrobe, threw him off. He took in the man's haggard face, his thick, round-lensed glasses and droopy mustache but still did not make the connection. Only as he arrived at the entrance of his building did Ricky realize that the stranger in the beret was the nerdy man he had seen the night before, the man who had been dressed so differently he might have been assuming a completely different personality as he had talked with Grace Kelly.

As he punched in the door code, Ricky turned and saw that the man in the beret was about to cross the street, about to approach him. At that moment, a blue, white and red police van came gliding up the rue des Martyrs, passing slowly between Ricky and the familiar stranger just as Ricky entered his building and closed the door behind him. He pushed the button on the wall. The lights in the lobby and stairwell clicked on and stayed on for the normal two minutes, giving Ricky enough time to climb the steps to his apartment, open the door and lock it behind him. He attached the door's safety chain.

Ricky did not turn on the lights in his studio. He crept through the shadows and stood in front of the long narrow window looking out on the rue des Martyrs. There was no sign of the police van. And Carmen and the mysterious man in the beret had both disappeared.

PART 3

Fatima

Nine

"YOU CAN CERTAINLY TELL who the Africans are at this party," the gorgeous woman with the wild black hair said as Ricky entered the garden.

It was late June 1998, one of the hottest days of the young summer. Ricky was already feeling a bit flustered when he arrived at Marva Dobbs's country house late. Having missed the train he'd wanted to catch, having had to wait another hour at the Paris station, Ricky knew he would be the last guest to show up for this Saturday afternoon lunch. He felt lucky to have been able to find a taxi at the Gisors station and, after the brief ride through the golden wheatfields, greeted Marva's husband Loïc at the front gate with an outpouring of abject apologies. The perfect host, Loïc acted as if Ricky were right on time.

"You know," Loïc said, leading Ricky into the kitchen, "I am married to this world-famous Paris chef but, here in the country, it is I who cook the grand meals."

"Smells like French paradise," Ricky said, taking in the aromas of the kitchen.

Loïc poured him a glass of white wine and sent him out into the garden, where he was greeted by the lilting, sardonic voice of the cinammon-skinned young woman in the Champagne-colored dress. At first, Ricky had no idea what she was talking about. He let out a nervous laugh and quickly scanned the crowd. Familiar faces all around. Sitting in canvas directors' chairs, in the open air, sweating slightly under the blazing sun, glasses of white wine in hand, were two black Americans, Marva Dobbs and Archie Dukes; one white American, Prunella Watson; and one white European, Archie's French-Italian-Spanish second wife, Claudia. But, lounging under the cool shade of a chestnut tree, were Juvenal Kamuhanda, a Rwandan whom Ricky had met on several occasions in Paris, and the luminous beauty who had welcomed him with her pungent social observation. She was the only person in the garden he had never met before and only after several seconds did he grasp the meaning of her comment.

"Mad dogs and Englishmen go out in the noonday sun," Prunella said. "Isn't that what Noel Coward sang?"

"He forgot to mention the rest of us fools," Marva replied, rising from her chair. She walked up to Ricky and kissed him once on each cheek.

"Glad we're all living up to our cultural stereotypes," Ricky said.

"I think you know most of the folks here, don't you?"

Ricky greeted the guests in the sunshine first, sharing a warm embrace with Archie Dukes, a brother in his late sixties with close-cropped salt-and-pepper hair and old-fashioned "Malcolm X" style glasses. Though he had graduated near the top of his class at NYU Law School, Archie had been unable to find a good job at any of the major Manhattan law firms back in the 1950s. He finally took a position with a French company that did a lot of business with the States. He moved to Paris with his wife and kids, thinking he would stay a year or two. Four decades later, he was a French citizen and a sort of griot of Paris's African-American expatriate community, a great storyteller who knew all the secret histories.

Next, Ricky exchanged kisses with Claudia. A fiftyish painter and

sculptor, pretty in a delicate sort of way, and bearing a shy and kindly
demeanor, Claudia spoke little English. But Ricky knew that, if Archie's
wife warmed to a subject, she could be extremely opinionated—so long
as the conversation was in French, or some other romance language. The
daughter of a Spanish mother and an Italian father, Claudia had grown
up in Cannes, in the South of France: a combustible cocktail of Latin
cultures. Some of Archie's old friends didn't know what to make of
Claudia. Everyone had loved his first wife, Ernestine, a charismatic sister
from East St. Louis. But Ernestine had succumbed to cancer soon after
Ricky arrived in Paris. Knowing that a lot of husbands of strong women
tended to die shortly after their wives, Ricky thought that Archie was
lucky to have found Claudia. And, though he couldn't say he knew her
well, he liked her enormously.

Prunella Watson threw her arms around Ricky and squeezed him
tight. Pru was also in her sixties and Ricky often thought of her as a
sort of white cousin of Marva's. Meticulously coiffed, with a high-class
fragrance about her, Pru was actually an unpretentious left-winger with
an earthy sense of humor and a globe-embracing lust for life. An Ohio
farmgirl, she had come to Paris to study French literature at the Sorbonne and fell in love with a prominent intellectual who ran with the
Sartre–de Beauvoir crowd. Prunella had had a few other husbands since
then—an Egyptian diplomat, a Belgian industrialist, a Czech poet—and
had published several books on subjects ranging from existentialist phi-
losophy to Middle Eastern politics. She was currently the chairwoman
of the Paris branch of Liberals Abroad and a hyperactive organizer of
political and literary symposia.

Finally, Ricky turned to the Africans who had had the good sense
to sit in the shade of the chestnut tree. "Ça va?" he asked, shaking hands
with Juvenal Kamuhanda. Tall and lean with an ebony complexion and
thick dreadlocks, Juvenal wore a silken-looking gray dashiki and black
pants. He was one of those men Ricky felt he'd like to be better friends
with—but they had never really had the chance to hang out together.
Juvenal ran a gallery, specializing in the works of Third World artists,
in the funky area near the Bastille monument. Ricky had gone to a half
dozen openings at the gallery over the years, and had noticed that Juvenal Kamuhanda always had a delectable-looking woman—sometimes

Asian, sometimes European, sometimes African—hanging on his arm. So Ricky assumed, with a sting of disappointment, that the hottie in the Champagne dress must have been the Rwandan's latest conquest.

"You've never met Fatima Boukhari," Marva asked, "have you?"

"I'm sure I would remember," Ricky said, feeling an erotic tingle just from grasping Fatima's hand.

"*Bonjour,*" Fatima said, flashing her iridescent smile, her coppery, high-cheekboned face glowing, as if lit from within.

"*Enchanté,*" Ricky replied. It was a common expression in French but Ricky had never meant it so sincerely. He truly was "enchanted."

"Fatima is getting her doctorate at the Institute of Political Science," Marva said, sounding like a proud aunt.

"*Sciences Po,*" Fatima said, referring to the prestigious university by its popular name.

"Yes, I know of it," Ricky said, trying his best not to gawk at the stranger who was not only beautiful but, obviously, very, very smart.

"And are you one of those Americans who is hopelessly in love with France?" Fatima asked, her voice lilting sardonically again.

"I don't know about the whole of France, but I *am* hopelessly in love with Paris. With the Eighteenth Arrondissement, anyway."

Ricky saw a flicker of recognition in Fatima's eyes. "*Ah, bon?*"

"Fatima thinks we expats are living in the past," Archie Dukes informed Ricky.

"Not exactly," Fatima hurried to respond.

"I refuse to be considered a relic of a bygone era," Prunella Watson said, patting her hair theatrically.

"You stepped into the middle of an argument," Marva whispered to Ricky.

"All I am saying," Fatima said, "is that you Americans who choose to live here have abandoned the most favored nation of the New World to live in a country that is very much a part of the decrepit Old World."

Everyone was sitting again and Ricky took the last empty chair, in the shade, with Juvenal and Fatima. He was beginning to doubt that the two Africans were boyfriend and girlfriend. He did not sense that invisible but usually detectable emotional rope that yoked an established couple together. Ricky was even more encouraged when Juvenal testily refuted Fatima's pronouncement.

"I lived in your so-called New World for five years," Juvenal said, "and I grew to despise it. I was very happy to return to Paris."

"Yes," Fatima shot back, "but you had already made the migration from Africa to Europe. You had already taken the step from an ancient world to a more modern one. Americans who choose to live here are only taking one giant step backward."

"I, for one, would take issue with your notion of progress," Archie said. "Do you really believe that America is more advanced than Europe? By what standard? And do you really think Africa is backward?"

Fatima took a sip of her wine and gave the shrug of someone who had never entertained a moment of self-doubt. Ricky was too intimidated to argue with her so he simply asked, "Have you ever been to America?"

"Of course," Fatima said. "I spent six month in New York. And I loved it. Absolutely. The energy, the passion, the ambition of the city."

"Yes, I know. I lived there, too."

"But you left. How long have you lived in Paris?"

"Eight years."

"And what, to you, if I may ask, is the appeal of Paris?"

Ricky paused for a moment, then said, "The food."

"À taaaaaaaaable," Loïc called out, as if on cue, with all the gusto of a Hollywood hillbilly hollering "Come 'n' git it!"

The midafternoon feast was laid out on a table beneath an arbor, rays of sunlight streaming through the grapevines that snaked in and out of the latticework. Loïc presided over the lunch with a proud and jolly hospitality. Marva Dobbs, so accustomed to being the hostess at her restaurant, was only too happy to let her husband run the show at their country home. Nearly forty years after Marva had met him, Loïc was still a fine-looking Breton, though now his blond hair was streaked with silver and the crow's feet of a frequent smiler crinkled upward from the corners of his blue eyes. The first course was escargots, sizzling inside their spiral shells. The guests used small, scalpel-like instruments to extricate the succulent snails, then savored the chewy goodness of the mollusks. But the best part was turning the empty shells upside down, letting the emerald-colored mixture of basil and garlic and olive oil pour onto your dish, then dipping thin slices of baguette into the sauce and munching on that tangy, soggy bread. The main course was *lapin à la moutarde*, rabbit stewed in mustard, with grilled potatoes and juicy string beans on the side. At once sinewy and tender, covered with that zesty sauce, Loïc's sublime hare flesh sent his guests into oooooh-ing, aaaaah-ing, mmmmmm-ing choruses of pleasure. Then it was on to the cheese course: Camembert, Comté, Chèvre: cheeses soft, hard and in between; mild, fragrant and seductively stinky. And complementing it all was a seemingly endless procession of bottles of Brouilly, a light red wine that was best served chilled, the perfect choice for a sultry summer's day.

The lunch table conversation, veering fluidly from English to French and back again, started out polite and convivial. The talk was of food and weather and travel, of the excitement of the city versus the tranquillity of the country, of the peculiar nuances of the two languages being spoken. But inevitably, this being the summer of 1998, the conversation turned to the travails of President Bill Clinton. The consensus at the table was that this whole scandal was ridiculous. The idea of a head of state being persecuted because he had received sexual favors from a young intern was bizarre and puritanical. And the fact that the controversy, the brewing Constitutional crisis, was both bizarre and puritanical made it idiosyncratically American. Here, at last, was a subject on which all of Marva and Loïc's guests could agree.

"And yet, you still want to go back to live in America?" Claudia said. It was already surprising that Archie Dukes's wife had asked her question in English—but even more startling was the pointed tone in which she directed her query across the table at Fatima Boukhari.

Fatima looked Claudia in the eye. "Yes, I do," she said.

"You know," Archie pronounced, "I've been thinking a lot about something Fatima said earlier this afternoon: that the great tradition of the black American expatriate in Paris is dead."

"I believe I said the American expatriate tradition in general," Fatima protested politely.

"Whatever," Archie said. "The point is I think you're right. Let's face it: Henry Ossawa Tanner, Josephine Baker, Richard Wright...

They're honored as historic figures. But no one in America today looks to black artists in Paris as polestars, guiding lights. And forget artists, for the moment. When I decided to settle in Paris back in the nineteen fifties, as a lawyer, it was seen as a form of protest, a rebellion against the racism of the United States. As a black man in America, I could not live up to my professional potential. As a black man in France, I could. Back then, expatriation was seen as a radical act. I sense that, today, it's seen as a sort of . . . fickleness."

"The fact is," Prunella Watson said, "that people who leave their native countries are always out of the mainstream. No matter where you're from, if you abandon your homeland to live someplace else, you're a weirdo."

Ricky saw Claudia lean toward Archie and heard her whisper, "*Qu'est-ce que c'est* 'weirdo'?" As Archie quietly translated, Pru continued.

"Just look at how few people actually do it. The vast majority of people, for whatever reason, stay in the general vicinity, at least in the country, in which they were born. The funny thing about America is that it is a nation of immigrants. Except for the slaughtered and disenfranchised Native Americans. And, of course, African slaves were not willing immigrants to the New World. But everybody else, or the ancestors of everybody else, *chose* to go there. And I suppose it's because most people's people went out of their way to get to America that folks in America can never really understand why any American would choose not to live in America. The issue isn't really so much that you choose to live in, say, France, but that you choose *not* to live in the U.S.A. And all of us who have left the States, whatever our background, share that sense of displacement. For forty years now, I've dealt with this not-so-subtle reproach from the folks back home. It's as if they're always chastising me: '*You left.*' I think they feel somehow rejected."

"But that was not always the case with African-Americans," Marva said. "Back in the sixties, I always felt that the folks stateside had a certain admiration for expats like me—and for Archie and Ernestine. For black people who had the nerve to say, 'To hell with it, I'm gonna make my own life, by my own rules, in Paris!' "

"Yes," Loïc said, "but clearly times have changed. Look at our

daughter. She is a university student in America. We had thought that
a *métisse* child would prefer France. But to our daughter, America is
where everything is happening. She loves it there."

"For all peoples," Fatima said, "it is the land of opportunity."

"*Mon Dieu!*" Juvenal practically shouted. "Surely you are not going
to sit here and say that America is not a racist country."

"Less racist than France, yes," Fatima responded coolly.

"You know what I think the big difference is between France and
America?" Ricky said. "When it comes to what I think of as *official*
racism, that is to say, racism on the part of the police, or racist political
rhetoric like the anti-immigrant rantings of a right-wing nut like Jean-
Marie Le Pen, I would say that France is at least as bad as the United
States. And it might very well be that when it comes to institutions—
corporations, universities, media outlets—there is as much or more racism in France than there is in America. The huge difference, though,
is in what I would call *everyday* racism, the attitude of normal people
you encounter on the street. And I can tell you, having spent the first
thirty years of my life in America and the last eight here that the sort
of petty insults and prejudices that a black person in the States just gets
used to, takes for granted, are often simply absent in Paris. The dirty
looks, the suspicious reactions, the snotty condescension, all the subtle
and not-so-subtle crap that white people in the States continually dump
on black people . . . well, it just doesn't happen to me here."

"That is because you are American, of course," Fatima said. "And
French people can instantly tell you are American. Even before you open
your mouth and reveal your accent, they can see from the very way that
you move, from your walk, your gestures, that you are American. And
your normal, everyday French people love black Americans. They love
your musicians and all your cultural heroes. They are naturally inclined
to be nice to you. But if you were Arab, or an African, you might not
find them so generous."

"Agreed," Ricky said. "All the same, I think your average white
person in Paris is just more chilled out when it comes to questions of
race. And the white Americans who come to live here chill out as well."
He gestured toward Prunella Watson. "I mean, look at us, Pru. Here in
Paris, we're able to get to know each other, have a great friendship. But

I would say that even in an ostensibly enlightened place like New York City, there would be all sorts of subtle barriers to our becoming friends. In fact, in New York, a lady like yourself, might even cross the street to avoid me."

"And she would be right!" Archie said, laughing.

"And who are you calling a lady?" Pru sniffed, feigning indignation.

"It might be that the problem in America today isn't so much racism," Marva said. "It's *racialism*. It's not just an oppressive system that discriminates against and crushes the poorest black people. It's more this pervasive, sometimes even unconscious, idea that your race defines you before anything else. The fact of whether you're black or white trumps love, trumps intelligence, trumps talent, religion, ideology and, yes, even class. And black folks buy into this racialist code every bit as much as white folks do."

"But a person's ethnicity *does* matter," Fatima said. "Look at you, Marva. You run a restaurant that specializes in ethnic cuisine."

"I didn't say ethnicity, or race, or whatever you want to call it, doesn't matter," Marva replied. She paused, seeming to grope for what she wanted to say.

"It is all a question of degree," Juvenal Kamuhanda jumped in. "Look at the world today. This obsession with ethnicity is the cause of more violent insanity than anything else. And it is not always a matter of black versus white. In the former Yugoslavia, they have these pathological blood feuds—and all the participants are white. Look at my home country of Rwanda. Everybody there is black. But how many hundreds of thousands of people were slaughtered four years ago, on the question of whether they were a Hutu or a Tutsi? This is where ethnocentrism taken to its ultimate degree always leads—to bloody madness."

Silence fell over the table. Finally, Loïc said, "Anyone for dessert?"

The mood lightened as everyone dug into their crème brûlée, cracking the brown and crunchy wafer-thin surface of the confection and scooping up sweet spoonfuls of the soft yellow cream that lay beneath. More cool Brouilly was poured and the conversation turned to the World Cup, the quadrennial global soccer championship that was being held in France for the first time in sixty years.

"Say what you will about ethnic issues in this country," Loïc said, "but France has the most integrated team in the whole tournament. The star, Zinedine Zidane, he was born in Marseille, but his parents were Algerian immigrants. And look at the other players. Marcel Desailly's people are from Ghana. Lilian Thuram is from Guadeloupe. Thierry Henry is from Martinique. And the goalie, Fabien Barthez, he is a white guy, but even he grew up in Africa!"

"They are an inspiration," Claudia said in her uncertain English. "Verily."

"Never underestimate the importance of sport," Archie Dukes said. "In America, when Jackie Robinson joined the Brooklyn Dodgers that was the first step toward integration throughout the society."

"Yes, the French will love their multicultural team," Fatima said, "until they lose and get knocked out of the competition."

"Who are you rooting for?" Prunella asked.

"Cameroon and Morocco were my favorites," Fatima replied. "But they've already been eliminated."

"Oh. And where are you from, originally?"

"Toulouse."

Juvenal seemed to jump in his seat. He looked as if he were struggling not to spit out his wine. After a big gulp, he said to Fatima, "You are French?"

"I was born in Toulouse."

"I thought you said you were African," Ricky interjected.

"My mother is from Cameroon and my father from Morocco."

"But but but," Juvenal sputtered, *"vous êtes française!"*

"I have three nationalities: Moroccan, Cameroonian and French."

"Et voilà!" Juvenal said, throwing up his hands, as if to say "That figures!" Ricky did not understand what exactly made him so angry. It was as if Juvenal now considered Fatima a fraud, a pretender, a fake African.

"But you're not rooting for the French team?" Archie asked.

"They are doomed," Fatima said authoritatively. "They will probably be knocked out by Paraguay tomorrow."

"But if they win," Ricky said, "they make it to the quarterfinals."

"Where they will most likely face Italy. And Italy will definitely beat them."

"Don't be so sure," Ricky countered. "The French have been looking real solid. They might be a team of destiny."

"I believe their destiny is to lose to Paraguay tomorrow."

Ricky and Fatima locked eyes across the table. "What do you wanna bet?"

Fatima smiled insouciantly. Ricky could see she relished a challenge. "Dinner," she said. "If France wins, I take you out, if Paraguay wins, you take me out."

"Let's turn it around," Ricky said. "Since I have faith in my team and I'm too much of a gentleman to make you pay, let's say that *when* France wins, I will treat you to a dinner."

Fatima laughed. "Fair enough."

Ricky and Fatima reached across the table and shook hands. Out of the corner of his eye, Ricky saw Marva and Loïc exchange knowing smiles. Then Marva winked at her husband. Ricky could tell she was pleased.

Ten

Sunday, June 28, 1998: France vs. Paraguay

RICKY WATCHED THE MATCH that afternoon at Le Bon Montmartrois. François had rented a wide-screen TV and set it up in a corner of the crêperie—but only for the duration of the World Cup. France-Paraguay was a particularly tense match. Ricky barely touched his piano. François made few crêpes and burned most of the ones he cooked because he couldn't take his eyes off the TV. When France finally won in double overtime, Ricky immediately pulled out his wallet and searched for the phone number he had been given at Marva's country house the day before.

"Fatima?"

"Reekee?" He heard that musical, gently mocking laugh of hers. "The game is hardly over and already you call me to gloat."

"I believe I owe you a dinner. Are you free tonight?"

"No, not tonight. Perhaps we should meet for France's next match."

"You're on. Where do you live, by the way?"

"Rue de Trétaigne."

"You're kidding. We're practically neighbors."

"Did you not know that?"

They scheduled the date. After hanging up, Ricky had to laugh. Back when he lived in the States, Ricky, like most American sports fans, didn't give a shit about soccer. Even after moving to France, it had taken him several years to learn to appreciate the sport. Now his pursuit of this beautiful woman was all wrapped up in what was known as "The Beautiful Game."

Friday, July 3, 1998: France vs. Italy

"Liberté, Égalité, Fraternité," Fatima Boukhari trilled sarcastically. "That is all—how do they say in New York?—a load of bullshit!"

It was halftime in another tense, scoreless match. The crowd in the Trattoria d'Amalfi, one of Montmartre's most popular Italian restaurants, was split right down the middle, half the diners rooting for the host country, the other half for Italy. There was no question whose side Fatima was on.

"You love France but you are a foreigner here," she told Ricky between bites of her saltimbocca. "I was born and raised in France so I can tell you what these French are all about. Like I say last week, they celebrate their multiracial team right now but wait and see how they turn on them when they lose."

"You're so convinced they're gonna lose."

"Of course. Italy almost won the cup four years ago. But France, they have never won a World Cup before. Why should they now? Besides, you are American. What do you know of soccer?"

"Frankly," Ricky said, "I'm more of a basketball fan. But I've seen all of France's matches in the tournament and I think they've got the desire. They *want* to win. They want it more than the other teams I've seen."

Fatima took a long sip of Chianti, eyed Ricky carefully over the rim of her glass, as if taking the measure of the man. He had felt weak in the knees when he entered the restaurant an hour earlier and saw her already sitting at the table, waiting for him. She was even more blazingly gorgeous than he had remembered. "Well," she said, "I think next time it is I who will be taking you out to dinner."

Even after double overtime, the score was still zero-zero. The outcome would be decided on penalty kicks. It was what is known as a shoot-out. A single Italian player would face the French goalie, try to blast the ball past him. Then a single French player would take his turn against the Italian goalkeeper. Back and forth it would go, until one team had, after an equal number of tries, outscored the other. The pressure was all on the keeper Fabien Barthez, the white Frenchman who had been raised in Africa, the fire-eyed competitor with the shaved head and the dark goatee. He made a spectacular save to give France the win, 4-3, in the penalty shoot-out.

"Pure luck," Fatima griped a half hour after the game, as she and Ricky sat side by side at a café on the rue des Abbesses, watching the passersby celebrating in the street. The underrated French team had just made it to the semifinals of the biggest sporting event on the planet— and this seemed to irritate Fatima immensely. "That Barthez, he gives me a pain in the butt."

"Why?"

They were on their second bottle of wine of the night, a Bordeaux, and Fatima knitted her brow in the pensive manner of a slightly, but still charmingly, tipsy woman. "To be honest, Reekee, this Barthez, he reminds me of somebody. Of my ix."

"Your who?"

"Bernard-Henri. My ix, I mean, my ex . . . boyfriend."

"How long has he been ex?"

"Eleven weeks and one day."

"But who's counting?"

"What?"

"Never mind. Tell me about him."

"Oh, he was a child of the *soixante-huitards*," Fatima said, suddenly letting out a lovely little burp. "*Excuse-moi*. How do you say, in English?"

"'Sixty-eighters. The nineteen sixty-eight generation."

"*Exactement*. The old hippies. They were revolutionary at the time.

But they, the parents of Bernard-Henri, they were *haute bourgeoisie*, despite their stated views. They had their little revolutionary interlude, then got on with life: father a doctor, mother a lawyer. Bernard-Henri, he grew up on the Boulevard Saint Germain, all the best schools, plenty of money and connections, but his parents they talk that leftist garbage and never ever live it. *Tu me comprends?*"

"Yes, I understand you."

"Anyhow, after university, Bernard-Henri, he became consultant with a management firm, the peoples who tell others how to run their business. Always I have been fascinated by world finance. I study international politics but it is the connection between the markets and politics that fascinates me the most. So I take this summer job. I was intern, like Monica Lewinsky."

Fatima and Ricky both burst into laughter.

"No," Fatima said, turning serious, almost severe. "I was most definitely *not* a whore, a little sucker. Most definitely not. I did my job as consultant. I met this Bernard-Henri. He was up-and-coming young man. Anyhow, we were friends in the office. I left the job when summer ended and only later did we become lovers. Okay?"

"Okay."

"Anyhow, he was nice French boy, a businessman, yes, but full of the rhetoric of the left, wanting to help the poor, his support for the ethnic and cultural integration of the society. He seemed like a good man, Bernard-Henri, very gentle and loving."

"So what went wrong?"

Fatima, for just a moment, seemed to fight back tears. Ricky worried that he was being too inquisitive—but he had to know.

"He is very ambitious," Fatima continued, her voice turning brittle. "And, after we had been together a year, he started talking all the time about the Internet and cyberspace and the New Economy and e-business and all that stuff. It became his obsession, his religion. I listened and encouraged him. Anyhow, he quit his job to become an Internet e-businessman. He said he would become the Jeff Case or Steve Bezos of France. I don't know what. He suddenly tried to be Mister Branché." Literally, *branché* meant "plugged in," but it was generally used as a demeaning term, sort of like "trendy."

"He got his mommy and daddy to give him the money to start his Internet company," Fatima continued. "He had no real product. Just this vague so-called start-up. Anyhow, he buys office space and hires people for no real jobs. He shaves off all his hair, he grows a goatee, wants to look cool like Fabien Barthez. And finally, he decides I am not cool enough for him so he drops me. Eleven weeks and one day ago."

Ricky saw a tear trickle down Fatima's cheek. "I'm sorry," he said.

Fatima poured herself another glass of wine. "It is nothing," she said, and sighed. "All I say is these French and their leftist talk, you must beware. Bernard-Henri is now with a little blond rich girl from the Seventh. You see what I mean? In the end, people revert to their true natures, they end up with their own kind. In spite of all the rhetoric of integration. Don't you agree?"

"No." Ricky waited for Fatima to respond but she just stared out at the busy street. After a moment, he said, "It sounds like Bernard-Henri really hurt you."

"Hurt me?" Fatima laughed dryly. "He cut out my heart and pissed all over it."

Wednesday, July 8, 1998: France vs. Croatia

"Dégueulasse!" Fatima hissed as she stood in Ricky's window, looking down at the transvestite and transsexual prostitutes on the rue des Martyrs. She shook her head and said it again. *"Dégueulasse,"* meaning, "This is something that makes me want to puke."

"I don't see what's so disgusting about them," Ricky said. "They're just out there trying to make a living."

"Don't tell me you are friends with them!" From Fatima's alarmed tone, Ricky wondered if she was beginning to question his sexual tastes.

"Not at all. I just see them as, I don't know, local color."

"Acch, that is because you are *voyeur*. You are cultural tourist. Searcher of exotica. You come to this foreign city, you look, you see, and anytime you want, you go home. But you have no moral sensibilitee, Reekee."

"First of all, this *is* my home. Second of all, I try not to be judgmental."

"And this is precisely my point. In order to be a moral person, you *must* judge."

"Let's eat."

Since France had beaten Italy, dinner was on Ricky again but he had decided that this time, they should watch the match in his apartment and order in the food. The couscous had been delivered from the North African restaurant a few doors down the rue des Martyrs. He ladled steaming heaps of the yellow semolina—granulated wheat that had the texture of finely chopped-up rice—onto their plates. He and Fatima helped themselves to the brown broth, pouring it over the couscous, then mixing in the carrots, chickpeas, potatoes and turnips, the juicy chunks of lamb, chicken legs and merguez sausage. Ricky had also ordered a couple of bottles of Algerian red wine. During the first half, Ricky and Fatima were too busy eating, drinking and talking to pay much attention to the soccer match.

"Pretty good couscous," Fatima judged, "but mine is much better. I will have to make it for you some time."

"Great," Ricky said. "Is it from an old family recipe?"

"Yes, my father's. It is my mother who prepares ninety percent of the meals in our family but when it comes to couscous, Papa is the big chef. And he taught me all his tricks."

Fatima talked a lot about her family that night. She was the eldest of three daughters. Her mother, growing up in Cameroon, had been actively discouraged from pursuing an education. But, against her family's wishes, she emigrated to France, to the university town of Toulouse, got her degree and eventually became an elementary schoolteacher. Fatima obviously loved and admired her mother but Ricky could tell that the family figure who loomed largest in her emotional life was Papa. He, too, had left his native land, Morocco, to get a university education in Toulouse. He had wanted to be a professor of French literature. How he worshipped the language's great writers: Molière, Voltaire, Racine, Rabelais, Flaubert, Balzac, Hugo, Zola, Gide, Proust. He was constantly spouting quotations from the works of his heroes. But brilliant as he was, Ahmed Boukhari was still a dark-skinned boy from the mean streets of Marrakech and the academic powers of France in the early 1960s let him know that, even with a doctorate, he stood no chance of ever gaining a university professorship. So he became a librarian.

"Sometimes, he makes me sad, my father," Fatima said. "There is something very spiritual about him. I think that part of him would like to go back to Morocco and become a holy man, a pure Muslim; to renounce worldly things, to wear a robe and study the Koran and pray five times a day. But then there is that secular side that he cannot suppress. He always says that he hates the French but he loves their literature and their wine. Many nights during my adolescence, I spied on him. He sat alone in his study after the rest of us had gone to bed, re-reading Balzac, sipping Saint-Émilion and crying softly to himself."

"And what about you?"

"What about me?"

"Do you wrestle with the secular and the spiritual?"

"Of course. I love my religion. I believe in Allah and the teachings of Mohammed. But it is hard to be pure, you know. One seeks a balance. I am a modern woman. I want to succeed in the secular world. I have opportunities before me that my parents never had. I do not wear a veil but I still consider myself a good Muslim."

France beat Croatia by a score of two goals to one. Ricky walked Fatima back to her apartment building, on the other side of the Butte Montmartre. There were people on the streets celebrating but the partying was somewhat subdued since, even though France had made it to the finals, the team would face the historically formidable Brazilian squad in the ultimate match. In any event, Ricky was happy that he owed Fatima at least one more dinner.

"It's funny," Fatima said as they traversed the hill, "but somehow, Reekee, you get me to talk a lot about myself."

"You make it sound like a bad thing."

"A girl has to protect her privacy."

"Sorry if I ask too many questions."

"It is all right."

"I've actually tried to restrain myself," Ricky said. "For instance, I didn't want to ask whether or not you were seeing Juvenal Kamuhanda."

"Juvenal!" Fatima hooted. "That predator! You think I would be interested in a man like him?"

"A lot of women are."

"Oh please! He has called my answering machine three time since we met at Marva's and I have never phoned him back."

Ricky tried not to show how reassured, how mightily encouraged, Fatima's comment made him feel. He just said, "Okay."

They stopped in front of Fatima's building. "So, I see you Sunday, yes?"

"Yes."

Fatima kissed him once on each cheek, as she had before—but now the kisses seemed to happen in slow motion, the soft touch of her lips on his face imbued with a new and tender intimacy.

"You know," Fatima said, "now France is really doomed."

Sunday July 12, 1998: France vs. Brazil

For days, Ricky had been telling anyone who would listen that France was destined to win it all. Those who bothered to listen laughed in his face. Brazil had won four World Cups, including the last championship in 1994. They had the rising young star of the sport, Ronaldo, on their team. Expert sportswriters, connoisseurs of the game, in the British, French and American press were unanimous in their predictions: Brazil would kick France's ass.

"They're wrong," Ricky blithely told Fatima as the match began. "Just remember, when this is all over, that I was the lonely prophet. Will you remember?"

"I promise," Fatima said. Like everyone else, she laughed in Ricky's face—but she did so with a certain affectionate pity, as if to say, "You poor deluded American, you don't know jack about this sport, do you?"

Fatima had suggested they watch the match at her apartment. Since Ricky was still winning their bet, he paid for the dinner: take-out Vietnamese. Ricky was impressed by Fatima's flat. She had a spacious living room and separate bedroom, a full kitchen, a bathroom that actually had a bathtub and not just a shower stall, and a little balcony. It made his studio on the other side of the Butte Montmartre look pretty cheesy. Fatima explained that her parents paid half the rent, but Ricky still couldn't help feeling outclassed.

By halftime, though, Ricky's self-esteem was making a major come-

back. Zinedine Zidane—nicknamed Zizou—the Marseille homeboy, son
of Algerian immigrants, the French phenom famous for his fancy foot-
work, had scored two goals by propelling the soccer ball into the net
with his head. Brazil was floundering, the golden-boy Ronaldo looking
listless on the pitch: rumor was he had passed out before the match, a
nasty case of pregame nerves. France was in control and, barring a
second-half collapse, well on their way to winning the Cup.

"You know who must be so happy right now?" Fatima said during
halftime.

Ricky was afraid she was thinking of Bernard-Henri, so he said,
"Your father."

"No. Karim."

"Who's Karim?"

"My first boyfriend. Back in Toulouse. His parents are also from
Algeria. He is fanatic for Zizou."

"Great," Ricky said, trying to conceal his sudden jealousy.

"You know, Reekee, I have had only two boyfriends in my life.
Karim and Bernard-Henri." There was a certain weightiness in Fatima's
tone, as if she were giving Ricky privileged information.

"So what's the story with Karim?"

"We met at university in Toulouse. He was a true love. We were
together for three years. But it had to end. He was more religious than
I was, more strict anyhow. He did not want me to have a profession.
And this, I could not deal with. In the end, Karim would have wanted
me to be a housewife in a veil. We broke up when I came to Paris for
graduate school. As much as I loved him, I could not suppress my own
ambitious. Do you understand?"

"Yes I do."

"I want to be a good Muslim and a modern woman. At the same
time. One must be allowed to be both."

"I agree," Ricky said, though he wondered if he truly comprehended
the conflict in Fatima's life.

The final score was a shocker, even for Ricky the lonely prophet:
France: 3; Brazil: 0. At the close of the match, the entire nation exploded
in ecstatic celebration. The streets of Paris were jam-packed with rev-
elers, flags flying, champagne flowing, a swirling, drunken chaos of

victorious exultation. On the Champs Élysées, the serious, heavy-browed face of Zinedine Zidane was projected onto Napoleon's Arc de Triomphe, along with the words *Merci, Zizou*. The next day, people would say that the city had not experienced such an orgiastic outpouring of joy since the great *Libération* after four years of Nazi occupation in 1944. And nowhere was the partying more wildly rapturous than in the Eighteenth Arrondissement.

Ricky and Fatima were out there, screaming and jumping up and down in the jubilant mob. They eventually found themselves in front of Sacré Coeur, at the highest point in the city, squeezed together in the human whirlpool, all of Paris laid out before them, sparkling magnificently.

"Now do you believe in France?" Ricky yelled above the cacophony.

Fatima did not answer. She just smiled her radiant smile, then lunged at Ricky, her left hand grabbing hold of the back of his head. Her mouth enveloped his in a splashingly passionate kiss. They went back to her apartment and made sweet love until the break of day.

"Let us not fight, Reekee. We have already discussed this before."

"I just don't understand how an intelligent person like you could be so completely narrow-minded on this one subject."

"Because it is not a question of intelligence. It is about faith."

Ricky and Fatima were sitting at a corner table in Chez Kamel, the Moroccan-Algerian-Tunisian restaurant on Ricky's block, sharing a couscous and getting on each other's nerves. Neither one of them could remember how, in the course of a pleasant evening, they had stumbled upon this disruptive subject, but now that they had, Ricky was unwilling to let go of it.

"Okay," he said, "forget about me. Pretend we never even met. But let's say you met another guy, a perfectly nice, I don't know what, New Zealander; a warm, smart, half-white, half-Maori guy from New Zealand. And the two of you fell in love. You had never been with anyone you loved so much. But the guy was an agnostic. Religion didn't matter to him. But he cherished you and you were totally in love with him and he proposed marriage. Are you telling me you would not marry that man because he wasn't a Muslim?"

"Yes, Reekee, this is what I am telling you."

"Well, I'm sorry, but I think it's a terrible, poisonous attitude. I feel the same way about whites who are opposed to marrying blacks and blacks who are opposed to marrying whites. It's the worst kind of segregationist thinking."

"This is not about race, Reekee. When I was going out with Bernard-Henri, my parents did not care at all that he was white. All they wanted to know was if he was a Muslim and I could see they were disappointed that he was not."

"Okay, sorry I mentioned black and white. My point is that bigotry is poisonous whatever form it takes, whether it's Jews who won't marry Christians or blondes who won't marry brunettes. I think this type of prejudice creates artificial barriers between people."

"Maybe there are natural barriers between people. Maybe they are not all artificial."

"I just don't understand how you, Fatima, could think this way. I mean, you don't live like some kind of fundamentalist."

"I am not a fundamentalist!" Now Ricky could see that Fatima was genuinely angry. "But I love my religion and I am committed to the continuitee of my faith in the next generation. Maybe you cannot understand this, Reekee, because you have no faith at all. You believe in nothing. And in that way you are as incomprehensible to me as I am to you."

That shut him up. Though he couldn't recall how they had wound up on this topic, Ricky knew he was the one who had started the argument. And, as is so often the case in relationships, the fight he had initiated was really about something else—it was a decoy for the problem that was actually troubling him. On this night in early March 1999, Ricky was feeling fed up with the on-offness of his romance with Fatima. It had been eight months since their first date and he still didn't feel that they were truly "a couple." Fatima kept him always off-balance. He tried to arrange his work schedule, trading shifts with Dominique, the other pianist at Le Bon Montmartrois, in order to be free for Fatima.

But Fatima was constantly cancelling appointments with him because she had to study for some big exam or deliver some paper or do research for her thesis. He would get sick of it, not call her for a week or two, then she would suddenly get in touch with him, suggest a date that night or the following afternoon. And, as much as Ricky might wish to blow her off, stand her up, give her a taste of her own medicine, he couldn't do it. He loved seeing her, talking to her, making love with her, too much. But he could never figure out what she really felt about him. Whenever he tried to discuss the nature of their relationship, she would skirt the issue, tell him she had too much on her mind for these kinds of conversations. Ricky wondered if he should try fucking other women. But for the past eight months, Fatima had been the only woman he was attracted to. She had absolute power over him. And, as much as he tried to hide that fact from her, she obviously knew it very well.

"You know," Fatima said, ladling more steaming broth over her couscous, "in many ways, you remind me of my ex. Bernard-Henri also had no convictions—"

"Damn it, Fatima!" Though Ricky had not raised his voice, there was a furious blast of heat in his tone. "I am so sick of hearing about Bernard-Henri. No matter what we're talking about, you have to always bring up Bernard-Henri. It's like he's your only point of reference for anything. And, look, I know he hurt you. I understand that. But sometimes it's like you think you're the only person who ever got hurt, who ever got their heart broken. Well I can tell you, you're not the only one. Okay?"

Fatima stared at Ricky across the table, clearly stunned. Finally she whispered, "Okay."

They ate in silence for a while, then Ricky said, "I was really hurt once, too. I never told you about it. But I was very much in love with a woman, back in the States. We were supposed to get married. I mean, shit, I was standing at the altar on our fucking wedding day, okay? Three hundred people sitting there in the church. And my bride didn't show up. She had left me. Run off with . . . with a guy I had known all my life." Ricky stared into his couscous as he spoke. He couldn't bear to look up at Fatima. He was afraid he would burst into tears if he did. But he could feel that she was staring unwaveringly at him. "Anyway," he continued, "I just want you to know . . . that . . . you're not the only one who ever got hurt."

Fatima reached across the table, caressed his arm. "I am sorry," she said.

"*Une rose, monsieur?*"

Ricky recognized the voice immediately. Looking up, he spotted the flower salesman, several tables away, clutching a couple dozen red roses, each wrapped in clear plastic. Paris in general, and Montmartre in particular, was filled with these roaming florists. They went from one restaurant to another, typically approaching couples and beseeching the man to buy a rose for his lady. Ricky had never bought a rose from any of the wandering flower men. When he was out on a date and one of the floral hustlers approached him, Ricky always replied with a polite "*Non, merci.*" But there was one particular salesman he had seen again and again in his neighborhood, a beige-complexioned man with an Indian accent who always wore a black-and-white checkered cap. Several years ago, when the flower man had heard Ricky speaking English to one of his dates, he broke into the language as well.

"Oh, why don't you buy a flower for the beautiful lady?" the man in the checkered cap had said, sounding, to Ricky's ear, just like Ben Kingsley in *Gandhi*. "It would make her so very happy."

"Sorry," Ricky said, "not this time."

Over the next three years, Ricky would often encounter the flower man in the checkered cap in a restaurant. "Won't you buy a rose for the beautiful lady?" the man would ask in his lovely Indian accent.

"No," Ricky would say. "Not tonight. But someday, I promise, I will buy a flower from you."

Eventually, Ricky felt that this exchange had become something of a running gag, a harmless comedy routine between him and the man in the checkered cap. The flower guy would see him on yet another date, urge him to buy a rose for that night's "beautiful lady," and Ricky would always demur, saying, "Someday . . . I will buy a flower from you."

And so it went on, month after month. The flower man's wheedling plea and Ricky's jolly little, "Someday . . . someday . . ."

Finally, in the spring of 1998, several weeks before Ricky met Fatima, he was out on a date with a Singaporean stewardess when the man in the checkered cap appeared yet again, offering yet another rose. "Some-day," Ricky said, laughing, "I will buy a flower from you but——"

"I don't need your somedays!" the flower man exploded. "Always I try to sell to you, I see you all the times and always you tell me 'Some-day!'"

Ricky was shocked. He had never taken their joking little exchange seriously. "I'm sorry," he began to say, "but——"

The flower man cut him off, screaming in anger, "I am trying to make a living and all you give me is somedays! I don't need your some-days!"

The manager of the restaurant approached the table but the man in the checkered cap turned and stormed off before he could be kicked out. As he pulled open the door he turned and called back at Ricky, "I don't need your somedays!"

Now, almost a year later, Ricky was sitting in Chez Kamel with Fatima and there was the flower man in the checkered cap, hawking his roses a few tables away. At some point in the past several months, Ricky had wondered what had happened to the guy. Had he returned to India to seek another line of work? Or maybe he had found another, more lucrative arrondissement in which to hector diners. But at this moment, when Ricky had just been on the brink of tears remembering his catastrophic wedding day, feeling utterly exasperated with Fatima, he could not have been happier to see his long-lost flower guy. The man in the checkered cap spotted Ricky, sneered, and was about to turn away, not even bothering to approach the table.

"*Monsieur,*" Ricky called out, startling Fatima. "*S'il vous plaît, mon-sieur!*"

The flower guy, almost grudgingly, came over to the table. "*Bon-soir,*" he said, as if he had never seen Ricky before.

"Tonight," Ricky said grandly, "I am going to buy a flower from you. In fact, I'm going to buy a dozen."

The flower guy, laying out twelve, plastic-covered roses on the table, beamed. He collected his 120 francs from Ricky then turned to Fatima and exclaimed, "Madame, this man, he really love you! For years, I try to get him to buy a flower from me and he never buy one. I see him with many beautiful ladies and never does he buy a flower. But tonight for you, he buy twelve. He loooooove you!"

Fatima and Ricky were both laughing hard now as other diners turned and looked. The flower guy kept going. "He love, love, love you, lady! He love you with all his heart!" Now everyone in the restaurant was watching and smiling and Fatima was laughing convulsively, covering her face with her hands in happy embarrassment. "I know this man," the flower guy continued. "You are the love of his whole life! Good night to you!"

And with that, the man in the checkered cap headed out the door. Ricky and Fatima spent the rest of the dinner laughing and talking about the flower guy. Then they walked over the hill, Fatima cradling her dozen roses. As soon as they stepped into Fatima's apartment, they were all over each other, kissing, stroking, squeezing, fumbling to get out of their clothes. They collapsed onto Fatima's couch, delirious with passion. Soon they were coming together in explosive bliss. It was the only time they ever made love without using birth control.

Eleven

ON MAY DAY IN Paris, the streets are filled with children selling lillies of the valley, sprigs of tiny bell-shaped white flowers. And throughout the city, on this particular holiday, the International Day of the Worker, labor unions stage *manifestations*, noisy but usually peaceful parades of workers flaunting colorful banners and making the usual demands for shorter hours, higher wages and earlier retirement. The *manifs* made driving through Paris even more nerve-wracking than normal but, on the morning of May 1, 1999, both Ricky and Fatima had forgotten the holiday. When Fatima showed up at his studio, looking even more bleary-eyed and sleep-deprived than he did, Ricky immediately suggested they take a taxi to the maternity hospital. He thought he was being not only considerate, but clever. Since this was a Saturday, Ricky figured a taxi would be able to zip down the nearly deserted big boul-

evards, getting them to the Clinique Beaucaire, in the Eleventh Arrondissement, in no time at all.

Half an hour later, as their driver maneuvered them through a maze
of crowded side streets, avoiding the big bouleveards which had been
blockaded for the workers' demonstrations, Ricky and Fatima barely
spoke. Ricky wanted to tell her about his meeting with Cash, about
Serena showing up at Le Bon Montmartrois, about Valitsa sheltering
Serena, the keys to his apartment being found in a dead prostitute's skirt
and the strange man with the glasses and droopy mustache who may or
may not have been stalking him on his block at four o'clock that morning. But he said nothing about any of it. He figured Fatima had enough
to worry about already.

Fatima, meanwhile, practically curled up in her corner of the backseat, her left elbow resting on the taxi door, her hand covering her
mouth, as if to prevent any words from inadvertently escaping. She wore
a floral-printed dress and her turbulent black hair was tied back in a
ponytail. Ricky wanted to reach across the backseat and touch Fatima
but he sensed an invisible force field around her, making contact impossible. He wanted to speak but did not dare risk saying the wrong
thing.

By the time the taxi pulled up to the Clinique Beaucaire, the trip
had taken twice as long and cost twice as much as Ricky had anticipated.
At the entrance of the maternity hospital, Ricky held open one of the
glass doors as a pale Frenchman pushed through a huge baby carriage.
The new father nodded to Ricky and said, *"Merci,"* as his dark-skinned
African wife followed him through the door. Ricky managed to catch a
glimpse of the small, amber-colored twins, fast asleep, lying on their
backs, in the carriage. The proud mother smiled at Ricky and Fatima.
In the hospital lobby, Ricky stood waiting beside a vending machine as
Fatima filled out papers at the front desk. Then they climbed the stairs
to the second-floor waiting room. The space was filled with big-bellied
women sitting in plastic chairs. Ricky was struck by the mélange of
ethnicities and classes in the room: the pink-complexioned, well-scrubbed
young ladies of the *haute bourgeoisie*, in their cashmere sweaters and
pearls; the African women in brightly colored robes and sandals; the two
Asian women talking quietly in the corner, speaking in a language that

Ricky guessed was Vietnamese; formidable-looking, olive-toned matrons, possibly of Algerian descent; a smattering of French hippie Earth Mothers dressed like Peruvian villagers. A half dozen or so multicultural toddlers blundered and tumbled about the room, squealing and spouting pre-verbal gibberish. And a bare majority of the expectant women were accompanied by nervous males doing their best to look calm and, however improbably, in control. White-clad nurses and doctors in blue surgical garb and tissue-like headgear that looked like shower caps, hurried back and forth across the waiting room, muttering importantly. Here was "socialized medicine" at its best: people of all backgrounds getting the exact same top-notch treatment and having to pay little or nothing for it. There were higher taxes in France than in the United States, of course. But what better use for them?

Ricky and Fatima took two of the few empty seats. There were twelve closed doors in the waiting room, eleven of them bearing white plaques with a doctor's name etched in black lettering. By chance, Ricky and Fatima were sitting right in front of the door of Fatima's gynecologist, Dr. Yassin.

"You okay?" Ricky asked.

Fatima gave him a weak smile. "I'm okay," she said, then looked away.

Ricky suddenly had to pee. He cast an eye toward the tightly shut door marked w.c. A queasy-looking Frenchman stood outside the "water closet," shifting his weight from one foot to the other. Not wanting to make the poor man any more tense than he already was, Ricky turned and stared at Fatima. She sat beside him, hands folded in her lap, her head bowed, eyes closed. God, she was beautiful. Ricky wondered if she was praying. He felt as if his heart was literally swelling, filled to the bursting point with love for her. But did she feel anything even remotely as strong for him?

Just as tears of longing were about to sting his eyes, Ricky felt the call of nature pressing more insistently on his bladder. Shooting a look toward the water closet, he saw that the suffering Frenchman had disappeared, no doubt relieving himself inside. Then Ricky's eye caught a woman he had not seen before, an expectant mother who must have been occupying the W.C. before the Frenchman. She sat in a plastic chair, amid all the other swollen women, completely veiled, covered, from head to toe, in impenetrable black. During his years in Paris, living in the Eighteenth Arrondissement, Ricky had seen countless women with their hair concealed under veils. And he had seen his fair share of women in more enveloping, dark *chadors*. But even the women he had seen in *chadors* had kept their eyes uncovered. Every other part of their bodies may have been enshrouded but one could at least see their eyes. That was not the case with the woman in the waiting room of the Clinique Beaucaire. Her entire head was cloaked in black. At first, Ricky wondered if the woman was able to see anything at all. But he quickly decided that there must be enough microscopic holes in the fabric for her to be able to view her surroundings. That was when he made a conscious effort not to stare at her. Having noticed the large round mound of her belly, Ricky surmised that she must be at least seven months pregnant. Despite his best efforts, Ricky could not help but look again at the totally veiled woman. And he wondered: If she was so committed to such an ancient rite, what was she doing in a modern hospital, one of the most technologically advanced maternity clinics in Europe? Was there a problem with her baby? Ricky sensed the slightest movement of the black-shrouded head and quickly looked away. He dared not stare at this scrupulously religious woman. That would be rude. But how did he know she was not staring at *him*? Ricky had always thought of this sort of dense veiling as a brutal form of "disempowerment." But this woman in the all-encompassing veil, at least within the confines of a Paris maternity hospital, was an incredibly powerful presence. When she so much as tilted her head, you noticed—you *felt* it. As a polite Westerner you avoided looking at her. But you could never be sure when the veiled woman was looking at *you*. That was her power. Call it superficial but it was, nonetheless, a palpable social advantage. Struggling not to stare at the carefully concealed mother-to-be, Ricky gazed at Fatima. Her eyes remained closed. She was completely unaware of the overpowering woman in the full-body veil.

"There he is," Dr. Yassin said, in French, of course.

She pointed to the faint shape on the small video screen. Ricky saw a ghostly white pattern, like a field of infared snow. Within the field was a darker oval—the embryonic sac. And within that dark oval space was a curled white figure, almost too tiny to perceive, shaped like an apostrophe, wiggling excitedly.

"My God," Fatima whispered. Perhaps unconsciously, she reached for Ricky's hand. They squeezed their palms together, tight and sweaty. "It resembles a little sea horse." She let out a high-pitched coo of a laugh.

Dr. Yassin, with her parchment-colored skin and bright blue eyes, smiled. "Congratulations," she said to Ricky.

"Thank you," he replied.

As Dr. Yassin turned off the sonogram screen and put the electronic probe back in its place, she said to Fatima, "But you told me you did not feel pregnant."

"I know," Fatima said, rearranging her clothes. "But now that I think of it, my breasts have been very heavy and tender. I kept expecting my period, but it never came. And when the morning sickness arrived, I dismissed it as stress. I'm working very hard at school these days."

Dr. Yassin turned to Ricky. Though she probably wasn't much older than Ricky, she had a vaguely intimidating, maternal aura about her. "I hope you are helping Fatima deal with all the pressures of life," she said.

"I try."

Fatima suddenly spoke to Dr. Yassin in Arabic. The obstetrician-gynecologist answered in the same tongue. Fatima said something else in the language she knew Ricky could not comprehend. Dr. Yassin, again, responded in kind. Ricky was stunned. He didn't understand why Fatima had decided to linguistically exclude him. He was about to ask, in French, what had just been discussed, when Fatima turned to him and said, in English, "Do you mind, Reekee, going outside?"

Standing in the waiting room, while Fatima and Dr. Yassin talked behind the closed door, Ricky looked for the woman in the all-encompassing, full-body veil. But she was nowhere to be seen.

Riding the metro back to the Eighteenth, Fatima tried to act normal. She spoke of Dr. Yassin, of how she had been the child of a French woman and an Algerian man, of her adolescence in war-torn Algiers, her struggle against the racism and sexism of the medical-school establishment in Paris. Fatima told Ricky of how Dr. Yassin split her time between her private practice in a largely Arab and Asian section of the Thirteenth Arrondissement and delivering babies in the Clinique Beaucaire. "It must be a beautiful thing," Fatima said as she sat beside Ricky on the number 12 line, the rubber-tired train chugging through the underground tunnels, "to spend your days bringing new life into the world."

"And what about you?" Ricky finally asked. *"Ça va?"*

"Ça va," Fatima replied.

"Alors, je voudrais dire que——"

"Speak English," Fatima snapped.

Ricky looked around and noticed that several passengers had seemed to perk up, to subtly eavesdrop. Fatima must have noticed that they had only pricked up their ears when they heard Ricky lapse into French.

"Okay," Ricky said. "I'd just like to say that, you know, you're not alone in this."

"I know."

"Is there something you'd like to tell me?"

"Yes." Fatima paused. "I have to go to the market. What time must you arrive at work?"

"Not until noon."

"Okay. So you have time to come with me to the market. We can talk there."

"All right. But can you tell me now what you talked to Dr. Yassin about? After you kicked me out of the office."

"Yes," Fatima said flatly. "We talked about whether or not I would keep this baby."

"Of course I am pro-choice," Fatima said. "Politically speaking. In my intellect. In my thinking. But when it comes to the other realm, the personal, the religious, it is not a question of pro or anti. It is something I never even considered. I never in my imagination thought I would ever be confronted with this choice."

"I understand," Ricky said.

A block and a half from the *mairie* of the Eighteenth Arrondissement, where Ricky had been questioned by Inspector Lamouche in the
Hall of Marriage, was a T-shaped outdoor market, composed of two long
streets, rue du Poteau and rue Duhesme, and filled with merchants
hawking fish and meat and wine and cheese, shoes and hardware, flowers
and jewelry, lingerie and household knickknacks. There were cafés with
tables spilling out into the street and, on this May Day morning, a
French version of a Dixieland band, five musicians blowing their horns
with more passion than professionalism, as the people of the neighborhood—the wrinkled old folks trundling on their canes, the young couples
pushing infants in strollers, the shrewd-eyed bargain-hunters haggling
with the shopkeepers, bedraggled panhandlers holding out their palms
and asking for a franc or two, the black-clad trendies nursing their Saturday hangovers: a swirling cavalcade of brown and pink and olive-toned
Parisians—animated this isolated northern corner of the city.

Fatima shopped for carrots; for potatoes and onions and turnips, for
chickpeas and chicken legs, chicken thighs and lamb chops; aromatic
grains, seasonings, herbs and spices and thin, snaky lengths of merguez,
a lamb meat sausage. Ricky lingered beside her. He felt a bit awkward,
as if he were distracting her; but, at the same time, going to market
together, he felt somehow more connected to Fatima—as if they were
more of a couple. Between stops at various shops and stands, they continued their conversation.

"I don't want to say the wrong thing," Ricky confessed. "But—is
abortion allowed under Islamic law?"

"There is no religion that looks kindly upon it," Fatima said, fon-
dling mangoes. "But there are many issues to be considered. You know,
Reekee, I have dreams of my own. What about my desire to go to New
York to live and work?"

"What about it?"

"Could I fulfill this dream of mine with a baby?"

"I don't know. . . . Could you?"

Chatting now with a mushroom merchant, Fatima ignored Ricky's
question. Only after they strolled over to a cheese stand did she say,
"You know, being a single mother could be worse than aborting a
child . . . in some people's philosophee."

"You don't necessarily have to be a single mother."

Fatima did not respond to Ricky's comment immediately. It was only once they had moved on to the butcher's shop that she said, "Marrying a non-Muslim could be worse, in the eyes of some, than having a child out of wedlock."

"And do you really care about the eyes of some?"

"I recognize that the opinion of the father is also important." Fatima did not elaborate, and the comment hung, portentously, in the air.

They walked in silence down the rue de Trétaigne. Ricky found it sad that this pregnancy, which should have brought them closer, had seemed to create yet another obstacle between them. He did not even know—and perhaps she did not know either—whether the wiggly little sea horse inside her had been produced by Ricky or by the ex-boyfriend Fatima said she had seen recently, the infamous Bernard-Henri. He was burning to ask Fatima if she knew who the father was, but some mechanism within him—be it a function of gentlemanly discretion or fear of the truth—stopped him from posing such a loaded question.

"So what do you do tonight?" Fatima asked, as they approached her building.

"I'm going to Archie Dukes's place," Ricky said, "for that monthly dinner."

"Ah, yes. And tomorrow night?"

"I'm free all day tomorrow. And tomorrow night."

"Well, I wanted to propose to you a dinner at my house. I am having over my friends Christophe and Eve-Laure. I am making couscous. I think that perhaps you would like to join us."

Ricky tried to conceal his excitement. For almost a year, Fatima had bragged about her couscous but she had never deigned to prepare the dish for Ricky. And though he had heard a great deal about Fatima's good friends Christophe and Eve-Laure, she had never introduced him to them. Trying to play it cool, Ricky shrugged and said, "Sure. I'd be happy to come by tomorrow night."

They stopped in front of Fatima's doorway. "You can come by tonight also, if you like." Reaching into the pocket of her jacket, Fatima pulled out a pair of silver keys. "Maybe now is the time," she said, placing the keys in Ricky's hand. "Come to me after the dinner at Archie's. Okay?"

"Okay. But it might be very late."

"That is all right." Fatima leaned forward, kissed him lightly on the lips. "See you tonight." She punched in the door code and entered her building.

Ricky strode proudly up the rue de Trétaigne, holding the keys to Fatima's apartment, rubbing them softly between his fingers, as if they were some sacred talisman.

Street mimes in Paris don't move very much. They don't climb imaginary ladders or tiptoe along invisible tightropes. In all his years in Paris, Ricky had never seen a single mime do a Marcel Marceau routine with all its busy movements. For Valitsa the Serb and all the other mimes who worked the Butte Montmartre, the real physical challenge was *not* moving. The hill was populated with men and women painted as alabaster statues, or dressed like eighteenth-century fops and courtesans in powdered wigs, or musketeers and conquistadors with swords and shields. The mimes stood on little pedestals, maintaining frozen poses, barely even blinking. Only when a passerby dropped a coin into the basket beside the pedestal would the mime actually move. Usually they made some dramatic gesture. The musketeer might draw his weapon, quickly slice the air with the sword, then suddenly freeze again, holding the pose until the next pedestrian dropped a coin into the basket and he burst once more into a brief pantomime.

On this May Day morning, Valitsa the Serb was doing her Cleopatra act. She stood stock-still on her pedestal, dressed in a gold lamé gown and towering Egyptian crown, her face and arms and hands covered in gold paint, her eyes made up with thick black mascara. When Ricky located Valitsa, in front of Sacré Coeur, her frozen pose suggested that she was beseeching the gods, her glistening gold face turned upward, hands above her head, reaching for the heavens. A cluster of tourists was gathered around her and when one of them dropped a coin into her basket, Valitsa spun around on her pedestal and assumed a completely different pose, standing on one leg, the other kicking up behind her, arms jutting out, wrists and elbows bent at sharp right angles. She froze in that stance, like one of the people in that old "Walk Like an Egyptian" music video. The tourists tittered with delight, threw more coins into the basket.

As Valitsa contorted, then froze again, she spotted Ricky in the crowd and gave him a wink. He edged closer to the pedestal. He was hoping Valitsa would take a break soon so they could talk. He wanted to find out how Serena was doing. It had been only eight and a half hours since Ricky had left his cousin's runaway wife at the Serb's apartment. A coin dropped into the basket and Valitsa bent and twisted her body so that her crowned head was leaning close to Ricky.

"Empress," Ricky whispered. "I need to speak with you. Can you take a break in the next couple minutes?"

Valitsa very slightly tilted her head, once to the left, once to the right. Ricky took that as a no.

"Okay," he murmured as Valitsa remained frozen. "I have to go to work. I'm off at six. Will you still be here? Can we talk then?"

Another coin clinked into the basket and just as Valitsa launched into her next movement, she gave Ricky a quick wink and a nod. She then reached into a pocket of her gown and pulled out a long thin snake. The crowd gasped in unison. Valitsa froze, holding aloft the blue rubber asp. Ricky chuckled. He knew what was coming: Cleopatra's suicide. He wished he could stay and watch but it was almost noon and he had to get to the crêperie.

Ricky played in a daze that afternoon, oblivious to the commotion around him in Le Bon Montmartrois. His fingers bounced along the keyboard but he was not even consciously aware of what tunes he was banging out. He was on auto-pilot. In his mind's eye, he kept seeing that wiggling little figure on the sonogram screen, that tiny "sea horse"—the child, or soon-to-be-child, that he and Fatima had created together. He felt, almost literally, a certain weight on his shoulders. And he liked it. He realized that the nine years he had spent in Paris had been the happiest of his life. There had been a frivolity, a lightness and airiness about it all that, until now, had only given him pleasure. But everything had suddenly changed in a joyous, scary and wonderfully heavy way. For the past nine years, Ricky had felt sublimely free, unattached, rootless. Nothing, however, could be more binding, more serious, more rooted in responsibility, than parenthood. Yet, as unexpected as the prospect had been, he felt that, on some mysterious level, he had been preparing for it.

"Are you all right?" François asked after Ricky finished his set. Wedged between his double counter, François continued to prepare crêpes as he spoke. "You have a strange air about you today."

"Fatima is pregnant," Ricky said in a low voice, not wanting Dominique or one of the waitresses to hear.

"Congratulations!" François said, his normally gloomy face lighting up. "Are you not pleased?"

"Oh, I am. But a little worried, too, I guess."

"I understand. I, too, was worried. But you will get over it. My two children have brought me nothing but joy. Is it money that worries you?"

"Frankly, I haven't even started panicking about that yet but I suppose I will."

"Then perhaps this is good timing, the news I have for you. A friend of mine, he runs the contemporary music program at a little music school, just outside Paris. He asked me if you would be interested in teaching jazz and pop there."

"Me? I've never taught before in my life."

"So what?"

"So . . . so . . . Why would he be interested in hiring me?"

"He has heard you play here many times. He likes your style. Anyway, he asked if I could give him your phone number. He would like to call you to set up a meeting. Okay?"

"Okay. But if I was teaching at a conservatory, wouldn't I have to give up my job here?"

"Of course. You didn't want to play piano in a crêperie your whole life, did you? And besides, you would earn more money. And a job like that would help you get your immigration papers. All this is very important if you are going to be a father."

"Yeah. I know you're right. But there's another thing I'm wondering about."

"What is that?"

"Is the baby mine?"

Ricky spotted Valitsa the Serb on the west side of Sacré Coeur. She was sitting on her pedestal, still dressed in her lamé gown, her flesh painted gold. But her empress's crown was resting at her feet, her hair was concealed beneath a black bandana and she was totally out of character, smoking a cigarette. Sitting on a pedestal beside her was another street performer, his hair and body covered completely in white powder and paint. He wore a white toga and had a wreath of olive leaves tucked behind his ears. He, too, was smoking a cigarette. Mimes in repose.

"Having a good day?" Ricky asked.

"Not bad," Valitsa said. "For early in the season."

The living statue stubbed out his cigarette beneath one of his san-dalled feet, said he should get back to work. He picked up his pedestal and walked off.

"Listen," Ricky said, "I just wanted to thank you again for taking in Serena. It's really generous of you. How was she doing this morning?"

"By the time I woke up," Valitsa said, squinting as she took a drag on her cigarette, "Serena had disappeared."

"What do you mean, disappeared?"

"I mean she was gone. It was nine in the morning and there was no sign of her. Her bag of luggage, everything disappeared."

"She probably just decided to go out shopping or something. She has a set of keys, right? She may have returned to the apartment by now."

"I don't think she is coming back," Valitsa said darkly.

"Why not?"

"You remember that box I showed you yesterday, in my closet?"

"How could I forget?"

"One of the grenades is missing."

PART 4

Legends and Liars

Twelve

ARCHIE DUKES GOT ALL choked up watching the Million Man March—broadcast live from Washington, D.C., in October 1995—on television in his Paris living room. He had no strong feelings, one way or the other, about the event's organizer, Louis Farrakhan. And while he liked the idea of a million African-American males gathering for a day of togetherness and reflection on the Washington Mall, he had too much work to do at his Paris law firm to seriously consider flying across the Atlantic to attend the march. But watching the event on TV, Archie was more moved, more emotionally shaken up than he had been since the death of his first wife Ernestine five years earlier. The march had somehow gotten him in touch with something he felt was lacking in his life. He had lived in Paris for nearly forty years and he did not miss the United States of America at all. But there was a certain aspect of the U.S.A. that he longed for, a very specific type of social communion.

Archie Dukes decided to do something about it. This was the origin of Paris's famous Million Man Dinners.

If it was true that the great tradition of the black American expatriate in Paris was indeed over; and if it was also true that all people who left their countries were "weirdos"; and if ethnicity really did matter—even if severe ethnocentrism was inherently dangerous—then it was also a verifiable fact that a great many African-Americans living in the City of Light in the 1990s felt the need to seek each other out, to share their lives and experiences in ways that they could not with people of other backgrounds; to form, however loosely or noncommitally, a community. There were organizations created for support and consciousness-raising: Sisterhood, a black women's group, was at the center of Paris's African-American universe, the sisters being popular not only for their feminist gatherings but also for their annual family affairs, the Thanksgiving Day feast and Juneteenth picnic; and the Minority Caucus of Liberals Abroad which arranged meetings where black Americans could debate all the political issues raging on the other side of the ocean. Then there were all the informal social circles: the book clubs and Bible study groups, the folks who met regularly at jazz clubs and the basketball nuts who congregated to watch videotapes of NBA games sent over from the States. And, of course, there were the Sunday gospel brunches at Marva's Soul Food Kitchen, where one could binge on flapjacks and grits while listening to glorious voices belting out beautiful black spirituals.

But for Ricky Jenks, the best of all the community functions were the Million Man Dinners. Since November 1995, on the first Saturday of each month—except for July and August—any African-American male who lived in, or even just happened to be visiting Paris was invited to Archie Dukes's home for dinner. The events were thoroughly ethnocentric, nationalistic, chauvinist and segregated: Not only were there no women allowed but no Caribbeans, purebred Africans, South Americans or Arabs. It was Archie's house and Archie's rules applied. And it was, as well, Archie's treat. He bought and cooked the food and provided most of the wine. There was no charge, no fee, no commitment demanded of anyone who showed up on any given first Saturday. As a simple gesture of respect, one was expected to bring a bottle of wine—and if it was of poor quality or vintage, you could also expect to be publicly ridiculed, in a good-natured way, by the host. The most thought-ful guests hung around for the cleanup afterward. But the Million Man Dinners were, by and large, Archie Dukes's monthly gift to his brethren.

By the dinner of Saturday, May 1, 1999, Archie's gatherings had become an honored ritual. Unless Ricky had been out of town or had found it absolutely impossible to arrange a swap with Dominique at Le Bon Montmartrois, he had attended all of Archie's dinners. And on this May Day night, he was particularly thankful for a respite from his suddenly crazy "real life." Riding the metro down to Archie's place in a blandly middle-class area of the Fifteenth Arrondissement, Ricky knew that, for a few hours anyway, he would not have to worry about Fatima's pregnancy, about the murdered transsexual prostitute who, inexplicably, had keys to Ricky's apartment in her possession, about his upcoming meeting with Inspector Lamouche, about his cousin's runaway wife who had probably betrayed his trust and run away yet again, stealing a hand grenade from his friend the illegal arms trafficker. For this brief evening at Archie's, Ricky would be able to forget his woes and just hang with the brothers.

It was a pretty typical crowd at Archie's this first Saturday night, about thirty black American men sitting at two long tables arranged in an L-shape, the usual mix of regulars, newcomers and passers-through, the usual absence of several of Ricky's buddies who, for one reason or another that month, had not been able to show up. Ricky always loved the range of generations and professions, of economic and geographic backgrounds at Archie's place: There were the serious old-timers who had arrived with other American troops after D-Day in 1944 and decided to stay; the next generation, Archie's generation, who had found them-selves excluded from the bounty of the post-war American Dream of the nineteen-fifties and early sixties and come to Paris to realize their human potential; the draft dodgers, black hippies and all-around noncomformists of the late sixties, seventies and early eighties who saw expatriation to France as one of a variety of alternative lifestyle choices; the younger men who had arrived in the late eighties and nineties and—Ricky and a few others expected—tended to be more careerist, many of them having been sent to Paris by their corporations back in the States.

Archie's guests usually included lawyers, chefs, translators, a singer, a dancer, several musicians, an architect, a photographer, a painter, a novelist, a fashion designer, accountants, academics, waiters, bureaucrats, construction workers, furniture movers and computer programmers. They came from all over the States, some of them in Paris on multiyear stints, some on short-lived adventures, others expats-for-life. Many had European wives or lovers, others were partnered with Asians, Africans or other African-Americans. But they were all gathered together at Archie's to get something they could not get anywhere else in Paris, at least not in such strong and concentrated form, a vague but powerful sense of interconnectedness that might be called brotherhood.

By eleven o'clock, the salad and main course had been devoured. The ragged carcasses of five huge roast chickens rested in five pans scattered across the two long dinner tables that were also haphazardly decorated with an array of empty and half-full wine bottles. Ricky was caught up in three different conversations careening around his stretch of table, sliding in and out of the simultaneous discussions. Chauncy, Ellroy and Cliff, Ricky's fellow hoop fanatics, were having one of those impossible sports debates about which team would have prevailed over the other, the Magic-Kareem-Worthy L.A. Lakers of the 1980s or the Jordan-Pippen-Rodman Chicago Bulls of the 1990s. The fact that it was a completely hypothetical scenario did not lessen the fiery passions of the debaters, though Ricky only poured gasoline on the flames when he insisted that the Frazier-Reed-Bradley New York Knicks of the 1970s would have whipped both teams. Meanwhile two long-time Parisians, Freddy and Harlan, were trying to advise two relatively new arrivals, Alonzo and Phil, on the best ways to navigate France's bureaucratic paper chase. Though Freddy and Harlan both knew what they were talking about, they disagreed vehemently on several arcane points, only confusing poor Alonzo and Phil, not to mention Ricky. In the third conversation, Sam, Jamal and Leon, all of whom were active in Liberals Abroad, were arguing over whether Bill Clinton had actually done any real political good for African-Americans or if he just liked hugging black folks. On those occasions when Ricky jumped into the fight, he took the skeptical point of view, pointing out that "welfare reform" had dumped half a million more black Americans beneath the poverty line. One other talk was getting Ricky's peripheral attention: Edgar, Cleavon and Ralph, three of the white-haired old-timers, were quibbling over when certain black expats had married, divorced, died, or "gone back," that is to say, returned to live in the United States.

The chair at the head of Ricky's table was, at the moment, empty. Archie Dukes must have disappeared into the kitchen to get more wine. Earlier in the evening, Ricky had considered asking Archie and the other veteran expats if they had known Serena Moriarty. But then he remembered that Serena had said she didn't hang out with other black Americans when she'd lived in Paris. And besides, Ricky reminded himself, this was his night to ignore the madness of the past two days. He tried to put Serena out of his mind.

"All right, y'all," Archie announced as he emerged from the kitchen, carrying a huge platter. "I've noticed you fellas don't seem to go for the cheese course." He took his seat and placed the round wooden platter in front of him. Ricky counted ten different cheeses on the tray. "Every month, I try to educate you bums with some of the finest *fromages* France has to offer. And usually, most of it goes uneaten. So tonight, I've busted out something special." Archie delicately lifted a circular mound of white cheese, partially wrapped in tissue-like paper, from the platter. "This here is a Langres," Archie informed his guests. "The French say it smells..." He paused for effect, then sighed, "... like an angel's pussy." He turned to Ricky. "Richard Jenks. You're a somewhat cultivated man. Take a whiff of this."

Archie reached across two other guests to hand Ricky the cheese. Raising the soft mound to his nose, noticing that a thin slice had been carved out of it, revealing a creamy yellow interior, Ricky immediately caught the fragrance. He inhaled deeply, then burst into giggles. The Langres had an unmistakable bodily odor about it, distinctly feminine, and, at the same time, sweetly, intoxicatingly perfumed. The scent was so familiar, yet so ethereally dulcet, and so completely unexpected in a slice of cheese, that Ricky could not speak—he was laughing too hard.

"Lemme get a hit of that," Wallace said, reaching across the table and pulling the cheese out of Ricky's hand. Wallace was in his fifties, an architect with an athletic physique. Though married to a French-woman, he enjoyed a reputation as something of a "player." Wallace held the cheese close to his nose, closed his eyes and sniffed. A lascivious smile crept across his face as he opened his eyes. "Oh, my Lord. If that's what an angel's pussy smells like, I can't *wait* to get to Heaven."

Wallace handed the mound to Cleavon, the snowy-haired elder sitting to his right. Cleavon took a whiff of the cheese, then jerked his head back, scowling. Just about everybody at the two tables saw his reaction and laughed. Edgar, one of his fellow World War II vets, said, "Cleavon think it just smells like pussy!"

Hunter, a translator in his early thirties and one of Archie's regular gay guests, also laughed but said, in half-serious exasperation, "Must we always end up talking about pussy?"

"Speaking of pussy," Ricky said. Once the laughter died down, he continued, out of sheer curiosity. "I have an honest inquiry to make. A friend of mine is trying to track down a sister who used to live here back in the eighties. Anyone remember a Serena Moriarty?"

There was much buzzing among the older expats. Fellas remembered Serena Buford, full-figured gal used to work as a secretary at the American embassy. Then there was Serena Rawls: Her husband was on a two-year stint in Paris, working for Proctor and Gamble—nice lady, very active in Sisterhood. And wasn't there another Serena, about twenty years ago, studying at the Sorbonne? She had a huge 'fro and was writing her dissertation on the Algerian war for independence. That Serena must have been about six feet tall.

"No, no, no," Ricky said. "The Serena I'm talking about is almost petite. She was a singer. And very light-skinned. In fact, she's a dead ringer for Mariah Carey."

This set off an eruption of horny exclamation. "Now you know I'd be all over *that!*" Wallace shouted above the clamor.

"Yo yo yo, Ricky," Garrett, a young chef, called out from the far end of the other table, clear across the room, "if I find her, do I get to keep her?"

Archie Dukes seemed baffled. "Who's Mariah Carey?" he asked.

"Aw, man," Wallace answered. "One of the biggest R&B acts of the nineties. High yellow gal, long brown hair."

"I don't know if I'd call her R&B," Alonzo said.

"And I don't know if I'd say she has brown hair," Jamal added.

"Every time she puts out a new video, her hair gets more blond."

"What is this shit with black women dying their hair blond?" Freddy blustered. "That chick in TLC. And the other one in that new group, Destiny's Child. Why are these sisters trying to look like fucking Christie Brinkley? If God had intended black women to have blond hair he'd have made them as stupid as white women!"

"Now, now, Freddy," somebody said.

"Encroaching blondness," Spencer muttered. He was a brother about Ricky's age who often described himself as "an obscure novelist." Spencer took a sip of his wine, then added, "Another sign of the coming Apocalypse. Pass that cheese."

"So I guess no one's heard of Serena Moriarty," Ricky said. "I think she was one of those black Americans who disappeared into France."

"Speaking of missing persons," Archie said, "you know who I thought of today when I read the newspaper? Lonnie John."

"You mean *Li'l* Lonnie John?" Wallace asked.

"Wasn't ever no *Big* Lonnie John," Archie replied. "Of course Li'l Lonnie John."

"Who's Li'l Lonnie John?" Ricky wanted to know.

"You mean to tell me you've never heard of Li'l Lonnie John?" Archie shot back, as if shocked by Ricky's ignorance.

"Sorry. Who is he?"

"He was a goddamned pimp!" snowy-haired Cleavon interjected. "Used to run them whores in the Bois de Boulogne."

"Not so," Archie said. "The Bois de Boulogne was where you had transvestite whores. Li'l Lonnie John pimped normal female whores in the Bois de Vincennes."

" '*Bois?*' " the newcomer Alonzo asked uncertainly. "What does '*bois*' mean?"

"I remember him well," Cleavon continued. "Short, light-skinned fella. One of them well-spoken hoodlums. Cut your throat just as soon as look at you."

" '*Bois*' means 'woods,' " Harlan explained to Alonzo. "The Bois, or the Woods of Boulogne, is just outside Paris to the west. The Bois de Vincennes is just outside Paris to the east. Basically, they're huge parks,

I mean, really huge, with public and private areas. Princess Di and Dodi were driving out to a mansion in the Bois de Boulogne when their car crashed."

"And the Bois de Boulogne," Freddy jumped in, "is also known for its chicks with dicks."

"Transvestite prostitutes," Harlan clarified.

"But the Bois de Vincennes," Archie said, "specializes in normal female whores and those were the kind Li'l Lonnie John used to pimp. Let's be clear about that."

"Wasn't Lonnie John a faggot, though?" Ralph, one of the elders, asked.

"Hell no!" Cleavon said. "And he'd slit your damn throat if you so much as called him a faggot."

"Could we please not use the word 'faggot'?" Hunter, the gay translator, asked.

"Sorry, brother," Cleavon said. "The point is Lonnie John was real short; he had a baby face and a high voice but he wasn't no . . . homosexual. He had women all over him. And I'm sure he fucked 'em all."

"For whatever *that's* worth," Hunter said cryptically.

"So these *bois*," Alonzo asked, "are full of prostitutes?" He was a pleasant, thirtyish computer programmer and on this, his second night at a Million Man Dinner, he seemed extremely disturbed by what he was hearing.

"Certain sections, yeah," Wallace explained. "Now, in the Bois de Vincennes, which, keep in mind, is enormous, there's a French army barracks. And across from those barracks is a long, narrow asphalt road. And all up and down that road you'll see these white vans that look like they've been sitting in one spot for years—because they have. These are basically four-wheeled whorehouses. The hookers take the soldiers, or whoever, in there to do their business."

"You seem to be awfully knowledgeable on this subject," Freddy teased Wallace. "Don't tell me you're a regular customer."

"Fuck no!" Wallace retorted. "I ain't never paid for sex in my life. Except for with my wife. And if you was married to a Frenchwoman, you'd know exactly what the fuck I mean."

"Lonnie John was a bad motherfucker," a low, crackly voice announced from the far end of Ricky's table.

"Say what?" Freddy called out.

"I say Li'l Lonnie John was one of the baddest black men Europe has ever seen," Ezra Peachtree growled. Ricky had met Ezra before at Archie's dinners. Almond-toned with a shaved head and long face that was at once youthful and strong, weathered and knowing, Ezra could have been anywhere between an old-looking thirty-five and and a well-preserved fifty—it was impossible to tell. He rarely spoke and gave the definite impression that he did not want to be asked any questions. Since Ricky only saw Ezra in gatherings of black American men, Peachtree's reticence was always respected. No one knew where he lived, what he did for a living, how long he had been or was planning to stay in Paris. But he was always welcome at Archie's. And now that he chose to speak, everyone leaned in close to hear his scratchy voice.

"I knew Lonnie John in the service. We were both on a base in Aviano, Italy. He used to run whores there, too. Precocious motherfucker. Anyway, he wasn't doin' nothin' a lot of American servicemen hadn't done before him. But Lonnie John was too bold about it. Did it too well, too . . . lucratively. So they kicked his ass out. Dishonorable discharge. That was when he came to Paris. Back in the early eighties."

Archie Dukes seemed as surprised as anyone by Ezra Peachtree's sudden burst of loquacity. "Exactly," he said. "That's what I always heard. After the military, Li'l Lonnie John decided to become a full-time pimp in Paris, or just outside Paris to be exact. He was the man who brought black pussy to the Bois de Vincennes. And the clients liked it so much, he got in trouble with the pimps pushin' white pussy."

"Now that's not what I heard," said Wallace, the knowledgeable player. "There had been black hoes in the Bois de Vincennes before. What was new was a black pimp. And a black American pimp who played by black American street rules, which is to say, if you fucked with him—"

"He'd slit your damn throat," Cleavon cried.

"And many a throat was slit out there, back in the day," Wallace said.

"But it wasn't Li'l Lonnie John doin' the throat-slittin'," Ezra Peachtree said. "So far as I understand, Lonnie would threaten you, but he
had his partner, Maximillian, who would inflict the punishment. He was
some Romanian dude, grew up in the circus. Parents used to do one of
them knife-throwin' acts, you know? Pops whippin' them knives at
Momma so they stick—*Thwaaaannnggg!*—in the wall just inches away
from her ears, her tits, her thighs. I don't know where Lonnie met him,
but Maximillian was the henchman, the enforcer, the throat-slitter. Max
the Knife. Crazy motherfuckin' Romanian."

Everyone at the two tables was silent, struck by the quiet authority
of Ezra's rarely heard voice.

"All right," Archie finally said. "If it wasn't Li'l Lonnie John slittin'
throats, musta been this dude Maximillian. But either way, Lonnie alienated the other pimps in the Bois de Vincennes."

"He was too good a businessman," Wallace said. "They didn't dig
his American capitalist tactics."

"So whatever happened to this Lonnie John?" Ricky asked.

"He was run outta France," Archie said. "Just as he was run outta
the U.S. military. The French gangsters got organized, chased him outta
the country. He tried to set up operations in Istanbul. Last I heard,
Lonnie John was in a Turkish prison."

"So if he wasn't takin' it up the ass then," Wallace said, smirking,
"he definitely is now." After hearing the groans of disapproval, mixed
in with the subdued laughter, Wallace turned to Hunter and said, "Sorry,
bro'." Hunter just rolled his eyes in mild annoyance.

"So what made you think of Lonnie John, Archie?" Cleavon asked
the host.

"I read in the *Faits Divers* today about a whore who had her throat
slit."

" '*Faits divers?*' " Alonzo, who had already seemed perplexed by the
evening's goings-on, now sounded utterly lost.

"Literally, it means 'diverse facts,' " Harlan explained. "You know
how in American tabloid newspapers the front page usually features
some sick murder or rape or whatnot? In France, all that shit gets
dumped deep inside the paper, in a column called '*Faits Divers.*' "

"Anyway," Archie continued, "I read today in the *Faits Divers* that some hooker got her throat slit up in your neighborhood, Ricky."

"Oh, yeah?"

"Oh, yeah indeed," Archie replied. "On your very block."

"Here we go again!" Hunter cried. "A bunch of intelligent African-American men and ultimately all we wind up talking about is pussy!"

"Speaking of pussy," Wallace said, "for all the talking we do, we never really address the question: How can you tell when it's good pussy?"

Wallace's query momentarily quieted the table. Ricky wondered if this was a straight line Wallace was presenting, if he was just laying the trap, waiting for some sucker to walk in so he could zap you with the punch line. Or was it a sort of riddle, some earthy-cosmic category of Delphic inquiry? Or was Wallace, the legendary player, sincerely looking for some sort of sexual counselling from his brothers? After a long, uncertain silence, Spencer, the obscure novelist, said, almost under his breath, but just loud enough for everyone at the two tables to hear him: "No seeds."

It was a long time before the quintessentially male laughter finally stopped.

After the usual 12:30–12:45 exodus of guests rushing to catch the last metro home, there were only about fifteen brothers left at Archie's place, sitting in pairs or trios, talking and drinking, surrounded by empty chairs, at the two long tables. Ricky was sitting beside Cleavon, polishing off a bottle of Cahors and listening to the old man's reminiscences about the glory days of the Café Tournon, in the heart of the Left Bank, where all the black American legends of the 1950s used to hang out. Cleavon knew them all: Wright, Baldwin, Harrington, Himes. "Ah, you shoulda been here then," Cleavon said. "Where were you in nineteen fifty-nine?"

"My mother's belly," Ricky said.

"Oh well," the old-timer replied magnanimously. "That's not your fault."

Cleavon was in the middle of a long and complicated anecdote when he abruptly told Ricky he had to go pee. As Cleavon stumbled off to the bathroom, Archie Dukes took his chair. "How ya doin', my man?"

"Good, Archie, real good. Thanks for another terrific dinner."

"My pleasure, youngblood, my pleasure." Archie poured himself a glass of the wine. "Listen, I talked to Marva Dobbs this morning. She told me about you finding this hooker's body—and your little encounter with the police."

"Yeah, I had a feeling you might have heard about it, the way you were talking tonight." Ricky and Archie both spoke quietly so as not to be overheard by the brothers nearby. "Don't tell me you think this Lonnie John guy is involved."

"Ricky, I just don't know. Lonnie, last I heard, was still in that Turkish prison. But one thing I didn't say earlier is that Lonnie John had a sister."

"Oh yeah?"

"Oh yeah," Archie said, his eyes glimmering behind his Malcolm X glasses. "Most folks don't know about her. Name was Cassandra. I met her only once, at Marva's restaurant, fourteen, fifteen years ago. Beautiful. One of the most astonishingly beautiful women I've ever laid eyes on. Anyway, Li'l Lonnie John was her pimp."

"What?"

"That's right. This motherfucker was so ruthless he pimped his own damn sister. Can you believe that shit?"

"She was a hooker in the Bois de Vincennes?"

"No way. She was too fine for the streets. Lonnie John sold her to private clients. Wealthy Frenchmen who'd fuck her in fancy hotel rooms. Lonnie knew he had to keep her under wraps. That's why most folks in this town who've heard of Li'l Lonnie John don't even know he had a sister. But I knew. And Marva knew. In fact, Marva knew Cassandra quite well. And when she spoke with me this morning, she was feeling very disturbed. She told me about your cousin and that wife of his."

"Did she?"

"Uh-huh. And she also told me about the photo of the wife you showed her." Archie paused to take a sip of wine. "I think you can guess where I'm going with this."

"You wanna see it?" Ricky pulled out his wallet, removed the photo of Cash's wife and handed it to Archie.

"Oh yeah," Archie said immediately. "That's Cassandra, all right.

Not a face one is likely to forget. Though I suppose she calls herself Serena now."

What Ricky felt at that moment was a simmering anger, though he tried not to show it. He was angry at Serena, or Cassandra or whatever the fuck her name was, for not telling him the truth about herself. He was angry at his cousin Cash for getting him mixed up in his marital psychodrama. And he was angry at Marva Dobbs. He almost told Archie that he had seen Serena/Cassandra the night before but decided against it. He needed to know more before he revealed anything else. "So," Ricky said, "why did Marva lie to me and say she didn't recognize her?"

Archie emitted a strange little laugh. "Well, youngblood, I think Marva may have felt like she was looking at a ghost. You see, Cassandra John contracted AIDS three years after Lonnie started pimping her. She died in a Paris hospital in nineteen eighty-seven."

"Get the fuck outta here."

"I kid you not, Ricky. Now, like I say, I only met the girl once and she looked fit as a fiddle. But Marva visited Cassandra in the hospital. In fact..." Archie spoke very slowly now, letting each word fall like a heavy blow: "Marva...watched...her...die."

"Jesus Christ."

"Now," Archie Dukes said, "can you explain to me how it is that your cousin is married to a dead woman?"

Ricky thought for a moment, then gave the only honest answer: "No."

Thirteen

WAS THAT LAUGHTER RICKY heard behind Fatima's door? Impossible. Fatima Boukhari was a studious young woman who ordinarily liked to be in bed by midnight. Ricky stood outside her apartment, holding the keys she had given him Saturday morning. For months, he had dreamed of being able to show up at Fatima's place at any hour, to enter her home in the middle of the night, slip into bed with her and hold her tight as she slept. But now, standing in front of the door, poised with the keys in his hand, Ricky wondered if he was hallucinating. How could it be that at two thirty in the morning, there was the faint sound of laughter coming from inside Fatima Boukhari's apartment?

Maybe, Ricky thought, he had had too much to drink. Or his mind was playing tricks on him after all the weird shit he had heard at the Million Man Dinner. During the taxi ride back up to the Eighteenth from Archie Dukes's place, Ricky's anger at Cash and Marva and Serena had subsided. Now, he was only angry with himself. He felt that, once again in this life, he had allowed himself to be played for a chump. Why was it that people felt they could brazenly lie to Ricky Jenks, trick him, use him, toy with his feelings? The word SAP must have been scrawled across his forehead. He didn't know what sort of fucked-up game Cash and Marva and Serena, or Cassandra or whatever the hell her name was, were playing. He only knew he wanted no part of it. As the taxi stopped in front of the building on the rue de Trétaigne, Ricky decided he would tell Fatima everything. At breakfast Sunday morning, he would relate all the bizarre events he had kept from her over the past two days. Fatima was so smart. She would definitely have good advice for Ricky on how to extricate himself from this mess that he should never have been involved in at all.

Deciding that the laughter could not possibly be emanating from Fatima's apartment—it must have been coming from across the hall—Ricky turned the key in the lock and pushed open the door. There was Fatima, dressed in a T-shirt and gym shorts, stretched out on the couch, her left leg suspended in the air. She was giggling merrily, covering her mouth with her hand to stifle the sound of her laughter. Standing at the end of the couch, slightly hunched over, holding Fatima's long and slender left foot, squeezing, fondling, massaging it, was Dr. Cash Washington.

"Obviously," Cash said, "you're suffering from a mild case of plantar fasciitis."

Only then did Fatima notice the man standing in the doorway. "Ree-kee!" she squealed.

"Yo, cuz!" Cash said, striding across the room and holding out his hand. "We've been waiting for you."

"Close the door!" Fatima gasped between giggles.

Ricky did as he was told, then offered his cousin a limp hand to shake. "What the fuck are you doing here?" he asked, so softly he might as well have been talking only to himself.

"I came back from Zurich a day early," Cash said, displaying his broad, telegenic grin. "I tried you at your apartment and at the crêpe shop but you weren't there. Your mom gave me Fatima's number last week. She said that you had said only to use it in an emergency and I figured, what the fuck, I guess this qualifies."

"What the fuck!" Fatima said, slowly sitting up on the couch. Ricky could not help but notice how her nipples pressed against the gray cotton T-shirt.

"So what's up?" Cash said. "Make any progress in our little research project?"

"None," Ricky deadpanned. He looked his cousin up and down. Cash was wearing an immaculate white shirt with a button-down collar and yellow "power tie." The pants of his black, pinstriped suit were sharply creased, his black shoes gleamed. Then Ricky noticed the two empty glasses on the coffee table, and the two bottles of champagne, one empty, one half full. Cash's pinstriped jacket was flung across an armchair. "How long have you been here?"

"Oh, about four hours," Cash said. "You really don't have any news for me?"

"Reekee! Why you never tell me about this wonderful cousin of your?" Fatima was clearly drunk, a fact that would have surprised Ricky under any circumstances but one he found particularly unsettling since she was pregnant. "You never tell me anything about your family. Why?"

"It was up to me to educate your lovely lady about our illustrious clan," Cash said, smiling winningly. "She knew nothing of our noble heritage."

Ricky did not respond.

"Let's go!" Fatima yelped, springing up from the couch. "Cash want to take us out on the town!"

"Most places in Paris close at two," Ricky said.

"Naaaaw." Cash shook his head. "I know a place that doesn't even get goin' till three, man."

"I go dress myself," Fatima said, disappearing into the bedroom.

Cash saw the worry in Ricky's face. "Relax, cuz. It's my treat. I've got a car and a driver waiting around the corner. You and your lady are in good hands."

Cash, nostrils twitching, took a big sniff of the air in front of him.

Ricky could hear the snot curdling in Cash's nasal canals. Remembering what Serena had told him about Cash's addiction, Ricky wondered, fleetingly, if his cousin had snorted cocaine in Fatima's apartment. But Ricky quickly ruled out the possibility. There was no way that could have happened. No way.

"Let's take the death route, Yuri!" Cash called out from the backseat of the limousine.

"Yes, doctor," the driver said, his black chauffeur's cap pulled down so low on his brow that Ricky could barely see his eyes in the rearview mirror.

"The what?" Fatima asked, sounding alarmed.

"You'll see," Cash replied. "Have some more." Fatima raised her glass and Cash poured fresh, fizzing champagne into it. A new bottle had been waiting for them in the cooler in the back of the limo. "Sure you won't have some, cuz?"

"No thanks," Ricky said. He stared out the window as the car sped down the nearly deserted rue d'Amsterdam, past the darkened windows of office buildings and the massive railroad station, the Gare Saint-Lazare. Cash wouldn't say where he was taking them. He wanted it to be a surprise. Fatima was all made up, black tumult of hair cascading down her shoulders. She wore a black velvet jacket over the same summery dress she had sported when Ricky first met her at Marva's country house: tantalizingly low cut, the same color as the bubbly wine she sipped from the fluted glass.

"Anyway," Cash said to Fatima, "to get back to what we were talking about earlier, you would love New York."

"I already love it," Fatima gushed. "I told you, I spent six month there."

"Oh, yeah, right. When was that?"

"The first half of nineteen ninety-three."

"Oh, girl, that was the olden times. Prehistory. Pre-Rudy. The city's totally changed since Giuliani became mayor."

"Yeah," Ricky said, "I hear it's like a police state now."

"No more so than Paris," Cash shot back. "Cleaner and safer than ever. The whole city's booming. Do you know there's a Starbucks in Harlem?"

"What is Starbucks?" Fatima asked.

"The McDonald's of coffee shops," Ricky said.

Cash ignored him. "My main residence is in Tarrytown, on the Hudson River. But I keep an apartment in the city. Whenever you come to New York and need a place to stay, just let me know, Fatima."

Cash pronounced her name in the American way: Fuh-TEE-ma. Usually, when people made that mistake, they could expect to be corrected. "You mean FAH-tee-ma," Fatima would say. But on this night, she let Cash go on mispronouncing. Maybe she thought it was cute, the way Cash said her name, just as Ricky had always found Fatima's squawky rendition of his name cute. Until this night, when it suddenly got on his nerves.

"Reekee was a fool to leave New York. Paris is totally dead compared to the Big Apple. I can't wait to get back!"

"Like the song says," Cash crooned, " 'If you can make it there, you'll make it . . .' "

He waved a hand in the air as he sang. And Ricky wondered: How did he get away with it? Dr. Cash Washington was always so transparent; his eagerness to charm, to flatter, to woo, was so nakedly obvious, Ricky would have thought that at least some people would be wary, maybe just a little bit skeptical, mistrusting of the act. But everybody seemed to fall for it. Ricky could see how Clementine Yerby would have been a sucker for Cash. She was the shy wallflower, the nerdy "late bloomer" who had rarely been asked out on a date. Oh, yeah. Clemmy would have been easy pickin's for cousin Cash. But how had he worked his spell on the likes of streetwise Serena Moriarty? Or Cassandra John, if they were one and the same person? Or was it that Serena-Cassandra had outcharmed the charmer? Who was zoomin' who there? Yet, Marva Dobbs, an extremely astute judge of character, had also been gaga for Dr. Cash. And now here was Fatima Boukhari, whose bullshit detector seemed to have been honed to a supersensitive acuity after her experience with Bernard-Henri, lapping up Cash Washington's flagrant lie of himself.

But hadn't Ricky also been duped by Cash? Even now. He looked at his cousin doing his best Sinatra imitation while his hand floated in the air, caressing the air, like a conductor lovingly directing an orchestra. Ricky had never noticed just how large Cash's hands were. They were beautifully formed, with the long, tapered fingers of a sculpture by Rodin. So unlike Ricky's chubby digits. A surgeon's hands. But then Ricky remembered that Cash's big hand, wafting like a butterfly in the back of the limo had, just last week, smashed a woman in the face.

Ricky wanted to blow Cash's cover, right here, right now. To tell Fatima: *"Open your eyes, damn it! This man is a coke-snorting drug addict! A wife-beating monster!"* But he decided to try to stay cool, see how the night played out, learn what more he could about this intrigue he had been sucked into. Thursday afternoon Cash had tearfully told Ricky how much he loved his wife, how desperately he needed to be reunited with her. But what did he really want from Serena? Ricky had taken Cash's money to find his wife but then wound up promising Serena he would hide her from Cash. Now Ricky wasn't even sure who Serena was. But he knew that it was a live woman he had met twenty-four hours earlier, not some ghost of a prostitute. And this Yuri, who was now driving them down the rue Auber: he was the Russian chauffeur who had shown up at Serena's hotel, trying to hunt her down. Ricky wanted to blurt out everything he knew. But he realized that, when you got right down to it, he had no idea what the hell was going on.

"And what about the Muslim communitee in New York?" Fatima asked. "During the time I lived there, I met no Muslims at all."

Cash frowned. "What did you want to meet them for?"

"I am myself Muslim."

"Oh, Well, you might want to consider changing your affiliation," Cash said matter-of-factly. "The Judeo-Christian tradition in America is very strong. When it comes to Muslims, Americans basically have two impressions. Either you're one of those dumbass Negroes in a bow tie, part of the Fruit of Islam, or you're an Arab terrorist in a turban."

Fatima looked confused. "Truthfully?"

"Would I lie to you, sweetheart? I figure if you're coming to America, you want to be part of the mainstream. And, as far as the mainstream is concerned, Muslims are either dumbasses in bow ties talkin' a lot of anti-white bullshit or they're terrorists in turbans, like those motherfuckers who tried to blow up the World Trade Center back when you were living in the city, in early 'ninety-three."

Ricky would have expected Fatima to be furious. Instead she nodded as Cash spoke, that sad and bewildered look still on her face. "I did not realize," she said.

"I suppose there is one other category of Muslim in New York but that would be taxi driver and I doubt you'd be coming to New York to drive a damn cab."

"Here we are, sir," Yuri announced. The limo glided into the fabulous Place Vendôme. In the center of the large plaza was a towering pillar, with a statue of Napoleon Bonaparte dressed as Caesar poised atop it. Surrounding the pillar was an array of some of the world's most expensive jewelry and fashion shops, the French Ministry of Justice and, of course, the Hôtel Ritz. Yuri pulled up alongside the three other limousines parked in front of the hotel.

"Finish your drink," Cash said to Fatima. She quickly obeyed, downing the rest of the champagne in her glass.

"I don't know if I'm dressed for this place," Ricky said.

"Okay," Cash barked at Yuri. "Hit it!"

The car bolted away from the Ritz, flying out of the Place Vendôme and down the rue de Castiglione. Fatima screamed.

"What the fuck are you doing?" Ricky yelled.

"It's the death route!" Cash cried over the *vroom* of the engine and the screech of the tires as the limo turned onto the rue de Rivoli, running a red light.

Ricky held onto Fatima, who was rigid in his arms, her mouth open, letting out a sustained squeal so high-pitched it was almost inaudible, like a dog whistle. "What's your fucking problem!" Ricky shouted.

"Okay," Cash said, "the paparazzi are on our tails! Riding their motorbikes, in hot pursuit as we make our escape!"

Yuri took a hairpin turn onto the Place de la Concorde. At three in the morning, there was sparse traffic around the giant Egyptian obelisk at the center of the plaza but the chauffeur seemed to take pleasure in passing dangerously close to the cars that were there. Horns honked frantically as Yuri weaved in and out of the traffic at an insanely high speed.

"All right, I get it!" Fatima shrieked.

"They were desperate to escape the paparazzi but those locusts were still bearing down on them on their motos." Cash spoke with a measured urgency, like a sportscaster describing a horse race. "Dodi screamed to the driver 'Faster, Henri Paul, faster!' "

"*Oui, monsieur!*" Yuri cried, playing along with the game.

"Are you out of your fucking mind?" Ricky screamed. He wanted to grab Cash by the throat but he had his arms full of Fatima who was clutching him in apparent terror as the car swerved around two other madly honking vehicles and tore down the straightaway of the Cours la Reine, the River Seine a passing blur on the left, the Eiffel Tower, all lit up, like a glittering toy against a purple sky, off in the distance but looming ever larger as they sped along the narrow road.

"Here is where the white Fiat appears," Cash continued in his rapid-fire narration of the chase. "Pulling up alongside the Mercedes. Dodi wants to tell Di what's going on, wants to ask her who these fuckers are but he knows she can't hear him and can't talk—her head is in his lap and her mouth is full! Dodi doesn't know that his driver is strung out on cheap wine and Prozac as he commands 'Faster, Henri Paul, faster! Fasteeeeeeeer!' "

"*Oui, monsieur!*"

Zooming into the mouth of the tunnel, Cash was bouncing in his seat, grinning like a crazed little boy. "We've lost the paparazzi on their motos but here comes the white Fiat, pulling ahead of us. And then— the white flash! Henri Paul is blinded! We're veering out of control! Aaaaaaaarrrrrrrrrrrgggggggggggghhhhhhhh!"

Yuri brought the limo within inches of the concrete pillars dividing the lanes in the tunnel. Ricky shut his eyes tight, anticipating a shower of glass in his face once the car hit a pillar. Fatima's fingernails were digging into his flesh now. He clenched his teeth, waiting for the shattering impact. Cash's theatrical holler, the screech of the tires and Fatima's blood-freezing scream deafened him. He knew they were all about to die.

Then, the car began to slow down. Ricky opened his eyes and saw Yuri guide them out of the brightly-lit tunnel, back into the dark night. There was the Eiffel Tower again, its spindly frame glowing like some skeletal spacecraft. The limousine decelerated to a pleasant cruising speed as Yuri drove toward the Place de l'Alma.

"And that," Cash announced, still grinning, "was the death route."

Ricky felt Fatima's body relax. They released each other from their terrified, pre-crash grip. Fatima slid away from Ricky on the slick leather seat. For a long moment, she was perfectly silent and still. Then her face quivered slighty and Ricky feared Fatima might start crying. Instead, she exploded in hysterical laughter. She leaned forward, clutching her belly, roaring with manic glee. Cash laughed along with her. Finally, when Fatima managed to get out a few words, she sputtered, "I—love—it!" She then succumbed once more to convulsive cackling.

Cash clapped his hands. "Bravo, Yuri."

Ricky saw the driver's face in the rearview mirror. Yuri grinned, displaying a mouthful of jagged, yellow teeth. His cap was still pulled down so low that Ricky could not see his eyes. But he guessed that the uniformed chauffeur was a young man, still in his early twenties.

"You didn't know I was this wild, didja?" Cash asked Ricky, as if he were proud of himself. Ricky did not respond.

Yuri slowly circled the so-called Princess Diana memorial. Even after 3 A.M. there was a small cluster of mourners gathered around the gold flame, bouquets of fresh flowers decorating the base of the torch, new photos of the dead royal plastered on the monument that had been appropriated for her.

Cash and Fatima were both laughing and applauding. And Ricky wondered if maybe Clementine Yerby, his ex-fiancée, had been right, the last time he saw her, all those years ago. Maybe Cassius Washington really was the devil.

"You are just jealous," Fatima said hotly. "Because your cousin is a success and you are not!"

Fatima's words were like a scorching slap across his face. Ricky didn't know how to respond so he simply turned away and looked across the room and out the long picture window at the gigantic Arc de Triomphe, its pale stone immensity bathed in golden klieg lighting. In all his years in Paris he had never been in any joint like this, the VIP lounge of

an exclusive nightclub called Les Enfants de l'Enfer. After the entertainment of the death route, Yuri parked the limo in front of the elegant
façade of a building in the ultra-rich Sixteenth Arrondissement. Emerg-
ing from the car, Ricky saw a uniformed doorman and a burly bouncer
guarding the entrance. But there was no sign over the door. Twenty or
so well-dressed Parisian yuppies stood outside, waiting to be allowed past
the velvet rope barrier. "We'll be back whenever," Cash said to Yuri.

Upon seeing Cash, the doorman smiled and bowed. *"Bonsoir, monsieur,"* he trilled, unhooking a length of velvet rope and nodding toward
Ricky and Fatima. "Zey are wiz you?" Assured that they were Cash's
friends, the doorman allowed Ricky and Fatima to follow the good doctor
into the club. Cash led them across a crowded dance floor. Ricky saw
the vacant eyes and hollow cheeks of fashion models, the thickly moussed
hair and well-toned torsos of their suitors. The clubbers moved stiffly to
the monotonous electronic beat, striking poses rather than really dancing,
in the shadowy blue light. Ricky finally saw the name of the place,
written in neon cursive over a mirror behind the bar: The Children of
Hell.

They followed Cash through a metal door and up a narrow staircase.
Cash paused in front of a wide door upholstered in brown leather, pressed
the buzzer beside it. A gorgeous Frenchwoman with artfully disheveled
hair opened the door and greeted Cash with a big hug and an ardent
kiss on each cheek. "So good to see you again, *docteur*." Cash introduced
Ricky and Fatima. "I am Esmerelda," the hostess said, somehow boast-
fully. "Welcome to ze VIP lounge."

Esmerelda escorted them into a large salon with red carpeting and
red walls, furnished with plushly cushioned divans, armchairs and
booths, all of them in varying shades of scarlet, crimson, ruby. There
were mirror-topped tables and glittering chandeliers. An older Frenchwoman with an elaborate platinum hairdo, dressed in a sequined gown,
was offering a passable rendition of "I Get a Kick Out of You," holding
the microphone too close to her lips as an emaciated, dull-eyed guy in
an oversized white dinner jacket banged away on the electric keyboard
beside her. The VIP lounge was filled with rich-looking men in suits,
mostly middle-aged, sometimes fat, often balding. But the women with

them were uniformly young and glamorous. They preened like starlets but were dressed like call girls, in microscopic skirts and lacy or leathery blouses cut so low they barely concealed their areolae—long-legged, long-haired vixens with the ripe and ready-to-fuck look of women in porno films. And all of these luscious babes were hanging onto oily bastards they could not possibly find attractive but who, obviously, could afford them.

Esmerelda sat Cash, Ricky and Fatima at a corner booth. Cash ordered a bottle of Dom Pérignon. Fatima gazed at the salon crowd in wide-eyed amazement. Even in her sexy, champagne-colored dress, Fatima looked like a nun in this joint.

"What the fuck, Cash," Ricky said. "Are you a regular or something?"

"Only since last night. One of my business associates brought me here."

"I thought you were in Zurich last night."

Ricky saw the surprise in Cash's eyes. "Oh, er, no," the doctor stammered. "I came back to Paris *two* days early."

"Is that so?"

Cash abruptly changed the subject, started talking about globalization. "We've gotta get on board. Black folks can't afford to be left behind." Ricky remembered what Serena had told him about Cash's desire to be a tycoon, to make his first billion by the age of forty. "I've got all my money in tech stocks," Cash bragged. "Mostly tech, anyway. We're living through a revolution right now. This is the age of the perpetual bull market. At least in America. The Clinton boom will keep going, even after Clinton. Al Gore is a fucking lock to be elected next president. Which means the good times are just gonna roll and roll and roll!"

Fatima excused herself to go to the *toilettes*. "Damn, Ricky!" Cash said as soon as she was out of earshot. "The bitch is *fine!*"

"Don't call her a bitch, bitch."

Cash gave a sheepish, naughty grin. "Sorry, cuz. All I'm sayin' is, man, you're doin' good for yourself. Real good."

"Uh-huh."

Cash took a long sip of champagne, nodded along with the lounge singer, who was now doing a clumsy version of the great standard "Love Me or Leave Me." Then he leaned closer to Ricky and said, "You really have no info for me?"

"None. Do you have any for *me*?"

Cash eyed Ricky suspiciously. "I think maybe you know more than you're telling me, cousin."

"And maybe vice versa."

"Hmmph. Well, I take it you haven't tried to find Serena. But has she tried to find *you*?"

"Listen, Cash, I got my own life to live, you know. I really don't have time to get involved in your domestic dramas. Drive us back to the Eighteenth and I'll give you back your thousand bucks. Frankly, I don't need the aggravation."

Cash nodded, his eyes glittering with a mixture of admiration and contempt. "Oh, yeah. I always thought you were much smarter, much slicker, than most folks realized, R. J. Everybody thinks I'm the smooth operator in the family. But it's really you. Ain't it?"

Ricky could feel the ancient anger percolating inside him. "If I'm so smart how did you manage to make such an ass out of me on my wedding day?"

"Hunh?" Cash let out a snorting laugh of disbelief. "Excuse me, cuz. But we were both played for a fool by that crazy bitch—and I hope you won't mind my using that all-too-appropriate word in this case—Clementine."

"Yeah, right."

"You damn right I'm right. The bitch was out of her mind, Ricky. That's why she ended up the way she did. You do know what happened to her, don't you."

"Cash, I don't give a fuck anymore. I—"

"Clementine killed herself."

For several moments, Ricky didn't breathe at all. He just stared at Cash, dumbfounded. When he finally exhaled, all he could say was "What?"

"So you didn't know," Cash said, oozing the common false sympathy of the bearer of bad news. "Clementine moved to Minneapolis, married some white dude. Everybody thought she was happy at last. Then, about a year ago, she gassed herself in their garage. No kids, fortunately. Nobody knows why she did it. No suicide note, no warning signs. The white dude freaked out, he's in some institution now. Anyway, like I say, Ricky, the bitch was crazy."

Ricky stared down at the glass-topped table. Though he was looking at his distorted reflection, he saw nothing but the blurry twinkling of the chandeliers, the bloodred paint on the ceiling above him. And all he could think was: Clemmy is dead. The three words kept running through his mind: Clemmy is dead. Clemmy is dead. Clemmy is dead.

"Hellooooo, boyz," a French voice cooed. "I'm baaaaaaaack."

Ricky raised his head and saw Fatima standing in front of him, a fresh layer of makeup—shiny lipstick, thick eyeliner, cakey rouge—on her face.

"You are a vision of loveliness," Cash said, rising from the table, letting Fatima slide into the booth and take her place between the cousins.

"This is my first time in a salon such as this," Fatima said, suppressing a giggle. "It is so . . . so . . . decadent!"

"I've always thought innocence was overrated," Cash said with a leer.

"Your life must be so exciting. I mean, you do your surgeries on the bodies of all these famous people, you travel the globe . . ."

Ricky noticed that Cash was looking about the room as Fatima tittered.

"You know," she continued, "Paris can be very boring. But, of course, Reekee and me, we do not know the side of Paris that you see, so—"

"Hey! There he is! There's Dr. Dmitri!" Without another word, he rose from the table and strode across the salon.

Cash was up and gone before Fatima realized he had stopped paying attention to her. When she finally noticed how rudely he had bolted, Fatima simply shrugged and took a sip of Dom Pérignon. Ricky, meanwhile, was looking at the man Cash had rushed toward. He had a sturdy, linebacker's build, a jowly, doughy face with a thin black mustache, waxy-looking and curled at the tips—a Salvador Dali mustache. He wore a black, wide-lapelled suit, a gray shirt and black-and-white polka-dot tie. What little hair he had was greasily styled in a comb-over across his knobby pate. Yet this repulsive man had each arm wrapped around a ravishing, scantily-clad young woman, a brunette on his left, a blonde on his right. When he saw Ricky's cousin approaching him, the seedy guy let go of his babes and called out, "Dr. Cash!"

"Dr. Dmitri!" Cash responded. Ricky watched as Cash and Dmitri embraced, exchanging a kiss on each cheek.

"Are you not having a good time?" Fatima asked.

"You're drunk," Ricky replied.

"*Et alors?*" Fatima said—the French version of "So what?"

"So I wish you'd show a little more intelligence."

"Oh, so now you think I am stupid, yes?"

"I don't think you're stupid. But I think you should be more wise about my cousin and whatever game he's playing."

"Ah, so you think I don't know what is going on? Cash told me all about his wife. How she stole his money and ran away from him. How he come to you for help and now it seem that you don't help him at all. You just take his money and fuck him over, like everybody else."

"Is that what he told you?"

"He told me everything."

"And you believe his bullshit?"

That was when Fatima slapped Ricky with the line about his just being jealous of his cousin, because Cash was a success and he was not. That was when Ricky stopped talking, turned away from Fatima and stared out the window.

"Greetings, my friends!" Cash's buddy was still several feet away from the table, but approaching fast, as he called out to Ricky and Fatima. The jowly, waxily mustachioed Russian in the suit that was probably very expensive but still looked cheap, stopped in front of the booth and leaned across the glass-topped table. "Don't get up," he said magnanimously to Ricky, who had remained firmly planted in his seat. They shook hands.

"This is Dr. Dmitri Zugashvili," Cash said, standing at his friend's side. "The business partner I mentioned to you, Ricky. He's been kind enough to let me stay at one of his apartments on the Left Bank. Yuri, our driver, works for him."

"Mademoiselle." Dmitri grasped Fatima's right hand, raised it to his lips and kissed it with a wet and noisy smack. *"Enchanté,"* he said, waggling his eyebrows.

"Enchantée," Fatima sighed.

"And what is the business you all are in?" Ricky asked.

"Health care," Dmitri responded instantly. "We are both healers and, as such, we are interested in bringing the best health to all the peoples of the world."

"Dr. Dmitri here is the finest orthopedic surgeon in Russia," Cash said, before quickly adding, "actually, in all of Europe."

Ricky remembered what Serena had told him about Cash's medical colleagues from the East seeming like "stone-cold gangsters."

"Dr. Cash, he is too kind," Dmitri demurred. "But everybody knows he is the finest orthopedic surgeon in the United States."

"Yes," Ricky said, "but I still don't understand what your business venture is."

"I told you, cuz, we're developing Centers for Athletic Wellness. In the States and over here, too."

"Oh. Is that why you had to go to Zurich? To deposit funds for your health spas into a numbered bank account?"

Dmitri shot Cash a look of alarmed suspicion. Cash glanced at Ricky, then turned to Dmitri. He flashed a sickly smile. "Well, yeah, you know," Cash mumbled. "Business."

Dmitri tilted his head, regarded Ricky through narrow eyes. "You understand, sir, your cousin, he is not only great doctor. He is visionary man of business. A true visionary. And those who share his vision, those who support him, they will stand to profit, to profit bigly. But those who wish to cause him problem, they will only suffer."

"Go fuck yourself," Ricky said.

"Reekee!" Fatima shrieked, aghast.

Cash shook his head, an incredulous half-smirk on his face. "Jesus," he said.

But Dr. Dmitri was cool. He continued to stare, slit-eyed, at Ricky. "It was a pleasure meeting you," he said. "Have a nice night." He turned around and walked back to the babes waiting for him at a table in the center of the salon.

Cash slid into the booth, still shaking his head. "Damn, Ricky. Damn."

"I have never in my life been so ashamed," Fatima said. "Please, Cash, accept my apologies for Reekee's behavior."

"I don't need you to speak for me, *Fatima*," Ricky said, making a point of pronouncing her name correctly. "You think you know what's going on here but you don't know shit."

"And what the fuck do you know?" Cash growled.

"I know you beat the shit outta your wife. Did you tell Fatima that?"

"Reekee, what nonsense do you talk?" Fatima glared at Ricky, inflamed with outrage. Then she turned to Cash, as if waiting for his denial. But Cash was silent. He looked away from Ricky and Fatima and stared into space. Ricky saw Fatima's anger melt into confusion. "Cash," she said quietly, "is it true?"

When Cash turned his head to face them, his eyes were wet. *Here we go again*, Ricky thought, *the wounded husband routine.* He'd seen it in the café in Barbès and now Cash was giving a repeat performance in Les Enfants de l'Enfer.

"Yes, Ricky knows I hit Serena. But what I didn't tell him was that it was in self-defense."

"Oh, please!" Ricky scoffed. "You told me Serena told you her big secret and you freaked out."

"Big secret?" Fatima asked, sounding even more bewildered.

"Yeah. Oh yeah," Cash said. "That's right—up to a point. But nobody ever really knows what goes on between a couple. Nobody outside of a marriage can ever really understand the passionate bond between a husband and wife. And maybe, Ricky, I'm just not as good a man as you. Not as kind, as tenderhearted. But when my wife, the person I loved most in the world, the woman I cherished, the woman with whom I had made a pact of total honesty, told me, after two years of marriage, after three years of being together as a couple, that she had been a prostitute, a common fucking whore who sold herself to men, who abused her body to such an extent that she couldn't even bear children— my children!—when she told me this, yeah, I freaked out, I lost it! I admit it. I was hurt and enraged. Because I had told this woman, my wife, everything about my past. And for the three years I had known her she led me to believe that she had been just as open and honest and unconcealing. Then I have to find out, from somebody else, from some total stranger, that my entire life with this woman was a lie! A sick, fucked-up lie! And when I confronted my wife with this lie and she finally, reluctantly, admitted how she had concealed the truth, and made a fool out of me, for three fucking years—well, I'm sorry, Ricky, but yes, I lost it. I said some things I probably shouldn't have said. I cursed her out and I called her all sorts of names. I am not proud of the way I reacted. And maybe a good and decent and tenderhearted man such as yourself would have responded in a kinder, gentler way. But I lashed out. In words. Okay? I lashed out verbally. I did not strike the first blow. That was Serena."

"She's five foot six," Ricky said. "You're six-one."

Cash shook his head again, with a bitter little chuckle. "So you think I shouldn't have defended myself? Lemme show you something."

He pulled off his pinstriped jacket, began unbuttoning his starchy white shirt at the waist. Fatima, still looking confused, cast a nervous glance around the salon, as if worried that others might be watching them. But Ricky, Cash and Fatima were in a corner booth and no one else in the VIP lounge was paying them any mind. Cash unbuttoned his shirt up to his midchest, flipped his yellow necktie over his shoulder, out of the way. First, Ricky saw only a lightly hairy expanse of brown belly. He was fleetingly reassured to see that cousin Cash had a fair amount of flab hanging over his belt. Then he saw the thick wad of white cotton, tape and gauze. Cash winced as he peeled away the bandages. Ricky and Fatima stared in wordless revulsion at the long, purplish gash that curved around the left side of Cash's midsection. The wound was still fresh. Ricky thought he detected black sutures knitting the flesh together. No real scar tissue had developed yet.

"Serena came at me with a knife," Cash said. "We were fighting, arguing, in the kitchen. And I admit, I said some harsh words. Next thing I knew, she was coming at me with a bread knife. Luckily, I was wearing a heavy sweater. It was a cold April day. Another half inch and she would have pierced a major organ. As it was, she only sliced some fat off me. But there was so much blood, she musta thought it was a fatal wound. I know I did. And as I lay there bleeding on the kitchen

floor, I saw my wife run away. I was the one who had to crawl to the
phone and call 911. Serena fled. Leaving me to die."

"*Mon Dieu,*" Fatima gasped. Ricky said nothing.

"My wife tried to kill me," Cash whimpered. "So, yeah, I hit her.
I hit her after she hit me, while she was stabbing me. Because I confronted her with the truth." Cash slowly put the bandages back in place,
buttoned up his shirt. When he spoke again, his voice was choked with
emotion. "Serena ran away, after stealing millions of dollars from me.
And left me to die. And you know what? I *still* love her. I forgive her.
And I want her back. Now you try and tell me what you *think* you know
about me and Serena. 'Cause what you will never—ever—know is
how . . . much . . . I . . . love . . . her."

Cash buried his face in his hands and began weeping softly. Fatima
looked shell-shocked. After a while, she started stroking Cash's shoulder.
"It's okay," she whispered consolingly. "It's okay."

Ricky still did not know how to respond, or what to believe. Mainly,
he just wanted to get out of this place. "Excuse me" he said, sliding out
of the booth and heading for the *toilettes.*

Even the bathrooms in the VIP lounge were painted red. Standing
before the scarlet urinal, piss pouring out of him like water from a
garden hose, all Ricky could think about was how exhausted he felt.
Over the past two nights, he had gotten a total of eight hours of sleep.
All he really wanted was to go to bed. Either with Fatima or without
her. He was too tired to care.

Heading back to the corner booth, walking across the red carpet of
the VIP lounge as the singer and her accompanist mangled "I Love
Paris," Ricky felt someone looking at him. With a quick, peripheral
glance, he saw Dr. Dmitri, sitting at his center table, flanked by his two
barely dressed babes, giving him that squinty, evil eye. Ricky, striding
past, decided that, even if this Russian surgeon-mafioso ordered a knee-
capping on him, he would still feel proud for having told Dr. Dmitri to
go fuck himself. Ricky saw Fatima and Cash in the distance, their heads
bowed over the glass-topped table. Ricky wondered if Cash was still
crying, Fatima still comforting him. Two men walked through the metal
door with the illuminated sign SORTIE DE SECOURS in small green letters
above it. The emergency exit. Both men wore black turtlenecks, black

leather jackets, black gloves, black pants and boots. And both of them had black motorcycle helmets on, with smoke-tinted Plexiglas visors covering their faces. Since Ricky's attention was focused on Cash and Fatima in the near distance, he thought nothing of the two men who briskly crossed his path as he approached the corner booth. Only when Ricky stopped right in front of the table did Cash and Fatima raise their heads. That was when Ricky saw the four lines of white powder laid out on the mirror surface. Seeing the pain and dismay on Ricky's face, Cash and Fatima both burst into laughter.

"What the fuck are you doing?" Ricky cried. "You're pregnant!"

With no thought at all, acting on pure reflex, Ricky spun on his heels and started to storm away from the booth.

"Reekee, it's a joke!" he heard Fatima say behind him.

"Chill out, cuz!" Cash bellowed.

At that moment, Ricky's focus shifted to the center of the salon. He saw the two black-clad men in their gray-visored helmets pull pistols from their jackets in perfect unison, like synchronized swimmers, and point their weapons, straight-armed and steady-gripped, at Dr. Dmitri. They stood directly in front of the Russian. Ricky saw the back of the doctor's nearly bald head. He saw him raise his arms in surrender, saw the two babes dive for the floor. He did not hear gunshots, but he saw six flashes of sparky light, three from each pistol, as Dr. Dmitri fell backward in his chair. Ricky heard the singer unleash a nerve-jangling scream. For an eternal moment, everyone in the salon was frozen. Everyone, that is, except for the gunmen, who calmly turned and retraced their steps, heading for the emergency exit. Then, as the singer's shattering scream continued to echo through the room, pandemonium ensued.

Ricky twirled around to see Fatima lunging toward him. In a spilt second, he realized that she must have first been trying to stop him from leaving, to explain this "joke" of the lines of cocaine on the table. Now, after the gunshots, she was reaching out to him in sheer panic. Ricky grabbed hold of Fatima and instinctively pushed her down, under the glass-topped table. They found Cash already there, clutching the metal table leg. "Don't move!" Cash shouted over the roomful of terrified cries. "Stay right here!"

From their vantage point under the table, they could see the crazed stampede in the salon, the well-dressed legs of men who were blundering toward any door they could find, the feet of women kicking off their pointy high-heeled shoes so they could better flee the scene.

"I'm leaving!" Fatima said, scrambling out from under the table.

"Don't!" Cash yelled.

But Fatima was already gone and Ricky immediately took off after her. She bolted toward the same emergency exit the assassins had used, violently pushing her way down the darkened staircase, past clumsier VIPs, Ricky close behind her. They stumbled out onto the sidewalk, amid a crowd of people scattering in all directions. Evidently, the chaos had spread to the downstairs disco, as Ricky saw many of the self-conscious dance floor poseurs running for their lives. Just as Ricky grabbed Fatima from behind, he felt Cash grab him from behind. "Over there!" Cash shouted, pointing. "Yuri!"

Ricky saw the chauffeur, standing in front of the limo, at the curb, flailing his arms wildly. They raced to the black sedan, tumbled into the backseat as Yuri hopped in the front and started the engine. "Get down!" Cash yelped, pushing Fatima to the floor. Before Ricky could join them, he saw a motorcycle speed by, with one of the black-helmeted killers driving, the other holding on tight behind him. As Yuri tore away from the curb, Ricky heard the familiar sound of French police sirens: *Weeeeee-WAAAAAH...weeeeee-WAAAAAAAH...weeeeeee-WAAAA-AAAA!* "Damn it, get down!" Cash screamed at Ricky. "And stay down!"

Fourteen

RICKY COULD HEAR FATIMA moaning. He was ravaging her, taking her from behind, in the corner booth in the VIP room of Les Enfants de l'Enfer. Fatima was dressed like the glamorous tarts they had seen in the scarlet salon, her short leather skirt hiked up over her bare ass. And Ricky, as his body slammed against hers, was also fully clothed, wearing the black pinstriped suit, the immaculate white shirt and yellow power tie his cousin had worn the night before. Ricky and Fatima seemed to be the only people in the VIP room. Yet, Ricky felt invisible eyes watching them as Fatima's body writhed against his, her moans growing louder. Then, appearing out of nowhere, was a man in a black motorcycle helmet, black turtleneck, leather jacket, pants, boots and gloves. His face was concealed by the helmet's misty gray visor. And he was pointing a gun directly at Ricky. Suddenly, the visor disappeared and Ricky saw the face of Dr. Cash Washington, smiling. With the blast of the gunshot,

Ricky woke up, frightened, sweaty, struggling to catch his breath.

"Uuuuuuhhhhhhnnnn." The sound Ricky heard was not an erotic moan but the strangled groan of a woman in pain. Fatima was lying beside him in the bed, on her stomach, both hands buried in her black forest of hair. The sky outside Fatima's bedroom window was dusty gray. Ricky turned and looked at the bedside clock: 11:44. Fatima abruptly rose from the bed and stumbled into the bathroom, slamming the door behind her. Ricky could hear her vomit splashing into the toilet.

Alone in the bed, Ricky tried to reconstruct what had happened after the shooting of Dr. Dmitri. He remembered huddling with Fatima and Cash on the floor in the back of the limo. When they finally felt safe enough to take their seats, Ricky looked out the window and was comforted by the sight of Sacré Coeur, its alabaster dome rising in the distance, growing ever closer. Yuri was taking them back home. For a long time, no one spoke. Ricky looked at Fatima, coiled in her corner of the backseat, legs crossed, arms folded tightly across her chest. Cash was wiping sweat from his brow with a white handkerchief. "Whoa," he sighed. Then, very slowly, a smile oozed across his handsome face. "Well," Cash said, "do I know how to show folks a good time in Paris or what?" He doubled over in raucous laughter. Ricky and Fatima remained silent. After half a minute, when Cash finally realized he was laughing alone, he abruptly stopped, straightened up in his seat. "Ah, well, never a dull moment, huh?"

Fatima glared at him. "There is something seriously wrong with you," she said, in a calm, cold voice.

Cash did not respond. Yuri stopped in front of Fatima's building on the rue de Trétaigne. "Good-bye," Ricky said, as he and Fatima stepped out of the limousine.

When they got in the bed, Fatima was shaking all over. Ricky held her, stroking her body, trying to warm her up. "I am so sorry," she said. "Please forgive me, Reekee."

"You have no reason to be sorry. There is nothing to forgive."

Fatima mumbled something in response as they both, more or less, passed out. Now, seven hours later, Ricky heard the toilet flush behind the closed bathroom door, heard the sound of running water, of Fatima brushing her teeth. She staggered back to the bed, collapsed beside Ricky.

"Are you okay?" he asked.

"I feel better since I throw up," Fatima said.

"Good."

"I want to say again, Reekee, how sorry I am."

"And I want to say again that you have nothing to be sorry about."

"Your cousin. I do not comprehend what happened. He called, I told him, yes, he could come over. I did not want his champagne but somehow he talked me into drinking a glass. And then another. And another. But it was more than the alcohol. He seemed to bring something out of me, some crazy woman I did not know was in there. I have no other way to explain."

"You don't have to explain."

"But I did not snort cocaine! That was not cocaine on the table. Cash said, 'Let's have a little fun with my cousin.' He had Esmerelda bring us four little paper bags of sugar. It was only sugar on the table and we did not inhale it. I know this was not a very funny joke to play on you but Cash persuaded me."

"Someone we both knew once said he was the devil."

"Oh no. He is all too human. But, tell me, why is he here? What is the true story about him and his wife?"

"I don't know the truth. All I know is what I've been told. I'll tell you what I know. But let's have some coffee first."

It took nearly an hour for Ricky to relate his encounters with Cash and Serena, Inspector Lamouche's talk of an embezzling doctor on the lam, Marva Dobbs's lie upon seeing the photo of the runaway wife, and Archie Dukes's recollections of Li'l Lonnie John and the sister he had pimped, Cassandra, who was supposed to be dead. But Ricky carefully left out certain details: the hand grenades in Valitsa's closet, one of which the Serb's guest may have stolen; the fact that Ricky's trunk had been tampered with and keys to his apartment were found in the dead hooker's skirt pocket; the fact that, as a "potential" murder suspect, he had a rendezvous with the police scheduled for Tuesday morning; and the quick, moist kiss Serena bestowed on Ricky in the lobby of Valitsa's building.

He and Fatima were sitting at the kitchen table, polishing off a pot of powerful espresso, as Ricky finished his tale. After a long silence,

Fatima said, "I wish you would not befriend Serbs. You know who they have been killing for the past decade, don't you? Muslims!"

"You're right," Ricky quickly agreed. "Before I met Serena I had decided to distance myself from Valitsa. Anyway, like I said, Serena isn't at Valitsa's anymore. I don't know where she is."

"Do you think she will try to contact you?"

"I hope not."

"No, Reekee, you must continue to try to help her. No matter if she was a prostitute. She must be protected from Cash. I think this man, he is very dangerous. Even before you showed up last night, I think I sensed a violence in him."

"Well, it was Serena who came after Cash with the knife."

"This is what Cash says. Who knows the truth? Maybe it was someone else altogether who stabbed him."

"Maybe . . . One thing I don't understand, though, is why a guy like Cash would get mixed up with a bunch of criminals."

"That is because you have never read Balzac," Fatima said. "Balzac wrote that behind every great fortune there is a crime. Your cousin wants to make a great fortune. He must think that he has to dabble in crime to do so."

Ricky hesitated before switching to a more important subject. "How are you feeling now?"

"Much better, though my head still feels like it weighs a hundred kilos."

"You weren't too traumatized by the murder we saw?"

"I barely saw a thing, it happened so fast."

"But all the stress. I was worried it might have affected the . . . the baby."

"You mean the little sea horse," Fatima said with a tender smile. She placed a hand on her belly. "I think it is all right."

"You have to be careful, though."

"I will be. From now on."

"So, I was wondering," Ricky said tentatively. "What if I converted?"

"What do you mean?"

"Became a Muslim."

Fatima let go a shrill, piercing cackle. "You are not serious!"

"How do you know? Maybe I am."

"Please excuse my laughter, Reekee. I just find it very American that you would think you can put on a new religion as you would a new jacket."

"First of all, I don't think that. And secondly, I thought you liked the way Americans think."

"Perhaps meeting your cousin Cash has changed my point of view. Do you think becoming a Muslim means wearing a bow tie and believing in the teachings of Farrakhan? The black American version of Islam has many elements of the real thing but it is not the same."

"I know that, Fatima. And not everyone is as narrow-minded as Cash. Malcolm X discovered a more orthodox Islam when he went to Mecca."

"Fine. Malcolm X was a truly religious man. But are you like that, Reekee? Let us get real now. When you are most honest with yourself, do you even believe in God?"

"Sometimes."

"I am afraid that is not good enough."

"So you think you have to be born Muslim?"

"I think it is a culture as much as a religion. And, yes, I do believe that growing up in that culture is important. You cannot just become a Muslim out of expediency, Reekee. Would you even be talking about converting to Islam if I were not pregnant?"

Ricky did not respond.

"You must ask yourself, Reekee, if you even want to have a child. You are a very free and easy guy. How could you support a baby, financially, I mean?"

"I could change jobs," Ricky said. "Maybe I could teach, be a professor of piano somewhere, at a conservatory."

Fatima smiled and shook her head skeptically. "Be serious, Reekee. Who in France would hire you as a music professor?"

At that moment Ricky was almost as hurt as he had been in the VIP room, when Fatima had told him he was jealous of Cash's success. "You don't have to be so negative about it," he said meekly.

Fatima reached across the table and pressed her hand against Ricky's

cheek. "You are such a sweet man. And I do appreciate it, you know? I
truly do." The telephone rang and she rose to answer it. *"Allô?"* She
made a worried face, then handed the receiver to Ricky. "It is for you."

He cautiously held the device to his ear, as if he were afraid it might
somehow contaminate him. "Yes?"

"Ricky . . . my heeeeeero," Serena Moriarty Washington purred. "It's
so nice to hear your voice again."

"Where the hell are you?"

"Bonjour to you, too," Serena sniffed. "I'm still right here in the
Eighteenth. I'm staying at a friend's place on Avenue Junot. I thought
maybe you'd like to come over and I can explain everything."

Ricky wrote down the address, said he could not come by until four
o'clock. After he hung up, Fatima said, "Don't forget we are having
couscous with Christophe and Eve-Laure at seven."

"I'll be back well before then," Ricky said.

Avenue Junot was the wealthiest street in the Eighteenth, a long, curving, steeply inclined boulevard, shaped like a giant horseshoe, looping
around the north side of the Butte Montmartre. There were hardly any
shops on the Avenue Junot. The street was lined with impressive apartment buildings and urban mansions that resembled small villas with
their wrought-iron gates and two-tiered balconies. Serena had given
Ricky the address of one of those magnificent private residences. The
name on the gate was WALDEMAR. Ricky pushed the button beside the
nameplate.

As he waited for a response, a rail-thin, middle-aged woman approached him, a neatly trimmed little white poodle trundling beside her,
without a leash. The woman's hair was artificially black—the color of
shoe polish—except for a dramatic streak of white at the front of her
head. She gave Ricky one of those Parisian stares, neither hostile nor
suspicious, just bluntly curious.

"Bonjour, madame," Ricky said.

"Bonjour, monsieur," the woman replied as she walked past and continued down the curve of the avenue, poodle trotting at her side.

"Oui?" Serena's voice sounded staticky in the small intercom.

"It's me, Ricky."

The buzzer sounded, Ricky pushed open the gate and entered a courtyard filled with plants and flowers. Serena stood in the open doorway of the mansion, wearing nothing but a red velvet bathrobe that extended only to the tops of her knees, and little white ankle socks. "Welcome," she said. When Ricky reached the threshold she stood on the tips of her toes and tried to kiss him on the mouth. Ricky quickly turned his head so that Serena's lips touched only his right cheek. Dropping back on her heels, Serena gave a sullen little frown, then ushered Ricky into the house.

"Nice digs," he said, trying to sound blasé about the opulence all around him.

"Glad you like it," Serena said, matching Ricky's self-consciously casual tone.

She escorted him through the cavernous foyer and into a high-ceilinged living room decorated with Persian rugs, African and Indian sculptures, huge abstract paintings, furniture that ranged from the antique to the ultra-modern, a long, sleek concert piano, a wide, swerving staircase with a mahogany bannister and a fireplace as big as a walk-in closet. The vast space was cluttered and chaotic but everything in it looked priceless. On the coffee table, Ricky saw a bottle of champagne in a silver bucket and a glass pitcher of orange juice. He had to stifle a laugh. Obviously, Cash Washington and his wife had similarly expensive tastes. What a shame they wound up trying to kill each other.

"Make yourself comfortable," Serena said, sounding every inch the lady of the manor. "I just made myself a mimosa. Would you like one?"

Ricky settled into a cushy leather armchair. "No thanks, I had a lot to drink last night."

"Aw, come on," Serena crooned, already mixing Ricky's drink. "Hair of the dog."

Her own hair fell over her shoulders in lush, amber waves and still looked wet from a shower. The bruise around her eye, so raw and prominent on Friday night, was only vaguely visible this Sunday afternoon, a faint discoloration. She handed Ricky his champagne and orange juice, plopped down in the armchair across from his and smiled coyly. "Aren't you glad to see me?"

"Why did you disappear like that? Valitsa wondered what the hell had happened to you."

Serena seemed taken aback by Ricky's hard-edged tone. "I wanted to call her but I didn't have her phone number."

"Then why didn't you let *me* know where you were?"

"I *did* let you know. I called you at Fatima's this morning, didn't I?"

"A full day after you left Valitsa's."

"I tried to phone you at your apartment yesterday," Serena said, sounding as testy as Ricky now. "There was never any answer."

"Oh . . . yeah . . . right. I haven't been home in a while."

"If you had been, I would have informed you that Saturday morning I finally got in touch with an old acquaintance of mine named Janusz Waldemar. He's a financial consultant who is very much involved in the art world. As it happens, he was just taking off to look at some statues he was interested in buying in Nepal and he offered me his house. I had to rush right over to get the keys because he had a plane to catch. I know I should have left Valitsa a note or something but I was in a hurry. Anyway, I felt bad about imposing on her and, as you can see, Janusz has a little more space than Valitsa."

"So I see."

"Not to mention a piano. So I've been able to rehearse for my recording session tomorrow. You do remember my recording session, don't you? With DJ Fabrice."

"Yes, I remember," Ricky said humbly. "I'm sorry to have sounded so irritable before. I was worried about you."

"So you really do care," Serena said, with a tongue-in-cheek pathos. She slouched in her chair, the red velvet bathrobe falling a little more open, revealing the fullness of her left breast. But the more she tried to be seductive, the less attractive Ricky found her. Serena was fake sexy, like those dolled-up women in music videos, preening and pouting. But, of course, that was Serena's ambition, wasn't it? To be one of those dolled-up women, to be the queen of the dolls.

Serena's sex-kitten phoniness was grating on Ricky. He decided to get tough again. "I've heard a lot about you in the past twenty-four hours."

"Have you?"

"I saw Cash again. Last night."

Serena sat up straight now, her ginger eyes quickly scanning Ricky's face. She reminded him of a cat sensing danger, bracing for an attack: wary, tense and alert. "Did you tell him we had met?"

"No. I told you I wouldn't sell you out to Cash and I meant what I said."

Serena maintained her taut posture in the leather armchair. "Thank you," she said, though there was not a hint of gratitude in her voice.

Ricky felt a frisson of sadistic pleasure. Finally, after three days of being manipulated by various people with their sundry secret agendas, he had the upper hand. "Cash showed me his wound. Pretty nasty."

"It was in self-defense."

"That's what he said about socking you in the face. Your bruise looks much better, by the way."

"I'm wearing makeup today. It still hurts like a motherfucker. Anyway, I told you Cassius tried to kill me. Was I just supposed to let him? I fought back so I could survive. I'm sorry I didn't tell you. Maybe I was afraid that if you knew I defended myself with the nearest weapon at hand, you wouldn't be as sympathetic toward me."

"Cash said you left him to die on the kitchen floor."

"Not so! I ran upstairs to call 911 and only once I knew an ambulance was on the way did I get the fuck outta there 'cause I didn't wanna have to deal with all the shit the so-called authorities were gonna hit me with when they showed up. I was trying to protect your cousin, Ricky. I didn't want people to know that the wife of this famous surgeon had to cut him 'cause he was beatin' the shit out of her!"

"Your hands aren't trembling today. They did the other night at the crêperie, when I told you I'd seen Cash. Was that because you thought he was dead?"

"Of course not."

"You just didn't expect him to be up and around, let alone traveling to France, so quickly. Is that it?"

"What are you getting at, Ricky?"

"What I'm *trying* to get at is the truth."

"Well, I *know* the truth, sweetheart. All of it. But I'm not gonna tell it to you till I know what lies Cassius has fed you."

Ricky should have gotten up and left: that was what he would think later. He just should have removed himself, right then and there, from this mess. But some baser instinct prevailed. He wanted to let Serena know that he was on to her, that as much as she might have tried to use him, he was still one or two steps ahead of the game. He had to show her that Ricky Jenks was nobody's sap.

"Cash told me your real secret. It's true, as you said, that you can't have children. But this is because your body was subjected to so much abuse. Back when you were a prostitute."

Serena didn't bat an eye. She remained rigid in her chair but raised her chin slightly, literally holding her head high. "For three years, in my early twenties, when I was desperate for money and didn't know any better, I was a call girl. And, no, I saw no reason to share this fact with my husband. But those three years had nothing to do with my infertility. If Cassius wants to believe some ignorant bullshit like that, well, that's his choice. I made a stupid mistake in my youth. But it's nature that made me barren. I was born with this curse. I didn't bring it on myself."

As touched as he was by the pain and the pride he saw in Serena, Ricky had to keep going, keep trying to provoke the truth. "And does Cash know your real name . . . Cassandra?"

Serena's eyes narrowed in a look of sheer hatred. Ricky worried that he had pushed her too far. He was relieved to see that there were no knives nearby. "You've been talking to that fucking bitch Marva, huh?"

"Cassandra John. Isn't that it?"

"Cassandra Serena John. And Moriarty was my mother's maiden name. So fucking what?"

"So does Cash know?"

"If he does, he didn't learn it from me." In an instant, Serena's defiance turned to vulnerability. Ricky could see tears welling in her eyes as she asked, "How is he . . . my husband?"

"Doesn't seem any worse for wear," Ricky said, struggling to maintain his tough-guy tone. "He says he still loves you. Even after the stabbing. He forgives you and wants you back."

"Really?" Serena asked plaintively.

"That's what he says."

She wiped her eyes with the sleeve of the bathrobe. "What else did he say about me?"

"Nothing, really. He wanted to know if you'd tried to contact me. I told him nothing. Do you want to see him?"

"Oh, God, Ricky, I don't know. Where is he?"

"He was staying somewhere on the Left Bank. Now I don't know. He took us to some snazzy club last night and while we were there the guy who was putting him up got shot to death."

"You're joking."

"I saw it with my own eyes. Two dudes in motorcycle helmets walked into the place and blew the man away. His name was Dmitri something or other. Called himself a doctor."

"Zugashvili! They killed him?"

"Six shots at point-blank range. I'd be very surprised if he survived."

"He was one of those gangster doctors I told you about. I met him in New York." Serena covered her mouth with her hand and looked genuinely frightened. "What the fuck has Cassius gotten himself mixed up in?"

"I don't know but I doubt I'll be seeing him again."

Serena took the hand away from her mouth, ran it through her silken hair. She stared into space and murmured, "Poor baby."

"But do you want to see him?" Ricky asked again.

Serena shook her head slowly. "I don't know, Ricky. I just don't know. It's hard for me to think about it right now. For the next twenty-four hours I just have to concentrate on—"

"Your all-important recording session. Yeah, I know."

Serena glared at Ricky again. "You really hate me now, don't you?"

"I have no strong feelings one way or the other. I've just been hearing a lot of confusing shit."

"Like what?"

"Like: Aren't you supposed to be dead?"

"Come again?"

"I heard that many years ago, Cassandra John contracted AIDS and died."

Serena threw back her head in gaudy, mocking laughter. "So, what, Ricky? You think I'm a fucking ghost? A zombie? The undead?"

"I'm just telling you what I heard."

"From who? That fucking bitch Marva?"

"First of all, I'd rather you didn't call her a bitch. She happens to be a good friend of mine."

"And she said I *died?* From *AIDS?* Sounds like wishful thinking on her part."

"Marva hasn't said anything to me about you. I just happen to know that she visited you in the hospital and thought she saw you die."

"Tcch." Serena sucked her teeth loudly and rolled her eyes. "That's just like niggas for you, ain't it? They don't just gotta bad-mouth you, they gotta bad-mouth you to death!"

"So, you were never sick?"

"I had hepatitis, Ricky. But I am not, repeat, not HIV positive. If you don't believe me, ask your cousin. We were both tested before we got married."

"Hepatitis?"

"Yes! I was in the hospital for a month and I have absolutely no recollection of Dame Marva coming to visit me. If she did, I was probably fast asleep and that . . . and *she* . . . went around tellin' people I had fucking died!"

"So why did you lie when I asked if you knew who Marva was?"

"Because I'd rather forget I ever met her. Marva was always insanely jealous of me. 'Cause I was younger and prettier than her and had a far better voice than she had *ever* had!"

"You told me you had no black American friends here."

"Very, very few. And I regret every one. 'Cause all these Paris Ne-groes do is sit around gossipping about each other. They think they're so damn sophisticated but they're worse than a bunch of dumbass coun-try niggas sittin' on their porches just talkin' shit all day long."

"And what about Lonnie?" Ricky asked. "Li'l Lonnie John."

Serena stared hard at Ricky, a completely unreadable look on her face. For a long time she said nothing. Then her whole body seemed to explode in violent sobs.

"Did you ever have a sister?" Serena asked.

"Yeah. Isabel. She's a judge in Miami. You met her at your wedding."

"Are you two close?"

"Very," Ricky said.

"Then maybe you can understand."

They were sitting at a stone table on Janusz Waldemar's patio. After Ricky had mentioned Lonnie's name, Serena sobbed for a full five minutes. Ricky had squatted beside her armchair, awkwardly patting her shoulder, hesitating to embrace her. When she finally quieted down, she said, "I need some air."

The air out on the patio was thick and humid, the somber sky above heavy with the threat of a downpour. But the only water falling in Waldemar's plant-filled alcove came out of the statue decorating the fountain, a leering cherub clutching his tiny member and spraying into the bubbling basin below. Though Ricky said he had had enough to drink, Serena had insisted they take the champagne and orange juice outside with them and she mixed two more mimosas before she was ready to talk of her brother.

"Lonnie and I are twins. We shared a womb. Can you imagine the sort of intimacy that creates? I doubt you can."

"So do I," Ricky agreed.

Serena consumed half her mimosa in one gulp. "It's really like Lonnie is part of me. And I'm part of him. Even though we haven't seen each other in years. It's like he lives inside of me. And I live inside of him. Does that sound sick to you?"

"No," Ricky lied. He had already leapt to the most perverse conclusion: that Cassandra Serena John and her twin brother had committed incest.

"What has Cassius told you about Lonnie?"

"Nothing. He's never even mentioned him."

Serena's Bambi eyes seemed to frisk Ricky's face. "Honest?" she said in her most childlike tone.

"Why would I lie?"

Serena was reassured. "Okay. It's just that Lonnie is the cause of a lot of the trouble Cassius and I have been having. I mean, the tension was building for a long time between Cassius and me. But Lonnie really set it off."

"Where is he now?"

"In Paris. I think. I've been trying to find him for days, but no luck."

"Wasn't he in prison in Turkey?"

A flare of suspicion went up in Serena's eyes. "Who told you that?"

"Some of those gossipy Paris Negroes you mentioned."

Serena, keeping her eyes on Ricky as if she expected him to make some kind of false move, downed the rest of her drink. "You do realize that none of those niggas talkin' about me ever even met me? And most of them never met Lonnie either."

"But is it true that he was in a Turkish prison?"

Having finished her own mimosa, Serena pulled Ricky's full glass across the stone table toward her. "You know," she said pensively, "my brother and my husband have an amazing amount in common. I didn't really appreciate that fact until a few weeks ago. They were both born to nice, respectable black families. Cassius's parents succeeded in the corporate world. Our parents, Lonnie's and mine, were successful in the military. Cassius is wildly ambitious and so was Lonnie. Yet they were both lured off the straight and narrow path. What is it about our men, Ricky? Why are so many of them, even the most advantaged, drawn to some kind of crime? I mean, Lonnie was on his way to becoming an officer, like our father. But he pissed it all away. My brother wanted to be a general. He had the brains to be the Colin Powell of our generation. Does anybody ever tell you that about Li'l Lonnie John? Fuck no. 'Cause Lonnie got into a little bit of pimpin', just as a sideline. And when he was more successful at it than the white boys in the force were, they discharged his ass. Dishonorable discharge. Can you even imagine how painful that was for our father, a retired air force major? A month later, I got rejected from drama school. And a month after that, my parents crashed their plane into the Pacific Ocean. Connection?"

"I doubt it," Ricky said. "What happened to your parents was an accident."

"Whatever. In any event, after that, Lonnie said, 'Fuck it, if I can't be the top dog in the U.S. military, then I'll be the top dog in crime! I'll be the richest damn pimp in Europe.' You see, Ricky, he still burned with ambition. He just channelled it in another direction."

"And he channelled you in the same direction."

Serena started on the drink she had mixed for Ricky. "Nobody has ever made me do anything I didn't want to do. Lonnie and I were alone in this world together. We decided to help each other as best we could. Like I said, like I tried to explain to Cassius, I was . . . in the business . . . for three short years. I'm not proud of it. Lonnie was sick with guilt when I got hepatitis. Even though the illness had nothing to do with my turning tricks, my brother felt responsible, like it was somehow his fault. Then, while I was in the hospital, Lonnie got the shit kicked out of him by some French gangsters. You see, once again, he was too successful for the white boys. Sick as I was—and despite the wishful thinking of Marva Dobbs and her ilk—my life was never in danger. It was Lonnie who almost died. When I got out of my hospital bed, he was still in his. They'd smashed his face up so bad, his mouth was wired shut. And, still, he fought to get the words out, to beg me to quit the business. He told me to go to America and start over. So I did."

"And Lonnie?"

"As you seem to know, he went to Turkey, started pimpin' there and wound up in jail. He got out a few months ago. After ten fucking years."

"You said Lonnie was the cause of a lot of the trouble between you and Cash."

"I did?"

Ricky wondered if Serena was drunk. "Well, yeah . . . About five minutes ago."

Serena lowered her eyes. "Oh . . . I shouldn't have said that."

Now Ricky felt he was beginning to understand. "Cash said he learned from a third party that you had been a prostitute. Was it Lonnie who told him?"

Serena looked up again, her face blank and inscrutable, as it had been when Ricky first mentioned her brother. "You don't miss much, do you?"

Ricky suppressed a gloating smile. Maybe he really was a natural-born detective. "Blackmail?" he asked.

Serena drank some more. She seemed to be bracing herself for some kind of big confession. "Lonnie and I hadn't spoken in years and years. Then he called me, out of the blue, a few months ago. He had seen, in that stupid magazine *Paris Match*, a profile of your cousin. And they ran a photo of Cassius and me at some banquet. I can't tell you how shocked I was to hear from him. I had made a whole new life for myself. I'd started from scratch in America. I really didn't expect to have any contact with Lonnie, ever again. He was such a little bad ass, I figured he'd manage to get himself killed in prison. And I convinced myself that it had happened: Lonnie had been murdered in prison. He was out of my life forever. I never told any of my friends in New York that I even had a brother."

"And you never told Cash either."

"Of course not. But then Lonnie called Cassius's office, talked the secretary into giving him our home number. It was so weird when I heard his voice on the phone. Like I had gotten in touch with some lost part of myself. I just broke down and cried. But I could hear in his voice how Lonnie had changed. He told me how happy he was that I had married a rich doctor—but he sounded much more bitter than happy. He told me he'd been struggling to survive since he got out of prison and he could use some money. I told him I hardly had any money of my own. Everything belonged to Cash. He didn't like hearing that. Anyway, we talked a couple more times, he said he was back in Paris. I sent him some money, through Western Union, but he said it wasn't enough. I was married to some rich nigga doctor, he said, so why was I holdin' out on him? He was my brother, my twin brother. He had always looked out for me. Why couldn't I do something for him? That's what Lonnie said."

"Bastard."

"Don't say that, Ricky. Please. You don't know how much I love my brother. And how much, in spite of everything, he loves me."

"Okay, yeah, but first he pimped you and then he tries to extort money from you. And when you gave him everything you had to give, he called Cash, right?"

"He sent him a letter."

"Telling him his wife had been a hooker and if he didn't pay up, Lonnie would tell the world."

"Something like that." Serena finished Ricky's mimosa. She looked totally exhausted; not sad, but drained.

"When's the last time you talked to him?"

"I called him as soon as I arrived in Paris. I told him what had happened when Cassius got his letter. Lonnie totally freaked out. He couldn't believe Cassius had hit me. I've never heard him so enraged."

"You didn't tell him about your self-defense with the bread knife."

"Jesus, Ricky, I don't know. Maybe I did, maybe I didn't."

"But you must know where Lonnie is if you've been talking to him."

"I had the number of his mobile phone. He said he was in Paris but he refused to tell me exactly where. I've called him probably fifty times in the past three days but there's never any answer. All I know is that if Lonnie finds out Cassius is here, he'll kill him."

"Would that be such a bad thing?" Ricky asked, surprised once again by his own cold-bloodedness. "I mean, you'd stand to inherit a bundle, right?"

Serena gave him her most earnest, wounded-fawn look. "Ricky—that's the love of my life you're talking about. Do you really think I want to see Cassius dead?"

Ricky shrugged. "I don't know what you want."

Now Serena shook her head, as if she were ashamed of Ricky. "You just don't get it, do you? I love Cassius the same way he loves me. Consumingly . . . violently. But the last thing I want is to see him dead. No matter how he's treated me."

"Sorry," Ricky said. "But it seems like somebody's gonna get ahold of Cash sooner or later. If it isn't Interpol or Russian gangsters it might very well be your brother. Which reminds me: Did Lonnie ever pimp a blond transsexual; tall, striking whore, looked kinda like Grace Kelly?"

"I don't know what the fuck you're talking about. Lonnie didn't deal with freaks. Not any that I know about. He pimped women. Real women."

"Okay, okay. And what about Maximillian?"

"Who?"

"Maximillian. Romanian dude. I heard he was Lonnie's enforcer. Out in the Bois de Vincennes. Used to slit people's throats."

"Sounds like the Paris Negroes have been tellin' you a lotta tall tales, Ricky. But maybe Lonnie did have some guy like that working for him. I wouldn't know. I wasn't a common streetwalker, like most of the chicks Lonnie handled. I was what is known as a high-priced call girl, Ricky. I only dealt with a certain class of client."

"Like Janusz Waldemar, you mean?"

Ricky thought this would piss Serena off. Why he wished to insult her, he did not know. But instead of seeming angry, Serena raised her chin again, looking hurt but proud. "Yeah," she said, "like him."

Janusz Waldemar's bathroom was almost as large as Ricky's studio apartment and much more elegant. Ricky sat on a throne-like toilet with armrests and a soft, upholstered back. Once he'd finished his business, he pulled the gold chain to flush the toilet and descended the three carpeted steps in front of the commode. Washing his hands, he decided he would apologize to Serena for having questioned her so roughly. Then he would get the hell out of there. And if Cash or Serena called him again in the next few days he would tell them to deal with their fucked-up marriage on their own and leave him out of it. And if one or both of them wound up in jail or dead, well, that wasn't Ricky's problem, either.

Stepping out of the bathroom, into the grand *boudoir*, Ricky saw Serena stretched out on the massive, brass-framed bed. "Come here, you," she said.

Ricky sat beside her on the black satin bedspread. He could feel goose bumps prickling his skin and hoped Serena didn't sense his nervousness. "I have to go," he said. "I just want to say I'm sorry for grilling you the way I did."

Serena propped herself up on one elbow, tossed her tawny hair. "I know it's only because you're concerned about me. You're such a good man, aren't you, Ricky?"

"I'm just a man."

"But you care about doing what's right. Don't you know how rare that is?"

Only then did Ricky remember another question he had meant to ask Serena. "By the way, you didn't happen to take something from Valitsa's closet, did you?"

"Like what?"

"Like a hand grenade."

This caused Serena to laugh uproariously. "What?!"

"You know, just your typical U.S. Army—"

"Oh my God!" Serena sputtered between giggles. "Here I am, feel-ing all embarrassed by my shady past and you've got friends with fuck-ing hand grenades in their closets!"

Ricky was laughing now, too, almost as hard as Serena, his body shaking on the edge of the bed. Everything seemed suddenly ridiculous. "Well, is that so unusual?" he tried to say with a straight face. "I mean, some women carry little spray cans of Mace, but Valitsa figures—"

Serena was rolling across the bed now, cackling hysterically. "Stop!"

"—you can never be too safe!"

Ricky found Serena's hysteria contagious. It occurred to him that maybe this was just a release from all the tension of the past few days but he couldn't help himself. He fell on his back, clutching his belly and laughing as crazily as Serena. They were lying side by side on the bed as their manic giggles slowly died down. Ricky turned and saw Serena's face, inches from his, on the black pillow. It would have been a basic impulse, the most natural thing in the world, at that moment, for him to kiss her. Instead, he abruptly sat up, planted his feet on the thick gray carpet. But just as quickly, Serena leapt from the bed, spun around and was now standing directly in front of Ricky. She placed her hands on his shoulders, wriggled her body between his legs. "I have to go," Ricky said weakly.

"I'm very attracted to you," Serena said. With a light tug at the velvet belt, her bathrobe fell open. Ricky stared straight into Serena's curly pubic triangle. He looked up and saw her almost perfectly globular breasts, their dark brown areolae and pert nipples. Serena stared down at him, smiling, her hair falling across her face.

"Don't do this," he said.

"What's the matter?" Serena purred, all throaty and theatrical. "Don't you want me? I want *you*."

Ricky's heart was beating at double time. He could feel beads of sweat popping all over his body. His mouth was actually watering. No, he didn't want her, but here she was, an undeniably gorgeous woman, brazenly offering her body to him. He didn't want her but something inside him said, *Take her anyway.*

"Don't you wanna fuck me?" she whispered, her body swaying slightly.

Well, did he? And what if he did? Wouldn't he be betraying Fatima? Of course. But hadn't she already betrayed *him?* Hadn't she told him she had been with Bernard-Henri recently? Fatima was carrying a baby, a little sea horse anyway, that might not even be Ricky's. She had mocked and humiliated him in front of Cash the night before. She had toyed with his emotions for damn near a year already. What the fuck did he owe Fatima? Nothing!

"Don't you wanna fuck Cash's woman?" Serena sighed. "He'd fuck yours. He *already* fucked one of yours."

At that moment, Ricky felt sick, nauseated with revulsion. He was suddenly revolted by the nearly naked beauty in front of him. And revolted by himself, revolted by the idea that he might fuck Serena purely out of revenge: revenge against Fatima, Cash, or the ghost of Clementine. He grasped Serena's wrists, took her hands from his shoulders and, with a movement that bordered on violence, pushed her away from him. "I told you I have to go."

Serena smiled enigmatically, wrapped her robe more tightly around her body, knotted the belt. "You're such a tease," she said. "Come." She turned and led him out of the bedroom, to the front door. "I'll call you tomorrow, after my session with DJ Fabrice." She kissed him once on each cheek. *"Au revoir."*

Walking up posh Avenue Junot, Ricky knew he had done the right thing, the virtuous thing. So why did he still feel kind of sick?

Fifteen

THE PROSTITUTE VALITSA THE Serb had nicknamed Carmen stood ramrod straight in front of 176, rue des Martyrs, seemingly transfixed by the memorial for her murdered colleague. By Sunday afternoon, the bright pile of flowers was two feet high. Someone had attached a large wreath to the front door with a color photo of the murder victim hanging in the center of the ring of flowers. A blue ribbon was pinned to the wreath, bearing a gold-lettered inscription: ADIEU, MIRABELLA. So, Ricky thought, that was Grace Kelly's real name. Though Ricky stood only a few steps behind her, Carmen was so taken by the tribute that she seemed oblivious to his presence.

Back on his street for the first time in a day and a half, Ricky had spotted Carmen from way up the block. Sunday afternoon was usually a quiet time for the action on Martyrs. But Carmen didn't appear to be "on duty." She just stood there in front of the flowers, as still and bleak as a statue in a graveyard. Ricky wondered if this was some sort of trap that had been set for him. He descended Martyrs cautiously, scanning both sides of the street, looking for the man with the glasses and the droopy mustache, half-expecting him to leap from out of a shadowy doorway, slashing away with his deadly blade. But the closer he crept toward Carmen, the more sure Ricky felt that he was not walking into an ambush. He stood directly behind her for a full minute before he spoke.

"*C'est vraiment tragique.*"

"*Oui.*" When she turned to face him, Carmen gasped and raised a hand to her mouth, her haunted eyes popping wide. "Monsieur Jank!"

"*Bonjour, madame,*" Ricky said coldly. He didn't know how Carmen knew his name but the fact that she did reignited his paranoia.

"I need to talk wit you, in the most urgent way." Ricky was startled to hear Carmen speak English. He responded in kind.

"Why?"

"Please," Carmen said in her thick Spanish accent. "We can go to café. There is no problem."

"I didn't kill her," Ricky said.

"I know, monsieur. That is why we must talk. I *do* know who kilt her. And I think you are in very big danger."

Down the hill and around the corner from Ricky's building was the Boulevard de Clichy, a long stretch of neon sleaze that marked the southwest border of the Eighteenth Arrondissement and the heart of Pigalle, or, as Ricky's old pal Charlie Jackson used to call it, Pig Alley. Paris's most famous "red light district," Pigalle managed the neat trick of being, at once, thoroughly seedy and completely nonthreatening. Up and down the wide Boulevard de Clichy, there were dildoes on display in shop windows, along with whips and chains, leather masks and nipple clamps and all variety of exotic undergarments. There was an array of venues, dominated by the towering, black-windowed Sex-O-Drome, offering private stalls for viewing lurid videos and DVDs as well as live sex shows galore: men with women, women with women, men with men, women who used to be men with whomever. The boulevard was populated by

shady guys in leather jackets who always seemed to be waiting for somebody; tawdry women standing in front of the sex shops, urging passersby
to come in and get off; and, during most of the year, huge flocks of
camera-toting tourists. The world-renowned Moulin Rouge was on the
Boulevard de Clichy, too, marked by an enormous fake red windmill, its
neon vanes slowly twirling. In 1899, this was where Paris's absinthe-
swilling bohemians gathered for good, dirty fun. By 1999, the Moulin
Rouge was a glitzy supper club frequented by gray-haired out-of-towners
eager to pay a small fortune to see a line of high-kicking cancan dancers.

The Hanoi Hideaway was one of the more *branché* joints on the
boulevard. It was located just a few doors away from the McDonald's
which had once been the Sunset Café, where Ricky had played piano
for Pierre Defenestre back in his early days in Paris. A painted bust of
Ho Chi Minh, complete with long goatee and piercing stare, greeted you
as you entered the twinkling dimness of the bar. The Hanoi Hideaway
seemed to be lit entirely by tiny white Christmas tree lights. A fake
gong hung over the bar, an antique rickshaw sat idle in the corner; there
were bamboo stools and bannisters and tables and one entire wall was
taken up by a huge, sixties-era poster painted in colorful, cartoony
Socialist-realist style depicting a green-uniformed soldier, a laborer in a
hardhat and a pigtailed teenager in what looked like a Girl Scout outfit,
each of them smiling and proudly brandishing an AK-47, their skin
tinted orange by the rising sun at the center of the tableau. The rifle-
wiedling comrades were surrounded by the elements of a productive
Communist society—factories, tall telephone poles and a radio tower
emanating rays of communication, the inevitable tractor. A long slogan,
inscrutable to Ricky, was painted in red calligraphy, across the bottom
of the poster. Young men and women of Vietnamese descent, dressed in
black satin, high-collared, double-breasted pajamas, waited on the clientèle. A recent Madonna song played on the sound system.

"You know," Carmen said, "Mirabella always liked you."

Ricky and the prostitute sat across from each other in wide-backed
wicker chairs of the type one might have seen on the verandas of French
colonial plantations in old Indochina. He had been surprised to learn
that the hooker Valitsa the Serb had always called Carmen was actually
named Carmen. She was not quite as feminine as her dead friend, whom

Valitsa had dubbed Grace Kelly but who had actually been named Mirabella. Despite her waist-length, glossy hair and artfully applied makeup,
Carmen had the strong jawline, the thick neck and large hands of a
natural-born male. But her gestures were dainty and demure as she
adjusted the hem of her short leather skirt over her crossed thighs and
lifted her foamy pink drink, a tiny parasol poking over the rim of the
glass. Ricky took a sip of his Orangina, tried to ignore the subtle stares
of customers who no doubt assumed that he and Carmen were intimately
involved.

"I'm amazed to hear that," Ricky said. "She always used to sneer at
me and call me nasty names."

"That was her way of flirting," Carmen explained. "In fact, she
thought you were very . . . oh, how do you say? . . . very . . ."

"We can speak in French if you like."

"No, no, it is good for me to practice my English. I live in Los
Angeles for three year and I like to go back someday. So, as I say,
Mirabella always thought you were very . . . ah . . . accchhhh . . . *mignon.*"

"Cute?"

"Cute! Yes! She thought you were cute."

"I would never have guessed."

"She had strange way of showing it, for sure. But that was Mirabella."

"You were very close to her?"

"Oh, yes. She was my best friend in the street. And I believe that,
except for her killer, I was last to see her alive."

"Really? When?"

"We have dinner Thursday night. Chez Kamel. Some hour later, she
is dead."

"I'm very sorry."

Carmen gave a sad smile. "Me also."

"Let me ask you something. The other night, Friday, when I was
coming down the street, it must have been four in the morning, I saw
you with a man in a beret. He had a mustache and eyeglasses. Do you
remember?"

"Of course."

"Is he the man who killed Mirabella?"

"Yes, I think so."

"And is his name Maximillian?"

"*Bon sang!* You know him?"

"No. But I have heard rumors about him. I know he worked for Lonnie John."

Carmen's big, dark eyes were filled with astonishment. "And you know Lonnie John also?"

"No, do you?"

"Not at all."

"I only know his sister, Cassandra. Do you know her?"

"No. I know only Mirabella. She tell me about Lonnie, she tell me about Cassandra and I meet this Maximillian only two time, both time last week."

"With Mirabella?"

"*Oui. Si.* I mean, yes, the first time. Second time, just me alone."

"Okay," Ricky said soothingly. Carmen was starting to seem a bit jittery and he wanted to calm her down. "Now, let me ask you another question. Did your friend Mirabella ever work for Lonnie?"

"You mean as whore?"

"Yes."

Carmen shook her head vigorously. "No. Lonnie John was not her pimp. He never pimp her. Most definitely not." For some reason, Ricky found this reassuring. At least, it corresponded with what he had already been told. Then, Carmen said: "Lonnie John was Mirabella's *boyfriend.* She call him always the great love of her life."

All Carmen knew was what Mirabella had told her. She stressed this again and again as Ricky ordered her one colorful cocktail after another, drawing, gently as he could, the information out of her. It all happened in the 1980s: that was what Carmen said. She was still in Madrid at the time, undergoing hormone treatment, saving up money for the big sex-altering operation, trying to make it as an actor/actress, hoping Pedro Almodovar might cast her/him in one of his movies. Meanwhile, in Paris, Mirabella, too, was still a mere transvestite, selling himself in the Bois de Boulogne. Carmen did not know how Mirabella and Lonnie John met; she only knew that it had been a *coup de foudre*—a lightning bolt, love at first sight. Lonnie was a pimp on the other side of Paris, in the

Bois de Vincennes. Lonnie John knew Mirabella's fondest wish, so he began giving the hooker the money that would pay for the hormone treatments and the surgery that would make him a her. But there were always problems between them, that was what Mirabella had told Carmen. Mirabella knew that Lonnie had a sister he pimped, knew that he was tortured over what he was doing to her, his flesh and blood, his twin. Then, while Mirabella was seeing a specialist in sex-change procedures down in Nice, Lonnie was attacked. For several days, he was unconscious, semicomatose. Surely, the gangsters who assaulted him had meant to kill him. When he finally came to, he told Mirabella, through teeth that had been wired shut, to forget she had ever known him. Mirabella returned to Nice to complete her sex change; stayed in the sunny South of France for a year. When she came back to Paris, she heard that Lonnie had gone to Istanbul, started pimping there. Another year passed. Then she learned that Lonnie was in prison.

"And is he still in prison?" Ricky asked, playing dumb.

Carmen took a quick look around the Hanoi Hideaway, as if she were afraid someone might be eavesdropping. She leaned closer to Ricky. "Mirabella tell me that Lonnie get out."

"When did she tell you that?"

"I don't know. Some month ago?"

"And had she seen him?"

"No. They telephone together. First, Mirabella, she is so happy. First time in ten year she talk to her Lonnie. Then, after some week, Mirabella is very angry, very mad, with him. It seem like she hate him."

"Where was he? In Paris?"

"I wish I know! I ask Mirabella, 'Where is he?' And she tell me, 'It is secret.' That was very much her, you know? I love Mirabella. Everybody love her, like you see from all the flowers at the door. But she had many, many secret."

Carmen felt that, despite her anger, Mirabella was expecting Lonnie John to show up sooner or later. Instead, it was Maximillian who made an appearance on the rue des Martyrs, last Wednesday night. Mirabella had told Carmen about him: that he was Lonnie's throat-slitting enforcer; that everybody hated him, especially the hookers he enjoyed subjecting to sadistic sex games; that many people believed Maximillian had plotted against Lonnie John; that Maximillian had tried to take over Lonnie's crew of whores after the American pimp left for Turkey; that Maximillian, failing as Lonnie's replacement, returned, in 1990, to his native Romania to cash in on the post-Communist bonanza of crime.

"I detest this Maximillian the minute I see him," Carmen told Ricky. "He is greasy man, with the odor of death. He scare me. But that night, Mirabella is very happy to see him. I think she think he will lead her to Lonnie John. So she is nice, much, much too nice to him. And this Maximillian, he look very rich that night. He have the clothes, the jewelry, the good air about him. It is all too much, I think. But Mirabella is all excited, hoping he is the emissary of Lonnie John."

"And was he?"

"That night, the Wednesday last, he say nothing about Lonnie. The three of us, Mirabella, Maximillian and me, we come here, to this place, to have drink. And this Maximillian, all he talk about is how rich he is now, how he get rich in Russia working for big-time gangster. He brag, brag, brag. *Dégueulasse!* How he collect the art, blah, blah, blah. But he sound like very ignorant man to me. No class, like you say in America. Rich, maybe, but no class. And still a killer. In his bone. One can see that. But Mirabella, she do not care. She seem impressed. And this Maximillian, he say he want to buy us both for the night. I tell them I have a regular client coming by at one, so I must be in the street for him. But Mirabella, she leave with Maximillian. It was a very hard night for her."

Only then did Ricky remember seeing Mirabella trudging up the rue des Martyrs on Thursday morning, her face looking haggard and uncharacteristically masculine in the brassy sunshine. Ricky had felt an abiding sympathy for Mirabella that morning. He was about to say *"Bonjour"* when he was preempted by Mirabella calling him a *"pauvre con."* After a night catering to the perversions of Max the Knife, was it any wonder she had been in such a particularly foul mood?

"What happened next?" Ricky asked, his need to know overpowering any sadness he felt for poor Mirabella.

"Next time I see her is Thursday night," Carmen said. Ricky could see she was warming to her story, getting into the pure telling of the tale. "Mirabella was all excited again. She tell me how cruel Maximillian had been in the bedroom. Very cruel. Very sick. The whole night long. But he had offered to her the hope of seeing Lonnie John. He said she must do him a favor and he would connect her with Lonnie. He said his boss is a Russian gangster name Dr. Dmitri."

"Named what?"

"Dr. Dmitri."

"That's what I thought you said."

"You know *him*, too?"

"Sort of. Go on. Please."

"And Dr. Dmitri want him to break in the apartment of an American who live in the rue des Martyrs. To search the apartment of this American."

Ricky remembered seeing Mirabella with Maximillian—who had, no doubt, been trying his best to look like an anonymous everyday nerd—on the rue des Martyrs Thursday evening, as he walked up the hill, on his way to work. He remembered how she had smiled and said *"Bonsoir, monsieur"* to him, knowing that she would soon break into his apartment.

"But why would Dr. Dmitri want my apartment searched?"

"I do not know. I think it is money they look for."

"But I don't have any money."

"Evidently, they think you do."

"And why did Maximillian need Mirabella's help?"

"It make everything more easy. She know the door code, of course."

"How?"

"How?" Carmen squinted at Ricky as if he'd asked the dumbest question she'd ever heard. "Every whore on the street know every door code on every building. We are there all the time. We see people push their code all night. How could it not be?"

"But if that's the case, why didn't Maximillian just pay one of the other hookers on the street to give him the door code? Why did he need Mirabella to help him?"

"Because he know she could get the key to your apartment, monsieur," Carmen said with an exaggerated politeness. "Mirabella know all the concierges on the rue des Martyrs. She went to your concierge, Madame Lavache, to get your key. She explain me all this at dinner Thursday night, Chez Kamel. Mirabella wait until she see you leave, then she go to your concierge and say that you tell her, Mirabella, that you lost your key and you need to give a copy to a friend you have coming over. You are at your job and cannot leave. But Mirabella is another of your friend. This, anyway, is what Mirabella say to Madame Lavache. Mirabella say that you ask her to ask the concierge for her copy of the key to your apartment. And later that night, after the concierge go home and you are still at your job, Mirabella and Maximillian could enter your apartment. Mirabella explain me all this at dinner, many hour before the break-in. She is all excited. She want to help Maximillian. At this time, she not really care about you. And she think all this will help her get to see her great love, Lonnie John. That is all she care about. To see Lonnie John again."

"So," Ricky asked, "what did they find in my place?"

"I do not know," Carmen said. "After dinner, when she tell me of the plan, I was never to see Mirabella again. Next thing I know, she is . . . dead." Carmen's voice cracked on the last word. She raised a hand to her mouth and looked away from Ricky, her eyes tearing.

Ricky squirmed in his plantation chair. He noticed other customers glancing nosily his way. Did they think that he had said something to hurt Carmen's feelings, that maybe she was his lover and he was breaking off the relationship, telling her it was time they both "start seeing other people?" Ricky had a sudden impulse to reach over and give Carmen a consoling touch, but he restrained himself—not because of the inquisitive stares of strangers but because he was still not quite sure he could trust the hooker who knew so much. As Carmen dabbed at her eyes with a little white cocktail napkin, Ricky asked, "What about Friday night, when I saw you with Maximillian on the rue des Martyrs? What was going on then?"

Carmen focused her tragic gaze on Ricky. "I want to say to you that I am very sorry for what I did that night. I was very scared. Maximillian had me in panic. You could have lost your life because of me, because of my fear, and I just want to say to you that I hope you can forgive me . . . please."

"What happened?"

"I was just standing in the street, waiting, between clients, and then,

from nowhere, like some evil spirit, this Maximillian appear. I tell him
'Go away,' but he grab my arm. He is skinny man but very, very strong,
like some skinny men are. I tell him, 'You kill my friend.' He act like
he do not understand. I say, 'Why you kill Mirabella? For Lonnie John?
Why Lonnie John want her kilt?' Maximillian say he kill nobody. But
I continue. I say, 'Who tell you to kill Mirabella, then? Dr. Dmitri?
Why? Why?' And then Maximillian, he open his leather jacket, and I
see, attached inside it, a very big sharp knife, almost like a machete. He
still grab me with the other hand and he say, 'I kill nobody yet but I
will kill *you* if you do not tell me what I want to know.' At this moment,
I am so scared, I cannot even think. I see what happen to Mirabella and
I am full of fear that I will be next. And Maximillian ask me, 'Who is
Reekee Jank? What he look like?' It was, like you remember, almost
four o'clock. Maximillian say he wait for you since two but he not see
you. I say, 'You want to kill him, too?' and Maximillian say, 'I kill you
right now if you do not tell me.' And, at just that second, I see you
coming down the rue des Martyrs. And I am so sorry but I was in panic
and I say then to Maximillian, 'That is him.' And, I believe, monsieur,
that the Holy Virgin must be looking out for you because as soon as
Maximillian turn to follow you into your building, the police drive by.
I walk away in one direction, Maximillian in the other, and your life,
it was saved."

Ricky asked Carmen if she had told any of this to the police. She
said there was no point. She was a whore and they wouldn't believe her.

"It is you who should go to the police, *monsieur*," Carmen said
earnestly. "You are American male. They will listen to you. But right
now, you must be vigilant. This is why I have to talk to you. Maximillian
is still out there."

Catching a glimpse of the clock on the wall, he saw that it was
almost six thirty. He was due back at Fatima's place in half an hour.
He thanked Carmen for her information and waved to the waiter, telling
the hooker he would pay the bill. "One more thing," he said. "I heard
that your colleagues on the rue des Martyrs think I was the one who
killed Grace . . . I mean, Mirabella. Is that true?"

Carmen winced. "Yes, there is some suspicion. But do not worry,
monsieur. We will . . . how do you say in America? . . . set them straight."

. . .

Walking together down the Boulevard de Clichy, then turning and climbing the rue des Martyrs, Ricky felt as if Carmen were his body-guard. During the short stroll from the Hanoi Hideaway to Ricky's build-ing, Carmen talked about Mirabella's distant past, her childhood as a flaxen-haired boy in Normandy. Carmen did not know what Mirabella's name had been back when he was a male. She knew that his parents were quite old when they had him. They had both been members of the French Resistance during the Nazi occupation. Mirabella said they had never disapproved of their only son's homosexuality but they both died before he changed genders. Mirabella liked to think her parents would have been supportive of her still.

As he and Carmen approached number 176, Ricky, out of the corner of his eye, spotted two of the night-shift hookers loitering across the street in front of the nursing home and looking their way. Carmen was also aware of the stares.

"Do not worry," she said. "Since they see you with me, they will know everything is all right. I will proclaim your innocence to everyone, *monsieur*."

"*Merci mille fois,*" Ricky said. Thank you a thousand times.

As Ricky reached to punch in his door code, Carmen suddenly leaned forward and kissed him once on each cheek. "Bless you," she said, then hurried up the street.

Ricky had barely had a chance to enter his lobby and close the door behind him when Madame Lavache, the plump and ruddy concierge with thick gray curls, came waddling rapidly across the floor tiles and threw her arms around him. She apologized profusely for having given his keys to Mirabella. She had raced back to Paris from Brittany when she learned of the murder. She had been periodically ringing Ricky's doorbell since ten o'clock Saturday morning but there was never any answer. Madame Lavache assured Ricky that the building's door code would be changed the following morning. She had already slipped no-tices under every tenant's door, informing them of the new three-digit, two-letter code that would take effect Monday. She said that she and her husband would stay in the ground-floor studio all night Sunday—

as they had all night Saturday—to make sure that no suspicious characters entered the building. And Madame Lavache told Ricky that her brother-in-law, a professional locksmith, was right there, in her apartment. They had been waiting all day for Ricky to return to the building so that the lock on his door could be changed, free of charge, of course. Ricky thanked the concierge for her thoughtfulness, said that right now he wanted to go upstairs and change clothes but he would let her know very shortly when the locksmith could come up and make the new installation.

"One more thing," Madame Lavache said. "The police were here yesterday. An Inspector Lamouche. He asked a lot of questions about you. He seemed quite suspicious of you. But I told him you are a good man, an innocent man."

"*Merci, madame.*"

As Ricky trudged up the stairs to his apartment, a grim nightmare scenario took shape in his mind: that he might actually be sent to prison, for the rest of his life, for a crime he didn't commit. That sort of thing happened to black men in America all the time. Maybe the same was true in France.

Entering his studio, Ricky saw the red number 1 flashing on his answering machine. He pushed a button and heard the voice of Cash Washington: "Yo, cuz, it's me, Sunday morning. I just wanted to say I'm sorry about last night. I didn't mean to put you or Fatima in a dangerous situation. As for me, I don't know what the fuck I'm gonna do." Cash's voice turned desperate and whiny. "I can't go back to the States, for various legal reasons. So I'm gonna have to stay in Europe for a while, maybe go back to Zurich. People tell me I might be safe there." After a short pause, Cash sounded more controlled, determined. "Anyway, I still want to see my wife before I leave Paris. I hope you're not hiding her from me, R. J. 'Cause if you are, you're gonna end up like that blond bitch in your lobby. That's not a threat, cuz. It's a guarantee."

Sixteen

FATIMA BOUKHARI HAD A notably different personality in each of the three languages she spoke fluently. In English, she was brutally direct. She wielded short, declarative sentences like blunt instruments. The choppy flow of American English—which is what Fatima spoke, as opposed to the more florid British English many French people learned in school— gave her natural candor an extra force. She said what she meant and she meant what she said.

Fatima was much softer in Arabic, despite the language's somewhat jagged rhythm. Perhaps it was because she spoke it mainly with her family. Ricky loved eavesdropping on Fatima when she talked on the phone with her mother or father or sisters, her aunts, uncles and cousins. Of course, he could not understand a word of what she said, but he adored the way she said everything, the relaxed and affectionate intimacy of her voice as she prattled away, making scratchy *acch*s and *ucch*s sound gentle and comforting. For Fatima, Arabic was the language of prayers and bedtime stories, of legends and ceremonies; it was the language of the clan.

French was her social tongue. And whenever she spoke the rolling, sumptuous language of her native land, Fatima seemed to take on all the complexity of the parlance. She became more sly and flirtatious as she wrapped her mouth around its convoluted structures. French was a language dripping with nuance and when Fatima spoke it everything she said seemed ripe with mystery and innuendo, a seductive elusiveness. Yes, she meant what she said but, given the artful dexterity with which she manipulated the language's serpentine syntax, what she said might have a multitude of meanings. Never mind her Islamic and African roots; when Fatima spoke the most romantic of romance languages, nationality trumped religion, ethnicity and race: She was a Frenchwoman, through and through.

Ricky didn't speak French fluently enough to have a different personality in his second language. In French, he sounded exactly like himself, only much dumber and without a sense of humor. Which is not to say that he spoke the language badly. After years of study with Valitsa the Serb, his command of the grammar and pronunciation was actually quite good. What he lacked was a feeling of ease. He was always acutely self-conscious in French, translating phrases in his head, pausing to rethink what he wanted to say, backtracking to correct slight mistakes, constantly apologizing for not speaking better. Ricky liked to believe that the huge obstacle preventing his French fluency was the fact that so many people in millennial Paris spoke English. Ricky told himself that if he lived in some isolated village in the countryside, he would be forced to speak French all the time and, through constant usage, might be much better at it. In Paris, he blundered along, doing his earnest best, pleased when people complimented him on his efforts, but always relieved when a conversation that had begun in French lapsed into English.

When Ricky and Fatima were alone together, they always spoke English. Only on those occasions when they found themselves among a bunch of Francophones, say, at some cocktail party, did Ricky speak French in Fatima's presence. She invariably made him feel more insecure, correcting his every little error, pursing her lips and impatiently making French sounds at him: *ooo, ewe, uuhh.* Eventually, Ricky would feel so intimidated, so stupid, that he clammed up. And once he stopped speaking, he would tune out the French conversation. He would watch Fatima chattering away with some other guest but lose any clear sense of what was being said. Then, when someone would ask him what he thought about the subject under discussion, he would mutter something completely inappropriate—comment on the political scene, for instance—while the talk had been of cinema. After which no one would bother to address him again, and Ricky would just stand there, with a wineglass in his hand, seething in impotent bewilderment.

But Ricky had never felt such a depth of helplessness and rage in the presence of French people as he did on Sunday, May 2, 1999, at Fatima's couscous dinner. Silent, smoldering, humiliated, he glared at Fatima as she babbled along, somehow conspiratorially, with the two guests who were not at all what Ricky had been led to expect. Once again, Ricky Jenks had been played for a fool. Or so he believed. And part of what made the experience so excruciating was that the evening had begun with such lovely promise.

"C'est pas grave," Fatima had said when Ricky called her from his studio at seven fifteen to say he would be late for dinner. Madame Lavache's brother-in-law the locksmith was still hard at work on Ricky's door. Ricky was apologetic in the extreme when he phoned Fatima. But the hostess was totally cool, soothingly repeating, *"C'est pas grave."* It was Ricky's favorite French phrase. To his American ear, the line came across as "Say pah grahv." This was what you said to reassure someone that whatever they had said or done was nothing to worry about. Whether a stranger had stepped on your foot or a loved one had unconsciously hurt your feelings, you could offer consolation by saying, "It isn't grave."

Fatima had a particularly beautiful way of saying it. At first Ricky was surprised that she had responded in French when he had spoken to her in English. Then he heard other French voices in the background and realized that Christophe and Eve-Laure had already arrived. While he found the prospect of speaking French for the entire dinner party a bit daunting, he happily braced himself for the challenge. He told Fatima, in French, that he would be right over. Just before hanging up, she tittered, *"J'ai une surprise pour toi."*

Bounding up the rue des Martyrs, Ricky gave no thought at all as to what surprise Fatima might have in store for him. Nor did he worry about the threatening message on his answering machine from Cash or the fact that Max the Knife was looking for him, eager to slit his throat. Since he knew these would not be dinner-party conversation pieces, he put them out of his mind. Instead, Ricky tried to concentrate on how happy he would be to finally taste Fatima's famous couscous and meet the wonderful couple she had mentioned so often. Ricky entered the Abbesses metro station, then went racing down the long, long spiral staircase, its twisting walls decorated with a mural depicting vibrant scenes of Montmartre. Standing on the platform, waiting for the train, he tried to remember the important details Fatima had told him about her friends. Christophe was a graduate school colleague, Fatima's closest comrade at the Institute of Political Science. Fatima had described him as looking remarkably like the young Dustin Hoffman and being full of "nervous Jewish energy." Eve-Laure, meanwhile, was a poet and literary critic, the daughter of a white Frenchwoman and a black man from Guadeloupe. Riding the train for two stops, tunnelling beneath the Butte Montmartre, Ricky thought that maybe Fatima would find some inspiration from Christophe and Eve-Laure's relationship. Maybe seeing the happy cross-cultural couple tonight would give her some hope for a future with Ricky and the child she was carrying.

Ricky exited the metro at the Jules Joffrin station, right in front of the *mairie* of the Eighteenth, bought a bouquet of tulips at the corner flower shop. He was whistling a giddy tune as he used the key Fatima had given him to open her apartment door. *"Bonsoir,"* Fatima sang as she glided up to him, wearing a long white dress. She gave Ricky a quick peck on the lips, then took him by the hand, leading him across the living room to meet the guests. He saw them standing expectantly in front of the couch and was instantly confused. The young man before him looked nothing at all like Dustin Hoffman. With his shaved head, goatee and stocky build, he was, in fact, a dead ringer for the goalie of the French national soccer team, Fabien Barthez. And the woman frowning beside the Barthez clone did not look even remotely *métisse*. She was a porcelain-skinned blonde with bright blue eyes and a pointy nose and chin. In the split second before Fatima introduced them, Ricky realized who they were. "This is my dear friend Bernard-Henri," Fatima said in French. "And his girlfriend Marie-Agnès."

"Enchanté," Ricky croaked. It was the last thing he would remember saying during the party. Bernard-Henri grasped his hand, pumped it hard and said something enthusiastic about how glad he was to meet Ricky at last. The hand of Marie-Agnès felt small and brittle as she greeted Ricky. She said something polite-sounding, the words barely escaping her thin red slit of a mouth.

"Christophe and Eve-Laure had to cancel at the last minute," Fatima explained. "At first, I was very disappointed but then I thought, 'Why not call Bernard-Henri?' "

"Why not?" Bernard-Henri said, grinning.

"I told you, Reekee, that I had seen him recently. But I had never met Marie-Agnès and I thought tonight would be the perfect occasion for us all to get together. Fortunately, they were free on such short notice."

This, in any event, was what Ricky thought Fatima was saying. As she spoke, Ricky could feel his understanding of the French language fly away, fluttering out of his brain. He stood motionless in the living room, dumbstruck and enraged, lost in a dual incomprehension: linguistic and emotional.

Why had Fatima done this? Was this her idea of a "surprise"? Ricky sat at the dinner table, unable to speak. He ate the couscous, but did not taste it, had to fight his swelling nausea even to swallow it. He downed glass after glass of Bordeaux, hoping the wine would dull his rage—but it only sharpened his paranoia. Why had Fatima done this to him? Sprung her ex-boyfriend, the object of her obsession, on him like this? Had she known all along that Christophe and Eve-Laure would not be coming to dinner? Was this couscous fest all a setup she and Bernard-Henri had arranged in advance? He watched Fatima jabbering with Bernard-Henri Henri and Marie-Agnès, hearing their voices, understanding nothing. He observed their gestures, their demeanors: Fatima with her hair-flipping flirtatiousness, reveling in her Francophonic personality, tossing off clever witticisms and sly asides; Bernard-Henri, animated and utterly full of himself, managing to exchange frequent knowing glances and old inside jokes with Fatima while constantly reaching over to stroke the shoulders of his current girlfriend; Marie-Agnès, bony and prim, not as loquacious as her fellow French citizens but seeming to enjoy herself and, Ricky perceived without comprehending the words, assiduously flattering the hostess on her cooking, her clothes and interior decoration, but with just the slightest hint of condescension, as if to say, "You're rather impressive—for a black woman who lives in the Eighteenth."

In the early stages of the meal, Bernard-Henri tried to chum it up with Ricky, making a few jovial, jokey remarks, trying to draw him into the conversation. Ricky, neither understanding nor caring what Bernard-Henri had said, responded with hostile grunts. Fatima shot him several dirty looks. Marie-Agnès, meanwhile, simply ignored the large, sullen black man at the table. Soon, Fatima and Bernard-Henri did the same. Ricky just sat there, swallowing the tasteless couscous, washing it down with full glasses of wine, marinating in silent, incoherent fury, his madman thoughts returning again and again to the same question:

Why had Fatima done this? What sort of coquettish little power game was she playing here? Did she just want to see Ricky squirm? Or was she trying to taunt Bernard-Henri and his posh girlfriend? By this point, Ricky had decided that Fatima had no idea who the father of her baby was. So perhaps she was taking a lighthearted approach to the dilemma, inviting her two lovers to the same dinner. Maybe she was behaving like one of those merry, amoral adulterers in some French film comedy. Why shouldn't two illicit cheaters get together for Sunday couscous with their respective, cuckolded mates? It was all in good fun, no? So what if Fatima did not know whose child she was carrying? Really, Ricky, thought, someone should be filming this romp. Call it *Les Deux Papas*. Or *Un Père de Trop*. Ho ho ho. By the end of the dinner, though, Ricky's ugly mood had befouled the air. As Bernard-Henri and Marie-Agnès rose to leave without having coffee or dessert, it occurred to Ricky that maybe Fatima, clueless as to her child's paternity, had brought the two suspects together so that she could decide who she would *say* the father was—regardless of the truth. If that was indeed the case, then Bernard-Henri, with his wealth, charm and whiteness, had definitely won the contest.

Ricky exchanged tepid handshakes with the guests. Fatima talked to them for a long time, in subdued tones, at the door, while Ricky uncorked a fresh bottle of Bordeaux, filled his glass to the rim. Once Bernard-Henri and Marie-Agnès had gone, Fatima sat beside Ricky on the couch.

"I really like them," she said, in English, "you know?"

"Yeah. I know."

"You were extremely rude, Reekee. I would like to know why."

"You would?"

"Yes, I would."

"Well, there's something I would like to know."

"That is what?"

Ricky looked Fatima dead in the eye. "Is the baby mine?"

Until that moment, Ricky had never seen a look of real horror in a person's face. Not shock or disgust—but pure, genuine horror. He watched Fatima's eyes widen and her mouth open in a soundless wail. It was the face of someone confronting a sight, an idea, a gross indignity beyond their imagining. And, as soon as Ricky saw the horror in Fatima's face, he knew he had made the mistake of his life. He felt as if he had opened a door to step into an elevator and found no elevator there. He was falling fast, plummeting down the dark, empty shaft.

Finally, Fatima spoke. "Of course," she said. "Of course the baby is yours."

"Okay, okay, okay," Ricky sputtered. "But, you know, you said, you said you had seen Bernard-Henri. You—you told me that! The other night, when you said you were pregnant, you also said you had seen Bernard-Henri!"

"Yes," Fatima said. She blinked hard several times, as if Ricky were shining a flashlight in her eyes. "Yes, I saw Bernard-Henri. Some time ago. And I wanted to tell you. Because I wanted to be honest. I know you have this obsession with Bernard-Henri, so . . ." Fatima's voice trailed off, disappeared into a defeated sigh, as if she could not find the words to continue.

"But why did you tell me that you had seen him at the same time you told me you were pregnant?"

The horror was fading now. Fatima's face was turning to stone. "I know you think I keep secrets from you, Reekee. But that night, I want to tell you everything. I want to tell you of the baby and maybe I also want to tell you that I had seen Bernard-Henri, just to be completely honest."

"Okay, but, but, but——"

"But you thought I had sex with Bernard-Henri?"

"Well, I, er, I, uh——"

"You thought Bernard-Henri was the father?"

"I thought, well, maybe——"

"You think I am a whore?"

"I never said that."

"You think I am such whore that I don't even know who is the father of my baby? You mistrust me so much? My God, Reekee . . ."

"Well, you know, honey, maybe it was just a cultural misunderstanding."

"Get out."

Ricky laughed nervously. "Fatima, I think what we have here is a failure to, you know, communicate."

"GET OUT!" Fatima shrieked. Now she was on her feet, screaming hysterically in Arabic. Ricky, suddenly terrified, leapt from the couch. He tried to approach Fatima, to put his arms around her, but she was flailing madly, whirling at him, a torrent of strange, violent language exploding from her mouth. Instead of embracing Fatima, Ricky found himself backing away from her, trying to apologize but being deafened by the scorching Arabic curses. "GET OUT!" Fatima shrieked again in English before returning to her tirade of indecipherable abuse. She threw open the door and, with a mighty shove, pushed Ricky backward, into the corridor. The door crashed shut in his face.

"Our *carrefour*," Ricky and Fatima used to call it. The word meant crossroads, and this one, the secluded, cobblestone intersection of rue Saint Vincent and rue des Saules, was the prettiest in the Eighteenth.

Back in their early days together, just that past summer, when strolling through the narrow lanes, up and down the hills and staircases of Montmartre, they would stop and sit in the ivy-lined alcove that was the Square Roland Dorgelès. It was a sort of miniature park, a small courtyard, raised like a stage, up a few steps from the sidewalk. There was a cluster of shady trees, lush plants, two wooden benches and a stone one along the wall. A foot-high stone barrier, more like a tall curb, bordered one side of the square. The iron railing surrounding the steps formed another boundary that defined the intimate space. There was a little plaque on the wall commemorating the man who had given the square its name. The first time they stepped into the alcove together, Ricky read aloud the words engraved beneath the small bronze profile: *"Je hais la guerre mais j'aime ceux qui l'ont faite."*

"I hate the war but I love those who made it," Fatima translated. "He is speaking of World War One. Roland Dorgelès wrote a famous novel about it, *The Wooden Cross.* The war disgust him but he had great feeling for the French soldiers who fought in it. He also wrote many stories about Montmartre. He lived up here."

"You're a walking encyclopedia."

"No, just the daughter of a librarian."

Ricky cuddled up to Fatima on the stone bench, took her in his bearish arms, nuzzled his nose in her crinkly, fragrant hair. Catty-corner to their alcove was the Lapin Agile. The favorite watering hole of thirsty artists like the young Picasso at the turn of the twentieth century, it was a popular tourist spot at the turn, of the twenty-first, featuring an unabashedly folksy cabaret act that encouraged group sing-alongs of old *chansons françaises.* On the outside, though, the Lapin Agile still resembled a tattered country cottage: pale pink façade, forest-green shutters, red tile rooftop, surrounded by a gnarly wooden fence, shaded by a leafy canopy. Above the doorway, under a protective if weather-stained glass frame, was the old painting of the nimble hare himself—a sort of nineteenth-century Gallic Bugs Bunny—hopping out of the pan in which his soon-to-be-skinned body should have been stewed, tall cap tilted jauntily between his long pointed ears, scarlet bow tie around his neck, matching sash around his belly, balancing a bottle of red wine on the back of his furry paw.

Directly across the street was a sprawling vineyard—not on the scale
of those in the countryside but huge for urban Paris. The vineyard was
enclosed in a high metal fence of the kind that Ricky always associated
with schoolyards and basketball courts. The fence surrounding the vineyard was painted green, in order to mesh with the verdant grape leaves
inside. At a diagonal from the vineyard, in the northwest corner of the
quaint crossroads, was the craggy stone wall of the small cemetery named
after Saint Vincent.

That first time Ricky and Fatima snuggled up together on the stone
bench, the *carrefour* was almost deserted. Strange for a summer's midnight. But it had just rained heavily, so the typical crowds of tourists
must have scattered in search of shelter. They could hear the muffled
voices of people singing inside the Lapin Agile and the faint chirping
of crickets, but that was all. Everything was so still, the *carrefour* illuminated by the soft, buttery glow of an old-fashioned street lantern. "I
feel like we just stepped inside an Impressionist painting," Ricky whispered in his lover's ear. Fatima sighed contentedly, wriggled even more
snugly in his embrace.

At just that moment, the Montmartrain came chugging down the
rue Saint Vincent. Ricky and Fatima laughed as the bizarre contraption,
a long white-and-red Little Engine That Could on rubber tires, rolled
along the cobblestones. A tour guide manned the driver's seat, beneath
the tall, fake, locomotive smokestack, droning into a microphone in
bored-sounding German, his voice echoing throughout the *carrefour*; that
first car pulled three open carriages behind it, each one packed with
tourists in T-shirts and baseball caps who stared blankly or snapped their
cameras at the passing scene as the Montmartrain disappeared down the
curving, sloping, ageless street.

"Ah, well," Ricky said. "Modern times intrude."

"I love these times," Fatima said. "This is our time."

"This is our *carrefour*."

And so they continued to call the spot, as if they owned it, through
the sultry end of summer, all through the chilly, brilliant autumn as the
grape leaves in the vineyard turned various explosive shades of red and
orange and yellow and the hordes of tourists gradually thinned out.
Ricky considered dates with Fatima rare and precious events. He could

never be sure when she would be free to see him, so he cherished every encounter all the more. And right up until it got too cold to sit in the Square Roland Dorgelès, Ricky tried to make sure that, as much as possible, he and Fatima made a stop at "our *carrefour*."

But tonight, in the wake of the wretched couscous dinner, three hours after Fatima had thrown him out of her apartment, Ricky sat alone on the stone bench, contemplating his stupidity. It was the first time he had returned to the alcove since the weather had begun to turn warm. Once again, the *carrefour* was nearly deserted. The rain had not yet come but the air was thick and clammy. Alone in the Square Roland Dorgelès, Ricky took in the ripe, tingling smell of the blossoming plants and trees. And once again, all he could hear were the sounds of a muffled French sing-along and chirpy crickets. He ached to have Fatima cuddled up against him. But he realized that he might never have that sublime sensation again. Just that afternoon, when Fatima laid her hand against Ricky's cheek and told him he was "such a sweet man," he had thought they were solid. The twist of some sort of binding commitment had been there—hadn't it? And then what happened? He splattered it all away in a madman ejaculation of sexual paranoia.

Cold drops of rain dampened Ricky's reverie of self-recrimination. He rose from the bench, clambered drunkenly down the short staircase of the Square Roland Dorgelès. Okay, so he was wrong to have suspected Fatima. But hadn't she suspected *him?* When he found her in his studio at dawn last Friday? She had called three times but never left a message because—despite Ricky's obvious devotion—she worried he might have been with another woman. "Well," Fatima would scoff if Ricky reminded her of her jealousy, "you are a *man!*"

As Ricky walked down the rue Saint Vincent, hands in his pockets, shoulders hunched against the drizzle, he realized that, on several argumentative fronts, Fatima had him trapped in a checkmate of political correctness and common sense. He was defenseless. There was nothing to do but confess his wrong and beg for mercy.

But when? Ricky had walked down to the broad, tree-lined rue Caulaincourt, going in the direction of Fatima's apartment. He still had the key. He could just walk in. But what if Fatima had put the little chain lock on? Remembering Fatima's frightening rage, Ricky doubted she would want to see him tonight. Give her time to cool off. Wait till the morning, when Fatima would be more rational and Ricky would, at least, be sober. He knew she had an eleven o'clock class down at Sciences Po. She would have to leave her apartment by ten thirty at the latest to make it to school on time. He decided to get up early (for him) and return to Fatima's apartment by nine o'clock, giving him an hour and a half to plead forgiveness.

Turning off rue Caulaincourt, heading back to his side of the Butte Montmartre, Ricky found himself walking again up the steep curve of Avenue Junot. He thought of Serena, of the way she stood above him and opened the bathrobe, boldly offering her body. Only then did he remember the sick message Cash had left on his answering machine. He had blocked it out of his mind all evening. What disturbed Ricky was not so much the fact that his cousin was threatening his life but that Cash seemed capable of making good on that threat or, as he termed it, guarantee. He began to recall his conversation with Carmen. Hadn't the hooker said that Maximillian was working for Dr. Dmitri? Why the hell would Dmitri order Maximillian to search Ricky's apartment unless Cash had told him to? And Cash knew Maximillian had murdered "that blond bitch" in Ricky's lobby. But how the fuck did Cash know Mirabella? Had he, through Dmitri, ordered Maximillian to kill her? Or had Cash ordered for only Ricky to be killed? Why? Because Cash thought Ricky was hiding Serena, maybe hiding some loot Serena had stolen from him? After all the questions he'd peppered Serena with that afternoon, the one he forgot to ask was whether it was true that she had stolen "millions" from her husband.

Maybe he should ask her now. If he kept walking up Junot, he would soon arrive at Janusz Waldemar's villa. He could press the buzzer, see if Serena was in. Where else would she go? Maybe she'd be happy to see him, maybe so happy she would thrust her naked pussy at him again. He knew it would be insane even to put himself in temptation's path. His main concern was salvaging his relationship with Fatima. What sort of monster would he be if he betrayed her now? Still, Ricky couldn't stop think about Serena's body. His mind was, in fact, so preoccupied with his vision of Serena's perfect breasts that he did not realize how close he was to the mansion. He saw the white ambulance first, blue light spinning silently atop it, parked in front of the wrought-iron gate. There were two police cars, as well, but no sign of the cops. Ricky figured they must be inside Waldemar's house. Ricky's heart seemed to have lodged in his throat, where it went into violent palpitations. Something had happened to Serena. Somehow Maximillian had found her. And killed her. On Cash's orders.

A crowd of about a dozen people was buzzing around the front gate, too curious to mind the steady drizzle. The lights were on inside the mansion, the door wide open. Ricky stopped and peered between two other sidewalk gawkers. He saw cops and medical workers milling around the foyer. "Hello, my friend," a familiar voice said.

Ricky turned and found himself standing beside the Indian flower salesman with the checkered cap. "Where is your beautiful lady friend?" the flower man asked, holding a batch of red roses, each one wrapped in clear plastic.

"At home in bed," Ricky said, shaking the flower man's free hand. "Do you know what happened here?"

"Yes. The owner of the villa was murdered."

"Waldemar?"

"No, Monsieur Waldemar sold this place two years ago. Did you know him?"

"Uh, no, not exactly."

"I did. I used to work as a gardener in many of the buildings on this street. No, Monsieur Waldemar lives in the Cayman Islands now. It was the new owner who was killed. A Monsieur Niculescu. Romanian."

Ricky's wooziness returned. "Maximillian?"

"Perhaps that was the man's first name. Did you know him also?"

"Not exactly," Ricky mumbled.

Then he spotted, through the open doorway, the pasty face, in profile, in the foyer of the villa. He saw the greasy-haired, green-suited man talking to a blue-uniformed cop in an authoritative, I'm-in-charge-here manner. No doubt about it: that was Inspector Lamouche.

"Yap! Yap yap yap!" Ricky looked in the direction of the shrill little bark. He saw the neatly trimmed poodle at his feet, staring up, somehow accusingly, at him. He turned and immediately recognized the woman

standing several feet away, and looking straight at him. She was the
poodle's owner, the emaciated woman with the dyed black hair dramatically streaked by that shock of white at the peak of her forehead.
The woman stood in a small cluster of people who seemed familiar with
each other. Neighbors of the dead man, no doubt. The Avenue Junot
Block Association. While the dog continued to yap at Ricky's feet, the
poodle's owner leaned toward one of her neighbors and, still keeping her
eyes on Ricky, whispered something in the man's ear. Now he was staring at Ricky, too. They were not giving him that blunt but harmless
French eyeballing. This was a "Let's Round Us Up a Lynch Mob, Bubba,
Go Get the Rope" kind of stare. And the fucking dog wouldn't shut up.
"Yap yap yap!"

   "Au revoir," Ricky said to the flower man.

   "Good-bye, my friend."

   Ricky walked briskly up the looping street, striding away from the
scene of the crime, away from Inspector Lamouche. Only once he got
to the top of Avenue Junot, and turned onto the rue Girardon, did Ricky
break into a run, just as the thunder cracked and a heavy rain came
pummeling down.

PART 5
Carrefour

Seventeen

RICKY OPENED HIS EYES at the first ring, found himself staring at the peeling ceiling, his apartment ablaze in sunlight. What day was it? What time? He turned and looked at the digital clock beside the sofa bed: 11:11. No fucking way.

The second ring. This was Monday. He had set the alarm for eight o'clock, had planned to go to Fatima's place before nine. He grabbed the clock and saw that he had failed to push the button that would have programmed the alarm, a mistake so stupid that Ricky could only wonder if he had, unconsciously, done it on purpose.

Third ring. The only person he wanted to talk to was Fatima and it couldn't be her calling because Ricky knew she had an eleven o'clock class. Unless she had skipped class because she was so upset from the night before and was now calling Ricky to say . . . what?

"*Bonjour,*" Ricky's voice said on the answering machine. He lunged for the phone. "Hello?"

"Monsieur Jank?" a deep French voice asked.

"*Oui.*"

"Good day. I believe you were awaiting my call," the voice said in stilted English.

Ricky could feel the hairs on the back of his neck tingle. "Oh, was I?"

"Yes. I am calling to find out when we can meet. There is much to discuss."

At first, Ricky wondered if this was a cop. Now, he was sure it was someone connected to Cash, maybe someone else his cousin had hired to murder him. "You're damned right there's a lot to discuss."

"I am sorry. I do not understand."

"Yeah, I'll bet you don't."

"You are Reekee Jank?"

"Of course I'm Ricky Jenks. Who the fuck are you?"

"Excuse me, I thought I had said. I am Monsieur Dumoulin."

"Oh, not *Dr.* Dumoulin. Like Dr. Cash and Dr. Dmitri. I thought all you motherfuckers were doctors."

"Well, I do have a doctorate in composition. I am sorry, *monsieur,* I seem to have said something to offend you. François Penin at Le Bon Montmartrois told me you were awaiting my call."

"Oh, shit."

"I direct a small music school in the city of Bobigny. I had thought you might be interested in teaching there but——"

"No, please, Monsieur Dumoulin, I've made a terrible mistake! I thought you were——never mind!"

When Ricky finally stopped apologizing, he made an appointment to meet the head of the conservatory at noon on Thursday. Monsieur Dumoulin sounded somewhat less than enthusiastic as they hung up. Ricky took a long, hot shower. Normally, he loved Mondays. Since the crêperie was always closed, Ricky knew it was the one day of each week he would definitely not have to work. But, today, as he got dressed, Ricky felt lost, helpless. He wondered if he should go to the police, as

Carmen had advised him, tell them everything he knew. Or thought he knew. Would it really do any good for anybody?

The phone rang. Hoping again to hear Fatima's voice, Ricky rushed to pick up the receiver. "Hello?"

"Bear?"

"Marva!"

"*Ça va?*"

"I guess I'm all right."

"What are you doing?"

"I was wondering the same thing myself."

"Listen, honey, I'm in my car right now, not far from your place." Ricky heard something unfamiliar in Marva Dobbs's voice, a certain grimness. "Can I swing by and pick you up?"

"Where are we going?"

"How'd you like to meet Li'l Lonnie John?"

"Are you serious?"

"Yes, I am. He's holed up in la Goutte d'Or."

"Holy shit."

"Do you want to meet him or not?"

"Yeah, I guess I do. There are a few questions I'd like to ask him."

Marva sighed. "You ain't the only one, Bear. That motherfucker's got a whole lot to answer for."

Paris's "inner city" was, in fact, an "outer city." It was called the *banlieue.* "The suburbs." There were many pleasant, and several wealthy, towns just outside the Paris city limits. But when Parisians spoke of the *banlieue,* they did not mean to evoke the backyards and white picket fences of American suburbia. Most of the areas ringing Paris's twenty arrondissements were bleak, impoverished neighborhoods, largely populated by the descendants of France's colonial subjects. It was on the outskirts of the city that one found vast housing projects, plagued by violent crime and gang warfare. But there were several pockets of the *banlieue* right inside Paris—and none was more notorious than la Goutte d'Or, that is to say, "the Drop of Gold."

Named for the white wine that had been cultivated from the vine-
yards that occupied the spot back in the thirteenth century, la Goutte
d'Or, since the time of France's Algerian conquest in the 1830s, had been
a beleaguered home to wave after wave of immigrants. Portuguese and
Spanish, Italian and Yugoslavian communities had carved out ram-
shackle enclaves for themselves over the decades. In the 1960s and '70s,
huge numbers of immigrants from the Caribbean and black Africa
flowed into the *quartier*. But from the mid-nineteenth century until the
waning days of the twentieth, la Goutte d'Or had been most famously
inhabited by the peoples of Northern Africa: the Arabs and Berbers and
Jews of Morocco, Tunisia, Algeria. During the late 1950s and early '60s,
while the war for independence raged in Algeria, la Goutte d'Or became
the main Parisian battleground for the conflict. There was nightly com-
bat between the police, Arab militants, and rival Algerian immigrant
factions. Decades later, the area still had a war-ravaged feeling about it.

La Goutte d'Or was defined by a network of narrow, intertwined
streets in the southeast region of the Eighteenth Arrondissement. Just as
it was often difficult to say exactly where touristic Montmartre bled into
Third World Barbès, so it was hard to distinguish where Barbès bled
into la Goutte d'Or, precisely where the bustling black and brown energy
of the street bazaar segued into the half-abandoned desolation of contemporary urban hell. There was raunchy rue Myrha, with its strung-
out bums, drug dealers and prostitutes; the young hoodlums hanging out
in the Square du Léon; and blessed Saint Bernard de la Chapelle, which
gave refuge to illegal African immigrants until the police violently
raided the church in 1996. And, of course, there was the long, blighted
expanse of the rue de la Goutte d'Or itself, dominated by a fortress-like
police station and rows of concrete-slab apartment buildings. No other
part of Paris reminded Ricky so much of America.

Ricky had done almost all the talking during the short ride from
his apartment to la Goutte d'Or. When he first entered the car, Marva
Dobbs greeted him with a kiss on each cheek and an apology.

"I'm sorry about the way I reacted when you showed me that photo,
Bear. It's just that I've had a lotta history with that child."

"Tell me about her," Ricky said.

"At this point, you know a lot more than I do. Why don't you tell me your side of the story first?"

By the time they reached their destination, Ricky had only told Marva about his first encounter with the woman who had gone by five names: Serena-Cassandra-John-Moriarty-Washington. He told her about their talk at the crêperie and the runaway wife's subsequent disappearance from Valitsa the Serb's apartment. He forgot to mention the missing hand grenade.

Marva seemed unsurprised by everything Ricky told her. "So," she said, "after Valitsa's place, Cassandra, I mean, Serena, wound up on the Avenue Junot."

"How did you know about Avenue Junot?"

Marva parked her Audi in front of a forbidding cement block façade. "Chinyelu told me. You're about to meet her, too."

As soon as he stepped out of the car, Ricky checked out the crew of tan-complexioned teenagers who were checking him out. There were four of them. Ricky figured they were *Beurs*—the French-born children of North African immigrants. They stood on the walkway leading to the building that, when compared with most of Paris's architecture, looked like a prison. They each sported a shiny warm-up suit, immaculate basketball shoes and a fashionable *banlieue* homeboy haircut: straight and greasy on top, totally shaved on the sides and the back of the head. One of them wore blue-tinted, wrap-around sunglasses. Another carried a boom box, blasting a French rap song. The smallest of the crew held a purebred, musclebound pit bull on a chain-link leash, spiked leather collar squeezing its bulging neck. The dog regarded Ricky with a quiet fierceness in its beady eyes, long white snout twitching. The boys from the 'hood gave Ricky that familiar Parisian gaze, brazen but nonthreatening. Ricky, after all, with his brown skin, black button-down shirt, baggy gray pants and black sneakers, was not completely out of place here. He might have been obviously American but he did not look like some lost tourist who'd stumbled into a bad part of town. And Ricky, for France, was quite a large man. So he did not feel intimidated— except, maybe, by the pit bull.

It was Marva he was worried about. The car she stepped out from

behind the wheel of was not ostentatious, but was clearly high-priced.
Like Ricky, she was obviously African-American. But, in her sharp black
Yves Saint Laurent pantsuit and Jackie O shades, she was also, obviously,
a bourgeoise. Ricky could see the crew's stares change from curious to
menacing when they spotted Marva coming their way. But Marva blew
right past them, striding insouciantly, as if she owned the pavement.
That was when Ricky remembered that Marva had been born and raised
in the Bedford Stuyvesant section of Brooklyn. She knew she was badder
than these wannabe hoodlums. Probably badder than the pit bull, too.
You could take the homegirl out of Bed Stuy but you could never take
the Bed Stuy out of the homegirl. The tough guys of la Goutte d'Or
seemed to blush in Marva's wake. Ricky followed her, trying not to
smile, through the cracked glass doorway of the building. Marva and
Ricky squeezed together in the coffin-sized, urine-scented elevator as it
clattered up to the fourth floor.

"When's the last time you saw Lonnie John?" Ricky asked.

"Must've been 'eighty-seven. He got up on the stage at one of the
gospel brunches. Impromptu. Sang 'Amazing Grace' like you've never
heard it sung. When he hit that line about 'a wretch like me . . .' Not a
dry eye in the house. Lonnie had a voice like an angel."

Marva pushed the light button on the fourth floor, but only half the
long corridor was illuminated. She rang the doorbell of an apartment at
the darkest end of the hall. A haggard African woman opened the door.
She did not look old so much as wrung out: baggy, bloodshot eyes and
mottled saddle-leather skin. She wore a *kente*-patterned robe and a shiny
but unkempt hair weave: purplish, synthetic-looking braids, clinging to
kinky scalp. Marva introduced her as Chinyelu. Ricky shook her skeletal
hand and said, *"Bonjour."*

The smell of burnt peanut oil filled Chinyelu's living room. There
was little furniture. In the corner, Ricky saw a small, pajama-clad girl
with cornrows, sitting cross-legged on the brown carpet, clutching a dirty
pink Barbie doll with blond hair. The girl had her back to Ricky. Her
attention was focused, silently, almost solemnly, on the image on the
wide-screen color television. Ricky recognized the young black actor,
quite a handsome kid, actually, though he could never remember his
name. But he remembered all too well the name of the character he

portrayed: the grotesque, squirming Urkel. Ricky had seen this American sitcom on several visits to the States. The character was supposed to be an intelligent kid, a nerd; but in every episode Ricky had managed to watch, the laugh track soared as Urkel engaged in the sort of bug-eyed, wide-grinning, body-contorting, racist minstrelsy that had ancient roots in American entertainment. Urkel conveyed the idea that no matter how smart a black student might be, he was still, at heart, a dumbass nigger. But Ricky had never seen Urkel like this before: dubbed into French. And there was Chinyelu's little daughter, eyes glued to the screen, savoring this cultural import, absorbing, in her own language, its images of black authenticity. Behold: the global village.

Chinyelu pointed to a closed door, decorated with a poster of the Spice Girls. *"Allez-y,"* she said. Go ahead.

Ricky followed Marva into the room, closed the door behind him. The only light in the small space came through the slits of half-closed Venetian blinds. The thin shafts of sunlight and bars of shadow striped the bed in the center of the room. Ricky saw the outline of a body beneath the red bedspread. Marva bent over, clicked on a lamp on a rickety-looking nightstand. There was Serena, amber hair spread across the floral-printed pillow. Her eyes fluttered open. She blinked hard at Marva. From the bewildered look on Serena's face, Ricky thought she must have been wondering if she was dreaming. When her eyes finally focused, Serena said, "Aw, fuck."

Marva stared down at Cash Washington's wife and said, "Hello, Lonnie."

"How you like me now, Ricky?"

Cash Washington's wife sat in a wooden folding chair, dressed in her velvet bathrobe, holding a glass ashtray in her lap and smoking a Gitane. She took occasional swigs from the bottle of Evian resting at her feet. Ricky sat in a matching chair, on the other side of Chinyelu's small bedroom, staring at his cousin's runaway spouse, in speechless astonishment. Serena was just as feminine as before, with her long wavy hair, one breast nearly hanging out of the robe, naked thighs crossed, huge fawn's eyes shining. But Ricky could not look at Serena now without sensing her buried gender. It was still a beautiful woman who sat before him—but only now did Ricky see the man who lurked inside her. He was there in the deeper timbre of her voice, in her looser posture, in that faint lump of an Adam's apple, the muscular hands and large feet. And he was there in the taunting way Serena addressed Ricky. Serena's theatricality, that show-bizzy mix of utter sincerity and utter phoniness, made perfect sense now. Because Cash's wife had always been playing a part. And playing it to the hilt.

Marva Dobbs, sitting on Chinyelu's bed, regarded Cash's wife with an admiring, analytic eye. "My compliments to your doctors," she said.

"Geneva," Cash's wife answered, as if naming the city explained everything, conjuring images of Swiss medical perfectionism.

"It really is remarkable," Marva continued. "I mean, the cosmetic aspect is one thing. You were always an effeminate man. But sitting here, looking at you, I feel like I don't even know who it is I'm looking at. You really did *become* Cassandra. Didn't you, Lonnie?"

"My name is Serena," Cash's wife snapped, womanish indignation underscored by a mannish threat of violence in the voice. "That is what you will call me."

"All right," Marva said coolly, "Serena."

"And it's God who made me." Serena took a slow drag on the cigarette, exhaled with authority. "You still believe in God, don't you, Marva?"

"You know I do."

"Then you should understand that who I am is the result of His will."

"Testify, sister," Marva said softly.

Now Ricky felt like an intruder. There was something deeply sad and intimate, angry and tender, in the way Serena looked at Marva and the way Marva looked back at her. Ricky wondered if he should excuse himself, go into the living room and watch Urkel with Chinyelu's daughter, let Serena and Marva share the mystery of their history alone. But he couldn't move. He had to stay, had to know.

"They met in the silent place," Serena said, staring straight ahead, her gaze seemingly focused on a point beyond Ricky or Marva, beyond this room, this realm. "Poor Cassandra, she was already sick, had been sick for a long time. Then Lonnie got his beating. Got beat into a coma, got beat to near death. And it was when he was in that space near death, that silent place, not-life and not-death . . . he saw Cassandra again. They met and they embraced for one last time. 'Cause they were twins. What happened to one, happened to the other. When one got hit, the other felt it. That was the way it always had been. And so when Cassie was sick and in the hospital, Lonnie got his beating and wound up in the hospital, too. And when Lonnie found himself in the silent place, his twin sister was there, too. And Cassandra said to her brother, 'Redeem me . . . Redeem us.' That's what she said, when they embraced in the silent place: 'Redeem me. . . . Redeem *us*.' "

She spoke in a bland, conversational voice but continued to stare straight ahead. Ricky listened to Serena-Lonnie, entranced, too freaked out to judge her/him.

"You know, the Lord has a soft spot for sinners. He wants to give the sinful a chance to earn their way into the kingdom of Heaven. The good He takes right away. Cassandra was goodness. She was sweetness and kindness and everything beautiful. It was her bad twin who corrupted her, who soiled her purity. But God took Cassandra twelve years ago. And He let the sinner live. That was the bad twin's punishment and his opportunity. So when Lonnie opened his eyes, when he returned to the earthly realm, he already knew Cassandra had died. And he remembered what she had told him in the silent place, when she was on her way to the next realm and Lonnie was returning to this one. Lonnie knew what he had to do for absolution. For redemption."

Serena stubbed out what was left of her cigarette. She took a long drink of mineral water, then lit up another Gitane. Ricky was not sure if she had only paused or was through explaining.

"What about Turkey?" Marva asked. "If you, I mean Lonnie, knew what he had to do, why did he go to Istanbul and get back into pimping?"

Serena looked Marva in the eye again. "Because knowing how you should live is different from living that knowledge. Lonnie had the knowledge in 'eighty-seven. But he wasn't prepared to live it. So he had to go to Turkey. Get his ass thrown in prison for two years. 'Cause it had to be that way. God knew what He was doing with Lonnie John.

God knew Lonnie had to sit in a cell for two years in order to understand his mission. Only once he got released, was he prepared to live the knowledge."

"Meaning," Marva said, "that he had to become Cassandra?"

"No, no, no," Serena said impatiently, as if annoyed by Marva's obtuseness. "Cassandra lived inside Lonnie already. It was Serena he had to become. And it was Serena who would live out Cassandra's dream. Live the life Cassandra had wanted to live before Lonnie corrupted her."

This is the craziest fucking shit I've ever heard, Ricky thought. But he was still too astonished to speak. He just sat in his folding chair, trying to assimilate all the weirdness, trying not to show how rattled he felt.

"And how did Lonnie pay for the transformation?" Marva asked. If she was as unnerved as Ricky, she certainly wasn't giving anything away. Marva addressed Serena with the polite curiosity of a hostess making dinner-party conversation. "Doctors in Geneva don't come cheap."

"Oh, Lonnie didn't lack for money. He had a good man taking care of his finances for him while he was in prison: Janusz Waldemar. And the two years Lonnie was in that Turkish cell, don't you know that Janusz didn't steal anything from him—not a single *centime*. All Lonnie's money was waiting for him when he came back to Paris. Janusz was a true friend." Serena smiled wryly. "He was also the only man who had ever fucked both Cassandra and Lonnie. But that's another story."

"And after Geneva," Marva said, "Li'l Lonnie John was gone and Serena Moriarty had been born."

"You always had an eloquent way of putting things, didn't you, Madame Dobbs?"

"Oh, I don't know. I just like to talk. So did Lonnie. And Cassandra, too. I've missed talking to both of them over the past twelve years."

"Cassie thought you were jealous of her."

"Oh, really? Well, if she did it musta been Lonnie who put that idea in her head."

Serena and Marva stared hard at each other now, both of them half-smiling, in a sort of fond contempt, like two well-acquainted battlers happy to be mixing it up again. After a lengthy silence, Ricky finally found the wherewithal to speak. "So, uh, Serena, when did you go to live in the States?"

"Why, Ricky Jenks!" Serena said, oozing sarcasm. "Are you still here?"

"More or less."

"I went to the States in nineteen ninety-three."

"To live Cassandra's dream?"

"Exactly. And you know what? I almost made it. 'Cause what Cassandra wanted out of life was a strong relationship with the Lord, a handsome and successful husband, and stardom."

"Well," Ricky said, forcing a smile, "two out of three ain't bad."

Serena squinted at him as she drew on the cigarette, then blew a cloud of smoke his way. "You're just like Cassius, aren't you? You bougie Negro hypocrites. I wish you could see your face right now, the way you're looking at me. Yesterday you wanted to fuck me. Today you look at me like I'm some kinda diseased fucking leper. Like you want to avert your gaze from this unsightly spectacle—but you just can't help yourself, right? You just have to look. 'Cause you know you still want some. You just hate yourself for still wanting it. Ain't that right, Ricky?"

"I think you've seen *The Crying Game* too many times."

"Oh, puh-leeeeze! Dil was a man pretending to be a woman." Serena slid a hand between her thighs. "And I'm *all* woman. You know that as well as anybody, Ricky Jenks. And you know you still want some."

"No. I don't."

Marva chose this moment to stare at the ceiling and pretend she didn't understand what was being said.

"I hope you're not as shitty a lover as you are a liar, Ricky," Serena said. "Maybe someday I'll find out. But in the meantime I'm goin' for three outta three. I will get the stardom that Cassandra deserved. You just watch me."

"And what about the handsome and successful husband?" Ricky asked. "You gonna keep him?"

"Maybe." Serena's eyes glistened with tears. "If he'll have me."

If Ricky had not known what to make of Serena before, he was now completely baffled. But, remembering how Cash had spoken about Serena, and seeing the hurt in Serena's face at this moment, the one thing

Ricky felt sure of was that Dr. and Mrs. Washington were, in their own tortured way, still in love. Aside from that one truth, Ricky didn't know what to believe about either Cash or Serena anymore. "So," he said, "the big secret Cash learned about you. It wasn't that you had once been a prostitute. It was that you had once been a man."

Serena's earlier bravado, the taunting sarcasm, had evaporated. "Yeah," she said, wiping her eyes with her velvet sleeve. "Ain't that a bitch?"

"And that's why you can't have children, of course."

"Of course."

"Lord have mercy, Cassie," Marva said, then quickly corrected herself. "I mean, Serena. Child, how could you think you could keep a secret like that forever?"

"I didn't think forever. I knew I would have to tell Cassius someday. I just thought if I could put it off long enough, then, by that time, he would love me so much that he wouldn't care. That he would be able to accept the truth."

"But he wasn't," Ricky said.

"Maybe if he'd heard it from me. Who knows? But instead he found out from some sick bitch blackmailer."

"Mirabella."

Serena tried to be cool but Ricky could see the startled Bambi-caught-in-the-headlights look in her eyes. "Uh . . . yeah . . . her."

"Who's Mirabella?" Marva asked.

"Why did you tell me all that shit about Lonnie trying to blackmail you," Ricky said, "when it was Mirabella?"

"Will somebody please tell me who in the hell is Mirabella?" Marva cried.

"The prostitute who had her throat slit."

"Because I knew you knew there was a Lonnie John," Serena said. "I had to tell you something, to explain who he was. I couldn't be sure how much Cassius had told you."

"But you were betting he hadn't told me that you used to be Lonnie."

"And he hadn't."

"Most definitely not."

"I'm confused," Marva said.

"Don't be," Ricky replied. "Here's the deal. Serena Moriarty, for-merly Lonnie John, moves to New York and, sometime in nineteen ninety-six, meets the man of her dreams—or of Cassandra John's dreams, anyway. One year later, Dr. Cash Washington and Serena Mor-iarty are married. Everything is peachy for a while. Cash becomes more and more famous and successful and more and more greedy and narcis-sistic. Serena, meanwhile, pursues her dream of pop stardom." He paused and looked at Serena. "Am I right?"

Serena stubbed out her second cigarette, immediately lit up a third. "Go on," she said tonelessly.

"Problems arise. Cash works crazy hours but discourages Serena's career ambitions. And, despite much effort, Serena can't get pregnant. Still, her big secret is safe. Anyone who knew Cassandra John knows she's dead. Anyone who knew Lonnie John thinks he's in prison. And none of those people live in America. Anyway, the marriage is already under some strain when Serena gets a call from Mirabella, Lonnie's ex-lover. It was Mirabella who saw the photo of Cash and Serena in *Paris Match* and instantly figured everything out. Mirabella was a transsexual, she knew Cassandra was dead, and realized that Lonnie had followed her—Mirabella's—lead, into womanhood. It was Mirabella who tracked Serena down, who called her demanding money. And when Serena couldn't pay her any more, Mirabella sent a letter to Dr. Washington. Cash confronts Serena. A big fight in the kitchen. Screams and accusa-tions. Cash hit his wife and she stabbed him in the belly."

"Stabbed?" Marva gasped.

"Self-defense," Serena said.

"Then you fled to Paris. You were panicked. Everything seemed to be falling apart. You tried to get in touch with Janusz Waldemar but found out he'd moved to the Cayman Islands. So instead, you hooked up with the man Waldemar had sold his villa to, your old buddy Max-imillian. And you paid Max the Knife to kill Mirabella."

"Who's Max the Knife?" Marva cried.

"Maximillian Niculescu," Ricky said. "Romanian gangster."

Serena blew another foul-smelling plume of Gitane smoke at Ricky. "My, my, you're not as dumb as everybody in your family says you are."

Serena's little dart hit the bull's-eye. Ricky flinched but quickly recovered. "So am I right?"

"Up to a point."

"Did you or did you not—"

"Now shut the fuck up!" Serena barked, pointing at Ricky, the lit cigarette dangling between her fingers.

There was that rage again, the bottomless fury that Ricky had perceived as the truest Serena. But now he knew the source. Back when Ricky was a kid in New Jersey, overweight and tall for his age, his father had warned him about short guys, telling him that the baddest dudes on the street were often the smallest. Because they had something to prove and they had to know how to fight dirty, to beat you with viciousness and guile rather than brute strength. Thirty years later, Ricky saw a gorgeous woman sitting before him but there was still a ruthless little pimp inside her, the pint-sized bad ass who had spent his youth making larger men pay dearly for underestimating him.

"If I'd been able to find that sick bitch Mirabella, I'd a killed her myself," Serena fumed. "I spent days huntin' that cunt but she wasn't in any of the places I expected her to be. So I figured, fuck it, she'd already wrecked my marriage, might as well let the bitch live. I would stay in Paris till I finished my recording session, then plan my next move. You're right about my looking for Janusz and finding him gone. But I had no idea he had sold his house to that scumbag Maximillian. I didn't find that out till Saturday morning when Maximillian called me on my cell phone at Valitsa's place."

"So you had had some contact with Max over the years?"

"Fuck no!"

"Then how'd he have your cell phone number?"

"At the time, I didn't know how the fuck he'd got it. He said to meet him at Waldemar's place. So I did. That's when I found out he'd gotten the number from my ever-lovin' husband."

"Because Cash, desperate to find you in Paris, had given the number to Dr. Dmitri and Max was now working for Dr. Dmitri."

"Who's Dr. Dmitri?" Marva cried.

"How do you know all this shit?" Serena asked Ricky. "Not from Cash?"

"No, not from Cash."

"The police then?"

"Does it matter how I know it? The only thing that matters is I know it."

"Will someone please tell me," Marva asked, "who in God's name is—"

"Dr. Dmitri Zugashvili," Ricky said. "He's dead."

"He and Max are suckin' each other's nasty dicks in Hell," Serena hissed.

"So lemme get this straight," Ricky said, "you didn't know Max worked for Dmitri and Max didn't know that Lonnie had become Serena—until a few days ago."

"I figured somebody musta killed Maximillian by now. He was the last person I expected to hear from—ever. And only when he called me and I went to meet him on the Avenue Junot Saturday morning did I find out that he hadn't been killed back in Romania, and that he'd hooked up with a bunch of Moscow gangsters. And that his boss was my husband's business partner. Small filthy world, huh?"

Serena flashed her wry smile again. Ricky was pleased to see that her rage had cooled somewhat. "Okay," he said, "I'm trying to figure out the sequence of events here. After your fight with Cash, you fled America. Cash, as he was recovering from his stab wound, called Dmitri, said 'I can't find my wife, I think she's in Paris. We're being blackmailed by some prostitute named Mirabella.' Is that what happened?"

"*Exactement.* And Dmitri said, 'Not to worry, my colleague Maximillian knows Paris. He will find both the whores—Mirabella, and your wife.' "

"And once Max located her, Mirabella told him what had become of Lonnie."

"And then he killed her," Marva chimed in. "Bastard."

"On Cash and Dmitri's orders," Ricky said.

"No, see, y'all didn't know Maximillian," Serena pointed out. "He didn't need nobody to give him no orders to kill. Max would act on his own initiative. He'd do it just for the buzz."

"So why did you go see him Saturday morning?" Marva asked.

"Old time's sake. I wasn't scared of Maximillian. And I figured maybe he could lead me to Mirabella. And when I first got there, every-thing was cool. He was impressed, like you all, by my transformation. We drank vodka and reminisced for a while. Then he tells me he's got a message for me from my husband: that if I don't meet with Cassius in Paris to give him back what I owe him and discuss the terms of the divorce, I'd end up like the other freak who had dared to blackmail him. That's how my ol' partner Maximillian let me know he'd sliced Mira-bella a new orifice. Not that the bitch didn't deserve it."

"And did Max mention me?" Ricky asked. "Did he tell you he and Mirabella had searched my apartment just before he murdered her in the lobby of my building?"

"Fuck no."

"Cash met with me Thursday afternoon and Thursday night he had my place searched, just in case you and I had met secretly and maybe you passed on some of the money you stole from him. How much did you steal, by the way?"

Cash's wife fluttered her eyelashes and went into her most flirtatious Serena persona. "I dislike the word 'steal,' " she cooed. "I was merely exercising a wife's prerogative. Cassius had become very secretive about his earnings. And I told you about those mysterious parcels in our home. Once the trust is gone from a marriage, what have you got? I couldn't stand Cassius ignoring my questions about money so I had to do some-thing to get his attention. I transferred sums out of accounts he didn't know I had access to. And I hid—from him—some of those parcels he had tried to hide from me."

"I reckon that got his attention," Marva said dryly.

"Mmmm-hmmmm." Serena looked proud of herself.

"And Cash used Maximillian as his emissary?" Ricky asked.

"You mean extortionist!" Serena was all lit up again. "Can you believe that shit? I don't know who pissed me off more. My old partner or my fucked-up husband. Imagine that scrawny, pasty-faced, circus si-deshow, Communist-bloc fuckin' refugee button man threatening me . . . me! Of all fuckin' people! To help make some bougie Negro from Jersey feel powerful? Fuck that fuckin' fucked-up bullshit!"

"And you conveyed this to Maximillian?"

" 'Conveyed'?" Serena sneered. "I told him, 'Yo, Max, just 'cause I *have* a pussy now doesn't mean I *am* one!' "

Marva burst out laughing.

"And then you killed him?" Ricky asked.

Serena took a swig of mineral water, seemed to consider how to answer the question, then said, "It was him or me."

"Damn, Lonnie," Marva said.

"When?" Ricky asked.

"Saturday," Serena replied matter-of-factly.

"So when I saw you Sunday afternoon..."

"Maximillian was moldering away in the basement."

"And it was late Sunday afternoon," Marva interjected, "that the neighbors started asking questions."

"Nosy fuckin' frogs."

"And you called Chinyelu, to see if you could hide out here," Marva continued.

"Who is Chinyelu, by the way?" Ricky asked.

"Old employee of Lonnie's," Serena said. "Look, all I needed was a place to stay until after my recording session this afternoon."

"So you left Waldemar's place before the police arrived?"

"DUH!" Serena shouted at Ricky. "Them nosy neighbors were askin' after you, too, my man. Who was that *'grand noir'* who came around Sunday afternoon? Sorry, Ricky, but you're in this shit up to your eyeballs, whether you like it or not."

No one spoke for a long time. Ricky, Marva and Serena sat in a loosely formed triangle, making brief eye contact with one another, then looking away. A whoosh of canned laughter, from the French-dubbed Urkel show, could be heard through the wall. In Chinyelu's bedroom, the silence lingered. Finally, Marva said, *"Un ange passe."* It was an old French saying, used to explain those awkward silences: "An angel passes by." That was why no one could speak. Ricky loved the expression. But never before had it felt so literal. He wondered if the spirit of Cassandra John had not indeed wafted through this room.

"Why the fuck did Chinyelu call you, anyway?" Serena asked Marva.

"She was worried about you," Marva said.

"Tccch." Serena sucked her teeth in exasperation.

"So what happens now?" Ricky asked.

"Y'all should get the fuck outta here and let me get ready for my session with DJ Fabrice."

"You're going through with it? After everything that's happened?"

"Fuck yeah! And right now I've got to shower, put my face on and warm up my voice, then I have to get my ass to his studio by three o'clock, so thank you very much for your concern but I'd appreciate it if y'all would get the fuck outta here."

"And then what? After your precious recording session?"

"I don't know, Ricky, all right? Probably, I'll go back to the States and deal with Cassius there. But the smartest thing for you and Marva to do is to keep your mouths shut and act like you never even saw me. And remember, Ricky: I coulda killed your cousin right there in our kitchen. I coulda slit his throat like I slit Maximillian's. And the reason I didn't do it is because I love him. I don't know what the fuck is gonna happen with us but there is no reason for you or Marva to concern yourselves with this—not anymore. Just leave me alone and let me go to this rendezvous with DJ Fabrice." Serena paused, then said, in a tight voice: "This is the only chance I might ever have to realize Cassandra's last dream."

Ricky did not know how to respond. He looked to his old friend. Marva Dobbs rose from Chinyelu's bed and walked over to Serena. She bent down and kissed Cash Washington's wife on the forehead. *Bon courage,*" she said.

Eighteen

THE BOULEVARD SAINT GERMAIN shimmered in that weird yellow light Paris sometimes has during those few precious months when the sun shines consistently, a light that always made Ricky think of the bright, curved brass mouth of a well-polished trumpet. Marva's Audi zipped down the avenue, past the lavish apartment buildings, the wide windows of chic fashion shops, their wares always displayed in tastefully minimalist style, the sidewalk café tables filled with rich old ladies and sleekly suited businesspeople. Here was the quintessence of Left Bank splendor.

"When Picasso was young and hungry, he lived in Montmartre," Marva once explained to Ricky. "Back then, he was struggling to *become* Picasso. Once he *was* Picasso, he moved down here."

La rive gauche. How did it manage to be both high-class and subversive? The Fifth, the Sixth, and the eastern half of the Seventh Arrondissements: the old stomping grounds of Sartre and de Beauvoir, of Richard Wright and Gertrude Stein, Miles Davis and Juliette Greco; Baldwin, Breton and Joans, Beckett and Himes and on and on and on . . .

Marva, the always striving genius of soul food, kept her restaurant in the unpretentious hills of the Eighteenth. But Marva Dobbs, the established Paris celebrity, made her home among the other stars of the media, the intelligentsia, and the world of creative entrepreneurship, the impassioned Socialists with expensive tastes who lived in the center of town, just south of the Seine.

After walking out of Chinyelu's grim building in la Goutte d'Or, Marva had told Ricky she was going home and asked if she could give him a lift somewhere. On the spur of the moment, he decided to drop by Sciences Po, Fatima's university, on the border of the Sixth and the Seventh. Ricky and Marva were both silent for much of the drive downtown, still stunned by their encounter with Serena. Then Marva said "How is Fatima, by the way?"

This was all that was needed to set Ricky off. He told Marva everything—about Fatima's pregnancy, the night on the town with Cash, his paternity paranoia and the debacle that was the couscous dinner—in one cathartic gush. "I don't know what to say to her, what to do," Ricky despaired as Marva stopped at the corner of the Boulevard Saint Germain and the rue Saint Guillaume, right down the street from the Institut d'Etudes Politiques.

"Sure you do, Bear," Marva said.

"I do?"

"You do."

"What then?"

"I gotta move this car before the light changes." Marva leaned Ricky's way, kissed him once on each cheek. "Go now."

"But what do I tell Fatima?"

"Tell her I say hi. Now go!"

If there was one thing Ricky hated more than unwanted advice from his elders it was elders withholding advice when they knew he wanted it. "Okay, bye," he huffed. Ricky entered the main hall of the university, searched for Fatima Boukhari in the bustling crowd of intelligent-looking twenty-somethings toting overstuffed knapsacks. He made his way to a sunny courtyard and immediately spotted Fatima pushing open a glass door and descending a short flight of stairs. She wore a simple black cotton dress and her hair was balled up in a bun at the back of her head. Only once she reached the bottom of the stairs did she see Ricky. Fatima froze. She seemed to be considering whether to turn and run back into the building. Ricky approached her quickly, before she could flee.

"Please, wait, I'm so sorry." Though he stood only inches in front of Fatima, Ricky dared not touch her. She looked up at him, impassively, inscrutably. "Please forgive me," Ricky continued. "There's no excuse for what I said, what I thought, how I acted. I was stupid, insecure, paranoid ..."

He paused and stared into Fatima's dark chocolate eyes, searching for some kind of absolution. "Go on," she said.

"Insane, irrational, idioto ..."

The faintest trace of a smile crossed Fatima's lips. "Keep going."

"Cruel, egotistical, macho, vulgar, disrespectful. . . . Did I already say stupid?"

"Oh, yes."

"Can we please go somewhere private, where we can talk?"

Fatima looked at the ground. "Yes. Let's go somewhere. Much has happened since last night. There are many things you do not know, Reekee, that I should tell you."

"I am moving to Morocco, one week from today. I do not know how long I will be there. But it will be a very long time."

Fatima and Ricky sat at the small sidewalk café table on the Place Saint Sulpice, surrounded by the stylish denizens of the Left Bank. Ricky felt dazed by the brassy sunshine beating down on them, by the constant whoosh of the streams of water gushing from the mouths of the stone lions that decorated the immense fountain at the center of the square, by the look of ferocious resolve on Fatima's face. All he could manage to say in response to her announcement was: "Why?"

"I reflected for a long while after you left last night," Fatima said. "I came to the realization that this was the time for hard decision. I called my aunt, the sister of my father, who lives in Marrakech. I told her of the pregnancy and begged her to keep it a secret between us. She vowed not to tell my father and mother. And she also promised to take care of me. This is something she has much experience in, helping pregnant young women who are not married. I will stay with her and if the child is meant to be born she will help me in deciding what to do with him. Or her."

"I don't understand. Are you talking about adoption?"

"Perhaps. We shall see. My aunt was very sympathetic when we spoke. We agreed to tell my parents that I am in Marrakech doing academic research. I have arranged everything with my professors here. My coursework is practically done, anyway. I must take one exam before I leave. Then there will be nothing more for me to do but write my dissertation. This can be accomplished in Morocco."

"But what about us?" Ricky asked, trying not to sound as overwrought as he felt. "I mean, I know I behaved badly but still I—"

Fatima cut him off, maintaining her calm and determined tone. "There is no longer any trust between us, Reekee. Perhaps it can be reconstructed but we do not know. I think we need this time apart."

"But it's my baby, too."

"You did not think so last night."

"Fatima, please, I beg you to forgive me. I've always felt so insecure with you. It was just a stupid misunderstanding."

"It speaks to deeper things, Reekee. Much of what has happened in the past few days has caused me to question how I live my life."

"What do you mean?"

"I mean that night with your cousin Cash. I was such a fool. And perhaps I have been a fool with you also. I think I must reconnect with my root. I have lost contact with my faith. I fear I have become too westernized."

"Fatima, you were born in France. This is a western country!"

"Naturally, you do not comprehend."

"But I want to. I really do. I think if we just spend more time together and talk this through, we will be able to comprehend each other. But if you shut me out of your life and move to Morocco then,

Jesus, Fatima, what hope is there for us to ever come to any kind of understanding?"

"There is something else."

"Are you listening to what I'm saying?"

"Yes, Reekee. It is you who are not listening to me in your very American way."

"What the hell—"

"I am bleeding."

Ricky felt as if he had been kicked in the stomach, all the air knocked out of him. He opened his mouth but no sound emerged. Fatima continued to stare implacably at him as he tried to speak. "I . . . uh . . . en . . . ahh . . ."

"It started last night," Fatima said. "After I talked with my aunt. I called Dr. Yassin this morning. She was very busy but agreed to meet with me on emergency. She did an examination, another sonogram. She said that perhaps the bleeding is nothing to worry about. Perhaps it will end soon. But she also said that maybe there is a problem. Dr. Yassin told me I should go home and stay in the bed for a few days. I will see her again Friday morning. If the bleeding has not stopped by Friday . . . then . . ."

Fatima stared down into her empty coffee cup. Ricky reached across the table and laid a hand upon her cheek. "Oh, my love," he said, "I'm so sorry. We have to get you home. I'll take care of you. If Dr. Yassin recommended bed rest then you shouldn't even be sitting here with me. Let's get a taxi back to the Eighteenth. I'll go to the market and buy everything you need. You've got to get off your feet."

Fatima looked up again, carefully grasped Ricky's hand and pulled it away from her face. "No. I must go back to Sciences Po now. There are several administrative issues I must deal with."

"I'll go with you. Then I'll take you home."

"No," Fatima said firmly. "I will go there on my own."

"But who's gonna take care of you these next few days?"

"Do not concern yourself with that."

"But the . . . the little sea horse . . ."

"If he is meant to be born, he will be born. If the bleeding continues, he was not meant to be born. It is up to Allah."

"Won't you please let me help you?"

"No, Reekee. I go back to school now. I will call you Friday, after I see Dr. Yassin. Until then, please leave me alone."

"I love you," Ricky said.

Fatima lowered her eyes. "Thank you."

Ricky walked all the way back to the Eighteenth. It took two hours for him to make his way from the elegant piers along the Seine to the tawdry homeliness of the Place Pigalle. Through most of the walk, he kept thinking of the snowy sonogram image of that tiny, wriggling proto-person. He couldn't know what would happen between him and Fatima but he desperately wanted that little sea horse to be okay, to grow and survive and become a baby. Ricky thought of what Fatima had said, about it all being up to Allah. Then he remembered the meeting with Serena in Chinyelu's bedroom that afternoon, the way the male-pimp-turned-female-singer had spoken of God's being responsible for the bizarre trajectory of her life. They were completely different people, Serena and Fatima, believed in completely different religions. But they both had this intense faith. Ricky had always been thoroughly agnostic, lacking the fierce conviction of both the believer and the atheist. He had never given much thought to questions of fate or destiny or cosmic design. It occurred to him that he had led a completely passive, even an accidental, life. He could not say that his way was any more right or wrong than Fatima's or even Serena's. But, as he reached the rue des Martyrs, Ricky felt the painful need of what Fatima and Serena both had: that unflinching sense that things happened for a reason. Was that why he kept thinking of the little sea horse?

The flowers had disappeared from in front of Ricky's building. Casting an eye up the block, Ricky spotted the two Tootsies, those matronly queens of the day shift, loitering outside a café. He absentmindedly punched in his old code and found the front door wouldn't open. He had to dig the notice of the new door code out of his pocket, then he punched it in and entered his building. The concierge's door was closed but he assumed she was on duty today. The light button worked just fine, keeping the spiral stairwell illuminated as Ricky climbed to the third floor. Knowing that Maximillian was dead, he felt safer than he had in three days. He turned his freshly minted key in the new lock, opened the door to his studio and had to stifle a sudden yelp of shock.

"Hello zere," Inspector Lamouche said. The detective sat in Ricky's one comfortable armchair, that enigmatic little smile on his pale moony face. There were three men standing around Lamouche—also plain-clothes cops, Ricky surmised. Two of them were nearly identical: beefy, broad-shouldered guys in black leather jackets, not quite bald, with thin layers of gray stubble on heads that looked as if they were made of concrete. Then there was the dude with the fifties-style black pompa-dour, pock-marked skin and a brown suede jacket. Tall and thin, he was not quite as imposing as the stubble-head twins but he had an unsettling glint of psychosis in his bright green eyes. Ricky knew he was in trouble if Lamouche had felt the need to bring along his goon squad. "Cloh ze door," the inspector commanded.

Ricky reluctantly obeyed, then decided to play it tough. "What the fuck are you doing in here?"

The three goons exchanged surprised looks. Lamouche's smile dis-appeared. "And to zink, I was so nice to you ze ozer night. I took you to ze Salle des Mariages, just to make you feel comfortable. And zen you *lie* to me!"

"I don't know what the hell you're talking—"

"Do not lie to me again!" Lamouche shouted. "You zink you are dealing wiz Peter Sellers here? I ask you about a black American doctor, an embezzler, you say you don't know him and now I learn he is your cousin! You try to make fool of me, Reekee Jank?"

Lamouche and his posse were glaring at Ricky but something in the eyes of the three goons indicated that they did not comprehend English. "Listen, Inspector," Ricky said in a calm but firm tone, "I'm sure we can—"

"You abuse my confidence," Lamouche said, cutting Ricky off. There was a pitiful edge of disappointment in his voice. "Always I am so nice to Americans, but you people do not ever deserve it."

"I still don't know what the hell you're doing in my apartment," Ricky shot back. "Have you got a search warrant?"

"I wipe my ass wiz your search warrant!" Lamouche exploded. "Now cuff him!" The goons clearly did not understand. Lamouche leapt from the chair. *"Mettez-lui les menottes!"* he shrieked.

While one of the stubble-head twins took hold of Ricky's arms and pulled them behind his back, the cop with the pompadour and the psycho stare clasped the handcuffs around Ricky's wrists. With Lamouche leading the way, the cops roughly pulled Ricky down the spiral staircase. As they hustled Ricky through the lobby, the concierge, Madame Lavache, ran up to him and said, "I am so sorry, *monsieur.* I promised not to give your key to anyone else but when the police ask, it is different!"

Ricky had no time to respond. The cops pushed him out the door and into a gray Renault. The stubble-head twins sat with Ricky in the backseat. The cop with the pompadour, meanwhile, mounted a motorbike, gunned the engine and took off up the rue des Martyrs. Lamouche placed a blue siren on the roof of the car, then sat behind the steering wheel. "You're making a big mistake," Ricky said. "I'm an American citizen and I demand to—"

Ricky was drowned out by the deafening two-tone wail of the siren. Other motorists rushed to get out of the way as Lamouche drove madly through Montmartre, into the heart of Barbès, then made a screeching turn onto the rue de la Goutte d'Or. He parked the Renault in front of the fortress-like police station. With Lamouche marching in front of them, the goons dragged Ricky through the main hall. The noisy space was filled with blue-uniformed white cops and black and brown young men, handcuffed like Ricky, sitting on wooden benches or being questioned by officers in front of formica counters. Lamouche pushed open a black metal door at the back of the hall, then led Ricky and the goons down a flight of stairs and through a network of dim basement corridors. Lamouche unlocked another heavy door and entered a stark, brightly lit room with puke-green walls. One of the stubble-head twins pulled Ricky into the interrogation room while the other remained outside in the dark corridor. Lamouche sat behind a gray metal desk, ordered Ricky to take the seat across from him. As Ricky sat down, he heard the door behind him slam shut. There was a second door in the room, tightly sealed, a few feet to the left of Lamouche's desk, and the beefy goon positioned himself in front of it. Adjusting his butt, Ricky discovered that the metal chair on which he sat was bolted into the concrete floor.

"I demand to speak with the U.S. embassy," Ricky said.

"Oh, we will be sure to place a call for you," Lamouche said. He slid open a drawer, pulled out a glossy, eight-by-ten photograph and dropped in on the desk, right under Ricky's nose. "You recognize zis person?"

Ricky looked down at the color shot of the bare-chested corpse, laid out on what appeared to be a slab in a morgue. The lips were slightly parted, beneath the droopy mustache; the eyes wide open, staring eerily at Ricky. There was a hideous, red gash across the throat. "Yes," Ricky said. "I recognize him."

"Aaaaarrrrrrrrgggggggghhh!"

Ricky jumped in his seat, turned in the direction of the tortured scream. The sound had clearly come from behind the door guarded by the stubble-head. But Ricky could not tell if it had been a man or a woman crying out in pain.

"Did you kill Maximillian Niculescu?" Lamouche barked.

"Of course not," Ricky said flatly.

"You were seen entering his home Sunday afternoon."

"So what?"

"Did you also murder Mirabella Darrieux?"

"Fuck no."

"You have already lied to me about your cousin. How do I know you are not lying now?"

"Look, Lamouche, I'm not answering another question until you allow me to contact the U.S. embassy. And unless you take these hand-cuffs off me right now, you are gonna find yourself in the middle of a major fucking diplomatic incident."

Inspector Lamouche leaned back in his chair, smiling cryptically again. "*Ah, bon?* Well, we certainly would not want zat to happen." He glanced at his henchman and gave a quick nod. The beefy cop opened the door he had been guarding.

Now Ricky could see clearly into the adjoining room. It was fur-nished in the same stark manner. And standing in the center of the space, wrists handcuffed behind her back, a black blindfold masking her haunted eyes, was the prostitute Carmen. Ricky could see the other stubble-head goon sitting in a chair behind her. And circling the statuesque hooker, muttering insults and threats in French, was the other cop who had appeared in Ricky's apartment, the green-eyed psycho with the pock-marked skin and the pompadour.

"I believe you know zis *putain*," Lamouche said.

"Yes," Ricky whispered.

At that moment, the elaborately coiffed cop slapped Carmen's face. "Aiieeeee!" the hooker screamed.

"Why is he hitting her?"

"She was arrested on drug charges," Lamouche replied. "Not for ze first time. We know zat she met wiz you Sunday. We ask her to tell us what was said, what she knows about zese murders and about you. But she refuse to talk about you."

The psycho cop continued to walk around Carmen, snarling at her under his breath. The blindfolded, handcuffed prostitute was still on her feet, but swaying slightly, as if she were about to topple over. *"Non, non,"* Ricky heard her whimper. *"S'il te plaît, s'il te plaît...."*

"She have no diplomatic status," Lamouche said. "She is criminal. Wiz a long record. So Bruno can beat her as much as he like."

Now Bruno slammed his fist into Carmen's stomach. The hooker crumpled to the floor. The psycho cop grabbed a handful of her long black hair and jerked her head up. His fist was poised to smash her in the face.

"STOP!" Ricky yelled. "Lamouche—make him stop!"

"Only you can make it stop," the moon-faced-detective said quietly.

"Okay, okay, okay. I'll tell you everything I know. Just tell him to stop hitting her."

Nineteen

WHO WAS IT RICKY Jenks had betrayed? Not Cash. Yes, he told the police everything he knew about his cousin's moves and motives. But what the hell. Somebody was bound to catch up with Dr. Washington sooner or later—Interpol, Russian gangsters, his knife-wielding transsexual wife. Any way you looked at it, Cash was doomed. So why should Ricky feel guilty about helping get the French police on the bandwagon? Cash might very well have tried to have Ricky killed. And besides, Cash would be safer in French police custody than he was on the run.

So was it Serena he had betrayed? As Ricky returned to his apartment after more than six hours in that vomit-colored interrogation room in la Goutte d'Or, he felt small and dirty. He was now a police informer, a collaborator. He told Inspector Lamouche everything he had learned about Serena, *née* Lonnie; let him know that she was the one who had knifed Maximillian. He said he believed it was in self-defense. Was that some kind of violation of trust? Serena had done nothing but lie to Ricky, to try to trick and manipulate him, from the moment they met. He had already done her a favor by letting her go to her precious recording session instead of reporting her to the cops that afternoon. As it was, Ricky didn't get around to telling Lamouche about DJ Fabrice until eight o'clock, stalling to give Serena enough time to lay down the tracks with her French producer. No, he had done Serena no harm.

For a long time, Ricky didn't bother to turn on the lights in his studio. He sat in the dark, stewing in his guilt, only now realizing that it had nothing to do with what he had said during his three hours talking to Lamouche. It was all about the subsequent three hours he spent sitting alone in that stark and putrid interrogation room. He knew, after Lamouche and the goons, having removed the handcuffs, left him alone in that basement cubicle that he might be facing arrest or imprisonment or deportation as some kind of accomplice in one crime or another. He knew that somebody else he knew might very well turn up dead soon. But all he could think about during those three hours was Fatima. He was so worried about her, alone in her bed, wondering if her pregnancy would survive. He worried that maybe the champagne and the stress of that night out with Cash had caused Fatima's bleeding. More likely it was the pain Ricky had inflicted on her—questioning her, insulting her, the way he had. Even if Ricky had not directly caused this crisis, his lack of trust in Fatima had smashed their relationship. This was why, after he was finally released from the police station, with no charges filed against him, and walked home from la Goutte d'Or, and plopped down on his sofa bed in the darkened studio, Ricky was sick with self-disgust. It was Fatima he had betrayed.

Red digits glowed in the dark: 11:44 on the alarm clock, in the tiny window on the answering machine: 3.

Beep. "Hi, Ricky...? It's Mom. I think it's about five in the afternoon your time. I know you don't work Mondays but I guess you're out. Anyway, I'm calling because it seems your cousin Cash is in some kind of trouble. Your Aunt Lenora called me this morning. She's in quite a state. Apparently Cash was about to be indicted for defrauding investors or donors in some health-care scam and his wife stole some money from him and they've both run off to Europe. Oh and his wife stabbed him. I'm sorry to bother you, sweetheart. I know Cash isn't your favorite person and this all sounds a bit nutty but could you please call me when you get a chance? Lenora seems to think that Cash and his wife are in Paris and maybe you could help find them. Anyway, Pops and I send you all our love. Say *'Bonjour'* to that exotic girlfriend of yours. Bye bye."

Beep. "Hello, Ricky. Are you there? It is me, Valitsa. If you are at home, please pick up.... Yes?... No? I need to speak with you very badly. It is now eleven o'clock. I have just arrived at my apartment. You remember you asked how you could repay me for my taking in your thieving sister-in-law or whatever she is. Anyway, you can repay me by coming over to my place right now. As soon as you get this message. I have some business associates coming by and I need your presence here. Just as backup. It is quite urgent so please come when you get this message. Please. *Merci.*"

Beep. "Ricky? Valitsa again.... Still you are not at home. It is now eleven thirty. I really need your help as in right now. I know I needn't remind you, Ricky, but you owe me. So please when you get this message call me back. Or better yet, just come to my apartment. Please. Oh, *merde.* I see someone out on the sidewalk. Anyway, please come. Hurry. I..."

Christ almighty, Ricky thought, *what now?* He immediately phoned Valitsa. Busy signal. He considered rushing up to her apartment but quickly decided against it. He had had his fill of dangerous situations the past four days. If Valitsa was as panicked as she sounded on her second message, then she should call the police. Ricky considered calling on her behalf. But during his three-hour grilling by Lamouche he had failed to mention the grenades in Valitsa's closet. So if he called the inspector now with this new information, it would sound particularly suspicious. Ricky decided to tell Valitsa to call the police. He punched in her number. Busy signal again. Damn. Ricky was starving. He knew he should go to Valitsa's, but he had to eat something. He went to the fridge, made himself a ham sandwich and washed it down with a bottle of Belgian beer. He phoned Valitsa again. Still busy. The last thing he wanted to do was go to the crazy Serb's apartment. Especially if arms smugglers would be dropping by to pick up that box full of hand grenades. But Valitsa was right. He did owe her.

Fifteen minutes later, trudging up the stairs of Valitsa's building, Ricky reasoned that there was nothing to fear. This would be a simple business transaction in which he would be an innocent bystander. The dealers would take their weapons, pay Valitsa or not, and go. They were professionals, right? It was only when Ricky got to the fourth floor landing, saw that the door to Valitsa's apartment was slightly open, a thin slit of light shining into the corridor, that his dread came rushing back. He gently pushed the door wide open and covered his mouth with his hand, suppressing a huge sudden sob.

Valitsa was lying on her stomach, in the center of the carpet, her head turned toward Ricky, her face partly obscured by lank black hair, but one eye clearly visible, wide open, staring lifelessly. She wore a brown tank top and black jeans. Her face, bare shoulders, arms and hands were a bright lime shade of green. Ricky noticed the green foam-rubber crown lying on the couch, beside a green gown and a plastic torch. Valitsa had been miming Lady Liberty tonight. She must have found out very late that her contact was coming. She had enough time to get out of her costume but not enough to shower off her green body paint. Ricky saw the phone lying on the floor, the receiver off the hook. Then he noticed the spreading stain, stretching across the darkly patterned Persian rug, from beneath Valitsa's body.

Ricky fought back his tears. He knew Valitsa was crazy, and on the wrong side of a repugnant war. But she was his friend and she didn't deserve to die like this. He backed into Valitsa's short hallway, saw that the closet door was wide open. Ricky didn't bother to peer inside—he knew that whoever had killed Valitsa would have taken the goods they had come for. He crept out of Valitsa's apartment. Covering his hand with his shirttail, he pulled the door toward him, leaving it as slightly cracked open as he had found it. Then he bolted down the stairs.

Out on the rue Berthe, Ricky knew Fatima was in danger. The fear came whooshing up from out of nowhere, seized Ricky's mind and squeezed tight. It was not so much instinct as conviction, the certain knowledge that Fatima was right now in some kind of life-threatening peril. Ricky bounded up the four steep sets of stairs that formed the rue du Calvaire, to the top of the Butte Montmartre. He strode across the Place du Tertre, breathing hard, pushing his way past the milling crowds of tourists and sidewalk sketch artists. He raced down the series of staircases on the rue du Mont Cenis, scared but lucid, prepared for anything. Fatima's street, pleasant, residential rue de Trétaigne, was nearly deserted. The elevator was waiting for him in Fatima's lobby. The key to her apartment was in his hand as he rode up to the third floor. He slid the key into the lock and realized as he turned it that the door had not been locked at all.

"Yo, cuz!" Cash Washington called out. He was standing by the tall windows in Fatima's living room, looking like a guy on his way to the golf course in his blue short-sleeved shirt with the tiny green reptile sewn on the chest, his hands stuffed in the pockets of his khaki trousers.

Ricky slammed the door behind him and went charging toward Cash—six feet, two hundred twenty pounds and ten years of accumulated rage, barrelling across Fatima's living room floor. He only saw the chauffeur peripherally, on the other side of the room, in his black cap and uniform, making some strange gesture with his arms folded across his chest. Ricky was reaching out to grab Cash by the throat. He saw the animal fear in his cousin's eyes, saw Cash raise his palm and say, "Don't, Rick—"

"FREEZE!"

The guttural bark stopped Ricky in his tracks. He turned and saw Yuri standing slightly crouched, feet planted firmly on the floor. His arms were stretched out in front of him, a pistol in each hand. His cap was still pulled down low. Ricky could barely make out Yuri's eyes, but he could see the late adolescent acne and peach fuzz on his cheeks. Remembering Yuri's lunatic driving on the Di and Dodi death route, Ricky figured this Russian kid was crazy enough to start blasting. After freezing in mid-lunge, Ricky relaxed his posture.

"Yuri's a big John Woo fan," Cash said, smiling. "He'll splatter you all over the room and think it's really cool."

"And you'd let him do it?"

"I'm a desperate man, cuz. I got nothin' to lose now but my life."

"Where's Fatima?"

"Check the answering machine."

While Yuri remained in crouching stance, guns thrust forward in steady hands, Ricky walked over to Fatima's desk, punched the playback button.

"Reekee, hello, it is me. I feel a bit silly leaving a message on my own machine but maybe you are there or will soon arrive. I just left a message on your machine as well. I am with Serena. She called my apartment tonight, in need of help. Of course, you did not tell me you had seen her today so I did not know of this complicated history. Well, I am with Serena and not of my own free will, if you catch my meaning."

Ricky heard Serena's voice in the background. She grumbled something but he could not make out the words.

"Anyway," Fatima's voice continued, "you are to meet Cassius at my apartment. We left the door unlocked for him. It is now a quarter past midnight. We will call again to give you further instructions. We will all have a rendezvous somewhere later tonight. Serena will not permit me to say where we are. But we will rendezvous somewhere in the Eighteenth. Okay? I cannot say more but I must let you know I am worried for the little sea horse. Okay. We call you back later."

"*Voilà*," Ricky heard Serena say in the background.

Beep, click, silence.

"What the fuck," Ricky growled.

"Serena called me on my cell tonight," Cash said. "First time I'd talked to her in ten days. She told me what she told you this afternoon. About the secret. Said she wants to meet in some neutral location so we can discuss a divorce settlement. Semipublic so that she feels safe. And she wants you and Fatima there as witnesses."

"You mean hostages," Ricky said.

"Whatever." Cash turned to his chauffeur. "Put those away, Yuri. And go out to the balcony. I want to talk to my cousin alone."

With a cinematic self-consciousness, Yuri tucked a pistol into a holster strapped under each armpit, then stepped through the door-sized windows. Ricky could see him out on the balcony, lighting up a cigarette.

"There's nothin' for us to do but wait, cuz." Cash took a seat on

Fatima's couch. "We might as well make the best of this quality time we have together."

Ricky sat down in one of Fatima's canvas director's chairs. He glared at his cousin, saying nothing.

Cash flashed his winsome "I Love Me" grin again, looking like Tiger Woods's jaded older brother. "How did it come to this?" he asked with a shrug. "Huh, Ricky?"

"You called *me*," Ricky said, through clenched teeth. "You said you needed my help. Remember?"

"I don't just mean the past few days. I mean how did we become who we are? How you? How me?"

"You mean how did you go from being a respected doctor to being a thief?"

"Ah, Ricky." Cash shook his head and sighed. "I have not done anything that thousands of white doctors haven't done before me. Every-body skims a little off the top in a project like this. Every-fucking-body does it—all these distinguished white men! But when a black dude comes along and does the exact same thing, the white boys don't like it. And I end up getting indicted. You don't see white doctors gettin' indicted for this shit. It's fuckin' outrageous. But I'm young and I'm black and I'm already at the top of my field. And those slimy white hypocrites who used to be the top surgeons to the superstars and who smiled in my face for years, conspired to bring me down. They acted like I was a member of the club—then they turned around and tried to destroy me. To make me the black scapegoat. The racial hypocrisy of the American establishment, man, it is just staggering."

"You call nine million dollars skimming off the top?"

Cash waved his hand dismissively. "You know, man, all I ever wanted was to show the white boys I was as good as they were. And I did! So now they wanna put me in jail for it. When all I wanted was my birthright. Damn it, man, too many of us have been cheated out of our birthright."

"What do you mean, 'birthright'?"

"I mean have you ever, in your entire life, met a white American named Washington?"

Ricky paused and racked his memory. "Actually, no."

"That's what I'm talking about! The first president of the United States. The so-called father of our country. A godammned Virginia slave owner. What happened to his bloodline? Where did his name go? Damn it, Ricky, all I ever tried to do was to take what should have always been mine!"

"So what happens now?"

"After we meet with Serena, Yuri's driving me back to Zurich. I'll keep a low profile there. But I won't have to stay any longer than January 20, 2001."

"I don't understand."

"That's when Clinton leaves office. Sometime between now and then, Bubba's gonna grant me a presidential pardon. He damn well better. Do you know how much money I raised for that horny bastard? I was throwing fund-raisers for him as far back as 'ninety-one! I was second only to Vernon in getting influential black folks on board. And who stood by him during this whole impeachment bullshit? Clinton owes a whole lotta black folks. But he owes me *personally*. And he knows it. If there's one white boy who won't turn on me, I hope it's Bill. But I might have to wait in Switzerland for a year and a half to find out. Do you know where I can find a good rib joint in Zurich?"

"Can't be done."

"Anyway, I'm sorry you got involved in all this."

"No you're not. You told Dmitri to have his hit man search my apartment."

Cash waggled his head sheepishly. "Okay, that's true. But I thought you mighta been in cahoots with Serena. Do you know how much money that bitch stole from me?"

"Did you also order to have me killed?"

"Jesus Christ, Ricky, I'm not fucking Michael Corleone!"

"Then why the fuck did you threaten me on my answering machine?"

"That was just for dramatic effect. I knew you knew where Serena was. But I never wanted anybody dead. Not even that French ho who sent me the blackmail letter. Was I happy to learn she'd been killed? Hell, yes! But, I gotta tell ya, Ricky, I'm pretty freaked out by this whole escalation of violence. I don't know who the fuck those people were who shot Dmitri the other night. I just know that assassinations were not something I bargained for when I went into business with these Eastern Europeans two years ago. But I'm through with all this shit. I just wanna get my ass to safe, neutral Switzerland and chill out till I get my pardon."

"But only after you see Serena?"

Cash swallowed hard. That wounded-husband look seeped across his face again. "Yes," he said. "I wanna look her in the eye one more time before her lawyers and mine go to war."

"Lemme ask you something, Cash. I've been wondering ever since I learned the secret. I mean, you're a doctor. How could you not have known?"

Cash bowed his head. "I guess you only see what you want to see." He took a small vial out his pants pocket, carefully uncapped it and poured the white powder on Fatima's coffee table. "I was so in love with her. And I loved fucking her so much. I just didn't see." Cash paused for a long time, staring at the little pile of coke. "Can you believe I didn't even ask for a prenup? That's how much I loved that woman."

"So you had no suspicions at all?"

"I denied them, man, that's what I'm tellin' you. Serena used to have this swishy little Brazilian friend. He was at our wedding. I don't even remember his name. Anyway, he made a joke once, at some party. Serena looked like she wanted to spit on him. I don't even remember the joke but I just thought he was a bitchy little gay guy, you know. Anyway, we never saw him again after that. I suppose there was some hint there. But, of course, once we started trying to have a baby..." Cash paused again, took a deep breath. He pulled a credit card from out of his wallet, starting slowly chopping up the cocaine with the plastic edge.

"Go on," Ricky said.

"Finally, we went to see a fertility specialist. We both went through a bunch of tests. I got a fax telling me my sperm count was fine, actually on the high side, to tell the truth. But I didn't get any results about Serena and when I asked her she said she was still waiting. After a few weeks, I realized she was being evasive. I called the specialist. I said,

'Hey, there must be something wrong. Tell me why we can't conceive.' And he just said, 'Ask your wife.' I kept pressing him but he kept saying the same thing: 'Ask your wife.' And here's the incredible part. I didn't ask her. 'Cause I was too scared to learn the truth. And who knows what she would have told me if I had asked? Hell, I'd have believed anything she said. Like with the missing parcels."

"The what?"

"Parcels. Packages stuffed with cash, man. Hundreds of thousands of dollars."

"Your skimmings?"

"Some of them, yeah. Anyway, these packages started disappearing from their hiding places. I confronted Serena. She blamed the maid. So we fired the maid. But the parcels kept disappearing. Serena blamed the new maid, so we fired her, too. Then she blamed her personal trainer, so we fired him. If Serena had told me it was me stealing from myself, I probably would have believed her. But then I get this letter, in broken English, telling me my wife is a man."

"*Was* a man," Ricky said.

Cash said nothing. He had divided the coke into four straight lines. He pulled a tightly rolled-up bill from his pocket, held it out to Ricky, who shook his head no. Cash hunched low over the coffee table, snorted up a line. He sat up straight again, wriggling his nose. "Sometimes, I ask myself, Why did she marry me? How long did she think she could get away with this lie? Why did she do it?"

Ricky remembered what Clementine had told him about why Cash had seduced her on the eve of her wedding. "Because," Ricky said, "she could."

"Anyway, I'm not gonna let some Frankenbitch freak rob me. This marriage is over and that fucked-up scientific experiment isn't gonna get a dime from me!"

"You know what, Cash? You're so whacked-out by the blow you've lost touch with reality."

"Yeah yeah yeah."

"Why don't you get some help?" Ricky said earnestly. "Go back to the States. Get into a twelve-step program or whatever."

"I don't need that crap."

"Take Serena with you. Maybe she could help you."

"Yo, R. J. Go fuck yourself."

"You're still in love with her."

Cash inhaled another line. "Bullshit."

"It's obvious."

Cash tilted his head and squinted at Ricky. "So tell me, cuz, what's 'the little sea horse?' "

The telephone rang and Ricky hurried to answer it. "Fatima?"

"Reekee. It is good to hear your voice."

"Are you all right?"

"I have not been wounded if that is what you mean. Though I do not know if I would say I am all right."

"When can I see you?"

"You and Cash are to meet Serena and me in fifteen minutes."

"Where?"

"Our *carrefour.*"

Yuri's nose was twitching as he guided the car along the cobblestones of the rue Saint Vincent. Ricky sat in the backseat of the limo, with Cash, giving the Russian driver directions and constantly telling him to go slowly, lest he zip right past the meeting place. Yuri and Cash had each done four lines of coke before leaving Fatima's apartment and Ricky could see that they were both buzzing.

"What's that?" Cash asked, pointing out the left side window. "Somebody's private garden?"

"It's a vineyard," Ricky said.

"No shit."

"Park right here, Yuri. Alongside the wall."

Yuri stopped at the small cemetery, at the northwest corner of the crossroads where the rue des Saules met the rue Saint Vincent; at the northeast corner was the Lapin Agile; the vineyard occupied the southeast corner and at the southwest corner was the Square Roland Dorgelès, that intimate, courtyard-like space, raised a few steps up from the sidewalk, like an outdoor stage. Though his view was obstructed by the trees in the center of the square, Ricky could just make out Serena and Fatima, sitting on the stone bench that ran along the ivy-lined wall of the alcove.

"Listen up, Yuri," Cash said. "I don't have a weapon on me but my wife might. If you see anything weird happen, get out of the car and start blasting."

"Gotcha," Yuri said with a twitchy nod.

Just as Ricky and Cash stepped out of the car, they heard a muffled burst of applause coming from inside the walls of the Lapin Agile. Ricky quickly scanned the area. Though it was after one o'clock, he counted about a dozen people strolling around the *carrefour,* mostly couples holding hands. Ricky and Cash climbed the steps of the Square Roland Dorgelès. And there they saw the two uncommonly beautiful women, sitting side by side, as close as cuddling lovers, in the halo glow of the street lantern.

"Hallelujah," Serena said in a deadpan voice, "it's rainin' men."

Cash's wife was wearing a beige safari jacket, crisp designer blue jeans and cowgirl boots. Her hair hung loose over her shoulders. The Samsonite suitcase rested on its wheels, beside the bench. Serena seemed utterly calm, in control. Fatima, meanwhile, was seething. She sat with her arms and legs tightly crossed, still wearing her long black dress, her hair still knotted in a bun. Fatima radiated anger. She kept her head tilted away from Serena, staring furiously up in the air. Fatima would not even make eye contact with Ricky when he appeared in the square. But she addressed him in a voice brimming with indignation.

"I think you should know, Reekee, that I have a gun in my back."

"Don't get too close, boys," Serena said sweetly.

Ricky and Cash stood a few feet in front of Serena and Fatima. "Goddamnit, Serena," Cash said.

"Don't use the Lord's name in vain, Cassius." Serena zapped him with her Bambi stare. "Do you realize this is the first time we've ever been in Paris together?"

"And whose fault is that?" Cash snapped. "You never wanted to come here. Too many bad memories, you always said. Only I didn't know it was your memories of being a fucking man."

"What makes you angrier, Cassius: that I wasn't truthful or that you didn't see the truth?"

"You are one sick fuck, you know that?"

"Did you just suddenly stop loving me, Cassius? Is that really even possible? That just because of this revelation you can shut down your love for me?"

"Oh, stop it! You lied to me for three years, stole six million dollars from me, tried to stab me to death and now I assume you wanna bankrupt me. Fuck you, bitch. A man's gotta draw the line somewhere. Would Lonnie John have let some bitch treat him like that and get away with it?"

Serena shook her head and sneered. "And would you have listened if it had been Lonnie John, a man, warning you about Dmitri and all those other crooks you were bending over for? Now you wanna try and play junior executive gangsta. And look at you. You're pathetic. A frightened little hamster boy."

"Could you two get down to business, please?" Ricky said. "Either wrap this up or let me and Fatima go."

"Ha!" Serena scoffed. "Please, don't *you* get started, Ricky Jenks."

"We don't need to be involved in this."

"Oh no? Aren't you gonna ask me how my recording session went, Ricky? No? Well, it was fantastic. And just as we were finishing up, Fabrice got a call saying the police were raiding his studio. Obviously, they had expected us to be there. No doubt someone told them we *would* be there. As luck would have it Fabrice had taken me to a completely different studio, on the other side of town. I had just enough time to get away before the cops found their way there. But the tracks have been laid, a contract has been signed and Serena Moriarty's first single will be released in two months."

"Bravo," Ricky said.

"Of course my totally unsupportive husband never thought I could do it, did you, sweetheart?"

Cash was silent for a long time. When he finally spoke, Ricky was startled by the tenderness in his voice: "Congratulations, Serena."

"Look," Ricky said, "even if I was forced to talk to the police, Fatima had nothing to do with it. Let her go."

"Everybody's a bad ass tonight," Serena bellowed in her deepest register. "Makin' demands and such. You think you bad, Ricky? Like your cousin here? Either one of you Negroes ever kill a man? Or a woman?"

Serena pulled Fatima even closer to her. Fatima continued to ignore everyone, glaring up at nothing.

"Now, I like Fatima here," Cash's wife said, returning to her girly voice. "But if I feel it suits my changing game plan, I will not hesitate to kill her. You dig? A stone-cold killer does whatever is necessary. And if you tell me Fatima is pregnant? Well, shit, that just makes me jealous. Hell, I'll kill her just to show you what a evil bitch I am."

"So what is it you want from me?" Cash asked.

"Well, there's the long term and the short term, honey. In the long term, I want—and I'm gonna get—at least half of everything you got. At *least* half."

"We'll see about that. What do you want in the short term?"

"Safe passage outta this country. I know damn well how you got here last week. Dmitri had you flown over on his private jet. Now, thanks to Ricky the Rat here, the cops are after me for killing Maximillian. And they'll probably try to nail me for crimes committed by Lonnie John in my past life. So what I want from you, Cassius, is a ride back to the States on Dmitri's plane."

Cash chuckled. "Serena, as I think you know, Dmitri is dead and I didn't inherit any of his planes."

"Don't fuck with me, Cassius! I know you can get me outta here. Now, what we're gonna do is have your driver take all four of us to the airport and you're gonna get me on one of those planes or I'll start killin' y'all. Fatima first."

"You're delusional, Serena. I can't snap my fingers and get a plane for *me*, let alone for you. Yuri's driving me to Zurich tonight. I can't risk being seen at an airport or I'll be extradited to the States."

"Motherfucker," Serena hissed.

"You're on your own. My lawyers will get in touch with your lawyers. But our whole marriage was a lie and you ain't gettin' another penny from me. Your ass is goin' back to jail."

"Now who's delusional? You won't have a pot to piss in when I'm through with you, Cassius. I intend to bleed you dry."

"Mon Dieu!" Fatima exploded. "How you Americans talk! Every dispute with you is about money, violence, revenge! Listen how you talk to each other. It is insane. You have been married for two years. What about love? Do you Americans even *believe* in love?"

Ricky, Cash and Serena were all flabbergasted by Fatima's outburst. They exchanged awkward glances, no one sure how to respond. Finally, Cash said, in a small, plaintive voice, "But, Fatima, I thought you *liked* Americans."

Fatima pressed her lips together tightly and resumed glaring at nothing.

"She's right," Serena said. "I did start out trying to talk to you about our love, Cassius. But I guess you don't believe in it anymore, if you ever did."

Cash stood with his hands on his hips, staring silently at the ground.

"You're wrong," Ricky said to Serena. "He does still love you. It's obvious."

"And you love *him*," Fatima said, still refusing to make eye contact with anyone. "You two should sit down alone and deal with this fact instead of threatening with guns and lawyers and money. What is wrong with you people?"

Ricky saw Serena's eyes twinkling tearily again, as they so often did when the subject was her husband. "Cassius," she said softly. "Would you like to do that? Go someplace where the two of us can talk? Alone. In peace."

Cash continued to stare at the ground. "I have to go to Zurich. And I have to leave right now. I don't know how long I'll need to stay there. But . . . would you like to come with me?"

Throughout this whole encounter on the Square Roland Dorgelès, Ricky had managed to discreetly scope the surroundings, casting furtive glances at the limo parked on the rue Saint Vincent, catching peripheral glimpses of the various couples strolling down the rue des Saules. He had the feeling that Serena, too, had been aware of everything happening around her. But now, all of her concentration was aimed at her husband. "Are you serious?" she asked, her voice cracking.

Cash finally looked up, meeting his wife's gaze. "Yeah. I am. Come with me."

Serena rose from the stone bench. Ricky saw the barrel of the shiny black pistol glinting in her hand. She stuffed the gun in one of the pockets of her safari jacket. "I'm scared, Cassius," she said. "Is this some kind of a trap?"

If Serena had been less focused on Cash, she would have noticed that a small crowd of people was filing out of the Lapin Agile. She would have been aware of the gray Renault that glided down the rue des Saules thirty seconds earlier and parked in front of the vineyard. Yuri had noticed it, because he stealthily emerged from the limousine just as the four plainclothes cops stepped out of the Renault. At that moment, the Montmartrain came chugging down the rue Saint Vincent, half-filled with weary-looking tourists. The driver, seated beneath the fake white smokestack, was droning lazily into his microphone, describing the sights in French-accented Italian. Out of the corner of his eye, Ricky saw Inspector Lamouche, the stubble-head twins and Bruno, the green-eyed psycho cop with the pompadour, striding across the rue des Saules at the same time that the Montmartrain traversed the *carrefour*. Ricky could no longer see Yuri. He was hidden by the rubber-tired locomotive. When Ricky looked Fatima's way, he could see that she, too, noticed the approaching goon squad.

"I'm fresh outta tricks," Cash said to Serena. "And I'm too drained to fight anymore. Come with me. Right now. Please."

Serena was standing only a few inches in front of Cash. Ricky thought they were about to kiss.

"*Bonsoir, mesdames et messieurs,*" Lamouche said, flashing his badge as he and the goons mounted the steps leading up to the square.

Cash spun around, saw the cops, then shot Ricky a look full of terror and rage. Serena was cool though. She just slid her hand into her jacket pocket, took hold of the gun. Fatima, meanwhile, rose from the bench, taking a couple of cautious steps in Ricky's direction.

Lamouche had a satisfied smirk on his moony face. "I would like to be as polite as possible. So, your papers please."

Just as the caboose of the Montmartrain passed out of sight, Ricky spotted Yuri, walking across the street in a strange, bowlegged crouch, arms stretched in front of him, a pistol in each hand.

"Lamouche!" Ricky screamed. "Behind you!"

In a John Woo movie, this would all happen in slow motion. In real life, paroxysms of violence happen extremely fast. Ricky sees many things, from different angles, seemingly all at once. He sees the flashes of light exploding from Yuri's hands, sees the grimacing, acned face, the eyes barely visible beneath the chauffeur's cap. Ricky sees Lamouche, Bruno and the stubble-head twins all reaching beneath their jackets. But Serena has already drawn her weapon. Ricky sees her standing perfectly still, calmly taking aim and firing a single shot. After that flash from her gun, Serena is propelled backward, a shower of blood bursting from her chest. Ricky reaches out and grabs Fatima by the shoulders. In what seems like the same instant, Cash bolts across the alcove, hurdles the high stone curb, lands gracefully on the rue des Saules and lopes, gazelle-like, across the street. Cracking gunfire and the screams of tourists ring in Ricky's ears. He sees people diving to the ground outside the Lapin Agile. Bruno the cop clutches his belly and tumbles down the steps. Ricky has flung Fatima to the ground and now he is down there with her, covering her entire body with his, pressing her against the stone wall. Fatima sobs convulsively in his arms.

There are no more gunshots. Ricky has his eyes shut tight, his face buried in Fatima's hair. He slowly raises his head. The odor of gunsmoke burns his nostrils.

"Are you okay?" he asks Fatima. "Are you hit?"

"N-n-n-n-oooo," Fatima sobs. "I don't think so."

Still holding onto Fatima, Ricky sits up, takes a look around. He sees Cash, across the street, scaling the fence of the vineyard, then dropping down on the other side, disappearing amid the leafy grapevines.

Ricky hears Lamouche, then sees the detective at the foot of the stairs, snarling orders into a walkie-talkie. He is kneeling over the body of Bruno, whose green eyes are wide open, unblinking. Ricky sees one of the stubble-head twins sitting on a wooden bench, breathing hard and holding onto his bloody shoulder. Ricky spots the other stubble-head standing on the rue Saint Vincent, gun in hand. Yuri lies at his feet, shot full of holes. Ricky hears sirens approaching: *Weeee-WAAAAAH, weeeee-WAAAAAAH*...

Just as Ricky is wondering what has happened to Serena, he sees her staggering across the *carrefour*. The bottom half of her safari jacket is soaked in blood. Red rivulets pour down her blue jeans. Serena stumbles like a drunk into the middle of the rue des Saules. Standing in place, she turns slowly around, three hundred and sixty degrees. In the middle of Serena's slow spin, Ricky gets a good look at her face. She is dazed but aware, trying to get her bearings. Ricky sees her take something from out of her pocket. She holds the object in both hands. Serena has finished her twirl. She stands facing the vineyard. Her left arm jerks wildly and Ricky realizes she has just pulled the pin from the grenade.

A blue, white and red police car screeches to a halt, inches in front of Serena. Throwing out her right arm in a gorgeous arc, she lobs the grenade high into the air. It falls into the dark green vineyard. Serena collapses, her head slamming against the cobblestones. And at precisely that moment the explosion goes off, a bright burst of red in the middle of the vineyard, branches and leaves flying into the night sky; a sudden, foul cloud of black smoke. After a chorus of shocked squeals from the innocent people cowering around the *carrefour*, a more horrific sound is heard. It is all the more shattering because people cannot see who is unleashing the tormented wail. But the voice is coming from inside the vineyard and Ricky knows it can be only one person shrieking in agony.

Twenty

"You have a very good lawyer," Inspector Lamouche told Ricky.

Silver-haired, suntanned Olivier Matignon turned to Ricky and gave him a discreet wink. Ricky had sat outside the detective's office, in the police station of the *mairie* of the Eighteenth Arrondissement, for an hour while the cop and the attorney discussed his case. When he was finally allowed to enter the office, Lamouche and Matignon were smoking long cigars, speaking in low, intimate voices. They shared a wry laugh, then Lamouche shrugged and said, *"C'est normal."*

But, as far as Ricky Jenks was concerned, there was nothing even remotely normal about this Tuesday morning.

"It is a sad day," Lamouche said after offering Ricky a seat, but not a cigar. "Zere has been much bloodshed. A very brave policeman, and a good friend of mine, Bruno Castillon, is dead. Zis person, Serena Washington, is also dead. Ze Russian driver, Yuri Ivanov: dead. Your friend

Valitsa Karodovic: dead. Add in Mirabella Darrieux, Maximillian Niculescu, Dmitri Zugashvili. Zat is quite a rare body count for five days in
zis town."

"And what about my cousin?" Ricky asked.

"Interesting enough, Dr. Washington lives. He has very bad burns
on ze face and ze hands, but he will live. Actually, he was quite lucky.
A few inches closer to ze grenade and he would have been blind or
killed. Anyhow, he is in ze hospital. When he is well enough, in a week
we hope, we will extradite him to America to face all ze charges he
must face zere."

Ricky nodded. "All right."

"And how is your *femme?*"

In French, the same word is used for *woman* and *wife*. Ricky wondered, for a moment, if Lamouche thought he and Fatima were married
before he answered, "It looks like she'll be okay."

Ricky had spent the night, under police guard, on a bench in a
corridor of the Clinique Beaucaire. Fatima was in a private room, her
gynecologist, Dr. Yassin, having rushed to the maternity hospital in the
middle of the night to tend to her. Fatima had suffered a mild state of
shock but, by sunrise, all her vital signs had returned to normal. And
her bleeding had dwindled to a trickle. Marva Dobbs showed up at
Beaucaire at seven o'clock Tuesday morning, accompanied by the lawyer
she had recommended for Ricky. The cops allowed Ricky and Olivier
Matignon to go to the hospital's cafeteria for an hour to discuss his case.
By nine o'clock, Marva had arranged for Fatima to be released under
her care. "Don't worry, Bear," she said to Ricky. "The mother of your
child will be safe with me."

Ricky, Matignon and the cops then headed for the *mairie* of the
Eighteenth.

"So what about me?" Ricky asked Lamouche, trying not to gag from
the thick cloud of smoke in the detective's office.

"Like I say," Lamouche replied with a respectful nod toward Olivier
Matignon, "you have a very good lawyer. You face no charges. Of course,
one could argue zat you wizzeld evidence from me when I ask you
certain questions. But maybe you just did not understand my accent in
English. Your accent in French is pretty bad, too."

Lamouche and Matignon had a good laugh over that, and Ricky reluctantly joined in. Once the chuckles died down, Ricky asked, "So who killed Valitsa?"

"Arms dealers, of course, also Russian. Like zis scumbag Dmitri. Zere is a war going on in Paris right now, for control of ze crime here. Many men from ze east involved. Like ze ozer scumbag Maximillian. We had no idea he was back in our country. Anyhow, Valitsa played a dangerous game. Like your cousin. But at least he managed to survive."

"American justice will deal with Dr. Washington," Olivier Matignon said.

"Yes," Lamouche agreed. "But only after he settles his business wiz ze *mairie* of ze Eighteenth."

Ricky was confused. "What do you mean?"

Lamouche's moony face was lit up with righteous anger now. "I mean someone has got to pay for ze damage zat was done to our vineyard!"

Until the afternoon of Friday, May 7, 1999, Ricky had never imagined how different Fatima Boukhari would look in a head scarf, her electric black abundance of hair concealed beneath the silky white fabric that also covered her neck and shoulders, framing starkly, but still beautifully, her coppery, angular face.

"The bleeding has stopped," Fatima had told Ricky that morning, after her appointment with Dr. Yassin. She phoned him at his studio to give him the news. It was the first time he had heard Fatima's voice since the shoot-out at the *carrefour* Monday night. "The little sea horse is okay. For now. But who can know what will happen in future month?"

Over the past three days, Marva had kept Ricky posted about Fatima's condition. He knew that Fatima was getting proper bed rest and tender loving care in Marva's Left Bank apartment. He also knew that Fatima did not wish to speak to him until after she had met with Dr. Yassin on Friday. And, according to Marva, Fatima was still planning to leave for Morocco on Monday, May 10. "Unless," Marva said cryptically, "she doesn't."

The sun shone brassily through the tall windows of Fatima's living room on Friday afternoon. She had invited Ricky over for mint tea. And to say good-bye. Ricky felt so guilty, he could barely look Fatima in the eye. He felt guilty for Fatima's pregnancy, for his mistrust of her, for exposing her to the wildness of Cash Washington, for, however inadvertently, placing her life in danger Monday night. Was it any wonder that, after her recent dealings with Ricky and his family, Fatima felt the need for moral cleansing?

"I want you to know," Ricky said, "that I understand your decision to go to Morocco. I respect it and I won't try to stand in your way."

"You are a good man, Reekee."

They sat beside each other, not touching, on Fatima's couch. Ricky looked up at Fatima, in her immaculate veil, but still had trouble meeting her gaze directly. "No, I'm not."

"You saved my life. At our *carrefour*. You protected me from the gunfire."

"It was my fault that you were in that situation in the first place."

"All the same, Reekee, you saved my life. And perhaps the life of our child. I want you to know I will never forget it."

"And I want you to know how sorry I am for all the pain that I've caused you."

They drank their tea in silence. After a while, Fatima asked, "Is there anything else you would like to say to me?"

Ricky struggled not to cry. "Just . . . again . . . that I'm really, really sorry."

Now he locked eyes with Fatima. *"Je t'aime,"* she said.

Ricky, stunned by her words, could only manage to say, *"Merci."*

Fatima leaned forward, kissed Ricky once on each cheek. "Now," she said, "I must pray."

She walked into the bedroom, closed the door behind her. Ricky could hear Fatima chanting softly in Arabic. He felt, in some strange, painful way, shamed by her faith. He placed his keys to Fatima's apartment on the coffee table, then, as quietly as he could, left.

"You know," Carmen said, "in a way, it is really quite a romantic story. A tragedy, yes, but romantic stories always are. Mirabella in love with

Lonnie, Lonnie and Cassandra in love with each other, Serena in love with Cash. Each of them dying from their cracked kind of love."

"Except for Cash," Ricky said.

"Yes. And this makes him the unluckiest of them all. The others, perhaps they are all happy together in the afterlife."

They were sitting in the Hanoi Hideaway late Saturday afternoon, Carmen sipping a foamy pink cocktail, Ricky nursing an Orangina. "And what about Bruno?" Ricky asked. Carmen had already told him that she knew the cop who had beaten her in the police station in la Goutte d'Or, the same cop Yuri shot dead in the Square Roland Dorgelès Monday night.

"I hope that he also has found peace in the next life," Carmen said. "You know, he and me, we had a story many years ago. I think I broke his heart. So, about once a year or year and a half, he like to arrest me and rough me up a bit. That was his revenge. He did not really hurt me last week. But I scream extra loud to make him feel better. You know how men are."

Ricky laughed. One major change in his life over the past week was that all the hookers on the rue des Martyrs said *bonjour* or *bonsoir* to him and he always returned the pleasantry. "Well," he said to Carmen, "I should be going now. I have to get to work."

"Yes," she said, downing the dregs of her cocktail, "me also."

As he played piano at Le Bon Montmartrois Saturday night, Ricky was already feeling nostalgic about his crêperie gig. His boss, François Penin, had told him that the head of the music school in Bobigny was eager to hire him. Despite all the madness of the past week, Ricky's interview with Monsieur Dumoulin on Thursday had gone very well. François had confided to his favorite pianist that Dumoulin was willing to tackle the mountain of paperwork required to hire an American like Ricky Jenks, who had lived in Paris for nine years on a loosely regulated tourist visa. Ricky was touched by François's happiness for him, his willingness to let him leave and take a more secure and well-paying job elsewhere. Ricky knew that, once his appointment at the conservatory began in

September, he would miss the crêperie badly. But he also knew François Penin would be his friend for life.

Knowing what had happened Monday night, François had allowed Ricky to take most of the week off and Dominique, the crêperie's other pianist, happily filled in for his colleague. Ricky had spent endless hours on the phone to America that week, explaining to relatives the bizarre saga of Cash Washington and Serena Moriarty.

"I gotta tell ya," Ricky's sister the Honorable Judge Isabel Jenks Douglas said, "everybody sorta knew."

"But nobody ever asked?"

"How are you gonna ask a question like that, Ricky? 'Excuse me, Cash, but did your wife used to be a man?'"

"Well?"

"I'm just saying a lot of us suspected something bizarre about Serena. I once considered doing a background check on her but I figured if Cash wasn't interested in such a thing, why should I be?"

"So Cash's friends and family accepted the fact that he was married to a transsexual?"

"It was always an open question. Don't you remember when Mom showed you Cash's wedding day video? She wanted to get your opinion on this while not saying anything to bias you. But you didn't seem to notice."

"Jesus, Isabel, this story just gets weirder and weirder."

"Yes, but the weirdest of the weird is Cash. He's maybe the only person who was totally shocked to learn the truth about his own wife."

Ricky had not spoken with Cash, who was still in a Paris hospital. Cash's parents had wanted to fly to Paris to give him moral support but Cash repeatedly told them not to come. Ricky assured his aunt and uncle that Cash was getting top-notch treatment for his wounds and would be returning to the States any day now. It was a strange situation for Ricky, having to reassure the family that all would be well with one of its golden achievers. Yet he was comfortable in his new position, calming the nerves of family members who had once pitied him but now looked to him for advice and consolation.

Ricky was in a John Lennon mode that Saturday night at the crêperie. He had already done his jazzy renditions of "Instant Karma,"

"Love," "Mother," "Jealous Guy," "Gimme Some Truth," and was now playing "Imagine." It was one of those songs that everybody knew but nobody ever truly listened to. Peace-loving people the world over sang Lennon's lyrics without ever really grasping the challenge he had laid before them. *Imagine no religion?* Even some of the most admirable people who had ever lived would not want to contemplate that. What was Martin Luther King Jr. without Christianity; or Gandhi without his Hindu faith? Fatima Boukhari loved Lennon's song but she would never wish to imagine a life without Islam. *Imagine no country?* What American, or Frenchman, could get along without at least a shred of patriotism? *No possessions?* Marva Dobbs had known Lennon personally but she would never want to live without her precious properties: her restaurant, her apartment on the Left Bank, her house in the French countryside. John Lennon was calling for simple human empathy and bonding to give meaning to life. Playing the song at the crêperie that Saturday night, Ricky realized this was an impossible vision. Certainly, he and Fatima would be unable to accomplish it. That was why he had to let her go.

But as he played, he kept thinking of something Marva had said to him over the phone that morning, a line she repeated again and again, without explaining what she meant: "Fatima is on the fence, Ricky. And you have to get up there with her."

"Yo, cuz!" Cash Washington shouted from the top of the grand staircase. Two uniformed police officers carried Cash, in his wheelchair, down the marble steps. Ricky waited for them in the lobby of the *mairie* of the Eighteenth Arrondissement. Cash was wearing his blue pinstriped suit, his crisp and snowy shirt, yellow power tie and sparkling black shoes. But his hands and head were covered, almost completely, in bandages. Only his dark brown eyes, his nostrils and mouth were unconcealed by the heavy white gauze. He looked like a Brooks Brothers mummy.

"Are you in pain?" Ricky asked, as the cops carefully placed the wheelchair on the floor.

"Oh, man," Cash said, "I've been shot up with way too much morphine to be in any pain!"

It was a little after two o'clock, Monday afternoon. Inspector La-mouche had phoned Ricky that morning to let him know when Cash would most likely be concluding his meeting with officials of the arron-dissement. When Ricky arrived at the *mairie,* he saw a black van parked outside and assumed this was the vehicle that would whisk Dr. Cassius Washington to Charles de Gaulle Airport for his flight back to America.

"I want to tell you how sorry I am," Ricky said, "about what hap-pened to your wife."

"Oh, fuck her!" Cash said. "I'm glad the bitch is dead!"

"I thought, the other night, that you two were on the brink of a reconciliation."

Cash threw back his bandaged head and laughed. "Do you really think if that piece of shit had got in the car with me that she woulda stepped out of it alive?"

Ricky stared down in amazement at his cousin. With only Cash's eyes and lips and the two dark holes of his nostrils visible, there was something even more powerful, more unsettling, about his natural ar-rogance and audacity. "I guess not," Ricky muttered.

"Yuri mighta saved me a bundle by shooting that freak. And I'm gonna need it, too. I just had to pay these damn frogs half a million dollars for their little vineyard and God knows what I'm gonna end up spending on legal fees in the States. I got Johnnie Cochran on the case and you know that motherfucker don't come cheap!"

"Well, maybe this will help." Ricky pulled the white envelope from his pants pocket, leaned over and stuffed it in the inner pocket of Cash's suit jacket. "That's the thousand dollars you gave me to find Serena."

Cash shook his head. "Damn, R. J. You're still a chump, ain't ya?" Ricky said nothing. "Lemme tell ya something, cuz," Cash continued. "I'm going back to the States and I'm gonna beat this rap. My hands are gonna heal and I will practice surgery again. And with the help of some very good doctors I know, eventually, my face is gonna be even prettier than before. And then, you know what? I'm comin' back here for *you*, cuz. You thought you could pull a fast one on me, huh? You and Serena both. Well, that freak is dead. But payback is comin' for you, fat man. Payback is comin'!" Cash unleashed a maniacal cackle. He was still laughing like a lunatic as the police wheeled him out of the lobby.

Ricky waited until Cash's black van had pulled away from the curb before he stepped out on the rue Ordener, into the brilliant May sunshine. He looked up at the clock on the façade of the *mairie*; ten past two. He knew that Fatima would also be leaving soon, heading for Paris's other airport, Orly, to catch a flight to Morocco. He knew what he had to do, but it scared him.

"Fatima is on the fence," Marva had said yet again, when Ricky spoke with her Monday morning. "And you have to get up there with her."

Ricky walked the two blocks to the rue de Trétaigne, bracing himself to go up to Fatima's apartment and make the bold gesture. There had to be a way, didn't there? A way to transcend religion, country, all these ideas we use to define ourselves. Turning onto Fatima's street, Ricky was startled to see a taxi right in front of her building. She was leaving earlier than he had expected. He saw the driver loading a suitcase into the trunk. And there was Fatima, in her silken white head scarf, closing the door to her building, approaching the cab. She turned around, clearly shocked to see Ricky racing toward her. The expression on Fatima's face seemed half-happy, half-horrified as Ricky walked right up to her and dropped down on one knee.

"Will you marry me?"

Un ange passe. That was what the French liked to say about these long silences. But as Ricky knelt on the sidewalk, staring up at Fatima's beautiful and utterly inscrutable face, an entire flock of angels seemed to pass overhead. He could almost hear their wings fluttering as he waited for her answer.